Lilies of Death

Jordan Hall

Copyright © 2009 Jordan Hall

ISBN 978-1-60145-683-0

All rights reserved. No part of this publication may be reproduced, stored in a retrieval system, or transmitted in any form or by any means, electronic, mechanical, recording or otherwise, without the prior written permission of the author.

Printed in the United States of America.

The characters and events in this book are fictitious. Any similarity to real persons, living or dead, is coincidental and not intended by the author.

Jordanhallbooks.com
2009

To Phyllis, who has helped me
more that she'll ever know. Thank
you for your kindness and friendship.
J.H.

To my dear
friend, Wendy,
All my love.
Jordan Hall 2009.

Chapter 1

Myrtle Bixby cast her eyes around the dingy room and had no idea that this was where she would end her life. She gawped at the dirty, rumpled bed.

"This is gross, couldn't you find anywhere better?"

"Not at this short notice. You know how I've been on about us trying this new sexual position. It'll do this one time."

Myrtle lumbered over to the bed and snatched back the covers. "I'm not getting in those filthy sheets. We'll have to do it on top of the bed."

"That's fine by me. Look what I bought today." He held out a gun.

She stared, her mouth slack. "Is it real?"

"Nah, it's just a replica. I got it to go with my camouflage gear." He waved the gun in the air. "It really makes me look like a professional mercenary now, doesn't it?"

She ran her eyes over his army combat clothing and raised her shoulders in a shrug. "Yes, I guess so."

"Wanna hold it?"

"What?"

"The gun." He offered it.

She stroked the cold metal and lifted troubled eyes to him. "Guns scare me."

The man flung an arm around her shoulders and crushed her body to his. She snuggled closer; laid her head on his chest and he placed the gun on the edge of a table.

He bowed his head and spoke in a low tone. "Are you ready for the ride of your life, honey?"

She nodded. He lifted her chin with his forefinger and gently kissed her lips. She responded by flinging both arms around his neck and pressing close so that the full length of their bodies touched from chest to knee.

He recoiled, not wanting her to contaminate him again and he could hardly stop himself from balking and shrinking from her hot, sweaty body. She repulsed him. After weeks of wooing, she'd at last agreed to try a new sexual position and he didn't want her to back out now. He was in the mood to kill, but he disliked killing unwilling victims. There was no fun in that—it was more exhilarating when they had no idea they were going to die.

His excitement mounted as his mind turned toward his next victim and he couldn't wait to begin the pursuit. The thrill of snuffing out a life in a gratifying dance of death ripped through him. He'd taken extra special care choosing this next prey, she was different from all the others. It had taken him years to find her; he had a valid reason to want her dead. Killing at random was not as satisfying as when he had a score to settle.

Hot color rushed to his face and he tried to hide his escalating irritation. "Then get on the bed and lie face down."

"Face down?"

Her consistent, nasal whine grated on his nerves. "Yes, that's what the book says."

"If I don't like doing it this way, I won't have to do it when we're married will I?"

"Married?" His brows twitched in a frown. "What do you mean?"

She gave a giggle and nudged him. "Oh, come on, you said that if I did this, we'd be together forever."

"Right, yeah, that's what I said, honey."

He wanted to get this over. Anger rose in him like a tidal wave, but he compelled himself to speak in a pleasant tone. "Come on then, get on the bed—I'm as horny as hell."

She screwed up her fat, ugly face and giggled again. "You say the cutest things."

He watched her take three, short steps to the bed in the corner, her wide ass jiggling. She waited by the bed, looking over her shoulder with a small smile, the corners of her mouth quivering. He nodded with encouragement. She hitched up her skirt, dropped her panties and crawled onto the sagging mattress, burying her face in the torn, dirty pillow.

"Is this okay?" was her muffled inquiry.

"Perfect."

By now, the crotch of his jeans was tight with his erection. He unbuttoned his pants, rummaged in his pocket and pulled out a small foil packet. Tearing it open with his teeth, he rolled the condom over and down the length of his swollen member. With the gun in his hand, he strode over to the bed. She had her legs closed, so he pried them apart with one knee and climbed on top of her. One thrust and he was inside her.

She wriggled. "Ow, that hurts."

"Relax and tilt your butt up," he continued his movements, laying the gun at his side and taking his body weight on braced arms.

As his climax approached, his body collapsed on hers and his hands grasped her neck squeezing as tightly as he could. She made a gurgling sound and struggled. He constricted her airflow until she was still and his body jerked in a climax. He lay for a moment, panting. Scrambling to his knees, he yanked up his pants, his insides contracting and his whole body tense while he delved into his pocket. He pulled out a silencer and twisted it onto the end of the gun's barrel, held his arm straight out, took aim and squeezed the trigger. A wooly, dull thud resonated around the small room as the bullet smashed into the back of her skull, splintering bone. His arm jarred with the recoil and his face creased in an evil, satisfied smirk.

He blew into the barrel of the smoking weapon as he'd seen cowboys do in the movies while he bent to pick up the spent cartridge. Now all he had to do was move her body to another place, he couldn't risk someone finding it in this seedy motel. Before stomping out the door, he turned and looked back. "Stupid little bitch!" He spat out the words and quietly closed the door.

The man dumped the heavy suitcase on the creaking porch boards and kicked open the mobile home door. The young redhead looked around with curiosity. It was nice to see something of the way her colleague lived. Although she'd worked with him for five years, she knew very little about his personal life except that he was crazy in love with his wife.

"This place'll be a bit dusty we haven't been here for months," the man said, carrying her bag into the bedroom.

"No, its fine, thanks." She rolled her head to gaze out the window at the heavily wooded area outside.

"I'll run down to the store and pick up some groceries while you get the feel of the place." He closed the front door, but poked his head back in. "Relax, everything's going to be okay."

She smiled. How could things be all right when she was living with an abusive, controlling maniac? Without her friend's help, she'd never have plucked up courage to escape. Although she was still far from being safe, this vacation home was the ideal place to plan a new life.

The siding-clad building sat on a large lot bordered by live oaks, their heavy branches dripping with Spanish moss. With one large bedroom and a living room, the small house was a perfect haven until she made further arrangements. Once she'd made a decision, she'd call a taxi to take her to the airport.

An hour later, she'd unpacked her things and had a shower in the small, well laid out bathroom when the man breezed in the front door carrying two brown, paper bags.

"It's going to be a cool night, so I'll chop some logs and bring them in before dark." He deposited the shopping on the counter.

"You mean you're staying tonight?"

"Yes, I told my wife I'll be out of town for an early meeting tomorrow morning."

She pulled her brows together in a frown. "You could have told her what we're doing. When I said not to tell anyone, I didn't mean your wife. I hate the idea of you lying to her on my account."

"She'll understand when I explain." His face split in a wide grin. "I'm the one guy whose wife *does* understand him."

He began unpacking the cans and packets while the woman stacked fresh items in the fridge. "Your wife sounds nice."

"She's more than nice. She's my best friend and soul mate as well as the woman I love. Do you want me to help you make the bed?"

She squirmed inside. Making a bed with a man was an intimate act. "No, I can manage thanks. Where will you sleep?"

"On the sofa, it may be old, but it's pretty comfortable. Anyway it's only for one night—I'll have to leave very early tomorrow—it'll take me a couple of hours to get to the office."

Her eyes lanced to his. "I can't thank you enough for what you've done. Without you, I'd never have had the courage to leave that…that…bastard and start afresh. You've been a good friend, how can I ever repay you?"

His face suffused with color and he jumped to his feet. "Just keep yourself safe and pick up the pieces of your life. Call us when you're fixed up somewhere and we'll come and visit."

"I'd like that, thanks."

The words hovered there between them and he coughed. "Right, I'll go and get those logs chopped." The corners of his eyes crinkled as he gave a quick grin. A cool blast disturbed the air when he opened the door and she shivered.

Her boyfriend had turned out to be a monster. She'd met him at a darts tournament where both companies they worked for were having an evening get-together for their employees. It was obvious he was a leader the way he organized the players into teams and presided over the scores. She'd felt his eyes on her most of the evening and when she eventually made eye contact with him, she was smitten.

They started dating and when he urged her to move in with him a few months later, she jumped at the chance, because by then she was crazy about him. Their love life was imaginative and fulfilling and it never occurred to her that he wasn't happy or that he needed more than one woman. However, when he began coming home late smelling of perfume, she realized she wasn't the only one and that the honeymoon was over.

She opened the freezer and reviewed the stack of neatly packed boxes. The Lasagna looked good, that would heat them up. Once dinner was in the microwave, she paced around the room, trying to keep warm. The strange sounds of the countryside unnerved her. Each time a squirrel ran up a tree or a raccoon scampered about, she tensed. She released a pent up sigh, crossed to where a portable television languished on a shelf and tuned to a news channel.

Cold air breached the room as the man carried in a large wicker basket piled high with split logs. He knelt in front of the brick fireplace and soon a roaring fire filled the grate. By the time the microwave beeped, tall flames with blue tongues licked the dry, crackling wood, radiating heat into the room.

They sat on the sagging sofa with trays on their laps eating dinner and watching TV.

"How long did you know this man before you began living together?" He asked between mouthfuls of food.

"Not very long, but he was so kind and charming then. After we'd been together a few months, he changed, always going out alone at nights. The first time I asked where he'd been, he went berserk and beat me."

"Did you ever find out where he went?"

"No, but he often came in smelling of perfume. I'm almost sure he was seeing other women."

"That's tough, but when did you first suspect he'd really hurt someone?"

She laid down her fork and leveled a scared look on him. "A few months ago, he came home late with his clothes spattered with blood. I pretended to be asleep, but I watched him hide a gun at the back of his sock drawer. Now you see why I had to get away—he's dangerous—he may even have killed someone."

"Well, you're quite safe here. By spring, you'll be in a new place and making friends. Let's clear this lot away and get some sleep."

She carried their trays through to the kitchen while he crossed to the bedroom, emerging with a pillow and a quilt rolled up in his arms.

"Are you sure you don't want me to help you make the bed?" He requested again.

In the doorway of the bedroom, she gave a negative motion of the head. "Goodnight and thanks again."

"Goodnight, sleep tight. I'll try not to wake you in the morning. Take care and remember to call when you're somewhere safe."

"I will bye."

He gave her a wink and she closed the bedroom door.

She ambled over to the window gazing up the street at the neighboring yard lights twinkling in the dark. Overwhelming feelings of being free from her boyfriend's clutches made her want to sing. The lights of neighboring mobile homes glimmered, the nearest one a few hundred yards away. Dancing in and out of the clouds, a sliver of a moon glinted in silver strips on a nearby creek. Trees in silhouette wafted in the gentle breeze, their branches reaching out surrounding the home. The atmosphere was one of tranquility. No phone and situated at the back of a large mobile home park in the center of the state at the bottom of a mile long dirt track, this place would be hard to find unless you knew it was there.

A loud thud woke her. She sat up, gripping the covers. By the bright shaft of moonlight streaming in the window, she peered at her watch and noted it was one-fifteen. Much too early for her friend to be dressing to go to the office. She strained her ears, but silence encompassed her.

Sliding out of bed, she pulled on a thin robe and padded over to the bedroom door. She reached out for the handle, but before she touched it, the door burst open. A tall, dark form advanced. Her heartbeat thundered in her ears. She turned to run. The man grabbed her robe and swung her hard against him. She screamed. Then her head jerked with the force of a backhanded slap that sent her flying across the bed.

"You fucking little whore! Did you think I'd let you get away from me? I've been following you and your stupid lover for months."

Fear kinked her insides into knots, as she inched across the bed. Quick as a flash, he was round the other side, hauling her by the hair onto the floor. The side of her head struck the nightstand, her cheekbone cracked on impact and an excruciating pain seared through her head.

"It's not what it looks like," she managed to stutter between little staccato gasps. "I've been helping clear this place out as a surprise for his wife."

"Liar!" he leaned down and wrestled her closer, still holding her hair. His face was inches from hers as he hocked up a glob of phlegm and spat in her face. "You'll never lie to me again, bitch."

His eyes were wild—wilder than she'd ever seen them—and she knew at that moment he was capable of killing. Her eyes skittered to the open door and she drew in a shocked breath. A pool of dark, red blood ringed the crumpled form of the man on the tiled floor in front of the sofa.

"What have you done to him?" She shrieked, bile rising in her throat. Her skull hurt and her knees felt boneless, they threatened to give way at any moment.

He bracketed her jaw and forced her head back round. "Go on, look at your dead lover."

"You'll go to hell for this!" She yelled through a curtain of crimson pain in one last attempt to stand up to him.

A raucous laugh thundered from his chest. "Not me, honey. You're the one who'll burn with your lover."

Her legs wobbled and she collapsed to the floor, hanging her head. The hopes of a new life seeped from her in abject defeat. All her plans had been for nothing. This monster was going to kill her, too. A stream of cold air swished past her as something sliced through the air. Bone and cartilage crunched as a searing pain bombarded her brain and darkness engulfed her.

He unscrewed the silencer and placed the gun on the nightstand before he went through to the living room to begin his clean up. First, he ransacked the man's jacket pockets pulling out a pair of nail clippers, some coins and a folded piece of paper with phone numbers written on it. Next, he rifled the pant's pockets, which revealed a wallet with credit cards, his driver's license and two bunches of keys. He deposited these items on the table before he went outside and crammed the only one that looked like a car key into the lock of the car parked under the carport. Once he'd established it unlocked the car, he scraped the key along the side of the pristine, shiny paintwork in a deliberate, vandalistic gesture before re-entering the house.

The man was a big sucker, so he dug in his heels, grabbed his ankles and dragged him face down across the tiles nearer to the door. A smeary trail of dark blood followed, glistening in zigzag patterns on the beige, tiled floor. Feeling uncomfortable in his pants, wet from his ejaculation during the killings, he bent to retrieve a small bag containing a change of clothes he'd hidden when he'd pried open one of the mobile home's windows. He re-entered the bedroom. Positioning the bag on the bottom of the bed, he gave the woman's body a swift kick as he crossed to another door poking his head in to check it was the bathroom.

He gathered up a bottle of mouthwash, floss and toothpaste, stuffing it into a cosmetic bag sitting on the counter. In the medicine cupboard, he discovered her perfume and deodorant, stashed those in the bag, and placed it beside her purse on the dresser. While the thought was still in his head, he retrieved one spent cartridge from the bedroom floor and the other from the tiles, pushing them down the side of the woman's purse. He prowled around the room, his eyes scanning it for evidence of her presence. Her glasses, a paperback book and her cell phone were on the nightstand, so he moved those over to the dresser. Last of all, he straightened the covers and made the bed.

He fired a hasty glance at the dead female and decided that he'd better get on with his work otherwise dawn would creep up on him and the last thing he wanted was to be seen around this neighborhood. He moved toward her and flipped her over so that she was on her back, her fixed, open eyes staring unseeing at the ceiling. She was a good-looking broad, flaming red hair, expressive green eyes a man could drown in, and a slim body with curves in all the right places. What a pity. She'd been a good fuck, but when she got suspicious about his comings and goings, he knew he had to silence her.

Her body was lighter than the man's was, and soon the two were prone together on the tiles near the door. He went outside and craned his neck making sure no one was around. The nearest property was several hundred yards away and plunged in darkness. He sat in the driver's seat of the car and backed it as close to the home as he could. Next, he climbed out and opened the passenger door.

Another swift look around verified all was quiet. He entered the front door, bent over the woman's body, swung it over his shoulder and carried it out to the car. Dropping her upright onto the passenger seat, he wrapped the seat belt around her and clicked the buckle in place. One body moved and only one more to go. Although he was tall with a good physique and worked out regularly, getting the man into the car wouldn't be easy.

He decided to drag him along the porch, down the steps and stash him behind the front seat. That action done, he doused the house lights, locked the door with another key from the man's bunch, climbed into the car and drove off.

A pre-dawn mist swirled around as he applied his foot to the accelerator and the car glided along. Once he'd passed through the park gates and maneuvered the bumpy dirt track, he drove along the main road for ten minutes. He pulled over onto a grassy verge and left the engine running. Now came the hard part, getting the man into the driver's seat.

He piled out, leaving the driver's door ajar, and opened the back door. With one foot inside the car, he leaned toward the body pushing with all his might until the man was in a sitting position. With sweat glistening on his brow, his arms encircled the body's chest and tugged until it bucked forward, knocking him off his feet. He pushed himself upright and rested, wiping perspiration from his brow and inhaling a few ragged breaths.

A cool wind rustled through the trees and an owl hooted somewhere, reminding him that he still had a lot of work to do before dawn broke. Springing into action, he lugged the heavy body along the damp grass and heaved it into the driver's seat. He buckled the seatbelt, cranked the steering wheel to the right and slid the transmission into drive. His last action before he closed the door was to toss in a plastic Calla Lily.

The vehicle crept forward, heading for the edge of a densely overgrown drop into a swamp. Wiping his bloodstained palms on his pants, he peeled his lips back in a reptilian grin and watched the wheels rotate, the front ones dropping from view. Damn. The car stopped, balancing on the edge. Without the momentum to send it over, the rear wheels remained on the grassy bank. He worked his face into a grimace and charged over, bracing his arms on the trunk. His face contorted with the effort of propelling the vehicle toward the edge until the mass of greenery consumed the car.

He inhaled a deep, restorative breath, dusted off his hands and started to jog. A few hundred yards down the road, he squinted back at the car's headlights illuminating the shrubs and trees creating a festive appearance. By the time the silver streaks of dawn heralded another day, the battery would be dead and all trace of the car and its inhabitants gone.

One hour later, he arrived back at the mobile home park, tired and sweating. Once he'd passed through the gates, he made a right-angled turn en route for the woods. He jogged slowly down the trails to the far side of the park and emerged a few yards from his pickup, which he'd hidden at the back of the home.

All was still quiet, so he bounded inside. The hands of the clock on the mantle were at ten after four, so he trotted through to the bedroom and zipped open his bag. He extracted a spray bottle of cleaner, a plastic bag of disposable cloths and placed a towel on the bed. With great gusto, he set about washing all trace of blood and gore from the tiles. The fire was still glowing, so he slung on another two logs and absorbed the welcome heat when they caught fire.

He stripped off his blood-spattered clothes and pitched them into the fiery flames along with the blood-soaked cloths, watching them ignite and disintegrate into ashes. He knelt down on the tiles and stared into the flames allowing his mind to wander. The heat from the raging fire burned red blotches on the top of his legs and lower body while he lingered naked by the grate, deep in thought.

He rose, picked up his towel from the bed and headed for the bathroom. Hot water scalded his burnt skin, so he adjusted the flow. He worked the soap into a generous lather as the spray of cool water cascaded over his body reviving him.

Now dry and dressed in clean jeans and a sweater, he wanted no trace of evidence left in the mobile home or any form of I.D., so he bustled around stuffing the man and woman's belongings into a black, trash bag. His last task was to wipe every surface clean with his damp towel and pick up his gun. This took some time and when he was happy that he'd eliminated all trace of himself and the victims, he extinguished the lights and crept out.

Chapter 2

Juno flicked the ash from his cigarette onto the grass by the yellow, police tape. A young, uniformed officer approached.

"Sorry sir, this is a police crime scene, please move on."

Juno puffed out his cheeks. "Yes, I know, Lieutenant Walker asked me to drop by. My name's Juno."

The officer threw him a wary look, swiveled on his heel and spoke into a two-way radio. Two lines of police tape cordoned off an entry and exit route to the forest. As the radio crackled, Juno pinched the glowing end of his cigarette between his thumb and forefinger before tucking the stub into the breast pocket of his denim shirt.

A few moments later, Lieutenant Zack Walker tramped from behind a sturdy tree dressed in coveralls holding out a rubber-gloved hand. "Hey, glad you could make it. How are ya?" He lifted the tape and Juno ducked his head and shoulders.

"I'm good, what's up? Your message said to get here as fast as I could."

"A murder, that's what's up. Some sonofabitch has killed this ugly broad. God, she's like a beached whale, but she still didn't deserve to die like this."

Juno held his breath and waited. Zack Walker was a homicide detective and finding gory remains was an everyday part of his job. He loved to elaborate on the sanguinary details leaving nothing to the imagination and causing Juno's stomach to roil.

The police officer stepped forward with a clipboard. He glanced at his watch and wrote down the time. "Name, sir?"

"Juno."

The officer looked at Zack. "Sir?"

"That's okay, Wilson, just log him as Juno."

The officer reached in a box and handed Juno protective clothing and surgical gloves. Zack launched into details of the crime and by the time Juno had donned the coveralls, he felt sick.

"A single bullet to the back of the head, execution-style." Zack held back the branch of a live oak until Juno passed. "The perp dumped the body here, probably hoping it wouldn't be found for some time, but after some ambient air tests, the M.E. thinks she's only been dead about twelve hours."

"Who found her?"

"A couple riding." Walker extended his index finger. "There's a riding stable about a mile up the road. Most people stay on the stables' property, but these folks rented the horses for a whole day and decided to ride in the woods. Here we are."

The crime scene manager was talking to the photographer while the pathologist handed the scene of crime officer a bundle of bagged swabs and sealed sample containers.

Zack waved a hand in the direction of the crime scene coordinator. "These guys have just finished, so I can let you see what I mean before the body's taken to the morgue."

Juno's insides turned to jelly as he stared at the portable, canvas tent erected over the murder victim. The few remaining members of the forensic team stood bunched in a small group speaking in low tones. He dogged Walker's footsteps to the opening and looked inside. A large, young woman lay prone on her back. The crime scene manager had already covered her head, feet and hands with individual bags and secured them with tape. The victim's cheap clothing was in disarray, her skirt lifted up to her shoulders revealing her naked, lower body. Juno turned his head away.

"Look at this," Walker pushed aside one milky, white thigh with the toe of his shoe. "Ever seen anything like this before?"

Protruding from the victim's vagina was a large piece of broken broom handle.

Juno emitted a small cry of astonishment. "My God! I hope she was dead before he used that."

"Yes, the pathologist said it was rammed up her post mortem. Just a minute." Walker bustled over to the nearby group and returned with a sealed plastic bag. "This was lying at her feet."

Juno stared at a plastic Calla Lily. "Is this significant?"

Walker lifted his shoulders in a shrug. "Maybe, one similar was left at a murder scene two months ago. I hope this is a coincidence and not indicative of a serial killer. I'd say we're dealing with a real sicko this time and I wondered if you could help."

As a boy, Juno discovered he was different from other kids when he had a vision of one of his friends trapped in quicksand. His mother hadn't laughed at him, as he'd suspected she would, but had contacted the boy's parents and two days later they rescued their son from a swamp, just in time. Other isolated incidents occurred during his teen years, and by the time he was in his twenties, he had the ability to receive vibes from articles and places he visited. He regarded this '*gift*' as a burden, not an asset. Seeing other peoples' sad demise was not something he cared for, but he had no choice. These visions interrupted his life for no apparent reason and afterward left him drained.

"Look, Walker, I can't turn my powers off and on. Sometimes I get no vibes at all, like that last case you called me in on."

The Lieutenant appeared not to hear and squatted down closer to the body. "Are you getting anything yet?" Walker pushed himself to his feet and fixed his dark eyes on Juno.

"I really need to be alone to get the feel of the place. Let me know when your guys are finished and I'll meet you back here."

A look of disgust crossed Walker's face. "You squeamish?"

"A little, but I work better when there's nothing to distract me."

"Like a dead body?"

"Yes, like a dead body. I know I write novels about people being murdered, but writing and reality are two different things. Seeing this poor girl lying here upsets me."

"Yeah, yeah," Walker flapped his hand, signaling Juno should go. "I'll call you."

The pathologist signaled to two officers standing at one side with a black, body bag to follow him. The three crossed to the body, so Juno turned and trekked back between the yellow tapes, his breath ragged. He nodded an acknowledgement to the uniformed officer who wrote down Juno's leaving time before he made tracks for his car.

A warm breeze ruffled his dark hair as he tore off his coveralls and rubber gloves and stuffed them in the trunk. Leaning against it, he lit a cigarette, drew the smoke deep into his lungs, flinging his head back as he exhaled. That first, long drag calmed his nerves and made him realize that he'd had no breakfast and was hungry. He flung the cigarette onto the road, ground it with his heel and climbed into his car.

The phone was ringing off the hook when Juno entered the front door of his house. "Yeah?" he gushed, out of breath from running.

"Mr. Juno, this is Charlie Addison of *Everyday* magazine. I believe your agent spoke to you about us doing an article on you."

Juno screwed up his face. "Yeah, but I'm really not into that sort of thing, I prefer my privacy."

"I understand, but my staff's very experienced and would only cover subjects you're willing to discuss. Your agent suggested Thursday. Is that still okay?"

Juno's mind raced. He silently cursed Edward for setting this up. "Er, yes, but I'm still not sure I want to do this."

"A great many readers love your books. Don't you think you owe it to them to do an occasional interview?"

"Mm, yeah, I guess so. Who'd be conducting it?"

"One of my top writers who's very intuitive and professional, Alex Martell."

Juno shrugged. "Okay, send this Alex along, but I'll only speak about my work, no personal stuff."

By the time Juno replaced the receiver, he wished he hadn't been so quick to agree. It was years since anyone had interviewed him. One of the reasons he'd moved to a house in an isolated region was to escape publicity. In addition, he needed seclusion to concentrate on his writing.

He gazed out the window at a large expanse of quiet backwoods. His ranch-styled house sat amid twenty-seven acres of rural outland. He mowed the grass closest to his home and around the dirt track that led from the main road to a concrete driveway, but he left the rest to grow wild. Leafy trees cast dappled shade around the house and the front yard where Juno sat pounding on his newly acquired laptop. On the other side of his property, a creek meandered nearby to where he'd built a timber-framed cabin, clad with rustic siding. During the winter months, when nights were cooler, he worked, ate and slept there. The intimacy of the cozy cabin appealed to him. Although he loved his house, it was nice to get away into this private place and watch wildlife frolic undisturbed.

A sudden idea invaded his mind. Thoughts spilled out one after another as his nimble fingers kneaded the keys of an old, Underwood typewriter.

Darkness had fallen by the time he looked up and realized he was hungry. A clock on the mantle chimed seven o'clock—no wonder he felt empty—he hadn't eaten in seven hours.

A loud thump sounded outside. He listened, knitting his brows as he pushed himself upright and tiptoed over to the window, standing to one side so that he had a clear view. The bushes outside rustled followed by scratching and whining.

A dark form materialized behind the glass. Juno flinched, his heart thudding. A face pressed against the window accompanied by a lolling, pink tongue and a sharp bark. My God, a dog, what a fright! His first instinct had been to rush through to the den to get his gun, but thank goodness he hadn't, he'd have felt foolish.

He opened the front door and a Labrador, the color of dark chocolate, pranced in. "Hello, boy." Juno inspected the dog's hindquarters. "Oh yes, you are a boy. What are you doing here? Are you lost?"

The dog's tail thumped the floor as he sat and tilted his head at Juno's words. Juno held out a hand for the animal to sniff before patting the dog's head and feeling for a collar. His neck was bare.

"Come on, let's find you something to eat." The dog trotted behind, his long tail swishing from side to side against the walls in the narrow hallway.

When he'd heated and eaten a pizza and the dog had wolfed a can of corned beef, Juno placed a call to the local sheriff's office, enquiring whether anyone had reported a lost dog.

"Well Fido, it looks as if you're staying with me for the time being. Whoever you belong to, either doesn't know you're missing, or doesn't care." The dog leaned forward and licked his hand. "I'd better find an old blanket for you to sleep on."

With the dog close on his heels, he entered the guest bedroom and extracted an old quilt from the closet. The dog leapt onto the bed and proceeded to meander in circles before curling up and snuggling down.

Juno grabbed a handful of loose skin on the back of the dog's neck and hauled him down. "Oh no you don't. You can sleep on the floor in my room."

Juno sat up in bed with a start. Sweat beaded on his forehead and his heart pounded as if he'd run a mile. The woman's face had been striking, but blurry. Shoulder-length hair framed an attractive, heart-shaped face with dark eyes—as dark as the depths of an ocean. When she'd smiled, her parted lips revealed small, white, even teeth. She'd thrown her head back and laughed, giving an impish grin.

This vision was different from the others he'd had before. His usual ones were in color, but this one was black and white and hazy. The woman's features had been hard to distinguish, but still conveyed beauty. He played the vision over in his mind, wondering who she was. She'd appeared at her ease and relaxed and not fraught with danger, so why the dream?

A warm, wet tongue licked his hand. He switched on the bedside light and looked into the dark eyes of the dog. "And who said you could sleep on the bed?" The dog laid his head on his paws giving him a soulful look.

Juno swung his legs from the covers and pulled on a robe. The dog followed and sat at the side of his barstool while he waited for a pot of coffee to brew. A contented moan escaped from the dog as Juno reached down to fondle the animal's ears. He mulled over his dream again and wondered if the woman had anything to do with one of the police cases. The vibes had been warm and pleasant, so it was unlikely that she was a victim of foul play.

Now he was wide-awake, he decided to work on his manuscript. Some of his best ideas came to him in the middle of the night and anyway, he needed to make a list of subjects he was willing to talk about for his appointment with the magazine correspondent later that day.

He fumed inside and regretted consenting to the interview. He now regarded his privacy as number one priority. The first few years of fame as a writer had been uplifting and exciting, but he soon discovered that it had its price. People pried into his private life, thought they had a right to know what he was doing and whom he was seeing. His love of the female species had enabled him to have any woman he wanted, and there had been many during the early years.

A disastrous, short marriage to a Hollywood starlet had cured him of philandering when she cited his adultery with several women as cause of the marriage breakdown, when in truth it had been her lack of enthusiasm in sex. Older and wiser, with seven successful novels under his belt, he sold his home in L.A. and relocated to Florida. His quest to find the perfect place to live had taken two years, but as soon as he'd set eyes on his present property, he knew he'd found it.

Daylight streamed through the Venetian blinds casting horizontal stripes over Juno sprawled on a black, leather sofa with the dog at his side. Sometime before dawn he'd flopped on the padded cushions, closed his eyes and before long was sound asleep.

A long, hot shower helped rid him of the crick in his neck. He toweled the dripping water from his hair and opened the kitchen door for the dog to go out. The animal hesitated and gave him a dubious look.

"It's okay. You can come back in."

Almost as if the dog understood, he frolicked around a clump of trees while Juno made breakfast. Halfway through eating scrambled eggs and toast, the phone rang. The dog was wolfing down the remnants of some leftovers, vegetables and a porterhouse steak bone when Juno reached for the handset.

"Juno," he muttered between bites of toast.

"Walker here, forensics are finished at the crime scene in the woods if you'd like to swing by this morning to get a feel of things."

"Okay, what time do you want to meet?"

"Nine-thirty?"

"I'll see you then." Juno hung up the receiver.

Getting involved with a police inquiry a year ago had been his biggest mistake ever. Local radio stations and newspapers had emblazoned news of a young child missing for nearly a week. When Juno descended into the depths of a dream one afternoon, he called the police and they referred him to Lieutenant Walker. He recounted what he *saw*, a child tied up in a shack near an old mill on S.R. 64. Dubious at first, the Lieutenant eventually arrived there with a backup team and found the child alive. Non-plussed by his experience, the boy had given detailed descriptions of his captors and their car, including the tag, and the police were able to arrest two men the following day. Now the lieutenant thought Juno could *see* something to help him with every major case.

The memory of his latest dream returned and he decided not to mention it to Walker. A vision of a happy, smiling woman was not going to help with this case. The woman in his dream had an aura of beauty something that couldn't be said about the latest murder victim.

The police had taken down the yellow tape when Juno arrived at the crime scene. Branches and twigs crackled beneath his feet as he tramped between the trees to a patch of flat earth surrounded by chalk marks, which indicated the place where the horse riders had found the victim. An eerie feeling swept over him and he swiveled round expecting to see someone, but the clearing was empty.

His eyes snaked around when rustling sounded low and to the right. He gulped and advanced two steps. Before he went any further, a rabbit hopped toward him and he exhaled loudly. The furry creature scuttled off and Juno rebuked himself for wanting some time alone before Walker arrived. Now he felt foolish that such a small creature had spooked him.

Noisy footsteps heralded the lieutenant's arrival. "Got here early I see," he said, bending low beneath a large branch.

"Yeah, sometimes I work better on my own, but there's nothing here but a creepy atmosphere."

Zack Walker leaned one arm against the trunk of a tree. "Yeah, death's strange. This murder's transformed perfectly peaceful woods into a macabre place of morbid interest. I just chased away a carload of teenagers hoping to find the murder spot."

Juno shook his head. "Why does death have such an appeal to the public?"

"It's the element of the unknown, isn't it?" Walker pulled a pack of cigarettes from his breast pocket and offered him one.

"Thanks," Juno slipped the cigarette between his lips.

Walker flipped his lighter, held the flame to the end of Juno's cigarette and then his own.

Both men inhaled deeply.

"I'm sorry to bring you here when I don't think I can help your case at the moment," Juno said. "But as I've explained before, these visions come when I least expect them. Who knows, I may never have another one again."

Walker gave a wry smile. "That's okay, I needed a break from the office. I only hope forensics have some evidence that'll give us a lead. I looked up the last murder two months ago and there's quite a few similarities. Once we get the autopsy and forensic reports, we'll be able to judge if the killer's the same guy."

"What makes you think the killer's male? A woman could quite easily have committed these crimes."

"Yes, I guess so, but more than likely it's a man."

Juno drew the cigarette smoke deep into his lungs and exhaled.

"The pathologist found numerous fibers on the victim that imply she was killed elsewhere and moved here. I can't see a woman lifting our victim. She weighs nearly three hundred pounds."

"Hmm, I see what you mean."

"If the same guy killed both women, I don't hold out much hope for any conclusive evidence, unless he's one of these perps that want to be caught and he's deliberately left us a clue. He'd cleaned up the last murder scene, so there was very little to go on."

Both men smoked in silence and Juno wandered around until he came to the place where forensics had erected a mobile tent over the victim. He squatted down, touched the grass and closed his eyes. Breathing deeply, he cleared his mind.

After a few minutes, he stood upright and dusted his hands together. "Sorry, nothing's coming to me, yet, but I'll hang around for a bit longer if you want to get back."

"Okay, call me and let me know how you get on."

"Sure thing."

The two men shook hands and Walker turned and retraced his steps.

Juno took a slow walk around the crime scene. The senior investigating officer would have ordered a fingertip search and anything important found his team would have sealed in bags to prevent any contamination. The grass and branches of the entry and exit route, which officers had sealed off with yellow tape, now lay trampled flat with constant foot traffic.

A brief wider search revealed impressions of horses' hooves in the dirt, which must have been as far as the riders came when they saw the body. His cigarette had burned down to the filter, so he ground it into some gravel with the heel of his shoe, and turned back. He sighed, lit another cigarette and walked to his car.

Chapter 3

The hinges squeaked when the door opened and a large brown dog flung himself at Alex. She grabbed the doorjamb to steady herself as a pair of green-flecked eyes bored into hers.

Startled, her lips tilted in a small smile. "Good morning Mr. Juno, I'm Alex Martell."

She extended a hand, which the man ignored, while his eyes raked her from head to toe before they impaled hers. Inside she squirmed under his scrutiny, but met his cold stare.

"But you're a woman!"

He rolled a cigarette from one corner of his mouth to the other while perusing her with narrowing eyes through swirling smoke. Dark hair with graying temples dipped over brows drawn together. The top button of his ragged jeans was missing, baring a small amount of tanned flesh. He was older than Alex had imagined—at least ten years older than she—an aging hippie.

When she'd unglued her tongue from the top of her mouth, she lifted her chin. "Yes, I'm a woman and we have a one-thirty appointment. Did I catch you at an awkward moment?"

"No."

A weighty silence hung between them while the dog licked her hand and Alex noted the man's bare feet poking beneath the frayed cuffs of his jeans. So, this was how a best-selling author dressed when he was off duty. A faded plaid shirt with rolled up sleeves hung open over a lean, muscled torso.

"I believe you were expecting me, my editor called and told you I was coming?"

His eyes continued to study her with disdain. "Nope." His tone was icy as he turned his back on her and strolled through the half-open door with the dog trotting behind.

Unsure what to do next, Alex rapped on one of the door panels. "Er, Mr. Juno?"

Several silent seconds ticked by before he barked. "Are you going to conduct the interview from out there or do you intend coming in?"

Alex stepped inside and closed the door. In the small foyer, an archway led to the living room with a few pieces of leather furniture and Juno leaning against the mantle shelf of a red, brick fireplace. He waved an arm in a curved gesture—an invitation to enter and she spurred her legs into motion.

"I'm a little confused. You said you weren't expecting me." She advanced through the archway and paused in the center of the room, clutching her briefcase with both hands.

"That's right. I arranged for a man to interview me. I'd never have agreed otherwise."

Alex's spine stiffened—another male chauvinist pig. She suppressed a sharp retort and withered onto a sofa, unbuckling her briefcase and pulling out her notepad and voice recorder.

He raised an arm and pointed an index finger. "You're not using that thing."

"You mean my recorder? Why ever not?"

"It's an invasion of privacy."

"But you consented to an interview."

"Not with a woman."

Couldn't this man speak? Did he have to shout? To think that at one time she'd thought he was the best thing since sliced bread and had jumped at the chance to come face to face with one of her favorite authors. Now she was regretting it and would have preferred to live with her romantic notions than to have had them dashed.

"Why are you so against women? What have we ever done to you?" Against her better judgment, her own voice had risen to match his pitch.

"Lady, it would take a month of Sundays to go into all that. Now get on with it."

Her chest lifted on a quick breath before she reached for her pen and list of questions.

"Can you tell me why you decided to move here from California?"

"No."

His hard expression told her that he was testing her patience, so she decided to let him play his little game and rephrased the question. "Does the move here mean you want nothing more to do with Hollywood after the fiasco the movie of your last book turned into?"

"No."

"No you've not abandoned Hollywood or 'no' the movie wasn't a fiasco?"

She gave him a sweet smile and he flung the remnants of his cigarette into the glowing embers of the fire. Despite his clean but disheveled appearance, she tried to ignore how sexy he looked as his green eyes flashed a warning. With a sudden movement, he plowed the fingers of one hand through his dark hair, which waved to the upturned collar of the plaid shirt.

'*One point for me,*' she thought, as he shuffled his bare feet on the rag-rolled rug. His chest heaved and he almost spoke, but he changed his mind.

"Continue," his hand sliced the air in a wave as if he were a king and she one of his subjects.

This man was both rude and obnoxious and she reminded herself to tell Charlie not to arrange any more interviews with petulant, pettish authors who had ideas above their station.

"When's your next book due for release?"

His eyes opened wide and he shook his head. "I really have no idea. My publisher would be the one to answer that. What kind of journalist are you? If these are the kind of stupid questions you intend to ask, then this interview is terminated here and now."

Anger and frustration seethed inside and Alex spoke through gritted teeth. "You're not being very cooperative, Mr. Juno. You won't talk about your personal life and you have no idea what's going on in your career, so I think you're right, this interview is terminated."

"Juno!" he bawled. "The name's Juno—not Mr. Juno—just Juno."

She continued ramming everything into her briefcase. "I see. Thank you for that one, little piece of information. I'm glad I'm not leaving here without any material about you." She sprang to her feet.

He crossed the short space between them in two strides and grasped her upper arm. "You give up too easily." A condescending smirk wreathed his face.

"Let go my arm and besides, I'm not a journalist, I'm a magazine correspondent."

He cocked one tantalizing brow as she tried to shake her arm free. His gaze was hot and intense as he pressed his face near to hers. For one split second, she thought he was going to kiss her and she held her breath. He suddenly released her and she almost fell.

"I didn't need you to tell me you're not a professional. Who are you? The editor's niece?"

The words were dripping with disdain and the emphasis on *'niece'*, caused tears to dew in Alex's eyes.

She raised her chin and looked him straight in the eyes. "You're the one who's supposed to be psychic, so you tell me." She slammed the door on her way out.

"Oh, Charlie, it was awful. He was hateful and he made me feel like that." Alex held her thumb and forefinger close together. "I've never met a man so rude and arrogant. You should have clarified I was a female before you sent me on this assignment. That man has a serious problem with women."

Charles Addison's eyes followed Alex as she paced the width of his office. What she lacked in stature, she made up with spunk. However, at this moment she looked defeated.

He reached out and drew her into his arms, stroking wispy bangs from her brow. "Sorry. He *was* a bit grumpy when I phoned, but I thought he'd be okay at the interview when he got used to the idea."

"No, it's not your fault. I badgered you into letting me do this interview. I guess I'm still not ready to undertake full duties, yet. Well, what they say about learning by your mistakes is very true. I learned a lot today."

She burrowed her face into his tweed jacket and he pulled her close. During her three-year marriage to John, she'd bubbled with happiness and had confided her hopes and dreams to him, but since her husband's mysterious disappearance, he'd watched her lose the will to live and her weight plummet.

When she'd returned to work after a short break, he'd allocated her small, easy assignments and bit by bit, the color had returned to her cheeks, but she'd begged him for something more challenging. He'd hoped that giving her what she wanted would make her more responsive to his needs. For years, he'd harbored deep feelings for her.

Alex's shoulder-length brown hair shone with golden highlights and she attracted attention wherever she went. Her eyes were an unusual shade of indigo, fringed with long dark lashes. When they first met, Charlie was sure she wore colored, contact lenses to make her eyes different, but he soon discovered he was wrong. The only women he'd come across with indigo eyes was the actress, Elizabeth Taylor and a female friend of his parents.

Medium height and slim with a neat figure, Alex barely reached his shoulder. His heart went out to her as she sagged into an armchair, and reached for a tissue.

"Don't let that conceited bum needle you. Why don't you take the rest of the afternoon off?" He tilted her chin with a finger and kissed a tear-streaked cheek.

She nodded, wiping away her tears and took Charlie's outstretched hand. "You always make things seem so unimportant and cheer me up. How did I ever get to be so lucky in finding a friend like you?"

"You know I want to be more than your friend."

Her face and eyes were serious as their gaze held. "I know," she whispered, "but please Charlie, don't."

He nodded in agreement and watched her trudge out the door.

After swinging by her office to lock the door, Alex visited the ladies' room to wash her tear-stained face. She stared at her image in the mirror and recalled the day she met Charlie. With work experience as a server, shop assistant and numerous other mundane jobs, she spent four years obtaining a degree in journalism. It was all she'd ever wanted to do. Her first job application was for a position on the staff of *Everyday* magazine and butterflies filled her stomach as she sat outside the editor's office.

The door opened and a tall man with a bushy beard emerged. He glared at her and lowered his brows in an expression of irritation. "Ms. Gray?" Alex nodded. "You'd better come in."

From the disgruntled expression on his face, Alex knew straight away that she didn't stand a chance. That made her even more determined not to show her disappointment when he rejected her. With a bounce in her step and a smile on her face, she followed him inside and sat on the offered chair.

Charlie didn't sit, but stood with his back to her, looking out the window. "Why do you want a job here?"

His first question took her by surprise, but she recovered quickly and realized that she'd nothing to lose by being sassy. This man had made up his mind about her the moment he set eyes on her. "Because I think I can write a report every bit as good, if not better, than the people you already have working for you."

"Think? You only think, don't you know?" He turned and his eyes met hers in a steady gaze.

"No, I don't know yet, but employ me and I'll prove I'm right."

His face creased in a small smile. "Are you always this straightforward?"

"Oh, no, most of the time I'm downright rude, but today I'm making an exception."

He laughed and sat on a leather chair behind the desk, grinning. "I like your spirit, Ms. Gray. A woman needs to be assertive in a man's world. Come to my office at nine o'clock tomorrow morning and I'll allocate you a small assignment. If I like what you do, I'll employ you. Is that fair?"

Alex gave a small affirmative motion, rose and held out her hand. "Most fair. I'll see you in the morning." With wobbly knees and head held high, she closed the door. Outside, her fist rose in triumph and she proclaimed. "Yea!"

Her trial assignment was to interview a local congressional representative with pancreatic cancer. Unknown to the editor, her adopted mother had died from this same disease and Alex knew everything there was to know about treatments and how the illness affected family and friends. Two days later, she handed in a heartwarming article written with understanding and poignancy and riddled with hope and emotions.

That had been four years ago. Charlie Addison had employed her and she'd been his close friend and star writer ever since.

Thirty minutes after leaving Charlie's office, Alex applied a coat of pink lipstick, combed her hair and rode the scenic elevator to the lobby. She exited the building by the front door and walked a block to a small, sandwich bar.

The man sped to the dark blue sedan and climbed in, assuming a pose with a newspaper, his eyes never leaving the building opposite. The automatic doors opened and closed and several people came out, sometimes in twos or threes and sometimes alone. Then he saw her. She stood outside the building and tilted her head backwards before setting off along the sidewalk.

When she reached the corner, he nudged the stick into drive and crept alongside the curb until he turned into a side road. Then he jammed on the brakes. She had disappeared. On either side of the street were cafes, restaurants and bars. She must have gone into one. Shit! He whacked the wheel in frustration and pulled into the parking lot of the first bar.

The time dragged. After an hour, just when he was considering leaving, he spied her as she sallied past toward the magazine's parking lot. He jumped from his car and ran to a red brick building at the corner, peering round. She stood on the sidewalk talking to another woman.

"Come on," he recited to himself. "Get going."

Right on cue, the couple separated and Alex climbed into a silver Chevy in the parking lot. Her companion waited until she was in the car before re-entering the building. The man hared back to his sedan and swung onto the main road, keeping a reasonable distance behind the Chevy. At one set of traffic lights, he almost lost her, but she was driving slowly and he caught up with her again once they were outside the city limits.

She executed a few turns and he inspected the older styled houses in a tightly knit community. Strange, he hadn't imagined she'd live here. He watched her pull into a driveway next to a Toyota and knock on a red-painted door. He sighed. It was obvious this wasn't her house. He needed to know where she lived to further his plan and his patience was running out. This was the third time he'd tried to follow her home and he'd already wasted too much time. Revenge had burned deep in his gut for a long time and once he'd settled this score, he could move on.

He parked a few houses away on the other side of the street, tuned the radio to a rock and roll channel, and leaned his head on the back of the seat. Every few minutes he monitored the driveway across the street to ensure that the silver Chevy was still there. By now, it was dark and he was hungry. Anger speared through him and he wished he could finish this tonight. He'd been planning this for months and now he needed closure.

A dog barking made him jerk upright. A woman held a large dog by his collar while his prey stowed several large boxes in the Chevy's trunk. In haste, they slammed the door and both women burst into laughter.

"Poor Caesar, he really wants to go home with me." His victim said.

"I know, but you're out at work all day and he'd only chew your place to bits."

The two women hugged. "Drive carefully."

"I will. Call me when you get back."

Silhouetted in the lighted doorway, the woman holding the dog waved while the other started the engine and backed onto the road. Once the Chevy moved off along the street, he released the handbrake and twisted the ignition key. Click...nothing. Click, click, and still nothing.

"Oh, fuck!" He blurted. "This damn starter motor!" He fumed inside as the clicking continued and he watched the red taillights of the Chevy disappear from view. Another wasted evening, next time he'd use a different car and make sure he got what he wanted. Lust for her blood and revenge burned deep inside. The more he thought about her, the more his rage threatened to erupt. Time was running out.

Chapter 4

The next day, Alex leaned back in her chair, glad the morning was over. Today was her third wedding anniversary and she'd thought twice about turning up for work. She knew Charlie would understand, but the thought of being on her own was worse than the sympathy she'd have to put up with, so she'd spent most of the time in her office writing about a young woman who was mugged and would never walk again after receiving severe back injuries.

The phone rang. The caller ID specified it was an internal call, so she picked up the receiver. "Alex Martell."

"Are you surviving?" Charlie queried in a concerned tone.

"Yep, how was your morning?"

"As bad as it goes. Do you want to get out of here and grab some lunch?"

Alex smiled. She knew this was Charlie's way of trying to help. "I'd love to."

"Good, I'll see you in the lobby in five minutes."

Alex stretched, massaged the back of her neck to relieve the tension and reached for her purse. A quick comb of her hair, a touch up of lipstick and she was ready. She locked her office door and took the elevator to the lobby. When the doors opened, Charlie was already waiting.

Alex arched an eyebrow. "You said five minutes. I make it only three."

Charlie took hold of her elbow. "Stop splitting hairs. I have a table booked for one-fifteen."

He hustled her out the automatic doors toward a small bistro. As Charlie pushed open the door, a bell tinkled and a dumpy, balding man greeted them.

He held out his hand. "Alex, Charlie, how are you both?"

"Fine, Enrico," they said in unison and all three laughed.

"Come this way, I have a nice table reserved for you by the window." Charlie and Alex followed Enrico. "In fact we have a lunch guest you might be fascinated by. Juno also has a reservation today. Is this table okay?"

Charlie nodded and focused on the door. "Sure, and speak of the devil, he's arrived."

As soon as Enrico assigned them their seats, he took off as fast as a greyhound and Alex watched him bow and scrape to Juno and a vivacious, female companion.

Sitting with his back to the door, Charlie looked over his shoulder and kinked his brow in a frown. "Enrico's leading them this way. He's probably going to seat them over there." He inclined his head toward an adjacent table.

"Oh, no, that's all we need."

Charlie's eyes swept over the extensive menu. "Forget him and enjoy your lunch."

Then Alex raised her eyes and stiffened.

"What's the matter?" Charlie asked.

"Don't look now, but Juno's pointing over here and Enrico's bringing them this way. If he introduces Juno, don't be polite, the man doesn't know the meaning of the word."

Charlie's knuckles were white as he gripped the menu. "What's happening now?"

"They're definitely coming this way." Alex admitted sotto voce.

Charlie routed in his pocket, pulled out a pair of dark, heavy-framed spectacles and donned them before pushing himself to his feet. Alex stared at the menu as the group of three paused by their table.

"Charlie, may I introduce Juno and Petra Zounes." Enrico's face flushed with pride as the two men shook hands.

"I believe you've met Alex," Charlie commented with tautness in his voice.

Alex raised her eyes and met a pair of green-flecked ones with brows lifted in interest.

"Alex, how nice to see you again." Juno's tone was as sweet as saccharin and laced with sarcasm. She cringed at the way he greeted her by her first name and wanted to kick him in the shins to take the smirk off his face. "And this is my friend Petra Zounes."

Alex's face muscles were stiff as she tried to smile. "Nice to meet you." She took the woman's offered hand.

"May we join you?" Juno asked before he turned to Enrico with a condescending smile. "This is a much nicer table than the other one over there."

Alex stared at Charlie willing him to refuse, but he declared in a non-descript tone. "Of course, it would be our pleasure."

Alex knew her eyes betrayed anger as they flashed Charlie a silent message. Juno waited until Petra seated herself before he sat and placed a tan, zipped, leather organizer and a bunch of keys on the table.

"So, you're the editor of *Everyday*." Juno said, placing his napkin across his knee. "How long have you been doing that?"

"Many years, five of them here in Geyserville." Charlie volunteered nothing more. "How long have you been a writer?"

"Much longer than that." Juno patted his companion's hand. "Petra helps with my research and corrects my typing errors."

"Don't you use the spell check on your computer?" Alex asked.

Cool, green eyes penetrated hers. "No, I still use a typewriter."

'*Well, good for you*,' she wanted to quip, but she remained silent.

Petra Zounes looked flustered at having to share a table with them. Her eyes looked daggers at Juno and her full lips drooped at the corners. Her flaming, titian hair was a contrast to a short, beige skirt and jacket, which emphasized long legs.

"Have you decided what you're going to have, Alex?" Charlie broke the awkward silence.

"Caesar salad and salmon," Alex replied, snapping the menu closed.

"Sounds good, I think I'll have the same." Juno quirked his brows at her with a smirk on his face.

"But we always have the same," Petra whined. "And I don't like salmon."

"So have something different for once. Now, Charlie, when are you going to send a real reporter to interview me?"

Charlie pulled his ear lobe and winked at Alex. "Well now, a little bird told me that interview's been cancelled and I've already reassigned another article to that section. I'm afraid we've other fish to fry right now. But why don't I contact you when we next have an opening."

Alex tried hard not to smile at Charlie's words as he turned a blank face toward Juno's questioning brows.

"Sounds good, Charlie, sounds good. Oh, great here's the salad, I'm starving."

Charlie returned Alex's smile and winked again as she dug into her food.

Fate must have been on their side. As they were finishing their entrée, Enrico summoned Charlie to an urgent telephone call. He bustled back, proclaiming a crisis at the office and they had to leave. The four shook hands and exchanged a quick farewell.

Once outside, Charlie groaned. "My God, Alex, I am so sorry. That man is the most detestable creature I've ever met."

"Then why did you agree to him sharing our table?"

"Mainly curiosity. I didn't think anyone could be as bad as you described. I'm only sorry I had to find out the hard way."

Alex pecked him on the cheek. "Do we really have a crisis at the office?"

"No, Irene phoned to say that my three-thirty appointment had canceled."

They laughed, linked arms and strolled back to work.

Angry words emanated from Charlie's office as Alex shrugged on her coat at five-thirty. Brett Etheridge, the assistant editor, slammed the door and marched past. Alex and Brett had been an item for two years before her father died and he usually took advantage of every opportunity to be alone with her. She suspected that he still had strong feelings for her.

"Goodnight, Brett," Alex cooed to his retreating form and poked her head round Charlie's door. "Are you going to be much longer?"

"Yes, but you go home. Brett's still against doing that story on Gloria DeSilva's adopted child, but he'll come round. Steven says he's managed to rake up some peculiar facts about her husband, too, so once I've cleared things with our legal bigwigs, I'll let Brett write the story. That'll give him a buzz."

Alex kissed Charlie's cheek. Almost six feet tall and at home wearing tweed jackets with leather patches on his sleeves, he reminded her of a cuddly teddy bear. His bushy, brown hair, which she suspected he had permed, a copper-colored beard and moustache all added to the aura of a gentle giant. Beneath this camouflage, she knew he'd served in the military, was a keep-fit fanatic, and worked out several days a week at a local gym. He smelled of pipe tobacco, chewing gum and toothpaste.

His strong arms cocooned her as he gave her a hug. "See you tomorrow, drive carefully." His presence was as soft as a warm blanket enfolding her.

She nodded. "I will."

The drive across town took Alex past the library, two cinemas and The Vaudeville Theatre, which had retained its name from the old Music Hall days. Once she turned up Patton Lane, on the way to Angerton, the road became narrow with two-way traffic. She wound down the window to ingest the fresh scents and hear the sounds of the countryside. Although her home was at the top of a quiet, rural lane, it was only a twenty-minute drive east from the bustling town of Geyserville in west Florida. Alex loved it here. She'd grown up a few miles away and her best friend Barbara Costello still lived next door to the house where her adopted father had raised her.

Jonty Gray had buried his wife soon after Alex's fifteenth birthday and had cared for her along with a housekeeper, Marion, who'd been her companion when her father worked away. Alex and Jonty's bond had gone further than a father and daughter relationship, they'd been best friends and confidants, too. When he died of a stroke four years ago, Alex's world had come to an abrupt halt. It was while she was mourning her father that she met John Martell. He was a junior partner in the law firm handling Jonty's estate and in a matter of seven months; they'd fallen crazy in love and married.

John was tall, slim and dark-haired. His quiet, unassuming nature had helped Alex through the second most devastating ordeal of her life. At fifteen when her mother died of pancreatic cancer, her father had been her rock. Now he'd also passed away and without John's help, she knew she'd have taken much longer to get her life back on track.

He'd made her see beauty in the environment and had taught her to laugh again. They took long walks on the beach and he spent hours listening to Alex reminisce about her life with her adopted family. His own parents had died within a year of each other. As an only child of older parents, he'd acquired an understanding beyond his years of compassion and love. These features had drawn Alex to him.

As the driveway of her house loomed, she noticed a bulb was out in one of the lampposts that bordered the driveway. Before she doused her headlights, a pair of shining eyes glowed in the dark—her cat had escaped again.

She turned off the engine and climbed out. "Here, Mitzi, Mitzi."

The shrubs at the side of the house rustled and the cat streaked across the driveway and through a hedge.

"Don't think I'm chasing you," she declared. "I've had a dilly of a day and the last thing I need is a cat that wants chased."

She was conscious of the resounding silence when she opened the front door and switched on a light in the foyer. A framed photo of John with his beloved car smiled at her from the hall table. He'd been crazy about cars and was ecstatic when he'd managed to acquire a used Jaguar XJS 12 that the original English owner had brought with him to the States. John knew almost everything there was to know about mechanics and he was at his happiest tinkering, servicing and caring for the vehicle. The chrome sparkled and he would buff the bodywork to a showroom shine every Sunday morning.

Alex placed her brief case on the floor and stared at John's photo. "Happy anniversary, darling." As she said the words, tears welled in her eyes and she wiped them away with the back of her hand. She sighed and trudged through to the kitchen. The bright fluorescent lights caused her head to pound and she rubbed her temples. This always happened when she came home. Her nerves became as taut as a piano string and she lost her appetite.

Five months had passed since John kissed her one morning and told her he had a meeting out of town and he'd be back the next day. Although nothing concrete had emerged from all the police inquiries, she now believed he was dead. Police speculations that he'd left her for another woman had never gelled. They'd been too much in love, John had doted on her.

Maybe she should consider selling the house and moving on. They'd only bought it two months before John's disappearance and it was all she had left of her life with him except a few photos and memories. Besides, if he came back he would expect her to be waiting. She sagged onto a tall stool, reached for a bottle of headache pills and urged herself to swallow two. The French doors rattled and she looked over at the cat pawing the glass.

"Oh, you want to come in now, do you? Then why don't you use the kitty door I paid a fortune to get installed?" She padded over and turned the key.

The cat moseyed in and was soon batting her food dish. "Well, at least one of us is hungry," she commented as she poured dried food into Mitzi's dish. She poked her nose in the fridge but nothing appealed to her, so she slammed it shut and decided to read.

She sprawled on the sofa with a glass of iced tea and picked up a romantic novel. After one chapter, her eyes grew heavy. She closed them for a moment and slept.

The jangling of the phone filled the silent room and her stomach lurched. Each time she slept, she re-lived the horror of John's disappearance and on waking, always steeled herself for bad news.

Her eyes noted the time as she reached for the receiver— eight-thirty. "Hello?"

"Hi Alex, its Barbara. How are you?"

"Tired, but I managed to get through the day. Thank goodness tomorrow's Friday. I feel like sleeping for a week."

"Well, you can sleep all day Saturday, but I want you here at our house for dinner at seven."

Alex groaned. "I don't think so. I hate being the odd one out at dinner. I'll just have something to eat here."

"Oh no you won't, if you don't come I'll have an odd number. Please Alex, you need to get out more. The reason you're so tired all the time is because you never relax." Her friend's voice became soft and low. "John wouldn't have wanted you to become a recluse."

"I know, but—"

"But nothing. Get yourself here for seven or you'll have me *and* Don to deal with."

Alex laughed. "And that's supposed to scare me?"

"No, just come, bye."

Alex hung up and traipsed through to the kitchen to put on a pot of coffee. Barbara was right. She needed to go out more to regain her confidence. Going back to her old neighborhood, where she'd been happy, would help. Her memories were all good. Barbara becoming her best friend at age ten, their high school prom, double dating and both ending up marrying men they loved. Except now, John was missing and Don was still here. She didn't grudge her friend happiness, but she despised her own loneliness.

"Doing anything special at the weekend?" Charlie asked as Alex prepared to go home the next afternoon.

"Not really, I'm going to Barbara's for dinner tomorrow. Her husband, Don's joined a golf club and they're having some new friends round."

Charlie threw an arm around her shoulder and cuddled her. "Well have a good time."

"I'll try, but it's hard going out on your own. People either regard you as a freak, a prude or look at you as if you have two heads."

Charlie threw back his head and guffawed.

Alex harrumphed. "It's okay for men, everyone accepts when you're single, but with women, they try to fix you up with a date. I hope that isn't the reason Barbara's invited me."

On that closing comment, Brett Etheridge walked in. "Well, you two look mighty cozy." His face tensed when he saw Charlie's arm around Alex.

"We were just having a private joke, Brett," Charlie said, removing his arm. "What's up?"

"I wondered if you could give me a ride home, my car won't start."

"Again, why don't you get rid of that old rust bucket, there's always something going wrong with it. What's it this time?"

Brett grimaced and shrugged. "Dunno, I've been having problems with it starting, it might be the starter motor or perhaps the alternator's not working right. I hope it's nothing too expensive, I'm a bit short of cash at the moment."

Charlie tossed an impatient glance at Alex and she thought he was about to make a snide comment, but instead he nodded.

"Okay Brett, give me ten minutes, there's a few things I need to take down to the vault before we go."

"Sure thing."

Alex smiled. "How've you been, Brett? We haven't spoken in ages."

"No, you've been busy and so have I. Any word on John?"

Alex worked her lips into a taut line. "No, I guess the police are still investigating, but no one's been in touch for weeks."

"Maybe you should call them?"

"Mm, maybe. So, are you still driving the same car you had four years ago?"

"Yep, it's still the same old jalopy. We had some fun in it, didn't we? I've bought another car, but my mother drives that." He laughed. "She won't drive the old one in case it breaks down on her."

"Wise woman. How is your mom these days?"

"She's good. A few months ago, she was invited to join the Red Hat Society, so she's enjoying meeting women her own age and going out with them. She really liked you and still asks me what went wrong between us."

Alex leaned back against the wall and looked down. "Nothing went wrong, Brett. I met John and the rest is history. I still regard you as one of my dearest friends."

He scowled. "That's not the same. I still love you, Alex, I always will."

There was a long silence in the room until Charlie returned. "Ready Brett?"

Brett nodded and gave Alex a wan smile. "Bye."

"Bye. Have a nice weekend, Brett—you too, Charlie."

Alex turned on her heel, rode the elevator to the parking lot and drove home.

Chapter 5

As soon as Alex entered the foyer, she caught a glimpse of her tired, drawn face in the mirror. Thank goodness it was Friday and she didn't have work the next day. She needed this weekend to recharge her batteries and get up to full speed again for Monday.

The conversation with Brett had surprised her. She was sure he'd be over her by now. Somehow, his love had almost turned into an obsession. It was as if he didn't want to get on with his life, but keep living in the past, and that scared her. People with fixations did crazy things, not that Brett had ever shown any signs of that, but she wished he would start dating and then he might realize that it was possible to love another woman again.

Saturday morning was another hot day. Alex donned a large brimmed sunhat, changed the bulb in the outside lamp and spent a couple of hours weeding the small garden at the front of the house. The weather on the Gulf Coast was too hot and humid to grow many flowers, but she loved seeing a splash of color in the front yard to brighten up the dark brown siding. Baskets filled with red and white impatiens hung on the porch while pink and white petunias stood as straight as sentinels lining either side of the driveway.

After a light lunch, she took her car to the carwash and with the threat of rain in a leaden sky, she returned home to spend the afternoon vacuuming the living room and dusting the den. Once she'd decided what to wear to Barbara's dinner, she showered and changed.

Dressed in a short-sleeved, black dress, with her hair held back in an ebony clip, Alex surveyed her reflection in the bedroom mirror before she called a taxi.

She rang Barbara's doorbell at precisely seven o' clock and watched her host approach through an etched glass panel in the front door.

"Alex," Barbara hugged her, "as always, you look fabulous. Is that dress new?"

"No, I wore it last Christmas to the ballet."

People milled around the living room as Barbara led Alex outside to the patio where her husband, Don, short and stocky with a deep Florida tan, was chatting to a tall, blond-haired man who dwarfed him.

Don leaned forward to kiss his wife's cheek. "Hello darling, have you met Darren Winters?"

Barbara shook the tall man's outstretched hand. "How do you do and this is my friend, Alex Martell."

Bright, blue eyes met Alex's and the man gave a small bow. "Pleased to meet you, Alex."

The four chatted about events in the local news until Barbara excused herself. An elderly man launched into conversation with Don, leaving Alex and Darren alone.

An awkward silence stretched for a moment until Darren spoke. "So, what keeps you busy, Alex?"

"My work, I'm a correspondent for *Everyday* magazine."

"Really? I have my own business, but I can't even write a postcard. I leave that to my staff."

They both laughed. "What kind of business do you have?"

"Nothing very exciting, my company makes and installs windows."

Alex nodded. "That's a great commodity and always needed, especially here on the Gulf Coast with the threat of hurricanes."

Darren held a forefinger to his lips. "Shush, don't say that too loud, June 1 always comes around way too fast."

They sauntered back inside and Darren led the way to a table in the corner of the living room laden with bottles and cans. "Can I get you a drink?"

"Thanks, I'll have some red wine."

Delicious aromas floated from the kitchen and feeling relaxed, Alex was glad she'd accepted Barbara's invitation. She took the glass of wine from Darren and watched as he poured himself a glass and took a slug.

"So, Alex, have you ever written about anyone famous?"

"Not really. I did a short interview with Juno recently, but I didn't get enough material for an article. I was rather limited with the time he gave me."

Darren pulled his brows together. "Juno? Isn't he psychic?"

Alex wanted to make a derogatory remark, but she didn't. "Yes, I believe so, although I was trying to find out about his latest book and when it'll be published, but he couldn't tell me, so we've shelved the article until we obtain more facts."

"I know a lot of writers live in Sarasota, but I didn't realize he was one of them." Darren drank a mouthful of wine. "Has he got one of those big, fancy houses on Longboat Key?"

"No, he lives out in the boonies. It took me ages to find it. I had to drive for miles after the turn off before I arrived at his house."

"Don tells me you and Barbara have been friends since elementary school. That's cool."

"Yes, she's the sister I never had. What about you? Do you have siblings?"

"I had a brother, but he died when he was ten. Shall we?" Darren held out his arm as Barbara announced dinner was ready and Alex didn't have chance to respond with an apology.

It was no surprise to find that Barbara had seated her next to Darren at dinner. He was on his own, too, and Alex supposed it was logical for her friend to seat them together. As it turned out, she enjoyed his company.

While he was relating the story of how his father had founded the window company, Alex studied him. She liked the way his facial expressions kept changing and the way he brushed his blond hair from his eyes. A sprinkling of freckles dusted his nose and cheeks and his wide mouth smiled with ease. He told her he was single and had never married.

Darren looked down at his plate and sighed. "I was at the end of my term in the military when my parents separated. My mom went into a deep depression and it took months of therapy to bring her out of it. The woman I was engaged to didn't understand why I had to be there for Mom, so we drifted apart and she eventually broke our engagement." He gave a wry grin. "Somehow I thought we'd get married and spend our lives together, I still miss her."

"I know what you mean. Sometimes I think I'm having a nightmare and that I'll wake up and my husband will be here, but deep down, I know he won't."

"I'm sorry, Barbara didn't tell me you're a widow."

Alex lifted her shoulders in a shrug. "I'm not—at least I don't think I am."

Darren's eyes opened wide in puzzlement.

Alex looked down and spoke in a soft tone. "My husband's missing. He hasn't been seen for months."

"How awful, I'm so sorry. What do the police say?"

"Not a lot. That he either wanted to disappear or that he left me for someone else." Alex tried to smile, but tears welled in her eyes.

"Cheer up you two and have another drink." Barbara pushed a bottle of red wine across the table. "Some of us are going to the midnight movie in Angerton. Wanna come?"

Lilies of Death

Alex dabbed her tears with a tissue. "No thanks, that'll take me way past my bedtime. I'll head on home if you don't mind."

"Are you sure you won't come?" Barbara pressed. "It's that new thriller starring Brad Pitt."

"I'm sure. Can I call a taxi?"

"Why don't you let me take you home?" Darren suggested.

"No really, I prefer to take a taxi."

Alex observed Barbara's head turning first toward her and then to Darren as she followed their conversation, proving her initial theory right and that her friend was matchmaking.

"Very well," Darren conceded, "but at least let me walk you down the driveway."

At nine-thirty when the first guests left, Darren escorted Alex into the foyer to wait for her taxi. She embraced Barbara and Don. "Thank you both for a lovely dinner. I hope you enjoy your midnight movie."

"We will. I'll call you soon, Alex." Barbara kissed her cheek.

The sky was clear and the moon's pale light bathed the driveway glistening with beads of rain from a recent shower. Alex's high-heel skidded on the wet path and Darren grabbed her elbow as he assisted her to the waiting taxi. "Careful, this surface gets really slippery when wet."

"I hadn't realized it had been raining. It was a lovely evening when we were on the patio."

"Ah, but that was nearly three hours ago—time flies when you're having fun."

She safely reached the cab and fell onto the back seat, rubbing her ankle. "Wearing these new shoes wasn't such a good idea. I usually scrape the soles on something rough so they'll grip better, but I must have missed this pair." She held out her hand. "Nice meeting you, Darren."

He shook it. "It was my pleasure, goodnight Alex."

She closed the door and the driver accelerated away. Soon they were bowling along the road and turning in the direction of Patton Lane. The driver turned into Alex's driveway and pulled up with the nose of his taxi close to her garage door.

"Here we are, ma'am. That'll be sixteen dollars."

Alex fished in her wallet and held out two bills. "Thank you, keep the change."

She kicked off her shoes the moment entered the foyer and locked the door. Barbara was right, she should get out more, but it was hard starting afresh at age thirty when all her friends were married or engaged. Besides, until she knew what had happened to John, she didn't want to move on with her life, maybe she never would. She'd made a point of not giving Darren her phone number, so she doubted she'd hear from him again.

Juno took a deep breath before knocking. A scruffy, middle-aged man, with a cigarette dangling from the corner of his mouth, opened the door. His worn, tweed jacket was rumpled with the breast pocket hanging off.

"Yeah?" he barked causing cigarette ash to sprinkle over Juno's shoes.

"I'm Juno, Lieutenant Walker asked me to stop by."

"Hey, Lieutenant," the man bawled. "Some guy's here. What's your name again?"

"Juno."

The man peered over the top of a pair of broken spectacles held together with a grubby Band-Aid. "Juno who?"

"Just Juno."

Lieutenant Walker hustled his menial aside and held out a hand, dragging Juno into the apartment. "Come in, the same killer's struck again."

"Are you sure?"

"Yep, he left another plastic lily."

Juno followed the Lieutenant through a small living room to a bedroom and his gut contracted when he spotted the remnants of a pool of dark, red blood on a bed.

The Lieutenant moved closer. "This was where she found her, lying face down on the bed."

"She?"

"Yes, the woman's neighbor, they were supposed to go to the movies. Apparently, the neighbor phoned to find out the time of the show and when there was no answer, she came round, found the door open and discovered the body."

Juno took a handkerchief from his pocket and covered his nose and mouth.

Walker fixed his dark eyes on him. "You okay? You look kinda pale. You're not going to throw up, are you?"

"No. Was there a break-in?"

"She either let him in or he had a key, there's no sign of forced entry."

The man who'd opened the door to Juno came through the doorway. "Hey Lieutenant, Sergeant Clancy's just returned. Can I go now?"

"Yes, but send her in here."

Juno pointed to the blood on the bed. "So this woman was shot like the others?"

"Probably post mortem. The pathologist thinks she died last evening from strangulation." Walker clenched and unclenched his fists. "This makes three murders now and we've still nothing to go on. Forensics only found one set of prints, probably hers."

"Sounds like your guy's very careful, but he'll make a mistake sooner or later, they always do."

Walker's face turned as red as a beet. "This isn't one of your books, Juno, sometimes serial killers aren't caught for years. I'm not having that happen on my patch."

Someone knocked on the open door and a dark-skinned, stocky woman strode forward. With hair cropped like a man's and the frame of a body builder, she was as formidable as any male officer Juno had ever met. There was no way he'd want to encounter her in a dark alley.

"Sergeant Clancy, this is Juno." Walker said.

"Sir," she gripped his hand in a vice-like handshake. "You that writer guy?"

"Guilty as charged," Juno gave her a grin.

She remained po-faced at his attempt at a joke and addressed her superior. "Everything's tied up here, sir."

"Good, I'll see you back at the precinct."

She turned on her heel and stalked out.

"Your sergeant hasn't much of a sense of humor," Juno remarked as they dawdled back into the living room. "Is she always that grim?"

"Clancy's okay, but she takes her work very seriously. She had a rough time growing up and is hell bent on catching perps that prey on women. You might not believe it, but she looks pretty good when she's off duty."

Juno found that hard to imagine, but maybe Walker liked his women as tough as old boots.

Zack Walker worked his face into an angry frown. "Well if you can't help just now, you'd better get the fuck out of here. Some of us have work to do." He swung round and Juno tailed him to the front door.

"Let me know when you're finished with the apartment and I'll swing by to see if I can get any vibes." Juno offered.

"Yeah, yeah, I'll call you." The Lieutenant waved a hand and closed the door.

Outside in the corridor, Juno leaned his hands on his knees and drew in a long, deep breath. In the fresh air once again, he jogged to the parking lot, climbed into his car, buckled his seat belt and fired the engine, trying to blot out the memory of the blood on the bed. He rammed the stick of his Mercedes into first gear and the car launched forward, tires squealing. With the car radio booming and the window wound low, his nausea soon vanished as he drove downtown to grab a beer and lunch.

Chapter 6

Alex jammed the key into the ignition, shoved the transmission into drive, and set off for home. She turned into her driveway with a pain in the pit of her stomach. Today had been particularly bad; her nerves had been on edge. All day John was on her mind. Perhaps the police were right and he had left her for another woman. She didn't want to believe that, but the longer he was gone, the more likely it was to be true.

The air had turned cooler since she'd left the office and as soon as she unlocked the front door, Mitzi darted in and through to the kitchen, tail as straight as a ruler. By the time Alex had retrieved the paper and turned on the light, the cat was stalking about, mewing.

"Cut it out, give me chance to fill your dish."

The cascade of dried food clinked into the aluminum dish and Mitzi swished her tail, rubbing her body against her ankles.

"There." She plunked the full dish down. "Now will you let me take a bath?"

Alex kicked off her shoes and meandered from the kitchen in her bare feet. In the bathroom, she turned the faucet on full and tipped a few drops of Calvin Klein's *Escape* bath oil into the gushing water. Rolling her head in circles to relax the tension in her neck, she removed her blouse, skirt and underwear. Next, she lingered by the tub while she tied her hair back with a band.

Warm water lapped against the back of her neck and softened taut muscles as a Barry Manilow CD played on her music system. A few strands of hair dangled in the water flapping against her cheek as she closed her eyes and tried to clear her mind.

Drifting on a cloud of soft warmth, the ringing of the phone failed to penetrate the first moments of total relaxation she'd experienced in weeks. Pleasant thoughts crept into her mind. Picnics with her parents and the way her mother entwined a strand of hair round her finger when she was thinking. Even when she was in intolerable pain, she still managed to laugh at one of Alex's jokes on the morning she died. Memories of the early days of her marriage when John and she discovered new things about each other and every day was better than the one before.

She stirred, opened her eyes and lifted one hand from the water. The tips of her fingers wrinkled like prunes, so she pulled out the bath plug and stood up. Feeling rosy and warm, she stepped from the tub winding a thick towel around her body. After she'd creamed her face and cleaned her teeth, she stuffed her arms into a terry robe and tied the belt. With her hair hanging loose, she grabbed an apple from a fruit bowl and curled up on the sofa to watch TV.

Ten minutes later, her cell phone rang. She didn't recognize the number and hesitated before pressing the 'talk' button. "Hello?"

"Alex? It's Juno."

Shock rendered her speechless and her jaw fell open. "How did you get this number?" She asked when she finally managed to make her tongue work.

"From your editor. I rang the office and asked for your home number, but he said he didn't have it, so he gave me your cell phone."

"*Thanks, Charlie,*" she thought. Then she issued a silent apology. At least Juno was being pleasant; something she'd imagined he was incapable of being.

He cleared his throat. "I'm sorry I was so hostile at the interview, but I'd had one hell of a day and I was under the impression that a guy was coming. Seeing a beautiful woman unnerved me."

By the time he'd finished mumbling the last sentence, Alex's face was glowing and her lips tilted in a smile. The high and mighty Juno was apologizing. This must be something for the record books.

"Apology accepted." She managed to speak dignified and business-like, despite the smile on her face.

"Would you allow me to buy you dinner on Friday as a sign of our understanding?"

"Um…well…"

"Please, I'd like to make amends."

"I'd like that, thank you." She was startled at her positive response. Why had she said that? The last thing she wanted was to share a meal and a few hours with this man. Well, it was too late now, she'd already accepted.

"Do you want me to pick you up?" He asked in a polite tone.

"No." Her retort was swift. "I'll make my own way."

"What kind of food do you prefer?"

"Anything, burgers, salad, Chinese."

"I was thinking of something a little nicer than those. There's a decent French restaurant on Old Polk Road. Do you know it?"

Alex reminisced for a moment—that restaurant had been one of John's favorites. "Yes, I know it."

"Seven-thirty on Friday?"

"Okay, thank you."

A few seconds of silence rivered between them before the line went dead.

Alex hung up and wondered why she'd agreed to dinner. Perhaps it was to pay back Juno for his supercilious attitude, or maybe deep down she wanted to see him again. His reputation as an inveterate womanizer intrigued her and she wanted to see what attracted all those women to him. He had the most expressive green eyes, was a handsome man and his psychic powers excited her. Yes—it was his clairvoyance that fascinated her—not the fabulous, flecked green eyes.

Alex was still lounging in her robe reading the newspaper when she froze. A woman's photograph smiled from the middle pages and the headline read, *'Third murder victim found.'*

She felt as if she was moving underwater as she read the short report. Her hands shook as she picked up the phone and called Charlie.

"Charlie?" she croaked, her eyes still glued to the picture. "Have you heard about this latest murder?"

"Yes, its shocking isn't it?"

Alex tried to control her fluttering insides. Her knuckles blanched as her hands gripped the paper. "What's going on, Charlie, this is a picture of me."

"What! Hang on a minute, let me get the paper and take a look."

Alex waited while rustling drifted down the phone. "She looks exactly like me," she mused. "It could almost be me."

"Have you got a sister or cousin who resembles you?"

"No I have no family, I was adopted."

"Hmm," There was a moment's silence. "Well photos can be deceiving and people say that everyone has a doppelganger somewhere in the world."

"Yes, but its scary when they've just been murdered and lived only a few miles away."

Lieutenant Walker closed the door, leaving Juno alone in the apartment. He strolled around scanning the neat room. Murano glass ornaments filled a curio along with Lladro figurines. Antique pottery gracing a Welsh dresser had intricate gold designs painted on it. Ratty, cream, velvet cushions decorated a worn, chintz sofa perched on a threadbare rug. Dotted strategically around the room were cheap pieces of furniture. How strange that the victim had expensive trinkets when the soft furnishings were all past their sell-by date.

Juno squatted in the middle of the floor and closed his eyes. His breathing was regular and deep as he cleared his mind and waited, but nothing happened.

Next, he ambled though to the bedroom and stood in the middle of the room, trying not to look at the bed in the corner. Again, he closed his eyes. This was hopeless; he was getting no vibes at all. As he turned to go, he came to a sudden halt at the sight of a framed photograph on the dresser. He was sure it wasn't there when he came before. Reaching out, he drew it closer. Indigo eyes smiled into his. This was the woman who'd interviewed him, Alex Martell. He'd only ever seen one other person with the same colored eyes as her, his mother. He grabbed his cell phone and called the lieutenant.

"Yeah, this is Walker."

"Is this photo in the bedroom the victim?" Juno held his breath.

"Yeah, that's her, Diane Bostock, a nice looking piece of ass, eh?"

"Diane Bostock? Are you sure that's her name."

"Yeah, her neighbor confirmed it, but she doesn't know if she has any family. They only met recently."

Juno pulled up a chair and straddled it backwards, gazing at the photo. "I think she has, I met her double a couple of days ago."

"Where?"

"At my house, she works for a local magazine and interviewed me."

"Great, where can I find her? This could be the break we've been waiting for. Have *you* come up with anything, yet?"

With the memory of the woman in his hazy dream, he almost said yes, but he held his tongue. Now he thought about it, the vision could have been Alex Martell or Diane Bostock. If he filled in their features, it could have been either one of them.

"Do you know what happened to this victim?" Juno asked.

"She was strangled first and then shot once in the back of the head with a 9mm. Like the others, she'd had sex prior to her death, but he'd worn a rubber, so there's no DNA. Forensics is still working on samples taken from the apartment. We're hoping they'll tell us something. I know they found a bunch of fibers and hairs. Other than that, we were hoping you could tell us more."

Juno shook his head. "Sorry, I've nothing at the moment. Let me have some of her personal items when the lab's finished, maybe I'll get something from those."

The shock of seeing the photo of the victim had unsettled him. He stood gazing at the picture. This woman was beautiful. The tilt of her head and her perfect smile alluded to a professional pose, but the lack of clarity led him to believe it was an enlarged snapshot.

He returned the chair to its original position, averted his eyes from the bed and left the room. Driving home, his mind kept wandering to Alex Martell. The feeling of relief had been enormous when he'd discovered she wasn't the murder victim, but why? She'd put him on his guard and rankled him from the moment they'd met. He'd felt tremendous triumph as hurt had invaded her eyes when he'd belittled her. Now he regretted his comments. She'd only been doing her job and, as Zack Walker said, '*she was a nice looking piece of ass.*'

In a way, she reminded him of Astrid, the one woman whose heart he'd broken and whom he'd killed. That first faltering smile Alex had given when he opened the door had set his pulse racing. For a fraction of a second, he thought she was Astrid with a different hair color, but then he remembered she was dead.

Ever since he was a teenager, women had always featured in his life. From the first day he lost his virginity to one of his mother's friends, he'd bedded more women than he could remember, usually on the first or second date, but Astrid had been different.

They'd gone out together for six months before they made love. To Juno, she was a paragon of beauty with long blonde hair, baby blue eyes and a smile that could melt the hardest heart. Her small breasts and tiny hips made him want to wrap her in cotton and protect her from the corruption in the world. She spoke in a low, husky voice and he doubted she could tell a lie. Her eyes held such candor and trust that he'd never forgiven himself when she discovered he'd cheated on her with several of her friends.

"But why?" Extreme hurt had radiated from her eyes. "Why, Juno? You said you loved me."

"Dammit, I do," he walloped the table. "I can't explain what happened. They just mesmerized me and before I knew what had happened, we landed up in bed together."

"You could have said no. I could never be unfaithful to you, I love you so much."

By now, her eyes swam with tears and he reached out to comfort her.

"No!" She pulled back as if he had a contagious disease. "Don't touch me, don't ever touch me again."

He was riddled with regret at the sight of her face distorted with pain. Again, he reached for her, but she lifted her chin high and stormed out. The intense sorrow he'd experienced when the authorities notified him that she'd been involved in a fatal head-

Lilies of Death

on collision minutes after leaving him had waned, but he knew he'd always mourn her and feel guilty.

Her sudden death had sent him to rock bottom and on a whim, he'd signed up for a two year term in the army. His Commanding Officer had persuaded him to enroll in one of the evening classes held on the base. With nothing better to do, he'd closed his eyes, stabbed a pin at the list of activities available, and ended up taking a writing class. That had been the turning point in his life, and by the time he'd completed his term in the military, he'd written his first novel.

His rise to fame had been slow, but it had given him the opportunity to seek solace with any available female. In his quest to forget Astrid, he'd plunged headlong into a disastrous marriage with Hollywood Starlet, Veronica Lawson. From day one, the marriage had been a farce. He didn't love Veronica and was only attracted to her sexually, but that had been a no-go, too. Abused by her uncle at a very early age, she was frigid and Juno was back to square one, bedding anything in a skirt.

After a swift divorce and nine years of tomcatting around, he fell in love with a young singer and they married after only three months. Again, that had turned into a fiasco when she was always on tour and he hardly ever saw her. This time, she divorced him for a guitarist in her band.

Now years later, when he'd at last found peace from his unfortunate marriages and had come to terms with Astrid's death, Alex Martell walked into his life.

Lieutenant Walker snapped closed the file and propped his elbows on the desk. He still had no leads on this latest murder. The autopsy established that the killer had asphyxiated the victim, placed her face down on the bed and shot her in the back of the head.

Whomever they were dealing with must be a psychopath. This killing was almost identical to that of Myrtle Bixby and the other woman two months before. He hoped they weren't dealing with a serial killer, but things were beginning to look as if they were. Some smart ass was befriending young women and killing them. As long as the media didn't get wind of the similarities they'd be okay, but if word got out about the lilies left by the killer, wide-spread panic would cause his superiors to step up the investigation. He was hoping he'd be on top of the cases long before that happened.

He'd heard nothing further from Juno. Shit! He hated outsiders poking their noses in, but the writer had helped them once before and had been accurate to the point of describing where the child was being held hostage. Perhaps that had been a piece of luck. However, his superiors had given him orders to ask for Juno's help, so he had.

His shabby office at the downtown precinct matched his gloomy mood. His personal life was a mess. He seized his jacket off the back of the chair and decided to stop work for the day. Lighting a cigarette, he was two steps from his desk when the phone rang. He sighed. "Yeah, Walker here."

"We've got something, Lieutenant." A male voice said.

"What?"

"A tiny hair, it was on the victim's clothing." His heart soared. "This hair's lighter than the victim's and has been treated with a colorant."

"Will you be able to identify the brand?"

"Probably not, but at least we have this for a match when you have a suspect."

"Thanks guys." He hung up the phone.

Finding a hair was good work and it might help eliminate the victim's friends and neighbors. At least this dame was good looking. The last one had been fat and ugly. She'd also had sex

Lilies of Death

not long before her death. That told them one thing about the murderer, if it was the same guy, he didn't care who he fucked.

News of the third murder had rocked the small community of Geyserville. Located fifty miles from the coast, this quiet, inland town was a direct contrast to the bustling, coastal towns of West Florida. The nearest, Sarasota, was situated on the Gulf of Mexico with sparkling azure waters. High-rise buildings flanked the waterfront and vacationers converged there for the endless activities, restaurants and shopping. During the cooler months, its population doubled when hoards of visitors flocked south to escape the northern winters. Many owned second homes, while others stayed all season, turning the city's roads into crowded chaos.

Zack tore open his desk draw and rummaged for his spare pack of cigarettes. Shoving them into his jacket pocket, he switched off the light and closed his door.

"You still here?" A young officer asked, hastily removing his feet propped on his desk,

"No, I'm just leaving, goodnight."

In the parking lot, Zack lit another cigarette. His wife hated smoking, so he always had one on the way home and then suffered purgatory for the rest of the evening. At his age, he was prepared to do anything for a quiet life. He had enough stress at work without his wife nagging him.

The engine of his old Buick started first time and he swung the wheel towards home. He pressed the button on the garage door remote and drove in, stubbing out the remnants of his cigarette in the ashtray. With bent shoulders, he lurched from the car and entered the kitchen.

His wife, Margo, was stirring the contents of a large pot with a wooden spoon with her brows drawn together. "You're late," she grumbled. "Dinner was ready hours ago. I'm reheating it for the umpteenth time."

Zack Walker kissed her cheek. "Sorry, honey, but there's been another murder and I—"

Margo raised her hands in the air. "I don't want to know. I've told you before, don't bring your work home. Keep the gory details to yourself."

Zack shook his head and entered the bedroom to change. He'd been in the house one minute and Margo was griping again. No wonder he chose to work fifteen hours a day. She never had a good word for him. Never encouraged him nor showed any passion in anything he did. He sighed. Oh well, what could a guy expect after thirty-two years of marriage. Yet he knew couples who were still in love and enjoyed doing things together.

When they were younger, Margo had thought it glamorous to be married to a Law Enforcement Officer, but she soon discovered that it meant many long hours on her own. Going to P.T.A. meetings and dealing with the household and the children's problems without him. Over the years, they'd grown apart. She had her own friends and him his work.

When he entered the dining room, Margo was ladling stewed meat onto two plates. He sat in his usual chair and spooned carrots and potatoes from a bowl in the center of the table onto his. They ate in silence.

"Done anything special today?" He asked hoping to disperse the strained atmosphere.

"No, your clean clothes are in your closet." She kept her head low, never meeting his eyes.

The silence continued and as she cleared the table, the phone rang. She gave Zack a disgusted look. "That'll be for you, *my* friends don't call this late."

She stomped from the room as Zack lifted the receiver.

"Lieutenant Walker? It's Juno."

"Hey, Juno, what's up?"

"I wanted to give you the phone number of that woman I told you about, the dead ringer for Diane Bostock. Her name's Alex Martell and she works for *Everyday* magazine."

"Okay, go ahead, give it to me." He wrote as Juno quoted Alex's work number. "Is this Alex related to Diane?"

"I've no idea, I don't know the woman."

"I'll swing by and talk to her. How are you getting on? Any progress?" His gut tightened with apprehension while he waited for Juno's reply.

"No, sorry nothing yet."

Zack turned his head when he heard a dull thud. Margo stood in the doorway with one suitcase on either side of her. His stomach contracted at the look of venom in her eyes.

"Look, Juno, I must go, call me tomorrow."

He hung up the receiver and faced Margo. "What's going on?"

"I'm leaving."

"Leaving? Going where?"

"Back to Chicago." Margo's eyes looked daggers at him. "I can't live like this any longer."

Zack kneaded the back of his neck while his gut churned. "How long will you be gone?" The cold look in Margo's eyes gave him his answer before she spoke.

"This is goodbye, Zack. I have to make a new start while I still have the nerve. You don't need me, you never have, only the kids needed me and they have their own lives now, but at least I can be near them."

Zack shook his head in disbelief. "Can't we talk about this? Can't I say anything to make you change your mind?"

"No, Zack. It's too late for that. When we moved here from Chicago, you said it was the first step to your retirement and that you'd cut back on your workload, but you didn't. I'm fifty-three-years-old. If I hang around until you decide to work less hours, I'll be too old and will have lost the courage to leave."

Zack's tongue felt thick. He tried to speak, but croaked. "I'm sorry."

"So am I."

Margo lifted the bags, turned her back and walked out.

Shock riveted him to the spot until the front door banged. Then he crossed to the window and watched the red taillights of his wife's car disappear. Thirty-two years of marriage was over. Maybe when Margo had time to reconsider, she'd come back, but Zack knew in his heart that she wouldn't. Anyway, he didn't want her back. She had finally ended this farce, something he'd longed for, but had never had the courage to do. He admired her for that.

Chapter 7

Zack's first instinct was to call Clancy. During the last three years, they'd become bosom buddies and he'd told her all about his marriage problems. She'd reciprocated and opened up to him, about her childhood.

One afternoon when she was twelve, she was walking back from the store with a bag full of groceries. As she turned the corner leading to the lane where her mother parked her trailer, five youths blocked her way. She turned away, but they followed and soon hemmed her in.

"What do you guys want?" She asked, her palms starting to sweat.

"What do you think?" The tallest replied, taking a few steps closer. "We want the same thing your mama charges for, only we want it for free."

Clancy knew exactly what he meant. Her mother entertained between five and ten men every day in the trailer and Clancy was used to hearing humping and groaning coming from the small bedroom.

The tallest youth knocked the bag of groceries from her hand and pushed her backwards. Another caught her and held her arms. She struggled. All five laughed.

"Get her down on the grass," the tallest one commanded and the others obeyed.

Fear caused Clancy to tremble and tears oozed from her eyes. "Don't hurt me," she pleaded, as two of them held her arms and two prized her legs apart.

The ringleader positioned himself between her thighs and unfastened the zipper on his jeans. Clancy stared in horror at his swollen manhood. His hand covered her mouth as he lay on top of her and thrust deep into her. The others all laughed.

"Go on, Jimmy, fuck her!" one cried.

"Me next, me next," another hollered, his hand pummeling her left breast.

For what seemed like hours Clancy's nightmare continued as one by one they all took turns and the ringleader raped her a second time. Her saving grace was a car driving down the lane otherwise the other four would have taken her again, too.

The five scurried away and Clancy clambered to her feet. She teetered the rest of the way to the trailer and fell inside the door.

Her mother was applying polish to her toenails. "Where've you been?" She barked. "I've been waiting for you to bring back the groceries."

Clancy stared at the rollers in her mother's hair and the slash of red that painted her mouth.

"I've been raped, Mama," she confessed quietly.

"Oh," her mother commented in a disinterested tone. "Did you get any money?"

"No!" Clancy hollered. "Don't you understand, five guys raped me?"

Her mother looked at her with cold eyes. "So, where's the fifty bucks." She held out her hand.

Clancy covered her face with her hands and sobbed. "I don't have any money, they raped me. I feel so ashamed."

Her mother crossed the small room and wrenched her head up. "Listen honey, rape or not, when a man fucks you, you ask for money. That's what we do around here. Now you've got experience, from tomorrow onwards, you'll have your own clients, it's about time you started earning your keep."

Therefore, for four years, Clancy had prostituted herself and entertained clients on the sofa in the trailer while her mother used the bedroom. Once word got around that a young girl was available, Clancy had a long line waiting at the door each evening.

Because her mother was usually in the bedroom, working or waiting for a client, she had no idea how many men her daughter entertained, so Clancy was able to stash away some of her earnings. Just before her sixteenth birthday, her mother went to the store, so Clancy pocketed her hidden cache and left the trailer for the last time.

A Greyhound bus took her to Tampa where she enrolled in the Police Academy. For years, she couldn't let a man touch her without feeling dirty. At twenty-five, she met and fell in love with a doctor and made love for the first time. However, he broke her heart after a courtship of five years when he divulged he was marrying another doctor.

She threw herself into her work and had no more relationships until she met Zack. Their sin was that they'd become lovers after one particularly long, drawn-out case. He was the father she'd never known. His love encompassed her and made her feel wanted and desirable. To all other men she'd had carnal knowledge of, she was an object of relief for their desires, not a woman with feelings and emotions. Even although he knew about her sordid youth, Zack still treated her as if she was a goddess and loved her with all his heart.

Regret overwhelmed Zack at the final breakdown of his marriage, but in a way, it was a relief. Now he could continue his affair with Clancy. The memory of her hard body against his and the way she made him feel, brought a rush of heat to his groin. Damn—her mother had taught her well, and although she'd only prostituted herself for a few years, she really knew how to please a man.

He grabbed his cell phone and called Clancy's number. It rang once before she answered.

"Margo's left me!" He blurted.

"Oh, Zack, I'm so sorry."

"I'm not. I'm coming over." He was shrugging on his jacket as he spoke.

"Now, but it's almost eleven?"

"So? Now I can stay all night."

He was already in the car by the time she replied. "Are you sure this is what you want? You're not acting on the rebound are you?"

"No, this is what I want and if I'm not mistaken, you want it too." He was already turning his car onto the main road on the way to her condo. "I'll be with you in ten minutes."

His body felt wired as he navigated the traffic, parked in the apartment guest area and rode the elevator to the third floor. The moment he knocked, Clancy tore open the door and fell into his arms. They wavered across the room and fell onto the sofa, arms wound around each other, lips melded together. Zack reached down, lifted the hem of her nightgown and began caressing her.

"Not here," she gasped. "I need more room."

Zack followed her into the dimly lit bedroom, ripping his sweatshirt over his head. A small lamp on the nightstand exuded enough light for him to watch Clancy tear off her nightgown and stand before him, naked. She was magnificent. Her dusky skin rippled with muscles as she lay on the bottom of the bed with her legs astride and began massaging her private parts.

Zack's erection strained at his jeans. In haste, he peeled them off, his penis pointing vertical to his navel. By now, Clancy was deep in the throes of an orgasm, so he knelt by the bed, pushed her hand aside and entered her. She cried and writhed with each movement, her muscles clamping his penis, until he slumped spent on top of her.

Lilies of Death

They lay side by side on top of the quilt, Zack's breath rasping in his throat and Clancy with her arms stretched high above her head.

"I love you, Clancy, but I think you already know that." Zack nuzzled her neck. She nodded. "I'll divorce Margo and we can get married."

Clancy tensed. "No Zack, I never want to be answerable to a man. I'm a loner and I need my freedom."

"But I'd never dictate to you. I admire your free spirit, that's one of the things I love about you. You've never made any demands on me or whined when I've had to break a date. Nothing would change."

"Then why get married? Marriage is for people who want children. You've already been through all that and I certainly don't want any. We can be happy just as we are, you living in your place and me in mine." Zack pouted. "Come on let's take a shower together." Clancy wiggled her eyebrows and Zack laughed.

"Okay, but his time I get to wash you."

She leapt off the bed and streaked in the direction of the bathroom with Zack trotting behind.

Friday evening, Alex left the office early and spent a lot of time trying to decide what to wear for her dinner date with Juno. First, she donned a blue, linen, business suit, but resolved it was too severe. Next, she twirled in front of the mirror wearing a peasant-styled dress with a tiered skirt, but abandoned that idea, too. She arrived at the restaurant feeling relaxed and smart in a pair of black pants, a crisp, white shirt and a lightweight jacket.

Juno was already in the foyer, chatting in French to a hostess and Alex couldn't help raising her eyebrows. She had time to study him before he saw her.

His profile showed a clear, tanned skin, full lips tilted at the corners and an aquiline nose. At six feet two inches, her head reached just above his shoulder when she was wearing high-heels. He wore his dark, springy hair longer than the current fashion. The back fell into deep waves while the shorter locks at the front curled and dipped over his brow. A black shirt with a button-down collar and a tan suede jacket topped black pants with knife-sharp creases. He spun round and his green eyes lit up with approval as they swept over her.

"Right on time," he noted, taking her arm. "I hate to be late, don't you?"

She murmured an agreement and allowed him to lead the way behind the seating hostess to a table at the back of the room. He thanked the woman in French. How affectatious. He held Alex's chair and waited until she sat before lowering his form onto the seat opposite. A busser filled their glasses with iced water and Alex took a sip to quench her parched throat.

All of a sudden, dinner with Juno lost its appeal. Being in close proximity to him unsettled her. She was conscious of his eyes watching her every move while she read the descriptions of delicious food.

"Didn't your mother tell you it's rude to stare?" she remarked, keeping her eyes fast on the menu.

After a long silence, she looked up and observed a faraway, vacant expression on his face.

"I can't get over the resemblance between you and that picture of the latest murder victim." He rubbed the side of his nose with a forefinger. "Did you know her?"

"No, I've never seen her before."

"Are you sure?"

"Positive, I have no family, I was adopted."

"Do you know for certain you have no family?"

The idea of having relatives hadn't crossed her mind for years. When she was a child and even a teenager, she used to fantasize that her real parents would turn up, take her home and introduce her to several siblings.

"I'm not certain, but none were ever mentioned."

"Have you ever tried tracing your birth parents?"

Alex shook her head. "I was told they were dead and a marvelous couple adopted me. When you're a child you don't question things like that or think about finding your family. As far as I know, I have no one."

Juno gave a wide smile and rolled his eyes. "This is not what I had in mind when I asked you to dinner. Let's order and enjoy the food."

Alex was surprised to find that Juno was an interesting dinner companion. He entertained her with stories from his days in the military and how he bombarded several publishers with queries before one of them gave him a contract.

"Do you enjoy *your* work?" He asked after the server had brought their entrees.

"Most of the time."

His eyebrows leapt up. "Is that a reference to my behavior?"

"Not really, although you were pretty rude."

His nose became thinner and more prominent as he drew in a sharp breath. "I've already apologized—"

"I know, and it was nice of you to admit to one of your short-comings."

"I did no such thing. I didn't want you thinking that I had anything against you personally."

"Really? Well, that's nice to know. So, what you're saying is that you always act that way when you meet someone for the first time?" She raised a quizzical eyebrow.

"No, of course not, I've already told you that you caught me on a bad day."

With his every word, the color in his cheeks crept darker and it amused Alex to think that she had the ability to rile him so easily.

"So you did, Mr. Juno, so you did."

As she deliberately included the salutation before his name, he clenched his teeth and his neck tendons stood out. Alex tucked into the delicious food, smirking inside. Somehow, she'd managed to turn the tables and enrage Juno, and that felt good.

The remainder of the meal they chatted about general subjects until Juno paid the check and they moved toward the exit. Alex caught sight of a waving hand and spotted Darren Winters dining alone. Their eyes met and she raised her hand in acknowledgement.

As Juno held the restaurant door open, he looked back and studied Darren. "A boyfriend?"

The cool night air hit her. "No, I'm a widow." She set off for her car with Juno following.

"I'm so sorry, I didn't know."

Alex reached her car and spun round. "Why would you, its not tattooed on my ass!"

Juno took a step backwards, his hands raised to shoulder level. "Whoa lady, I can see that this is a sensitive subject so I won't pursue it."

He held out a hand and Alex took it. Much to her surprise, he raised it and brushed it with his lips. "Thank you for a delightful evening and allowing me to apologize. Drive carefully, goodnight."

He turned on his heel and disappeared into the murky shadows.

Alex leaned back on her car with closed eyes. The tension of being with Juno had at last erupted and she hadn't been able to restrain herself from snapping. She didn't want his pity because she was on her own. Maybe it wasn't his intention to sound patronizing, but he had.

As she bent to unlock the car, a thick, dark shadow loomed. Her heart hammered. She struggled with the key. It wouldn't fit. She flinched with fright as a hand touched hers.

"May I?" Alex looked up into Darren Winters' boyish face. Her heart was still in her mouth as he took her key and unlocked the door. "These parking lots should be much better lit. I always have trouble finding the lock, too."

"Thanks," Alex managed to muster, her heartbeat now returning to normal.

"Where's your date?" Darren asked, looking all around.

"He wasn't my date, it was business."

Darren held the door as she slid onto the front seat. "Well, he should still have waited until you were safely inside your car."

Alex tried to smile, but her insides still churned. "I'm fine and thanks for helping me with the key."

She fired up the car and roared out the parking lot, her breathing now normal. Dealing with these two men in one evening was too much to handle. The first was a narcissistic, overpowering psychic and the second an unattached man who dined alone. As far as she was concerned, she was glad this evening was over and that she need never meet either of them again. However, unknown to her, fate had decided that was not how it should be.

Chapter 8

He'd waited an hour for Alex to come out of the *Everyday* building. This time there would be no mistakes, he was driving a different car. Her Chevy pulled out into the traffic and he waited until she was round the corner and out of sight before he cranked his engine. As he approached traffic lights, he saw her ahead in the inside lane, so he flipped on his indicator and pulled over, two cars behind. He hummed and tapped his fingers on the steering wheel while he waited for the lights to change and the line of cars to move forward. His prey signaled a right turn, so he did the same.

Now on State Road 70, she continued driving at a steady speed toward Arcadia until she reached State Road 17 and there she made a left turn. This was more like it. Excitement gushed through him and he fidgeted in his seat as she approached and drove straight through the next town and out into the countryside. This was better than he'd hoped. If she lived in an isolated locale, his job would be much easier and besides, he liked being around grass and trees.

Raised in Pittsburgh, he'd never had chance to enjoy the countryside, so now it was a remedy for all his ills. He loved to drive into the middle of the state, find a creek, do a little fishing and make his plans. All his best thoughts came to him in this environment, so if she lived out of town, his job would be much easier to execute. Execute—that's precisely what he was going to do—shut the little bitch up for good. However, before he finished her off, he intended to make her suffer as he had. Make her realize why he'd chosen her and why she had to die.

The thrill of seeing the fear in her eyes caused him to have a strong erection and he wriggled in his seat as he followed her to the top of Patton lane. At the stop sign, she turned right onto a narrow road with flat, open scrubland on both sides. The road ahead shimmered with heat waves creating the illusion of puddles in the dips, and he turned down his air conditioning a degree. After driving for ten minutes, they passed a house set back from the road. Another half-mile further on, a decorated mailbox approached, and she swung into the driveway of a small house, parking in front of a two-car garage.

He brought his car to a halt and sniggered. No need for a big garage now, she only had one car. The other was at the bottom of a steep incline covered in shrubbery. Laughter threatened to erupt and he had to control himself as he watched her unlock the front door and disappear inside.

He stuck his hand in his pocket and pulled out a chain with two keys attached. One of them opened the door of the mobile home, so the other must be the key to this house. Now all he had to do was plan how and when he was going to kill her. He'd already eliminated two another rivals, her husband and Diane, so now he could take his time, no rushing. The killing of this victim was going to be special. Something he would always remember.

Juno fidgeted. A shudder of alarm ran through him and he couldn't shake an uneasy feeling. When he had misgivings, it usually meant that the visions would start along with violent headaches. He tried to concentrate on writing, but he was restless. Perhaps now was a good time to visit his cabin. The dog could roam free and taking long walks often helped dispel his discomfort.

Grabbing a sports bag from his closet, he flung in a change of clothes, underwear and stuffed a pair of running shoes down the side. He kept the cabin well stocked with canned and frozen food in case he decided to go there on a whim. The shower room sported an array of medicines and toiletries, so he didn't take any of those.

With his laptop slung over his shoulder, he whistled and the dog came frolicking in from the kitchen. "Come on, let's go."

He flung open the front door, locked it and started jogging. When he was halfway to the cabin, he pulled to a halt. "Oh, shit! There's no food for you there."

The dog cocked his head and waited.

"Never mind, you can eat people food for a few days."

He set off again with the dog loping at his side and he was no sooner inside the cabin when his cell phone rang.

He flipped it open. "Yeh, Juno."

"Hi sweetie, it's Petra." Her saccharin voice whined down the line. "Have you any pages needing proof-read?"

This was always the line she used when he hadn't contacted her for a few days. He tugged on his lower lip. Damn, he'd been hoping for a few days peace and quiet. The attraction he'd felt for her at the beginning was waning fast. After a relationship of almost two years, her clinging attitude had finally got on his nerves, so because she'd called his cell phone, he decided to give her the brush-off.

"No, I'm not at home at the moment and lately I've found it easier to work on my laptop."

"But you always said you prefer typing on your Underwood."

"I know I did, but you were the one that persuaded me to get a computer and I like using it, now. I'll call you when I get back in a few days, bye."

He snapped shut his phone, ending the conversation in a hurry before Petra could ask where he was. What he'd said wasn't a lie, he wasn't home, by no stretch of the imagination could the cabin be called that. It was basic in that it only had a portable air conditioner, two small bedrooms off a reasonably good sized living room, and a shower room next to the kitchen.

Nevertheless, he loved coming here. As a boy, he'd never been allowed to go camping or slum it with friends. His mother had felt it was below her son's station. Because she'd been raised and protected within a wealthy Pennsylvanian family and had never wanted for anything, she couldn't understand why her son wanted to rough it with friends, so he'd remained at home in the luxury of his parents' mansion taking escorted trips to Europe.

As soon as he was demobbed from the military, he moved to California where he began writing and enjoying the good life. When his father died, his mother sold the house in the northeast and bought a home in Boca Raton. He'd thought long and hard before moving to central Florida, but once his mother married a wealthy businessman the family had known for years, he decided that she lived far enough away for her not to meddle in his life. Now he lived how he liked and did the things he wanted without any interference from his mother.

His first task was to examine the food supply to see what the dog could eat. Out of the freezer, he withdrew a T-bone steak with freezer burn and placed it on a plate to defrost. A brightly packaged, frozen pizza caught his eye, so he took that out and set it next to the steak on the counter.

By now the back of his head and neck was pounding, so he ambled into the shower room, tugged open the vanity drawer and swallowed two Tylenol with a handful of water from the faucet. Before he reached the sliding door into the kitchen, the room began to spin. He managed to grab the shower door before sinking to his knees on the bath mat and spiraling into a haze.

He sat in the back of a car with a woman driving and the sign for Geyserville flashing past. The car hurtled on, its headlights splitting the darkness until it slowed and swung into a driveway of a small house clad with dark wooden siding.

All of a sudden, the vision changed, he was in a darkened room. He heard scuffling and someone screamed. Through swirls of mist, a woman lay on her back with dead eyes staring straight ahead. Crouched over her was a figure in dark clothing, laughing.

Juno groaned as nausea swamped him. He hung his head and drew in a long, therapeutic breath. Dragging himself upright with the help of the shower door, he willed his jelly-like knees to support him, and staggered into the living room, collapsing on a chair.

The dog trotted over and licked his hand while he leaned his head back, breathing deeply. Slowly the nausea subsided and the room steadied. The dog's tail thumped on the hardwood floor and Juno reached over to fondle his ears.

"Its okay boy, I'll be fine in a minute and then I'll get you some water."

Almost as if the animal knew what he'd said, the dog's tail wagged faster.

Juno sat thinking. Although he'd looked into the woman's dead eyes, he hadn't taken note of her face. With the uncanny likeness between Alex Martell and Diane Bostock, he wasn't sure if either had featured in his vision, or if it was some other woman.

Now Juno felt almost normal, so he pushed himself to his feet and crossed to the kitchen sink to fill a large bowl with water. The dog drank and drank as if he'd just crossed the Sahara and Juno realized that almost two hours had passed since he'd set off from the house. This always happened when he had a vision; he lost all sense of time.

He splashed cold water over his face, dabbed it dry with kitchen paper and opened the cabin door. The dog romped out,

Lilies of Death

pausing at a nearby tree to lift his leg. The air was hot and humid and burned Juno's lungs as he took deep breaths. With arms akimbo, he surveyed the peripheral wasteland. His house was out of sight, but he was able to make out several mobile home parks located on the main road. Most of them were vacation homes, their owners from Geyserville, Bradenton or Sarasota that liked to fish in the creek.

As Juno whistled, the dog leaped from the shadows and dashed past him into the cabin. He slammed the door and crossed to the kitchen, tearing open the box containing the pizza.

The dog sat at his side while he placed the pie in the microwave and set the timer.

Juno eyed the dog. "I suppose I should give you a name," he bent to pet the animal's back. "What about Rover? Sultan? Max?" The dog wagged his tail. "You like that? Okay, I'll call you Max."

The microwave dinged. Juno took out the sizzling pie, inserted the half-frozen steak, set the dials and pressed start. By the time the steak was cooked, the pizza was at an edible temperature and Juno sat eating it with Max at his heels.

Alex woke with a start and froze. She lay as still as a statue, listening. Then she heard a noise—footsteps. She relaxed telling herself that she'd been dreaming and closed her eyes. A moment later, they shot open. There was the same sound again—it was footsteps. She slithered from beneath the covers onto her knees beside the bed. With her left hand, she stretched as far as she could onto the middle of the bed frame and felt the cold metal of the loaded gun John kept there. She sat on her heels and listened. Silence was deep around her. Now she was beginning to doubt that she'd heard anything at all. She angled her head to one side and waited. Cramp ripped through her calf, so she struggled to her feet just as she heard the click of a door catch.

Now she was sure that someone was inside her house and a cold chill ran down her spine. One step backward took her to the nightstand and the phone. She lifted the receiver and with her eyes glued to the bedroom door, she dialed 911. The phone didn't connect. With trembling fingers, she pressed '*off*' and then '*talk*' again. Her stomach gave a sickening jolt—no dialing tone—her cell phone was downstairs in the kitchen.

She placed a hand over her mouth to repress a small sob of fear, her eyes scanning the room for a place to hide. There was only the closet. Hysteria threatened to choke her as the sound of a steady tread approached. On her knees once again, she dropped onto her stomach and crawled under the bed. The footsteps ceased. The door handle turned. Faint light from the landing window filtered through the doorway. Alex closed her eyes, gripping the gun with her arms outstretched.

"Hello? Anyone here?" A man's voice asked.

A flashlight circumnavigated the room and Alex held her breath.

"Hello? Police."

Alex stared at a pair of black boots poking beneath dark green pants with a stripe down the side. She was about to reveal her whereabouts, but stopped. Maybe this wasn't the police. Her heart banged against her ribs as she watched the black boots turn and tramp out. As the man made his way downstairs, Alex slithered out and tiptoed over to the window. Once she heard the front door slam, she peered out and watched a white sheriff's car, with a telltale green and gold stripe along the side, back out of the driveway.

She let out a pent-up sob and flopped onto the bed. Once her breathing was more normal, she pulled on a robe, ran downstairs and bolted the front door. Still holding the gun, she flipped on the light switch. Nothing happened. Keeping her back to the wall, she scuttled into the kitchen and jiggled the back door's handle. The lock was still firmly in place. Next, she tried the French doors, but they were fastened tight.

Feeling more secure, her mind teemed with questions. How did her front door get open when she'd locked the house before she went to bed? Her one hand groped in a drawer and pulled out a candle and matches. Lighting the wick, she placed her gun on the counter and stared at a plastic lily. How did that get there? Before her legs gave way, she slumped on a barstool.

Now that her initial terror was passing and common sense kicked in, she realized there must be a power outage and that was the reason her cable phone didn't work. She craned her neck, peering out the window at distant neighboring houses engulfed in darkness. *Well they probably will be at four-thirty in the morning,* she thought, as she filled the kettle and placed it on the lit burner of her propane stove. Still, there was the question of her unlocked front door, and the lily.

Once she'd made a pot of coffee, had a shower and eaten an early breakfast, she decided to call the local sheriff's office from her cell phone. A young female answered as soon as the call connected.

"Sheriff Potter's office, Ann speaking."

"Yes, my name's Alex Martell and I live at 1620 Halcyon Lane. Was an officer sent to my address tonight?"

"One moment, please."

Music filled Alex's ear. With the phone tucked between her chin and shoulder, she sallied over to the dishwasher. By the time her dishes were stacked, a man spoke in her ear.

"Ms. Martell?"

"Yes."

"We sent an officer to your house when we received a call saying there'd been a break-in."

"Really, who called?"

"Um," The sound of shuffling papers carried down the line. "Er, it was anonymous."

This was weird. Alex pondered the reply. "Well I was asleep upstairs and as far as I know, there's been no break-in. I hid when your officer woke me. How did he get in?"

"When he radioed in the report, he said the front door was wide open and no one appeared to be home."

"I see, thank you." Alex hung up with a knot in her stomach.

Something strange was going on. She would never go to bed without securing the house and where had the lily come from? There was no sign of a break-in and she was the only one with a key, except John. John! This could mean only one thing. Either John had returned or someone had managed to get hold of his keys. He kept his office and car keys together and the house and mobile home ones on a separate bunch. She had a sinking feeling in her stomach. John would never return without making his presence known, so that left the alternative. Someone was out there with his house keys.

She knew she would never feel safe now, so as soon as it was light, she decided to change the house locks and tell Charlie what had happened. There she was, planning to run to Charlie for help again. Somehow, she'd allowed him to become a substitute for her father, which she knew was unfair when he was in love with her.

Chapter 9

Zack had called the H.R. department of *Everyday* magazine and obtained Alex Martell's home address before he and Clancy paid her a visit. They both stood on the top step of a siding-clad house and Zack rang the doorbell. A young woman opened the door. He exchanged a look with his companion when the woman's face turned chalky white. Her eyes swiveled to the official car parked in her driveway and she gripped the doorframe.

Walker held out his I.D. and Clancy followed suit. "Alex Martell? I'm Lieutenant Walker and this is Sergeant Clancy, may we come in?"

The woman closed her eyes. "Is it John? Have you found him?"

"No, ma'am. We'd like to ask you some questions about a case we're investigating."

The woman stammered. "Oh...er...yes...come in."

Zack and Clancy followed her into a neat living room and waited until she sat before Zack spoke. "You mentioned someone called John."

She gulped and nodded. "Yes, my husband, he's been missing for several months."

"And you've filed a missing person's report?"

"Yes, months ago, but he's never been found."

"Well, this is a big country, ma'am, and if someone wants to disappear, it shouldn't be too difficult." Clancy remarked, looking up from her notebook in which she'd been taking notes.

The young woman's brows drew fretfully together. "Yes, I understand. What did you want to ask me about?"

Zack couldn't take his eyes off Alex. She didn't only resemble Diane Bostock, she could have been her twin. They were of equal build and height and she had the same, unusual indigo eyes. He felt as if he were seeing a ghost.

"A young woman was murdered a few nights ago and her resemblance to you is remarkable. Did you know her?" Zack held out the photo of Diane Bostock, which he'd removed from the frame in the bedroom.

Alex reached out a hand and took it, her eyes opening wide. She took a deep breath and expelled it in a sigh. "Whoa, this is scary. She really *does* look like me. I saw her picture in the paper, but this really brings it home. No, Lieutenant, I don't know her and I've never seen her around here either."

"What about your family, Mrs. Martell? Could you have a sister you're not aware of?"

Alex continued staring at the photo and shrugged. "It's possible. I was adopted as a baby. The attorney told my new parents that my birth parents were killed in a car wreck when I was an infant and that I had no other family." She turned enormous indigo eyes to Zack. "I'm sorry, but that's all I know."

Zack took the photo and returned it to a file. "As far as we can gather, until recently the victim was living and working in St. Petersburg, so why did she come to Geyserville? Who or what was she looking for here?"

He hadn't expected an answer to his rhetorical question and was surprised when Clancy mused. "Maybe to look for her twin?"

Alex's eyes opened wide. "What?"

Zack shrugged. "Do you know any details of your adoption? The attorney who handled it or in which state it happened?"

Alex declined with a shake of her head. "I was raised right here in Geyserville. My adoptive parents only told me that an attorney arranged everything. There was never any mention of me having a twin." She smiled and Zack's stomach flip-flopped.

This woman was beautiful. "I was lucky, they were wonderful people."

Zack studied her for a long, ponderous moment. "Well, ma'am, due to the coincidences in this case, we may need to investigate your adoption details along with the latest murder victim's background." A startled look flashed across Alex's face. He held both hands up, palms facing her. "Believe me ma'am we've no intention of prying into your private life. We just need to establish if there's a connection between you and the victim."

"What good will that do?"

"We don't know," Clancy, piped up. "But in a murder investigation sometimes the smallest detail helps."

"I see. Of course, please do anything you need if it'll help."

Zack rose and held out his hand. "Thank you for seeing us, Mrs. Martell."

Alex shook it and raised her eyes to his. "Will you let me know if you find out anything?"

"Sure thing."

Alex rose and Zack followed her to the front door with Clancy in his wake.

Once outside, Zack paused and fastened his eyes on Clancy's face. "Dig up what you can on her husband's disappearance. A missing person and three murder victims—makes me wonder if there's any connection." He lifted his brows in a questioning manner.

"You mean he could be the perp?"

"It's possible. Maybe killing Diane Bostock was a substitute for the real thing."

"His wife?"

He flung an arm around his partner. "Who knows, who knows?"

The next afternoon, Clancy tapped on Zack's doorjamb and sashayed in. "Guess what?"

"What?"

"By all accounts John Martell was a saint and crazy about his wife. He's a partner in a law firm and no one has a bad word to say about him. Everyone at his office is eagerly waiting for his return. The senior partner even employed a P.I. to see if he could find out anything, but he came up empty."

Zack Walker rubbed his chin. "That's strange. Why would a man like that disappear?"

Clancy shrugged. "He's a model husband and apparently he and Alex have a vacation home out east and used to go there for romantic weekends. But there's also another lead I've been following."

"Which is?"

"One of the female law clerks resigned and left the same Friday John Martell was last seen."

Zack's gut gave a twinge. Now this was more like it. There was nearly always a woman involved when a man went missing. "What do we know about her?"

Clancy looked down at the paper in her hand. "Her name's Sandra Barrett. I've been to the address the Company had on file for her, but the property's empty, she must have moved. Neighbors told me she lived with a boyfriend and that she often had signs of physical abuse. Sandra was very friendly with the woman next door, but she told no one she was leaving." She sucked in air between her teeth. "Now what?"

"Could be we have another missing person."

Zack considered all this data, but it wasn't going to help them solve the murders, unless there was a connection. He let his mind wander. Perhaps John Martell hired someone to dispose of his wife, so that he could be with Sandra Barrett, and the assassin killed the wrong woman, her double, Diane

Bostock. It was a possibility, but unlikely. In addition, what about Myrtle Bixby and the other victim, there was no way to connect them to Diane?

"Good work, Clancy." Zack struck his desk. "Damn, now we have another case to investigate. What time does your shift finish today?"

"I'm only on until seven, then its home to a nice hot bath and bed."

Zack's eyes ran over her firm figure. At his age, he was sometimes too tired at the end of a long day to think about anything except a shower and bed, but tonight he wanted to be with Clancy. Her statement told him she needed privacy, so he decided to stay at the office and work late.

"Tomorrow, see what you can find out about Sandra Barrett's boyfriend, she might still be with him, but I'll lay odds she isn't, and that she's in the same place as John Martell."

"So you think they've run off together?"

"I didn't say that. I said they're in the same place." Zack raised his eyebrows.

"Six feet under?"

"Maybe, who knows, but it's up to us to find out. After all these months Alex Martell deserves to know if she's a widow."

"So you think they're both victims?"

"I'll bet my 401K on it. What did the initial investigation into John's disappearance find?"

"Nothing. They ruled out foul play and he's just listed as missing. Seems as if no one's done anything other than assume he's taken off and left his wife."

"And what do you think, Clancy?"

"After meeting his wife and hearing how perfect this guy is, he's either a schizo or he's a victim."

Zack nodded. "And it's my bet he's a victim along with Sandra Barrett."

"See you tomorrow." Clancy spun on her heel and left his office just as the phone rang.

Zack lifted the receiver. "Walker."

"Juno here. I know you were waiting for the autopsy report, but you said they thought that Diane Bostock was strangled before she was shot."

"Yes and that's been confirmed. Why?"

"I've had a vision."

Zack's heart leaped. "You saw it? You mean you know who killed her?"

"No. I saw a form in dark clothing strangle someone, but I never saw faces. I'm sorry."

"No matter. What's important is that you've had a breakthrough. Keep in touch and let me know how things progress and I'll do the same. Maybe we can crack this case together."

Juno laughed. "I'd like to think so, bye."

Zack hung up the phone and sat with the tips of his fingers together. Maybe having Juno on this case wasn't so bad after all. He was a nice enough guy and didn't interfere. With nothing concrete to go on, they needed all the help they could get.

Two days later, Alex turned the corner to her office and saw Darren Winters waiting outside.

He rose and his mouth widened in a smile. "Hi, I was passing and dropped by to see how you're doing."

Alex held out her hand. "I'm fine. So you remembered where I work?"

"Sure thing. This is a beautiful building. Is it new?"

Alex unlocked her office door and Darren followed her in, his eyes sweeping the room and taking in every aspect of the stylish décor. On the fifth floor with one large, tinted glass window, it offered panoramic views of the distant town of

Geyserville and beyond. Beige, plush carpeting covered the first half of the floor while the back part was polished, oak hardwood, which matched the desk and trim on a black, leather chair. In an alcove, equipped with a coffeemaker and cups, comfortable armchairs flanked an ultra-modern, glass and stainless steel coffee table.

"Wow, this is something else." Darren mused. "Are all the offices this big?"

"Most of them, but Charlie's is the biggest."

"Charlie?"

"The editor." Darren nodded. "So, how's the window market these days?"

"Okay, business is good. I know your magazine does editorials and I was considering having you write one about my company, so I thought I'd swing by to find out what I could. You can never get too much exposure."

Alex piled her briefcase on the desk and booted up her computer. "Give me a minute to load the program and I'll be able to let you have some prices. What size were you thinking of?"

"I've no idea, maybe a double-page spread."

Alex whistled. "That would be pretty expensive. Let me print out our rates and then you'll have a better idea."

Once she had the printout, she handed it to him and it was his turn to show surprise. "Wow, I see what you mean. Maybe you could do a write-up, take some pictures and then give me a quote?"

"Of course, that's what most companies do, but I really think Dave Saez, our Homes and Garden writer, might be the best person to do your write-up, I know nothing about industry."

Darren gave her a downcast look. "I really wanted you to do it. I had to have a reason to come here and see you and now you want to palm me off on someone else." He pouted.

Alex laughed. "Oh, I see, so this was just a ploy."

Darren shrugged. "Just a little one, but I really want to have an editorial done and who better to do it than *Everyday* magazine."

The phone rang and Alex reached for the handset. "Excuse me. Hello, Alex Martell?"

Alex heard Charlie's gruff voice. She replied to his rapid questions and replaced the receiver. "I'm sorry, but Charlie's called a staff meeting, so I really must go."

Darren stood. "No problem. Can I take you to lunch, so that we can discuss a time for you to come and visit my workshop."

"Yes, I'd like that. Meet me in the lobby at one."

Darren grinned. "Great, see you then."

Outside in the corridor, Alex locked her office door. Other members of the magazine staff poured past as they shook hands.

"See you later." Alex waved and joined the scurrying throng.

It was one-fifteen when she emerged from the glass elevator in the lobby and Darren greeted her. "Hi, ready?"

"More than ready. I'm sorry I'm late, but the meeting went on longer than expected. The legal department has a problem and everyone has to be notified when there's chance of a lawsuit."

"That's nasty, does it happen often?"

"Now and again when writers don't validate their facts." Alex pointed north as they sashayed along the sidewalk. "There's a nice little Italian bistro round the corner, unless there's somewhere else you'd rather go?"

"No, that sounds good, let's eat there."

Five minutes later, they sat at a table overlooking the outside, dining patio. After perusing the menu and ordering a bottle of Valpolicello, they both chose the Chicken Alfredo.

Alex leaned back sipping her wine feeling at ease in Darren's company. She liked his boyish manner and his silly jokes made her laugh. For too long she'd been tense and on tenterhooks. Between John's disappearance and the local murders, she'd had no respite for months. It felt good to relax with a new friend.

"Where is your window workshop?" She asked.

"On Northgate Business Park in Sarasota. Do you know it?"

Alex shook her head. "No, but I've heard of it. When would you like me to make a start?"

"As soon as possible, just whenever you can fit me into your schedule."

The server brought their entrée and the delicious aroma made Alex realize she was hungry. She never ate breakfast and sometimes only a sandwich for lunch, so this was a nice treat. Charlie sometimes brought her here or to one of the other restaurants, but only at the beginning of the month. Once the magazine deadline drew near, everyone stayed late and Charlie often worked fifteen hours a day.

During the meal, Alex suggested that she visit Darren's workshop the following afternoon. She had an appointment with a prominent businessperson at three-thirty on Lido Key, so she would be able to fit both engagements into her schedule. He agreed and the rest of the time, they spent getting to know each other.

Alex was surprised to learn that Darren had been born in Great Britain and that his family had relocated to the United States when he was twelve. They'd settled in the northeast, where his father had founded a window company and Darren had joined the family business as soon as he'd completed a short spell in the marines.

"This was not what I intended doing with my life," he revealed, as he stared out the window. "But when my parents split up and Dad moved away, I decided to keep the firm going and buckled down to the task of making it my life. After a year apart, my parents got back together again, but Dad never returned to work. He and Mom traveled a lot until she got sick and died."

"That must have been hard."

"Yes, when Mom passed on, Dad spent more time traveling before he resumed contact with an old friend of the family. After they married, I sold the business and moved to Florida. However, before long I missed having my own company, so I restarted another window venture here." He lifted his palms up to his shoulder. "And that's the story of my life."

Alex grimaced. "And much more exciting than mine. I've always lived around here and apart from visiting Nashville once, I've never been out of the state. My husband, John, traveled a lot when his father was in the air force, so he was content to stay put. I'd like to travel, but the time's never been right."

"Have the police found out anything about your husband, yet?"

"No. The more days that pass, there's less chance they will."

Darren stroked her arm. "I'm sorry. You must be going through hell. I think you're very brave to carry on with your life."

"What else can I do? I can't shut myself away because my husband's missing. I may never know what happened to him. The police have told me I can have him officially declared dead after he's been missing a certain length of time, but that's little consolation." She studied her watch. "I really should be getting back. I've a lot to get through this afternoon."

The server brought the bill and Darren handed Alex a business card. "Call me in the morning if you need directions to find the workshop."

"No, that's okay, I'll find out from the Internet. Thanks for lunch, I enjoyed it."

"Me, too. See you tomorrow."

When Alex reached the corner, Darren was still standing in the bistro doorway, so she waved and headed back to the office.

Chapter 10

Alex drove north from State Road 72 until she reached Fruitville Road where she turned onto U.S. 301, and made a left turn into Northgate Business Park. Winters' Windows was easy to spot with its bright, red sign adorned with a golden crown. The metal building was in pristine condition, painted cream with red trim and several trucks parked on the wide, concrete driveway, bore the same eye-catching, crown logo.

Round the side of the building, Alex entered by a glass, swing door. A young receptionist looked up and smiled. "Good afternoon, may I help you?"

Alex returned her smile. "Yes, Mr. Winters is expecting me. I'm Alex Martell."

"Please take a seat and I'll let him know you're here."

Alex sat on a button-backed, leather chair and surveyed her surroundings. The L-shaped reception desk covered half the back wall along with samples of window styles with before-and-after photographs of happy customers. The rest of the waiting area consisted of chairs, similar to the one she sat in, a coffee table with magazines and several plaques from safety councils.

Darren breezed in wearing overalls and a hard hat. "Hi, you found us okay?" he held out his hand and Alex shook it.

"Yes. Once I knew I had to get on the 301, it was easy. Well, this all looks very impressive and I love your logo."

"Shall we?" Darren stood aside for Alex to pass. "Hold my calls, Vera. I'll be in conference with Mrs. Martell."

In a large, airy workshop, several men all dressed the same as Darren operated machinery and carried sheets of glass and strips of vinyl. Once they'd turned into a corridor, the noise lessened and Darren led the way to his office. It was plain and

Lilies of Death

functional. Cream-painted walls were bare, except for a clock with a loud tick, mounted behind a leather-topped desk, a computer and two chairs. The reception at the front of the building was sumptuous compared to this.

Alex sat on one of the chairs and opened her briefcase. She tugged out a notebook, pen and voice recorder. "Do you have any objections to me recording our interview? It makes it a lot easier when I'm reviewing my notes."

"No, fire away. I'll tell you all I can and you stop me if you have any questions. What about photographs?"

"Bob Hernandez will give you a call when he has an opening. He's an excellent photographer and we use him for all our editorials."

"Great, let's get started."

The next two hours flew by and when Alex's watch beeped, informing her that it was three o'clock, they wrapped up their conversation. She packed everything back into her briefcase and they stood. "That was intriguing, Darren. You've given me a real insight into how your company works."

"It was a pleasure. You will call if you need anything else or if you have any questions."

"Of course, I'm sure to come across something."

"Good, we can have lunch again, or maybe even dinner or the theatre?"

Alex hated giving a negative reply, so she said, "We'll see," and followed him out.

Back on U.S. 301, Alex turned south, then right onto Fruitville Road and left onto U.S. 41 on her way to Lido Key. She was half way across the newly constructed, concrete bridge to the island, when her cell phone rang. She'd left it in her car during the interview with Darren, and it was the office notifying her that her three-thirty appointment had been canceled. As she was already on John Ringling Boulevard and almost at St. Armand's Circle, she decided to park and window shop.

Although she seldom bought anything in this exclusive shopping district, she loved to browse. Getting a parking place was no easy exercise this late in the afternoon, but she managed to get lucky and drove into a space on the circle, just as another driver pulled out.

Distant piano music made her head for the sound, which she knew came from one of the restaurants. She'd eaten an early lunch to make sure she arrived in time for her one o'clock appointment with Darren, so when she reached the restaurant, she decided to sit under an umbrella on the sidewalk and order something to eat.

The afternoon sun was hot on her shoulders and she was glad she'd worn a long-sleeved blouse buttoned up to her neck otherwise her fair skin might have burned. The pianist played Lara's Theme from Dr. Zhivago and she closed her eyes tapping her toes in time to the tempo. A shadow crossed her and her eyes snapped open. Sitting opposite was Juno.

His eyes crinkled at the corners when he smiled. "Hello, we must stop meeting like this."

Annoyed, she crossed her arms and stared. "I don't know what you mean."

He raised his shoulders in indifference. "It doesn't matter. What are you going to order?"

"Just coffee and a slice of carrot cake." *'And what's it got to do with you,'* she wanted to add, but didn't.

"Allow me," He spoke in a silver-tongued tone to the server and ordered two coffees and two slices of carrot cake.

That could mean only one thing; he'd invited himself to her table. Inside she fumed and tried to ignore the strained silence that descended when the server left.

"So, Alex, is this work or pleasure?" Juno leaned back in his chair, his eyes narrowed against the afternoon sun.

She hated the way he always stressed her name and she tried to keep her voice non-descript, but she knew it sounded harsh. "A bit of both. My three-thirty appointment canceled, so as I was already here, I decided to stop and have some refreshment."

He planted his elbows on the table and leaned closer. "You really have the most beautiful eyes."

Heat surged to her face. This man was incorrigible. One minute he barked derogatory remarks and the next he uttered compliments. How did he expect her to know what he really meant? She cast her mind back to the day of the interview and remembered his angry, green eyes. Admiration shone in them today and she felt as if she were drowning.

A phone rang. Juno fumbled in his shirt pocket and flipped open his cell phone. "Yeah?"

After a few seconds of listening, he rose and leaned on a nearby tree. Alex watched his eyes darting around. "Yeah, I'm at The Spotted Dick restaurant on St. Armand's Circle." A pause as his caller spoke. "I can do that." Another short lull followed. "How long will you be? Okay, thanks, bye."

With one hand, he curled his fingers up into his disheveled hair, and Alex's knees liquefied. How could one man be such a monster and yet be so attractive and sexy. He was the most diverse character she'd ever met and worst of all, she found herself wanting to know him better.

Juno closed his phone and sat down again. "Sorry about that, my publisher always calls at the most inopportune moment."

The server brought their order and Alex shook herself out of her reverie and concentrated on stirring sugar into her coffee, keeping her eyes low on her carrot cake. Sparks of anger fizzled inside. This man was a renowned, inveterate womanizer who expected her to fall at his feet because he'd made one flattering remark about her eyes. The thought disgusted her and she pursed her lips, frowning.

"Something wrong?" Juno bent his head and tried to get her to look at him. "Are you sensitive about the color of your eyes?"

"No, I never think about it until someone mentions it." She persuaded herself to look at him and instantly wished she hadn't. His hair fell over one eye, he cocked his left eyebrow in an evocative action, and his green eyes twinkled.

She continued to stare at him and he raised his other brow. "Something is wrong. Have I a dirty mark on my face or a zit erupting?"

"No, I'm sorry to be so rude staring like this, but—"

"But what?"

He waited for her to speak.

She was about to continue when a woman swaggered over to their table.

"Juno darling, what are you doing here?"

Petra Zounes looked fantastic in a black and white, polka-dot sundress, which accentuated her golden suntan. Her long, titian hair shone in the sunlight and hung down her back in deep waves. She'd emphasized her blue eyes with shadow and liner and was batting half-inch-long, false eyelashes at Juno.

She looked down her nose at Alex. "Oh hello, you're that magazine person, aren't you?"

Every muscle in Juno's handsome face tensed. "Yes, Alex works for *Everyday* magazine."

Petra perched on the edge of one of the spare chairs and leaned over to look at Alex's plate. "What's that you're eating? It looks full of calories."

"Its carrot cake and delicious," Juno replied, tucking into his.

"Carrot cake? Can one really make cake from carrots? How disgusting."

Juno and Alex exchanged a look and he smirked. "You can make cake from anything, my favorite's broccoli."

Petra's eyes opened wide. "Really? I had no idea."

It took Alex all her time not to laugh and she covered the lower half of her face with her hand while feigning a cough. Her eyes met Juno's again and they swapped a knowing smile.

Petra rose from her seat. "Sometimes it makes me glad that I was raised in New York when I see some of the things you Southern people eat. Are you coming, Juno?"

"Where?"

"With me of course." She glowered at Alex.

"In a moment, Alex and I are discussing business. I'll meet you at your car."

She gave Alex a supercilious smile before strutting away without another word.

Juno used his chin to motion toward the retreating Petra. "There goes one spoiled woman." He shook his head. "Sometimes I wonder why I ever allowed her father to talk me into her helping me. She's about as much use as an ashtray on a motorcycle."

His simile brought a grin to Alex's face. Then she realized why she felt drawn to him. She admired anyone who used expressive, descriptive phrases. They had the love of words and writing in common, and were kindred spirits.

"Why are you grinning?" he asked with knitted brows. "Sometimes I don't know how to read you."

"Me, too. Why did you tell Petra that trash about cakes?"

"Because she's so gullible, she'll believe anything I tell her. That's what I like about you. You've got common sense, something found in not too many people these days."

Alex glowed inside. His praise meant the world to her, but she'd make sure he never knew how she felt.

The server refilled their coffee cups and placed the check on the table. "It looks as though they're trying to tell us something," he picked up the check, looked at it and laid some bills on top. "I hadn't realized that everyone else is ordering dinner."

Alex glanced around, chewing her bottom lip. "My goodness, I'd better get home, Mitzi needs fed."

"Mitzi?"

"Yes, my cat. She's only a street cat, but she still tries to run my life."

"I know what you mean. My dog'll be champing at the bit, too. Do you live here in Sarasota?"

Not many people knew her address and she was reluctant to start giving it out. "No, I live near Geyserville, and I can be back home in less than an hour."

"Lucky you, I've another twenty miles further to go."

"I know," She quirked her brows at him. "I came visiting once, remember?"

He rolled his eyes. "Of course silly me." He held her elbow and helped her from the seat. "Where's your car parked?"

"Over there," She pointed halfway round the circle to her Chevy. "Thanks for the coffee and cake."

She faced him and their eyes met and held. "Drive carefully." He quipped and turned away.

The delicious aromas coming from the restaurants made Alex's mouth water as she set off round the circle in the opposite direction.

Cars whizzed past in their quest to find a parking space close to the restaurant of their choice. When she was almost at her car, she placed one foot on a pedestrian crossing. A dark sedan pulled out, but slowed as it approached. Alex continued.

The vehicle suddenly accelerated. Alex froze. She stared at the driver. With the windshield tinted almost black she could only make out the vague shape of a male figure. The car engine growled. Her heart thudded. Someone screamed. Her brain responded. She bent her knees and tried to spring forward. Her whole body jarred as the car's bumper smashed into her right leg and jettisoned her onto the opposite curb where she landed on her right shoulder. The car roared past.

A hand grabbed her shirt and wrenched her onto the grass. "Are you all right, ma'am? Did that driver hit you?"

"He should have stopped," another voice said.

"Did anyone get a look at his tag?"

Several people spoke and Alex looked up at a small crowd through a haze of pain.

"Call 911," a woman's voice floated through a fog.

A figure squatted next to her and she looked up into an elderly man's worried face. "Please, give her some air," he ordered and undid the top button of her shirt. "Are you okay, ma'am?" He petted her hand. "Don't try to get up, there's an ambulance on its way?"

She nodded, excruciating pain spearing through her before the gray, swirling mist returned. Somewhere in the back of her mind, she heard sirens wailing and remembered someone moving her.

A high-pitched, steady beeping infiltrated her brain. Still in a daze, she was conscious of someone being close, but tendrils of the gray mist still closed around her and she couldn't fight her way up through it. Footsteps echoed and then a voice spoke low and hoarse.

"You should have died, Alex, but I'll get you next time and then you'll beg me to kill you."

Her heartbeat accelerated and her whole body trembled. She flung her head from side to side. "No!" She shouted, "No, go away!" The footsteps sounded again and she lapsed into oblivion.

A cool hand touched her brow. "Mrs. Martell, are you awake?"

Alex opened her eyes, but images were blurred. The room tilted and she gripped the bed. "Help me, somebody's trying to kill me."

A young, smiling face swam before her eyes. "It's okay you're in hospital now and quite safe."

"No, he wants to kill me." She urged as the fog gradually cleared and she looked into the kind face of a nurse.

"A car hit you, but I'm sure it was an accident."

"No he was here, he said he'll kill me next time. Who was in my room before you came in?"

The nurse straightened the covers and tucked them under the mattress. "No one was here, Mrs. Martell, I think you must have had a bad dream."

"It seemed so real. Are you sure no one was in here?"

The nurse smiled. "I'm sure. You've had a nasty shock. I'll bring you some water and tell the doctor you're awake."

The door to her room swung several times after the nurse left and Alex racked her brain to remember exactly what had happened. Had she been dreaming? She was sure she'd heard footsteps before and after the voice spoke. When the nurse left the room, her shoes hadn't made a sound.

Her head ached, but her mind was now lucid. She was convinced someone had been in her room even although the nurse denied it. Could trauma cause her imagination to run riot when she believed the driver of the car deliberately drove straight at her. She didn't know anymore. Now she'd gained the full scope of her faculties, the verbal threat seemed somewhat incredible. Besides why would anyone want to kill her?

Satisfied that the threat had been a trick of her mind while she was regaining consciousness, she closed her eyes and rested.

After the doctor examined her and gushed about how lucky she was not to have broken any bones, he confirmed she could go home the next morning, provided she didn't drive.

"I can't," she told him. "I was going to my car when the accident happened. It must still be parked at St. Armand's Circle."

"Well, I'd advise you to keep off that leg as much as possible. The pressure bandage will allow you to get around in moderation, but the bruising is deep and will take a few weeks to fade. I recommend keeping the bandage on for at least a week. We'll send you home with some painkillers to get you through the first few days and by then an over-the-counter one should do the trick."

"Thank you, Doctor." Alex held out her hand.

The doctor took it in both of his own. "Remember you're very lucky to have escaped with such light injuries—you could quite easily have been killed."

Alex shuddered at his words. Was that someone's intention?

After the nurse helped her sit up, a young man carried in a tray with her dinner. She was sipping soup when her door swung open and Charlie bustled in.

"My God, Alex, what happened?" He leaned forward and hugged her.

She clung to him, tears welling in her eyes. "Oh Charlie, it's so good to see you. How did you know I was here?"

"Brett heard about a hit and run on the police scanner and called to get the victim's name for his column. I came as soon as I found out it was you. How do you feel?"

"Sore. My legs took the brunt of the hit, my right one's the worst, it's in a large bandage. I ache all over and I'm covered in bruises, but I'm alive." As she finished the last word, she hiccoughed a large sob, and tears poured down her cheeks. "The doctor says I can go home in the morning."

Charlie reached out and embraced her. "There, there. You've had a terrible ordeal and are still in shock. Once you get home tomorrow, you'll feel much better. I wish I could take you home, but I have to be in St. Petersburg by nine, but I'll ask Brett to come. What time do you want him to pick you up?"

Alex sniffed and swiped away her tears with the back of her hand. "He'd better wait until about nine-thirty. Are you sure he won't mind?"

"My dear Alex, Brett would go to the end of the earth for you. Surely you know he's still in love with you?"

She nodded.

He kissed her cheek. "You get a good night's sleep and I'll see you soon."

"Goodnight, Charlie." Alex leaned back on the puffy pillows and closed her eyes. A few minutes later, the door swished.

"Are you finished with your tray?" The nurse asked, poking her head in.

"Yes, I'm not very hungry."

The nurse picked up the tray and left.

True to plan, Brett arrived at nine-thirty and accompanied her wheelchair to the hospital entrance before loping toward the parking lot for his car. Once Alex was safely ensconced in the passenger seat with her belt buckled, Brett drove off.

"How's the leg?" He asked as he turned north on US 41.

"Painful, in fact I hurt all over. It wasn't as bad as this yesterday."

Brett swung right into Fruitville Road, and pulled in behind a line of traffic waiting at a red light. "Do you still live on Halcyon Lane?" he enquired, swiveling round to look at her.

Alex tensed. "Yes, how do you know where I live?"

"You sent me an invitation to your house-warming when you and John first moved in, remember?"

She remembered. Unlike Charlie, who'd flung his invitation back at her without opening it.

"Stop rubbing it in, Alex." He'd blurted.

She'd moved her head from side to side puzzled. "What do you mean, Charlie?"

He fidgeted and hung his head. "I know how happy you are with John, you tell me every day, but don't expect me to come to your fancy new house and watch you cooing over each other, that would kill me."

"But I—"

He held up his hands. "Just forget I said that. I won't be coming." He rushed from the room, banging the door.

That was the day she realized Charlie Addison was in love with her.

Of course she remembered the housewarming party, it had been quite a night, Brett had arrived with a gorgeous redhead and had congratulated her and John on owning such a beautiful home. The guests were much too drunk to drive and it was two in the morning before they all left in a flotilla of cabs.

Brett pressed his foot on the accelerator and tailed the vehicle in front. "You gave us all quite a shock when we discovered it was you who'd been involved in the hit and run. Did you get a look at the driver?"

"Nah-uh, the windshield was tinted almost black. All I could make out was a shape, but I'm sure it was a man."

"The police have taken statements from several people, who witnessed the accident, but none saw the tag, it was covered with brown paper."

Alex felt her insides shift. The only reason someone would hide the tag was if the accident was planned and they didn't want it seen. The words spoken in her 'so-called dream' came rushing back, and worms of fear crawled around inside her stomach.

"I think someone deliberately tried to hit me, Brett," she confessed. "I know I sound neurotic, but something happened in the hospital."

"What?" Brett jammed on the brakes and veered into a side street.

Alex soon regretted mentioning her suspicions. She had no idea who or why someone wanted to hurt her. It could be a stranger, or someone she knew, and talking about the threat might alert the perpetrator.

She twisted in her seat and faced Brett. "I guess I'm still in shock and being stupid. A nurse said a man called to ask about my condition and didn't give his name. I think I'm letting my imagination run away with me. I'm sorry I startled you and made you pull over."

"That's okay. Sometimes when things don't make sense, we try to find a reason to justify them. I know Charlie called, but the call disconnected before he could leave his name."

"That's probably it then."

Brett executed a swift u-turn and merged into the lane of traffic on the main road. Alex sighed, pleased that she hadn't revealed her true suspicions, and glad that Brett had accepted her white lie. They drove in silence with a radio chat show discussing the economy, until Brett turned into Halcyon Lane.

"I really like it out here. There's lots of nice countryside and it's always so peaceful and quiet."

Alex smiled. "Yes, I like it, too." She extended her right index finger. "Here we are, just after this bend on the right—the brown clapperboard house."

Brett pulled into the driveway, slipped the transmission into park, and secured the handbrake. He leaned over the back of his seat and lifted a pair of crutches.

He looked at her and grinned. "Charlie sent these. He said not to dance too fast or you might fall over."

Alex chuckled. "He's a sweetheart. I have no idea how to use them. I'll probably end up flat on the floor."

Brett climbed out the car, ran round to the passenger side and opened the door. "Well don't fret about the crutches now. I'll carry you into the house."

Alex fidgeted, flustered. "No, Brett, it's all right, I can manage."

"I have my instructions from Charlie, so get out your key and don't argue."

He leaned down, scooped Alex into his arms as if she were as light as angel cake, and carried her to the front door. Alex inserted her key into the lock; Brett carried her over the threshold and straight into the living room where he placed her gently on the sofa. That done, he fled from the room, returning a few moments later with the crutches and propped them against the sofa arm.

Once again, he left returning with a bowl of Calla Lilies. "Someone left these beside the garage door. Shall I put them here?" He placed them on a side table close to the sofa.

Alex rooted around looking for a card, but there was none.

Brett stood flexing his hands together. "Right, point me toward the kitchen and I'll make you some tea. You still drink tea, don't you?"

Alex nodded. "Yes I still drink tea. The kitchen's through there." She flapped a hand behind her.

While Brett was making the tea, Alex shuffled into a comfortable position, and lifted both legs onto the sofa. Her right leg throbbed. Her whole body ached and she would have preferred to take some painkillers, go to bed and sleep. Although she'd slept most of the night, she was extremely tired and felt as if she could sleep for a week.

Clinking sounded. Brett carried in a tray laden with china cups and saucers, a sugar bowl, a milk jug and a plate of cookies. He placed it on the coffee table and sat in an armchair. "Shall I pour you a cup?"

"My, my, you've used my best china, I feel flattered."

"Well my mom always says that drinking out of something fancy when you're not feeling well makes you feel better."

A rush of affection swamped her. Brett was one of the most considerate people she knew, and his mother was a gem. "You know what they say," she quipped. "'Mother knows best.'"

Brett lifted the teapot, poured the brown liquid into a cup and handed it to her. "This is just like old times," he said, filling his own cup. "Remember how we used to drink tea before we went to a movie?"

"Yes, I remember. We had some good times together."

Brett slouched deep in the chair and Alex was conscious of his eyes following her every move. She looked up and their eyes met and held.

"Are you going into the office today?" Alex asked, breaking twenty seconds of silence.

"Uh-huh, Charlie's up in St. Pete's, so I'd better get going in case a crisis crops up."

"Thanks for bringing me home, I really appreciate it." Alex reached over and touched Brett's arm. He stiffened and rose.

"You're welcome. Take care, I'll see you soon."

He strode into the foyer and closed the front door behind him.

No sooner had Brett driven away than Alex heard the sound of a key turning in the lock. Her whole body tensed and her hand crept toward a large, stone ashtray on the table while her eyes never left the doorway.

"Anyone home? Alex are you back yet?" Barbara's voice preceded her into the living room as she stuffed a key into her pocket and juggled a large bouquet of roses. She grinned. "Hi there, I'm glad you gave me a key when you changed the locks, I was hoping to get here before you arrived. How're you feeling?" Barbara kissed Alex's cheek.

The tension left her body and Alex sagged against the cushions. "I feel like I look—a mess."

Barbara's eyes swept over the tray on the coffee table and she raised her brows. "Did I miss the tea party?"

"No, Brett brought me home and made tea. Would you like some?"

"You mean doe-eyed Brett who swoons every time he sees you?"

Alex giggled. "He's not that bad, but he does still have a thing for me."

"That's unhealthy after all this time. Shall I pour you another cup?"

Alex motioned the affirmative.

Barbara refilled Alex's cup before she went to get another one for herself and poured in the tea. Then she turned serious eyes to her friend. "I heard a report of the accident on the evening news, but they didn't give the victim's name. I nearly fainted when I read this morning's paper and found it was you. I called the hospital, but they told me you'd been discharged." She leaned over and placed a hand on Alex's arm. "You really must be more careful."

A sudden chill reverberated through Alex's entire body. She shivered and grasped the top of her arms. "It wasn't an accident.

Somebody tried to kill me." As she spoke slowly and quietly, Barbara stared at her bug-eyed.

She grabbed her teacup and gulped down a mouthful of tea while Alex informed her about the threat she received in hospital before she was fully conscious. All through her narrative, Barbara remained silent with a shocked expression. Alex had never known her friend to be flummoxed. Usually nothing fazed her, so for Barbara to remain silent for such a long time was unheard of.

"I don't know what to say," she eventually spoke with a dazed look. "Why would somebody want to kill you?"

"That's what I want to know. I wondered if it might have anything to do with John's disappearance. Was he involved in something I didn't know about? All I know is that I'm scared, really scared."

Barbara knelt in front of Alex. "Then why don't you go away when you're feeling better? I'm sure the magazine'll give you some time off in these circumstances."

"No, if someone really wants me dead, that'll only prolong the issue. As soon as I return, they'll try again. I can't live the rest of my life looking over my shoulder. I have to face this here and now."

Barbara wrapped her arms around her. "My God, you're brave. If it were me, I'd run as far as I could." She gave a chuckle. "You always were the courageous one. Even at school, you'd stay to fight the boys, whereas I'd run home crying. However, don't you think this is a little different? This is your life we're talking about, Alex. Go away somewhere and let the police deal with this madman."

"I'll think about it. Thanks for coming, you're a good friend."

Barbara intertwined the fingers of both hands and held them up. "Remember our secret signs?"

They both laughed and Alex interlaced her own fingers mimicking her friend's gesture. "Is it really twenty years ago that we devised these codes? I'm surprised we still remember them."

"If you're finished with your tea, I'll take this lot through to the kitchen." Barbara stacked the cups and saucers and lifted the tray. "Can I get you anything else while I'm through there?"

"No thanks, I'm fine. I *can* walk, but the doctor told me to take things easy."

When Barbara returned, she cuddled into the corner of the loveseat and pressed the button to extend the footrest. "So, how's it going with Darren Winters? A little bird tells me you've been seeing him."

"We've met twice and both times it was business. I'm writing an editorial about his company."

Barbara grinned and waggled her eyebrows. "Is that the best he could come up with?"

"What do you mean?"

"Oh, come on Alex, the guy's smitten by you. Couldn't you tell it was just an excuse to get to know you? All Don's heard since he met you is, 'Alex this' and 'Alex that.' He's quite a catch, single, his own business and a nice house on Siesta Key. You could do worse."

Alex ran her fingers through her hair. "I'm not interested. I still love John and when he comes home, I'll be waiting."

Barbara snorted. "You mean, *if* he comes home. You need to move on with your life and not live on hope. I think it's time you faced reality and considered that perhaps the police are right and that he left because he wanted to."

Tears stung Alex's lids as she shook her head. "No, Barbara, not until I get some evidence. Even if John did want to leave me, I still think he'd have at least left a note. He'd never have gone without letting me know."

All this talk of John made Alex weepy. Her friend was only trying to help, but sometimes Barbara's bluntness grated on her nerves and she wished she knew when to stop. A headache hammered in her temples and round the back of her head and she hoped her friend would go soon to allow her to sleep. She closed her eyes and leaned her head back.

"You look tired," Barbara pushed in the footrest and rose from the loveseat. "I'll put these flowers in water and then I'll go and let you rest."

Alex opened her eyes and smiled. "Thanks."

Once the roses were in water, Barbara carried them through and placed the vase on the writing desk. "I see someone else also sent flowers."

Alex scowled at the bowl of lilies. "Yes, I think it must be from the girls at the office."

Barbara pulled a moue. "Someone ought to tell them that you only send lilies for a funeral." She gave Alex a hug. "Bye, call me if you need anything."

"I will."

When the front door clicked, Alex stared at the lilies and shuddered. She pulled forward a large, puffy cushion, laid her head on it and slept.

Chapter 11

The next morning, Zack Walker was in his office drinking coffee and scarfing down a burger. He'd spent the previous night with Clancy and was exhausted. They'd made love twice before midnight and once again before he left to return home. The effort of keeping pace with Clancy's libido was wearing him out. She once told him that she used a vibrator the evenings they weren't together to satisfy her needs. Of that, he was glad; he couldn't perform more than once every night. Twenty years ago, he'd have welcomed it, but not at his age.

He wiped the sweat from his brow with his shirtsleeve. Just thinking about Clancy tired him out. He picked up the report on his desk and read it again. The police had responded to a 911 call at St. Armand's circle where a young woman had been involved and survived a hit and run accident.

He laid down his burger when he saw the victim's name— Alex Martell. He formed his mouth into a straight line as he read statements taken from eyewitnesses. From this report, it sounded as if this was no accident, but deliberate.

He grabbed his jacket off the back of the chair, stuffed the last of his food into his mouth, and left the office.

"I need a woman officer. Who's on duty?" His eyes scanned the dry-wipe board displaying that day's schedule.

"LaTour's in the lunch room." Someone shouted.

"Go get her and tell her to meet me at my car."

Zack fished in his pocket for his car keys and trotted down a flight of stairs that led to the yard at the back of the precinct. A small figure rounded the corner of the building and met him at the entrance to the parking lot.

"Where are we going, sir?" The young brown-haired woman asked, slightly out of breath.

Zack unlocked the car and Minnie LaTour slid into the passenger seat fastening her seat belt. "To interview a hit and run victim."

Zack swung the wheel and joined the line of traffic driving east from Geyserville. Twenty minutes later, he parked outside Alex Martell's house, climbed the steps and rang the doorbell. When no one answered the door, he consulted the accident report.

"She was discharged from hospital yesterday and should be home," Zack said, closing the file.

"Maybe she didn't come here, sir."

Zack squinted at the small woman beside him and rang the doorbell again. He heard faint tapping, the door opened a crack and he held out his badge and official police ID.

"Mrs. Martell, Lieutenant Walker and Sergeant LaTour. May we come in and take a statement about your accident?"

The door opened wider and Zack just managed not to exclaim at the sight of Alex's swollen, bruised face. She leaned on a pair of crutches and slowly shuffled backwards allowing them access.

Alex wobbled into the living room followed by LaTour while Zack closed the door.

"Do you need any help?" Minnie asked as Alex swung one crutch and wilted onto the sofa.

"No, I'm fine, thanks. It's getting up that's hard. That's why I took so long to answer the door. I haven't mastered these things yet." Alex motioned to a chair. "Please sit down."

Zack lowered his frame into an armchair, his eyes sweeping the room, taking note of the bowl of lilies and a vase of red roses. "What can you tell us about the accident?"

Alex held her palms upward and shrugged. "Nothing more than you already know. A car was coming when I stepped onto the crossing, but he slowed, so I kept walking. Then he drove straight at me. For a moment, I was paralyzed with shock. Then the car hit me and flung me off the road. After that, everything's hazy."

Minnie looked up from taking notes. "Did you see who was driving?"

"No, all I could see was a shape, but I think it was a man."

Zack leaned forward with his hands on his knees. "How do you feel, Mrs. Martell?"

"Sore, bruised, but the doctor said that—"

Zack looked her straight in the eyes. "I know what the prognosis is. How do you feel about what happened?"

For a fleeting moment, a scared look flashed across her face and then she shrugged. "These things happen. I'll need to be more careful in future."

Zack arranged his face into a serious expression. "Mrs. Martell. Neither you nor I are stupid. First, a young woman is murdered and she just happens to look like you. Then someone tries to run you down. I think you're in danger. Do you have any idea why?"

Alex's lips trembled and tears filled her eyes. "No, I don't know why anyone would want to harm me. As far as I know, no one has a grudge against me." She lifted troubled eyes to Zack. "But I am scared."

"Is there anything else you can tell us that might help or make us understand why this happened?"

Zack noticed a second's hesitation before Alex spoke. "No, I wish I knew what was going on."

"Well, in light of what's happened, I'm going to put in a request for you to have protection. How'd you feel about that?"

"Okay, but what kind of protection?"

"Once you feel better, I'll have Sergeant Clancy seconded here. You remember her, don't you? She was with me the last time we met."

A look of profound relief crossed Alex's face and she gave a wan smile. "Thank you, I'd like that."

The officers both stood and Zack nodded toward the flowers. "I see you've already received some gifts from well-wishers."

"Yes my friend Barbara brought me those." She flapped her hand at the roses.

"And the lilies?"

Alex shook her head. "I've no clue, there wasn't a card with them. They'd been left by the garage door."

Zack exchanged a look with Minnie and held out his card. "Call me if you think of anything else. In the meantime, I'll get the paperwork started and try to get Clancy allocated to you as soon as you're fit to resume work. Don't bother coming to the door, we'll see ourselves out."

By the time a week had passed, Alex was walking without crutches and she decided to remove the pressure bandage. Her leg underneath the padding was itchy and she longed to relax in a long, hot bath. She winced when she peeled the last of the cotton wadding from her leg. Her entire calf was almost black and her swollen foot colored purple and yellow. Her leg muscles were weak and rubbery and she had difficulty keeping her balance. Determined to overcome her injuries, she spent time each day massaging her leg and doing simple exercises. Her body and facial bruises had begun to fade, so toward the end of the second week, she returned to work.

She limped into reception amid a flurry of questions about her condition and made light of her escapade, making out it had been her fault. However, the spoken threat continued to ring in her ears. Ever since John's disappearance, strange things had been happening. Charlie was the only one to whom she told the truth about the accident.

"What! My God Alex, you might have been killed." He exploded.

"The police think that's what the driver intended, but who would want me dead? I've never done anything to anyone."

"Not that you're aware of," Charlie muttered, pacing back and forth in front of her desk. "You said the police are going to give you protection. When does that start?"

"I don't know. I rang the lieutenant and told him I was starting back to work today."

Charlie smoothed his hand over his beard. "You really need to be careful, Alex, it sounds as if there's a maniac loose out there."

That thought turned her stomach and a bubble of panic lodged in her throat. She plunked on a chair, her shoulders rigid. "I'm scared, Charlie, really scared. What's going on? Could John have been involved in something illegal?"

Charlie sighed. "I've no idea, but it's most unlikely. You just have to hang in there. Why don't you go and stay with Barbara for a while?"

"But, that means involving someone else. If I'm in danger, they might be, too. No, I can handle this by myself and I know just what I'm going to do."

Alex didn't go straight home that evening, instead she drove northwest to the Manatee Convention Center in Palmetto to visit a gun show. She made tracks for the booth offering handgun instruction, defined what she wanted and signed up for a course, which began the following month. If she was going to protect herself, she needed to know the proper way to handle a gun.

She had no clue where John's permit was, so the next step was to buy a new gun and when she'd completed her training, apply for a concealed weapon's permit. A man at the Smith and

Wesson booth sold her a compact 9mm pistol and gave her the application packet she needed to apply for the permit and a copy of Chapter 790 of the Florida Statutes to read. Before her training course started, she'd have plenty time to have a passport-style, color photo taken, visit her local law enforcement agency for them to fingerprint her, and to sign her application in the presence of a notary.

In the meantime, she had John's gun for protection and if she ended up injuring someone and facing prosecution, she would deal with that when it happened.

Two days later, Zack Walker phoned to say that his superiors had turned down the request for protection. "I'm sorry, but the County Commissioner feels it's unjustified."

"It's not your fault, but thanks for trying." Disappointment speared through her as she hung up the phone.

Her injuries made her feel vulnerable. If someone chose to chase her, she couldn't run. The bruised skin on the right side of her body was still tender and pains coursed through her. Now would be an ideal time for the assassin to strike. She flopped on the end of the sofa feeling miserable. Then her adopted mother's words returned to encourage her. *'Only you can make it happen. Nothing is going to fall from the sky and hit you on the head; you have to be the one to do it.'*

Now she felt better. Her mother had always been able to make things seem right. Even now, fifteen years after her death, Alex still relied on her words of wisdom. At that moment, she vowed to begin an exercise regime to help speed up her recovery. When her assailant struck again, she wanted to be fit enough to fight back.

During the next two weeks, Alex's recovery was rapid. Her bruises faded and her strength and morale returned. Several times her thoughts strayed to Juno. In a way, she'd expected

Lilies of Death

him to contact her when he heard about the accident. But then again, maybe he didn't know about it.

The weather had changed. At last the humidity had dropped. During the day, the sun was still warm, but by evening cooler air descended. Alex loved when the weather changed. It gave her chance to spend more time in the garden, weeding and planting. Each evening she'd spend an hour at the back of the house filling planters on the patio and mowing the grass.

She stood up and stretched. Her stomach rumbled and she realized she was hungry. Pulling off her gardening gloves, she entered the kitchen and called a pizza delivery company. While she waited for dinner to arrive, she mixed and picked at a salad.

As the doorbell rang, she grabbed her wallet and opened the door. Brett Etheridge, the assistant editor, stood there.

"Hey, Alex, I tried calling earlier, but you weren't in."

"Yes I was, but I was out in the back yard weeding. I thought you were the pizza delivery boy."

Brett grinned. "Sorry, no such luck. But the reason I phoned was to see if you wanted to go to dinner."

"Not this evening Brett. Anyway, I don't think it's such a good idea for us to pick up where we left off. We're both older and wiser and I know I've changed since we split. It's almost four years."

Brett leaned on the doorjamb and hung his head. "I don't expect to pick up where we left off, but can't we still be friends and maybe even start over?"

Alex didn't want to disillusion him. He'd been a broken man when she'd told him she was in love with John and they intended to marry, so she changed the subject. "Whatever happened to that redhead you brought to the Christmas party? She was beautiful."

Brett pouted. "It didn't work out, we both wanted different things from life."

"Most people do, Brett. That's what makes life so fascinating."

"Not you and me. As I remember it, we both wanted the same things."

"Maybe then, but as I've already said, I've changed and you probably have, too. It's never a good idea to try to go back."

The truth was, she didn't want to start a relationship with Brett again, there was always a chance that John might come back.

Alex shook her head. "I'm sorry Brett, but I think we'd be better keeping our meetings to the office for now, at least until I find out for certain what's happened to John."

"And what if you never do?"

Alex shrugged. "Only time will tell how I feel, but thanks for dropping by."

"Anytime." Brett caressed her cheek with his forefinger. "I'd do anything for you."

"I know, goodnight Brett." She leaned forward to peck his cheek, but he turned his head and her kiss landed on his lips.

He placed a hand on the back of her neck and pulled her close, deepening the kiss.

Someone coughed and Alex pushed Brett away.

The pizza boy held out a box. "That'll be $11.99."

Alex handed him a twenty-dollar bill. "Thanks, keep the change."

She flounced through the open front door and slammed it. Damn Brett, after four years, he should have gotten over his obsession with her. Everyone at work sympathized about John being missing, but Brett was the only one who assumed it was permanent. He always spoke as if his disappearance was final. Alex would never accept that unless someone gave her definite proof.

Chapter 12

Three days later, the phone rang on Zack Walker's desk. On hearing that Alex Martell was waiting to see him, he stubbed out his cigarette in the ashtray. "Send her in," he mumbled.

The door opened and the first thing he noticed was Alex's ashen face and dark shadows under her indigo eyes. This was one scared woman. He pulled forward a chair, his eyes sweeping over her.

She smoothed down the seat of her cream pants before lowering her body onto the hard, wooden seat. Despite her fragile appearance, she still looked beautiful. Long hair framed her heart-shaped face and shone with golden highlights. Navy blue shoes matched a cream and navy, nautical-looking, striped top, decorated with a striking, red appliqué. She had painted her nails the exact same shade of red.

"Good morning, Mrs. Martell. Can I get you some tea or coffee?"

The shining hair bounced on her shoulders as she shook her head. "No thanks, Lieutenant, I'm here to report an attack."

Zack immediately sobered and grabbed a pen. "Go ahead, I'm listening."

Alex related how she arrived home the previous afternoon late, tired and hungry. Mitzi was nowhere in sight, so she kicked off her shoes, perched on a kitchen stool and flexed her feet. Once she'd filled the cat's dish, she concentrated on whisking an omelet for her own dinner and wolfed it down in a matter of minutes.

While she was clearing away her dishes, angry clouds spilled out huge raindrops battering the windows. The wind whipped the rain into a frantic whirlpool while lightening ripped through the darkness. Alex shuddered. Thank goodness she'd made it home before the storm. By now, low-lying districts would be flooded and the waterfall of rain would have brought traffic to a standstill.

Before she drew the curtains, she stared out at the turbulent sky. By the glow of the light from the window, she saw Mitzi huddled beneath a hibiscus bush. "Oh, no!" She cried.

She made a beeline for the kitchen door, leaving it open, and sprinted barefooted over to the bush. Raindrops struck her like needles and soon she was soaked to the skin. The wind buffeted her about. The cat struggled in her arms. Alex gripped her tighter. Mitzi's claws raked her forearm.

"Stop fighting me." Alex yelled above the noise of the thunder.

She bowed her head and strode out for the kitchen door. An arm grabbed her from behind. In her fright, she released the cat. A gloved hand covered her mouth. Her mind was racing, twisting and turning. Rain pounded her head and shoulders. She grasped her hands tightly together, jerking her right elbow into her attacker's stomach. For a fleeting moment, he loosened his grip. Alex swung round. She skidded in the mud. He grabbed her shoulders. His torso was now slightly below eye level. Her pulse raced. She lowered her head and butted it into his ribs. He yowled. She wiped the rain from her eyes and stared up into evil eyes behind a black, ski mask.

With each breath, her chest felt heavy. The man bawled again. Without thinking, she raised her right knee with as much force as she could muster, ramming it upwards into his groin. The man doubled up. Alex turned and ran into the kitchen, slamming and locking the door behind her.

A sob caught in her throat as she raced upstairs and reached under the bed for John's gun. With her back to the wall, she sat on the floor, aiming the gun at the bedroom door. Her whole body quaked. She shivered with the cold, her wet hair plastered to her head and her clothes dripping. Thunder clattered and lightening flashed. If the man gained access to the house, she'd never hear him moving around above the noise of the storm. Her only hope was to stay put and shoot anyone who came through the door.

Rainwater dripped from her hair down her face, so she reached for a tissue on the nightstand. As she wiped away the water, she crept sideways along the wall toward the bathroom. She groped behind her back for the handle and opened the door. Once inside, she turned the lock and leaned back, exhausted.

Her body still shaking, she placed the gun on the vanity and reached for a towel to dry her face and hair. With her back to the bathtub and her eyes glued to the door, she hastily stripped off her wet clothes and toweled her body dry. Now what? She wrapped the towel around her body, placed her ear to the bathroom door and listened. All she heard was the rain and wind still bombarding the house.

With caution, she opened the door a crack. Her eyes swept the empty room. Feeling braver, she reached for the gun and inched her way along the bedroom wall. Her face contorted when the closet door creaked. She rammed her hand in and selected a pair of jeans and a sweater. Before she had chance to put them on, a loud clatter sounded downstairs. She froze for a millisecond, hugged the clothes and scampered back into the bathroom.

Once safely ensconced, she rammed her legs into the jeans and pulled the sweater over her head. The air was hard to breath and her heart thudded as if it might jump right out of her chest. She sat on the edge of the bathtub repeating over and over something she'd once read. "No one ever died of fright, no one ever died of fright."

This was small consolation when she was upstairs alone and there was a possibility that a maniac was on the loose. She stood, straightened her shoulders and opened the bathroom door. If she were going to die, she would die fighting.

Her eyes scanned the bedroom. It was the same as she'd left it. The door to the landing was ajar. Clasping the gun with two hands, she approached it. Her throat was dry with no saliva as she tried to remove the lump in her throat. On tiptoes, she poked her head round the door. A loud clap of thunder shook the house. She suppressed a scream.

Breathing rapidly, she took one step. Now, she could see right down the stairs to the shadowy foyer. She transferred the gun to her right hand, clutching the banister with her left. One by one, she descended the stairs, holding the gun out in front of her. There was no doubt in her mind that she had the ability to shoot the perpetrator. Her whole body pulsed with tension, but her mind was clear. She was in full charge of her faculties.

Someone knocked on the front door. She stumbled to a sudden stop.

"Alex, its Charlie, are you all right?"

It took a moment for the words to filtrate through to her brain. She almost fell down the last few steps. "Oh, Charlie, thank God it's you." She removed the chain and unlocked the door, falling hard against him.

He enveloped her in his arms. "I guessed your power might be out, so I brought over some flashlights."

Relief flooded through her and she clung to Charlie like a limpet. Unable to speak, sobs wracked her entire body.

Charlie closed the door and stroked her hair. "Come on, there's no need to go to pieces, it's only a storm."

Alex's wet hair flew in wild array as she shook her head. "No, he was here." She was still having difficulty breathing. "He attacked me when I went to get the cat."

"Who did?"

"Him, a man in a ski mask. He could even be inside the house."

Charlie switched on a flashlight and took the gun from her. He started to mount the stairs, but she stalled him. "He's not up there," she whispered and nodded in the direction of the kitchen.

Staying behind Charlie, she doused the flashlight and followed. He nudged open the kitchen door and assumed a firm stance, holding the gun outright in both hands. "Freeze, I have a gun."

There was silence except for their breathing. They waited. A shuffling sound came from a corner. Alex clutched the back of Charlie's jacket. "Come out and you won't get hurt." Charlie signaled for Alex to turn on the flashlight.

The bright beam showed Mitzi fleeing across the kitchen, meowing. Alex's knees went limp and she grabbed the doorjamb. Beside the counter lay a broken vase and a baking tray. The clatter she'd heard when Mitzi knocked them over.

"There's your culprit," Charlie quipped, but his expression changed when he turned and saw Alex grasping the doorframe. "Come and sit down, you've had a nasty fright."

He helped Alex over to a stool. "Thanks, Charlie."

He crossed to her propane stove, lit the four burners and the room filled with light. "There, that's better. You sit still and I'll make some tea, then you can tell me everything."

Charlie sat on an adjacent stool with a tense face listening as Alex related what had happened. "Did you get a good look at him?"

"Only his eyes behind the ski mask." She quaked. "They had so much hate in them."

"What about his build and the clothes he was wearing?"

Alex ran the incident through her mind like a videotape. She closed her eyes and tried to picture her assailant. "He was big, dressed in a dark anorak and dark pants. That's all I can remember…oh, and dark gloves, he wore gloves."

He winced at her words. "That's not much to go on, that could be anyone." The muscles in his jaw knotted. "You have to think hard, Alex. Who could hold a grudge against you?"

"I don't know." She wailed, shaking her head in an exaggerated movement. "As far as I know I haven't crossed anyone." Every inch of her body ached and her limbs felt heavy as she wracked her brain.

"What about Brett?" Charlie suggested.

"Brett Etheridge? Why would he want to hurt me? He loves me."

Charlie pursed his lips. "He's obsessed with you—that's not love. Sometimes rejection burns deep enough to turn into hate."

His words hit her in the stomach like a baseball bat. Her attacker was of the same height and build as Brett. However, she found it hard to believe that he'd want to hurt her.

"You need to suspect everyone, Alex. This person knows where you live. How many other people know that?"

"Not many. I didn't even know *you* knew where I lived, Charlie." Her brows raised in question. "How did you find out?"

"From Barbara, I was worried so I called her."

Alex smiled. "Thanks, Charlie, you're a true friend." She leaned over and hugged him. For once, he didn't smell of pipe tobacco and toothpaste, but nondescript.

"You're welcome. It's late, why don't you go to bed and I'll sleep down here on the sofa."

"Shouldn't I call the police?"

"There's not much point now, the man'll be miles away."

Alex motioned a nod. "True, I'll get you a pillow and some blankets."

She climbed the stairs, her knees no longer feeling like jelly and took the spare bedding down to Charlie. After one more hug and a brief kiss on the cheek, Charlie settled on the sofa and Alex went upstairs. In the safety of her bedroom, she undressed and lay listening to the thunder rumbling in the distance. The knowledge that she had a protector for the night dispersed all her fears and in a short time, she was fast asleep.

The man socked his fist into the open palm of his other hand. Things were not going the way he'd planned. He knew his victim was feisty by the way she'd handled her husband's disappearance. Somehow, she'd survived when he hit her with his car and now he was the one in pain from when she'd butted his ribs and kneed his balls. He'd underestimated her and hadn't reckoned on her being a fighter.

Goddamn her eyes, her beautiful eyes. He'd felt a rising sense of trepidation when she'd looked up and the thought that she might recognize him, filled him with dread. That would have spoiled the game. He didn't want to reveal his identity until the time came for the kill. The shocked expression on her face would be worth waiting for. The knowledge that he'd tricked her into thinking he was her friend when all this time hate simmered in his gut, increasing his desire for her blood. However, before that, he wanted to enjoy making love to her and punishing her the way she'd tortured him with her rejections. She had to suffer. She had to die.

Over the years, his other victims had given him immense pleasure. The beginning of the game when he'd courted them and gained their respect and confidence. His detailed plan to hoodwink them and finally the kill, but this one was proving harder than all the others put together. By now, he should have completed the deed, but she was too spirited and spunky and his patience was running out.

'*Calm down,*' he told himself. Perhaps he should pull back and let life return to normal. If she began feeling safe again, he'd be able to strike when she least expected it. Yes, that was what he'd do. Become her closest friend and confidant before he struck. He threw back his head and laughed with one hand holding his sore ribs and the other his bruised balls.

After Alex had finished relating the details of the attack and had signed a statement, she exited Zack's office, turned the corner toward the main exit of the police precinct and bumped into someone. She looked up into Juno's green eyes, her heart turning upside down at his closeness.

"Excuse me," he gave a slight bow, "as I said before, we must stop meeting like this."

Her tongue felt thick and she couldn't muster her usual quick repartee. "I'm sorry."

"Are you okay?" Juno placed a hand on her arm to detain her. Before she could answer, his face became serious. "Something's happened."

He shepherded her toward a bench in the deserted corridor and persuaded her to sit. His nearness bothered her, so she attempted to slide away, but he bracketed her jaw with his hand and turned her to face him. "Tell me what happened."

The look of concern in his eyes caused tears to roll down her cheeks in silent rivers.

His expression softened, and he draped an arm around her shoulder, pulling her close. "Tell me Alex, please, I want to help."

The warmth and softness in his tone brought out the longing she felt for him. She raised her eyes to his again and felt as if she was drowning. The rest of the world seemed far away, as their eyes fused together. With one smooth motion, he dipped his head and his lips brushed hers. He curved his hand round the back of her head and a small groan escaped from her tight throat.

The pressure of his lips was soft and her body quivered with desire as his tongue parted her lips. He kissed her hungrily and she responded by running her fingers through the back of his hair. He lifted his head and a heavy sigh seeped out as he looked at her with tender eyes. They stared at each other in silence. Unanswered questions echoed inside her head.

"Now tell me what happened," he implored.

She brushed the last of the tears from her face and once again described the previous evening's occurrence. Juno sat with a stony face listening to every word, his eyes never leaving her face. When she'd finished, he pulled her into his arms and she sagged against him. "I'll murder him, I'll bloody kill him!"

Alex pushed him away. His look of extreme anger shocked her. "No, the police'll deal with him. Lieutenant Walker thinks the same man's responsible for both the hit and run and this attack, so he's putting in another request for protection. This time he thinks I'll get it."

A puzzled expression crossed Juno's face. "What hit and run? Has there been another murder?"

"No, someone ran me down a few weeks ago. I'd only just recovered when this attack happened."

"Dammit, I must have been in New York when the car incident happened. I had to go and visit my publisher. Has Lieutenant Walker got any leads?"

"Not as far as I know. The way things are going, I'll be dead before they find him."

Juno placed his hands on her upper arms and gave her a gentle shake. "I will not let that happen. I'll hunt down this bastard and kill him."

"No, please Juno, let the police handle it. You might get hurt."

His eyebrows lifted with curiosity. "Are you concerned about me?"

Blood rushed to her face. "Yes—no one else should get hurt—it's me he's after." Stillness settled over them and her gaze swung up to his. "Deal?"

He hesitated for several heartbeats. "Deal. I'm glad Walker's trying to do something to protect you."

Juno pulled her to her feet, curved his arm around her waist and steadied her while she negotiated the steps to the exit. At the bottom, he wheeled her round to face him. "Where are you going, now?"

"Home."

"Which is where?"

Lieutenant Walker had told her not to reveal where she lived to anyone. She looked at her feet and mumbled. "I'm not supposed to tell anyone."

He uttered a curse word. "Dammit, Alex, I'm helping the police with these cases. Walker didn't mean me. Anyway, if I were the killer, I'd already know where you live."

She braved another look at him. "Okay, okay. I live on Halcyon Lane."

"That's pretty isolated. How close is your nearest neighbor?"

"About a half-mile away, but Mr. Jennings is in his eighties."

Juno chewed his cheek, deep in thought. "And the protection?"

"The Lieutenant wants Sergeant Clancy to stay with me. If The Commissioner agrees, she'll start later today."

His eyes searched her face. "Clancy's good. You'll be quite safe with her. She's built like a Sumo wrestler and I think Walker has the hots for her, but she'll look after you."

Alex wanted to blurt out that she'd rather have him stay with her, but she didn't. Because Juno had kissed her when she was vulnerable, didn't mean he felt anything for her except compassion. This man with a caring nature was very different from the hostile one she'd interviewed. Every time she encountered him, he produced a different side of his personality.

Juno held out a business card. "My home and cell number's on here. I don't give this to anyone either, but call if you need me, I can get to you quicker than the police."

She stared at the card in her hand. "Thanks."

"You're very welcome." Juno kissed her cheek and every inch of her tingled. "Drive carefully." He loped across the road to his dark blue Mercedes and winked before he closed the door.

Alex stood rooted to the spot, watching him drive away. Then something crossed her mind. Why had Juno come to the precinct? He hadn't entered the offices once he'd met her, so why had he been there?

Chapter 13

All afternoon as Alex shopped for groceries and paid some bills, she kept looking in her rear view mirror monitoring the traffic behind, but no one appeared to be following her. Then if they were an expert, she doubted she'd be able to detect them.

At last, safe in the confines of her home, she relaxed and made a pot of coffee, making sure she'd locked all the doors and windows. At five-thirty, the doorbell rang and she peered through the peephole before opening the front door to a tall woman who showed her police I.D.

"Mrs. Martell?" She held out a hand the size of a man's. "I'm Sergeant Clancy."

"Oh, yes, I remember you."

The woman wore a denim shirt and matching jeans with a small, sports bag slung over her shoulder. A large pizza box was in her other hand. "I brought dinner." She held out the box.

"Nice to see you again, thanks for the pizza." Alex noted that the other woman was many inches taller than she was and despite her size and masculine appearance, her dusky face was round and feminine. Her nose and lips had no trace of Negroid features and her black, spiky hair was as straight as a die. At most she was an octoroon with beautiful, high cheekbones and skin the color of burnished copper.

"Glad to be of assistance," Clancy let her bag fall to the floor. "Shall we start with a guided tour of the house? I need to pinpoint anywhere with easy access that might need reinforced."

Alex led the way into the kitchen and Clancy examined the door to the outside. "I'd like to get these boarded up," she rattled the French doors. "Even when they're locked anyone could get in through these small panes. They only need smash the glass in a couple of the lower ones and climb in or force this lock. It's very flimsy."

Fear pulsated through Alex at the thought that she'd been at risk all this time. "Of course, anything you say, I can call someone tomorrow. There's plenty of plywood in the shed we keep to board up the windows in hurricane season."

"No need to get anyone in, I can do it myself. You can show me the shed later when I've explored the rest of the house."

Alex ushered Clancy through the downstairs rooms and she picked up her bag before they climbed to the first floor. "This is good," she flung one arm wide at the top of the stairs. "If we get trapped up here, we have the advantage. Which is your room?"

Alex opened the door and Clancy roamed around scrutinizing the window and the door to the bathroom. She battered on one of the panels. "This is a good strong door. If there's any kind of crisis, you hole up in here, lock the door and lie in the bathtub."

A flutter of anguish filled Alex. "But why?"

Clancy stared, her face solemn. "If there's shooting, you'll be protected by the tub."

Alex drew her lower lip through her teeth. "Do you think it might come to that?"

"Who knows, we need a plan in case something happens. Now, do you want me to sleep upstairs in the guest room or downstairs on the sofa?"

"I don't mind, you choose."

Clancy shook her head. "No, Mrs. Martell, you choose. If the intruder injures me when I'm downstairs, I can't protect you. If I'm asleep upstairs, I might not hear someone breaking in, but at least there's a better chance of us getting him before he gets us."

Alex felt the blood drain from her face. "You're speaking as if he's definitely going to break in."

"Well, we think there's a big chance that he will, that's why I'm here."

Alex felt as though she'd been slapped. Until now, she hadn't realized the seriousness of the situation. "I'd prefer you to sleep in the guest room. I'll show you the way."

Clancy dumped her bag on the bottom of the bed and inspected the adjacent shower room.

Together they returned downstairs, Alex gave Clancy the key to the shed, and in no time at all, she was nailing plywood to the architrave around the French doors while Alex heated the pizza and set the table.

Alex couldn't help wondering why Clancy wore her hair the way she did. Although she was a tall, big-boned woman, her physique was definitely feminine. With longer hair and a touch of make-up, she'd be very attractive.

They ate the pizza in silence and when Alex looked up, Clancy was watching her. "Are you married, Sergeant?"

Clancy's eyes were downcast. "Nope, never have, never wanted to be. Please call me Clancy. If we're going to live together, we should be on first name terms."

"I agree and you must call me Alex." She drew in calming draughts of air. "I'm so glad you're here. This is the safest I've felt in a long time."

The next morning the phone rang at six-thirty. Alex picked up the receiver at the same time that Clancy raced into her room.

"Hi, Alex, it's Charlie. Sorry to call so early, but I've just received word from my sister-in-law that my brother's been injured in an accident at work, so I'm taking two weeks vacation to visit him."

"Oh, I'm so sorry, Charlie, I wanted you to meet Sergeant Clancy, the police officer who's been assigned to protect me."

"Well, if things aren't too serious, I'll try to get back by the end of the week. In the meantime, Brett's taking over, so be nice to him."

Alex groaned. "Okay, you take care and I hope your brother's condition isn't too serious."

She disconnected the call and turned to Clancy who was leaning against the doorframe. "That was my editor. He's had to go out of town to visit his brother, but you'll still get chance to meet everyone else at the magazine."

Now they were both wide-awake, the two women, pulled on robes and went downstairs to make an early breakfast.

Clancy took two eggs from the refrigerator, whisked them into a glass of milk and held the mixture out to Alex. "Drink this."

Alex wrinkled her nose. "Raw eggs?"

"Yes, while I'm here, I'm going to try to prepare you for when your attacker strikes and the first thing is to build up your strength."

"And the second thing?"

Clancy smiled. "The list's too long. Let's just take it one day at a time."

After the first few days together, Alex and Clancy had formed a firm friendship. They were total opposites in that Clancy was self-sufficient, and able to defend herself with unarmed combat, while Alex had always had someone to look after her.

Alex drove the two of them to the magazine each morning, and Clancy sat reading a book in one of the comfortable armchairs in Alex's office, accompanying her wherever she went in the building.

Brett called a few times with queries, but Alex never had chance to introduce him to Clancy. She knew that when Charlie was away, he took his responsibilities very seriously and didn't fraternize with anyone.

Every evening Clancy instructed Alex in ways she could defend herself. "Wherever you go, whether you're with me or alone, try to be mentally aware. Always park where it's brightly lit and there's other people around making sure you carry your keys in your hand along with a kubaton."

Alex was puzzled. "What's that?"

"It's a small, round piece of wood, about this long," Clancy opened the span of her hand. "You can buy one at any martial arts store. If you slam it into the side of someone's head or sternum, it will cause them considerable pain giving you the opportunity to run away. Another good place to use it is the back of their hand. There's lots of nerve endings there and it hurts like hell."

Alex sucked in her breath and took jerky-written notes. The more Clancy elucidated the more she realized how vulnerable she was. She had no sports training and compared to the other woman, she was lacking in strength and stature.

That weekend, Alex attended her first gun-handling lesson and the instructor taught her to remove the safety catch, exhale, take aim and squeeze the trigger without taking her eyes off the target. Clancy sat on the sidelines observing and when they arrived back at the house, she complimented Alex. "You did really good for your first lesson. Now here's what I want you to practice."

She proceeded to squat, rise and kick, first using one foot and then the other. "Okay, now you do that until you're exhausted. We've only a short time to work together and I want you to strengthen your legs."

Alex copied Clancy's actions, but she only managed a few squats before collapsing in a heap on the floor. "Ow, that hurts!"

The next day Alex's thigh and calf muscles complained with each step and it took her all her time not to hobble from the elevator to her office.

Darren Winters had an appointment to read the proofs of his editorial, but he called to cancel, so Alex put everything in the mail.

Two days later, he called. "This is great, Alex. The way you've written this article makes the company sound really upmarket. Thanks very much." Alex glowed at his praise. "Can I take you to dinner to celebrate?"

"Dinner?" Alex watched Clancy pull her eyebrows together and give a negative movement of her head.

"I'm sorry, but...er...but while Charlie's on vacation, I'm really too busy, maybe another time."

"You bet. I'll hold you to that."

She hung up and was surprised at Clancy's sharp tone. "How long have you known *him*?"

"Not long. I met him at my friend Barbara's when I went to dinner a few weeks ago. Why?"

Clancy fired an irritable glance at her. "You need to be very wary until this felon's caught. Don't trust anyone."

"But it can't be Darren. He's a friend of Don's. And what possible reason could he have for wanting to hurt me?"

Clancy looked frazzled and annoyed. "Your attacker has some kind of grudge against you. To us it might be something quite simple, but to this psycho it's enough to fuel his fire. How tall is Darren? Could he have been the man in the ski mask?"

"I don't know it was pitch dark and pouring rain."

"But you said you looked into his eyes. What color were they? Blue? Brown?"

Alex spoke in a rush, words stumbling over one another. "I've told you I don't know—I was scared and in shock—fighting for my life."

On the tenth day, Clancy came down to breakfast with her sports bag in her hand and Alex felt sick. "You're leaving?"

Clancy dropped her bombshell. "Yes. Lieutenant Walker called me on the radio this morning. I'm sorry Alex, but the County Commissioner won't sanction your protection any longer."

Alex drew in a shocked breath and she tried to control her trembling hands as she ran her fingers through her hair. Her thoughts ricocheted all over the place wondering what she should do now.

"You know I'd stay if I could, but orders are orders." Clancy said. "They only allocate protection for so long."

Words stuck in Alex's throat and she gestured that an apology wasn't necessary. "What now?"

"You're on your own again, I'm sorry."

The news that the police had canceled her protection decked Alex for a moment leaving her feeling disconnected from the world. They'd stripped away her warm blanket of security and she felt exposed and unprotected. She spent a sleepless night agonizing what to do and by dawn, she'd reached a decision.

The next morning, she knocked on the door of Brett's office. He smiled when she entered and indicated a chair. "Hi, Alex, what's up?"

"I'm going to take some leave, Brett. I need to get away for a while."

His face fell and a distressed frown pulled his brows together. "Is everything all right? It's not bad news is it?"

"No, nothing like that, but there's something I have to do and I don't know how long it'll take."

He pulled a moue. "Sounds mysterious, can I ask what?"

"Sorry, no, it's something personal. I hate to leave you short-handed while Charlie's away, but this is important."

Brett lifted his shoulders in a shrug. "No matter, Charlie's returning on Monday, so that shouldn't be a problem. Can I do anything to help?"

Alex shoved her chair back and held out her hand. "Thanks for the offer, but I'll be okay. I'll clear out my desk and finish later today. See you, Brett."

She felt his eyes boring into her back, so she turned. Brett still had the same disturbing frown on his face when Alex smiled, closed the door, and leaned against it with her eyes closed.

After Clancy expanded on why she was leaving, they'd had a long talk. Between them, they'd narrowed down the identity of her stalker to four possibilities.

"That's if it's someone you know," Clancy said, writing down the fourth name. "More often than not, it usually is."

Alex stared at the list. She found it had to believe that any one of these names wanted to hurt her, especially, the last name.

"It couldn't be Juno," she remarked, "he'd just left me when that car ran me down." Her heart was constantly heavy when she thought of him and he inspired a passion in her that she'd never felt before.

Clancy's eyebrows sprang into perfect arches. "He could have run to his car, put on a ski mask and tried to run you down. Remember he's a writer and has an imagination."

Alex couldn't believe that. The same applied to the other three suspects; she refused to believe that any one of them wanted her dead. She folded her arms and leaned back in the chair. "Well, where do we go from here?"

"He obviously knows you've had police protection and has pulled back. Now I've been removed, he'll feel safe and try again, so you need to be very, very careful."

Those words rebounded like a death knell and lodged in Alex's throat. "Y-You make me sound like a lamb ready for slaughter." She announced when she finally found her voice.

"That's exactly what you are. Go over in your mind everything I've shown you so that it becomes a natural reaction and you don't have to think what to do. When he strikes, the most important thing is to get angry. Get so angry you can't see straight—that'll get your adrenaline flowing and help you defend yourself."

Untamed fear shot through Alex and her breath hissed in a quick intake.

"Remember the pressure points behind the ears and under the nose. If you smack your palm into his nose, it'll cause his eyes to water and give you the advantage. Box his ears and use anything you can find as a weapon."

Alex nodded in agreement, fear darting up her spine. This life and death situation made her want to stay locked in the house, but she knew she couldn't do that. Her life would never be her own until the police caught this person. She was determined to endure this ordeal even although she'd become nothing more than live bait.

Clancy hugged her. "Remember the forms we practiced? Block and punch, block and punch. He won't expect you to have a gun or to fight back, so don't be afraid to shoot and most of all, don't let him sweet-talk you. Remember this man wants to kill you, so disable him by shooting him in the leg or anywhere else you can." The two women embraced again.

Alex had one more question for her mentor. "What's your first name, Clancy? Is it really so bad you never use it?"

Clancy clicked her tongue. "You promise you won't laugh?"

"Promise."

"It's Abigail."

Clancy's dark eyes penetrated hers and Alex's expression never changed. She tilted her head and surveyed the other woman. "It suits you."

"Well, I haven't used it in years, I prefer Clancy."

Chapter 14

The next morning, Zack Walker roamed around his office, his mind teeming with thoughts. He'd been trying to get in touch with Alex Martell, but she wasn't at work or answering her home or cell phone. Where would she be likely to go? She had no family, so that left friends.

He summoned Clancy to his office. "Call her friend, Barbara Costello, maybe she's with her, and also speak to the people at the magazine, maybe she mentioned where she was going to one of them."

Clancy zoomed into action and charged from the room.

Zack placed his glasses on his nose and opened a folder. He'd only had a short time to read the report when it first arrived, so he picked up the first page and poured over each word with care.

A group of hikers had discovered an abandoned car at the bottom of an incline leading to a swamp on the road from Zolfo Springs to Arcadia. Branches of neighboring bushes had overgrown it, which implied it had been there for some time. What intrigued Zack, was the occupants of the car—a tall, dark-haired man in his thirties and a redheaded woman—both with a single bullet in the back of the head, and a plastic lily on the floor.

He took off his glasses and rubbed his eyes. Forensics was spending the morning at the car site and then they'd have the vehicle towed away and the occupants taken to the morgue. He'd bet his boots that these were the remains of John Martell and Sandra Barrett. The awful thing was that after months of living with the unknown, he couldn't contact Alex to notify her of their find.

According to the report, the killer had shot both victims with a 9mm bullet, the same caliber the killer of Myrtle Bixby and Diane Bostock had used. In each case, the perpetrator had left behind a plastic lily, conveying that the same person had murdered them all. Zack was almost sure that forensics would prove all four bullets came from the same gun. If this was so, then the heat was on to find a connection between these cases.

Someone rapped on Zack's door and Clancy walked in. She waited until he'd finished reading before she spoke.

"By all accounts, Alex told no one where she was going. No one at the magazine knows why she's taken leave. Her friend, Barbara Costello, said they'd only spoken on the phone recently and was shocked to hear about this latest attack."

"Hmm," Zack said, tweaking his ear. "She probably didn't want to scare her."

"Barbara also said that she has a key to Alex's house, so she'll keep an eye on it in case she returns."

"Okay. Sit down, Clancy, I want you to read this report."

Juno berated himself for kissing Alex. That innocent gesture had sparked something deep inside that he was trying to understand. He recalled the first time he'd seen her standing on his doorstep the morning of the interview and how his gut had contracted. Then rage had consumed him at the sight of this beautiful, fragile creature when he'd been expecting a man.

Women were nothing but trouble. Several years ago, he'd made a pact not to get emotionally involved anymore. *'Love them and leave them'* was his motto, and yet he felt different about Alex. She crept into his mind during his waking hours and disturbed his dreams.

His gut felt weird and a strange feeling niggled inside. Something was wrong. He'd called Zack Walker to find out about any recent developments and had been mentally winded when the lieutenant asked if he knew where Alex was.

"What do you mean?" He snapped. "You're protecting her."

Zack spoke with a slow drawl. "Not anymore, that ceased yesterday, Clancy's back on normal duties again."

Those words were like a knife in Juno's heart. A sixth sense told him Alex was in danger and his heart skipped a beat. He still couldn't fathom why he agonized about this woman whom he hardly knew, but somehow she'd wheedled her way into his soul.

"Dammit, Walker, are you saying she's disappeared?"

"Dunno, she's taken leave from her job and isn't answering her home phone or her cell. I thought you might have some ideas."

"Well, I don't. It sounds as if she's gone away to escape the attempts on her life, and I can't say I blame her."

"Yeah, she was scared witless after that car incident." There was a pause on the line before Zack spoke again. "I don't think she's the kind of person to run. In fact, Clancy told me she'd given Alex some basic instruction on keeping safe and that she's learning to shoot."

Juno faltered his mind racing. "Didn't you say that she and her husband have a vacation home somewhere?"

A loud noise resounded in Juno's ear and he guessed Zack had struck his desk. "Yes, you're right, maybe she went there. I'll get Clancy onto that right away. You don't happen to know where it is, do you."

"Sorry, no, but there's several mobile home parks not far from me by Highlands Hammock State Park."

Zack bade him farewell and Juno hung up, venting his anger with a volley of curses. His body was taut with rage as he prowled around his living room, trying to decide what to do next. He should let the police deal with this and not interfere, but unseen threads drew him toward Alex—not because she was helpless and needed his assistance—but because he was convinced that his last vision had been of her and the killer.

Grabbing his jacket off the back of a chair, he hitched it over his shoulder by an index finger and went outside to his car. When he swung the wheel of his sedan and pulled up in *Everyday's* parking lot, he noted the absence of Alex's silver Chevy. Once inside the building, a young receptionist greeted him and directed him to Brett's office. He rapped on the door and a gruff voice shouted, "Come in."

A large room yawned before him with one full wall constructed of tinted glass and a striking panoramic view. A gray, plush carpet embossed with red swirls covered the floor. Mounted on one wall was a large, framed photo of Alex and Brett in a romantic pose. Juno's insides contracted—they looked good together. Brett sat with his back to the window behind an L-shaped desk that dominated the room. He rose and held out his hand. "Juno, I'm sorry, but Charlie's not back until Monday. Is there anything I can do?"

Juno's eyes swept the room and returned to the photo. "I believe Alex is on leave. Did she mention where she was going?"

Brett's brows hooded his eyes before he raised them and glared. "No, and even if she had, I don't see how it's any business of yours."

The frostiness in Brett's tone shook Juno and a shudder of alarm ran through him at the other man's cold, remote stare. He was receiving disturbing vibes from this character and hairs on the back of his neck bristled. "I'm helping the police with these recent murders and we believe Alex is in danger, especially after that incident with the car."

Brett grunted. "Well then, it's up to the police to interview me, not you."

"I believe Sergeant Clancy already called you this morning."

Brett nodded. "That's right and I told her everything I know. Now if you'll excuse me, I have a very busy morning." He crossed the room and held the door open.

Juno turned and looked again at the photo on the wall. "For an old friend, you don't seem very perturbed."

Brett pursed his lips. "And for a new friend, you seem more than overly interested. Good day, Mr. Juno."

Outside in the corridor, Juno assessed his short conversation with Brett. Either the man was hiding something or he was still in love with Alex and thought he was protecting her. The other prospect was that he was the man the police were looking for. Something about the assistant editor's body language and manner had alerted Juno's senses. Brett had oozed strong, mixed vibes and Juno was having a hard time analyzing them.

Next, he strolled down the corridor until he arrived at a door marked with Alex's name. He turned the handle, but the door was locked. Footsteps sounded from behind and he spun round to see a smiling, young woman approaching. "Hi, are you looking for Alex?"

"Yes."

"She's taken some leave."

"Do you know how long she'll be gone?"

The young woman pouted. "No, but you're the second person who's been looking for her today."

Juno tensed. "Oh, who else wanted to see her?"

The woman rolled her eyes with a smitten look on her face. "That dishy new client, Darren Winters. I offered to help, but he turned nasty, saying that he wanted to see only Alex." She took a step closer to Juno. "Maybe I can help *you*?"

Juno smiled, "Maybe you can. Do you know where Alex's gone?"

"No, but that's what the other guy wanted to know, too. Why is it that no one wants to know anything about me."

Juno chucked her under the chin. "Because you're here and absence makes the heart grow fonder."

She giggled and Juno made tracks for the elevator, deep in thought.

In the lobby, he approached the receptionist. "Hi. Can you remind me of the name of Darren Winters' company, I seem to have forgotten it?"

"Sure, just a moment." The woman pressed a few computer keys. "Here it is. It's Winters' Windows in Sarasota."

Juno snapped his fingers. "That's it. I had it on the tip of my tongue, thanks."

So, Darren Winters was anxious to see Alex, was it for business or pleasure? He would soon find out.

In a way, Alex was glad that Charlie wouldn't be back until Monday because she wanted to run and tell him her plans. Instead, she spent the morning vacuuming and cleaning the house. After lunch, she sorted through her closet, packed two suitcases, loaded them into the trunk of her car and drove to the grocery store to stock up with food. If she was going to continue exercising and practice her shooting, she needed solitude. She hoped her stalker would take his time finding her, so that when he did, she'd be ready for him. Every time this thought entered her head, her knees shook.

Clancy had given Alex her private cell phone number to call anytime, and once she was ready, she would. In the meantime, she needed to be alone, and didn't want anyone knowing her whereabouts, not even the police.

The silver Chevy purred through Zolfo Springs and along State Road 66. When her turn off approached, Alex braked, swung onto the dirt track leading to a mobile home park and slowed her speed. Spanish moss, dangling from low, tree branches, brushed the roof of the car as it rocked and jounced over bumps and potholes until it arrived at the entrance gate and a smooth, paved road. She passed several homes on carefully tended sites, drove around the perimeter of the park to the very back and the location of their home backing onto dense woods.

John told her he picked this location because of its size and the isolation from all the other buildings. The home sat on a large landscaped lot at the back of the park, the nearest neighbor a few hundred yards away on the last street lit by lamps.

Alex climbed out and stretched. The evening sky had dimmed to twilight and moving purple shadows lurked around. Loud, rhythmic chirping of cicadas and the scuttling of nocturnal nightlife surrounded her. A thin slice of moon reflected in the creek turning the water's shining surface into silver ribbons. She opened the trunk and unloaded the suitcases and food.

Once inside the home, she closed the curtains and locked the door. A strange odor permeated the air and she wrinkled her nose. By the time she'd put the groceries away, the nauseating aroma had turned her stomach sick.

She turned the air conditioner down and rooted in a kitchen cabinet for air freshener. With can in hand, she began spraying. Then she froze. John's cell phone was perched in the fruit bowl where he always placed it. This could mean only one thing; he'd been here after the last time she'd seen him.

Her knees gave way and she plunked onto the sofa, taking a meticulous look around. It was months since they'd last been there and yet there was hardly any dust settled on the side tables. She hurried through to the bedroom and jerked to a stop when she saw the made bed.

The police had assumed that John had left her for another woman. Were they right? Had this been where he'd held his love trysts? That thought turned her stomach. With urgency, she stormed into the bathroom and began ransacking the cabinets. With shaking fingers, she raked around in the drawer and withdrew an orange lipstick.

"Oh, no," she wailed. Smothered by feelings of defeat, she leaned her hands on the counter and gazed at her image in the mirror. A pale face molded in anguish stared back and she spoke aloud. "Well, Alex, now you know for sure. All his business trips were a cover for...this." She gesticulated at the bed.

Disappointment, hurt and finally anger swept over her. She didn't know if John's affair and her being in danger was connected, but one thing was certain, she may be a sitting duck, but she wouldn't give up easily. The knowledge that John was not the man she thought he was, gave her strength and courage. She intended to fight for her life to the end.

Unable to bring herself to sleep in the made-up bed, she grabbed a blanket and pillow from a closet and curled up on the sofa. Soon the sound of the water in the creek lapping against the bank and the muffled hooting of an owl lulled her to sleep.

Chapter 15

The call from the police had unnerved Barbara Costello. Usually Alex confided everything to her, so it had come as a shock to learn that her friend was in trouble. She clenched her hands together feeling insecure. With her husband, Don, away on a business trip, she was alone at nights except for her Great Dane, Caesar.

She petted the dog's strong back. "You'll protect me, won't you, boy?" The obedient dog remained seated while she picked up her purse and reached for her car keys. "Now guard the house, I won't be long."

The garage door opener whined as she sat in her Toyota and started the engine. The traffic heading out of town was heavy and it took twice as long as usual to get to Patton Lane. By the time she reached Alex's house and parked in her driveway, thunder rumbled and the sky had darkened to the color of lead.

The exterior of the house looked the same as always. The curtains were open and the sprinkler system was watering the front yard. With key in hand, Barbara opened the front door and a pang of sorrow ran through her at the sight of John's smiling photo. Poor Alex, it must be awful not knowing what had happened to the man you love.

She hated it when Don was away. His longest trip had been two weeks, which was nothing compared to the agony Alex had suffered during the last five months. By the dim light from the kitchen window, she laid her purse on the counter before clicking on the light. Above Mitzi's dish was an automatic feeding and watering unit. Not knowing how long her friend would be away, she topped up both.

A stroll though the downstairs rooms revealed everything was normal, so she climbed the stairs to the second floor, pausing to peer through the landing window, as a flash of sheet lightning lit up the sky. Torrential rain battered the house and landed in large splats on the driveway. Her childhood fear of storms and the dark made her quake. This was no fun. The sooner she could get home the better. Once she'd poked her head in the bedrooms and bathrooms, she began descending to the lower floor.

The lights flickered. She halted, gripping the banister with both hands. A few seconds later, the lights came on and she exhaled a long breath. A tremendous volley of thunder rattled the windows along with a strobe-like flash of lightning. The lights flashed again and this time they stayed out. One step at a time, she felt her way downstairs to the foyer, her heartbeat as loud as the continuing thunder. The house was in complete, claustrophobic darkness. Lack of power had extinguished the outside lights along with those inside.

Barbara swallowed hard and the noise of the storm masked her anguished wail. Her heart fluttered around in her throat and she thought she might faint. The blackness pressed close around her and she could hardly breathe. With faltering steps, she reached the front door and wrenched the handle. It turned, but the door was stuck fast. She tried again.

A sob escaped from her tight throat and her knees wobbled. "Please open, please open," she chanted under her breath, tearing at the door handle with both hands, but the door didn't budge. This was ridiculous. Fifteen minutes ago it had opened, so why not now. She gave a scared laugh and decided to leave by the kitchen door.

Hand over hand, she teetered though the darkness, feeling her way around the kitchen cabinets. One hand encountered her purse, so she tucked it under her arm and both hands combed the wall for the key that normally hung on a hook by the door. It was empty.

A shiver of fear ran through her when she realized there was no way to escape. The French doors were boarded up, the front door was stuck and the kitchen door key missing. She tried to think, but her mind was a fog. She felt her way around the room until she came to the kitchen window. Her fingers probed the frame, but the window had a fixed pane.

She swung round and bumped into something, dropping her purse. Her loud scream filled the room. Moments later a gloved hand covered her face. A strong arm encircled her chest. She struggled, couldn't breathe, her heart raced.

Her assailant kicked the back of her knees with his foot. They gave way and she toppled backward. A shoe came off. Her muffled sobs broke the silence. She continued to struggle, twisting her body and kicking her legs, but he held her firm lowering her to the floor.

For a split second, her mouth was uncovered. Her hopeless shriek rent the still air. A heavy body fell on top of her. All the air in her lungs escaped in a whoosh. A hand grappled with her lower clothing. Her gasping, open mouth failed to fill her lungs. She lay motionless on the floor as the other hand wrested her legs apart. Her brain was numb. She wanted to fight, but blackness threatened to consume her.

His rigid flesh was between her thighs and probing her cleft. Fear rose in her throat. Warm breath panted in her ear. "At last you're mine."

With a surge of horror, she flung her head from side to side, gulping in air, "No! No!"

Positioned above her, his thick, hard penis ravished her. Pulse pounding, panting for breath she lay paralyzed as his male hardness assaulted her. He moaned and ground his lips against hers while his straining manhood continued to pump into her.

Shock rendered her immobile. Her brain couldn't absorb what was happening. Then reality hit her in the chest and a surge of anger consumed her. She fashioned her hands into fists and battered the back of his head with all her might. Unable to see his face, she raked her long nails downward, pulling threads in a ski mask.

"You little bitch!" He blurted, his hands circling her neck.

Her fingers grappled with his as her throat closed and she started to choke. Loud buzzing filled her ears. Fireworks exploded behind her eyes before she descended into a swirling vortex.

The man pressed hard on her throat, fury invading his brain. She lay very still. He removed one hand to wipe beads of sweat from his brow and with the other felt her carotid artery, no pulse. With stooped shoulders, he sat back on his heels, panting. Now she was dead because he'd allowed his temper to rise to the limit. Frustrated, he slapped her hard across the face.

Damn this storm, it had made him crazy. He'd wanted to relish the moment when he revealed his identity and take pleasure in seeing the shock on her face, but he'd botched things and now it was too late.

He scrambled to his feet zipping up his pants. What he'd hoped would be an exhilarating experience had turned out to be a big disappointment. After years of tracking her down and all the months he'd planned her death, he'd botched it. He stamped his foot and ripped off his mask.

The lights blinked and went off again. He wavered around in the dark, felt a kitchen stool and plumped down. Light flooded the room and this time stayed on. He swiveled round and looked at her body.

Horrified, he gaped. This was not Alex. Relief and exuberance swelled inside and he flung back his head and laughed. He bent over the body flipping the female's face toward him with his foot. Ripples of laughter threatened to erupt as he stared at Barbara Costello.

His beloved Alex was still alive. God had given him another chance to complete his plan. All he had to do was find her. If the police knew Alex had gone away and her house was empty, it could be a long time before anyone discovered this body, so he decided to leave it intact. He'd felt no thrill at this killing, so there was no point in shooting her as he had the others. He tugged a plastic lily from inside his jacket and laid it on the counter.

He chuckled as he pulled a key from his pocket and placed it back on the hook by the kitchen door. Next, he toed off his running shoes, carried them through to the foyer, and placed them beside the front door. In thick woolen socks, he scooted back and opened the door of the cabinet under the sink, withdrawing a cloth and a bottle of 409. Taking great care to cover every inch, he sprayed and washed the floor from the kitchen door to the body. He paused for a few moments, waiting until the floor was dry before flipping the body onto the washed section.

Lastly, he lobbed the plastic lily on top of the body and carried on cleaning right through to the foyer where he pulled back the upper and lower bolts he'd shot when Barbara went upstairs. Then he laid the cleaning items on the bottom step of the stairs and crammed his feet into his shoes.

Luck had been on his side. When the storm had extinguished the lights, Barbara couldn't see the bolts and panicked, fleeing into the kitchen. His original plan was for Alex to see them in place when she descended to the foyer, thus demonstrating she was not alone in the house, and instilling fear into her. However, fate had intervened changing things around and his stupid mistake had turned out fortuitous with the help of the unexpected storm.

Alex had slept soundly and was surprised to see there had been a heavy shower of rain during the night. Raindrops on the grass sparkled like crystals in the early morning sunshine. The air freshener had lessened the sickening smell inside the mobile home, but she still didn't feel hungry. She stripped the bed and stuffed the sheets into the washing machine along with the clothes she'd worn the previous day.

Her commitment to continue exercising was stronger than ever and her only regret was that she'd spent months pining over John's disappearance when he hadn't thought twice about bringing another woman to their special place. No man was worth it. She picked up her five-pound weights and began a vigorous exercise regime. An hour later, she was hungry, so she opened a tray of prepared salad, and gobbled it up while she watched the news on TV.

After a refreshing shower and changing into a jogging suit, she grabbed a hammer, some nails and a box. Her intention was to walk deep into the woods and reconnoiter the myriad of trees by the creek where she could place her targets. It was a beautiful day, the humidity low with a breeze drifting from the east, causing gentle ripples on the creek's surface. With arms akimbo and head flung back, she studied a flock of geese flying overhead in a 'V' formation.

At the sound of a strange noise, she swung round with her hands shaped into fists. A squirrel carrying some nuts ran along the ground and clambered up a tree. She smiled. It was so long since she'd been in these woods that she'd forgotten how much wildlife lived there. She must learn to relax.

In a small clearing, she spied a sturdy tree with a wide trunk, which was perfect. She sauntered over and banged in two nails, one at the top of the target, and one at the bottom. With her back to the tree, she paced out ten feet and marked the spot with a branch. This was her starting range. Once she'd perfected shooting from here, she'd increase the footage between her standpoint and the target.

She knelt by the box and withdrew her ear protectors and pistol. The full clip held twelve rounds and further increased the weight of the twenty-two ounce firearm. She decided to begin with some exercises to get used to the weight.

Ear protectors in place, she stood with her feet apart and aimed at the target. She didn't fire, but lowered the gun, aimed and lowered it again. This sequence she repeated twenty times, getting faster with every move. Now she was ready to start.

Clancy's words reverberated through her mind. *"Firm stance, safety off, aim to get through the other side, exhale and squeeze, keeping your eye on the target."* Her first round missed the tree. The second clipped the bark on the right side. The third missed again. She took several deep breaths and worked her shoulders to release the tension.

Her next shot was a lot more controlled and struck the edge of the target. The following two went wide, but the fourth smacked into one of the concentric circles. When she'd used all twelve rounds, she examined the bullet-ridden bark and scrutinized her work. One bullet had nicked the edge of the target and another was a respectable hit.

That was enough for her first day. Her arms ached with the weight of the weapon, so her next goal was to strengthen them. The gun rendered safe and repacked in its box, she picked up her tools and tramped back along the trail.

Juno parked outside Winters' Windows and entered the building by a glass door. He clarified the reason for his visit to the receptionist and poured coffee into a Styrofoam cup while he waited.

The door opened and a tall, blond-haired man ambled through. He held out his hand and Juno rose. "This is a pleasure. It's not every day we have a famous author drop by. Please come through."

Juno picked up his Styrofoam cup, followed the man down a corridor to an office, and sat in the offered chair. His eyes swept the bare room and landed on a ski suit complete with ski mask hanging from a hook.

"Now, how can I help you, Mr. Juno?"

Juno cringed. Even although it was his correct surname, he hated when someone called him that—still, it was better than the Christian name his parents had bestowed upon him. He recalled how other children had teased him and called him names during his schooldays. At university, he'd chosen not to reveal his first name and that was the start of being called Juno.

"I believe you went to visit Alex Martell yesterday. May I ask why?"

Darren's eyebrows twitched and the muscles in his jaw tensed. "It was business. She's written an editorial about my company and we needed to finalize the details."

"So you expected her to be there and didn't know she'd taken leave?"

Darren nodded his face still stony. "What's this all about? Has something happened to Alex?"

"Why would you say that?" Juno leaned back and surveyed the man on the other side of the desk. He was not relaxed, almost agitated. His face was pallid and he kept running one hand through his hair. Juno looked askance at the ski clothes. "I take it you like winter sports."

Darren jumped to his feet and began folding the clothes into a tight bundle. "Yes, I've been back from Colorado for more than a week, but I keep forgetting to take the clothes home. Why are you asking these questions about Alex?"

Juno decided to lie and maybe generate a reaction. "Because there have been two attempts on her life, and the police want to know her whereabouts, so they can protect her."

"My God!" Darren marched back to the desk, his face awash with emotions. "What kind of attempts?"

Juno gave a blasé shrug. "The usual kind, someone tried to poison her and then shoot her."

Darren shook his head and pursed his lips. "Poor Alex, how terrible. Do the police have any leads?"

"Only that the person wore a ski mask."

The color drained from Darren's face and his eyes opened wide. "You don't think it was me because—"

"No, no, of course not, but it *is* interesting that you have a ski mask in your office when you live in Florida." Juno quirked his brows and stood. "Thanks for seeing me, Mr. Winters. You will let the police know if you hear from Alex."

Outside in his car, Juno ran the conversation with Darren through his mind. If he was the one who wanted to hurt Alex, he'd hidden it well. The vibes he'd exuded were mixed— anger, frustration and excessive reactions when Juno spoke about Alex. Even although he'd only made her acquaintance recently, he could have orchestrated that for his needs. Darren Winters was definitely a suspect along with the two other men on Clancy's list.

His main task now was to find Alex. She had his home and cell phone number, but he doubted she'd call him unless she was stranded, and couldn't get hold of Clancy or the police. Sometimes she filled him with such rage that he wanted to shake her. She was the most annoying woman he'd ever met and why he'd kissed her was still a mystery. He recalled the way she'd looked, vulnerable and scared and his heart fluttered.

Zack Walker gulped and took a deep breath before he lifted the sheet and gazed down at the decaying face fringed by matted, red hair. This corpse was wearing a nightgown and a thin robe. Then he moved to the next slab and stared at the man who was clothed in gray pants and a white shirt with rolled up sleeves. He rubbed his chin wondering why the two bodies were clothed differently.

The M.E.'s report said that the killer had shot both victims elsewhere and moved them to the car. Neither had ID, so it was Zack's job to get in touch with the suspected victims' dentists to verify identification, but he'd bet any odds that these were the rotting remains of John Martell and Sandra Barrett.

Vomit rose in his throat and he turned away. No matter how many years he'd been working in homicide, he'd never been able to get used to seeing decomposing corpses.

He thanked the technician and hastened out, taking long rasping breaths to clear his senses of the smell and taste of death. There was no doubt in his mind that the detailed report of both autopsies would pinpoint the times of death around the time John Martell went missing.

Back in his office and his stomach back to normal, he summoned Clancy to his office. She breezed in and waited until he spoke.

"How's the investigation going?"

"Okay, I've contacted the attorney that handled Alex Martell's adoption, he's retired now and out of town, but he'll be back in a few days. As far as finding out about the Martell's vacation home, there's nothing to go on. I've researched all the County records and neither John nor Alex Martell has their name on anything other than the house in Halcyon Lane."

"Shit!" Zack swore under his breath. "Any ideas?"

"Maybe someone else owns the house and lets them use it. I've got the guys checking on what family John Martell has.

Also, I've been trying to contact Barbara Costello, but so far I haven't spoken to her. I'll let you know what I find out as soon as I do."

"Good work, Clancy. Why is no one ever available when we want them?" He ran his eyes over the woman in front of him. "Doing anything tonight, Sergeant?"

Her teeth were very white in her dark face as she smiled. "What did you have in mind, sir?"

"I thought I might do a little investigating myself. The kind that entails discovering the color of your underwear."

Clancy pretended to look affronted. "Really, Lieutenant, are you sexually harassing me?"

"Yes."

"Good, I'll expect you at seven."

Clancy spun on her heel and marched out, giving Zack a cheeky grin before she closed the door.

Zack's heart swelled with love. He still couldn't believe his luck at finding romance at his age. He couldn't remember how he'd felt about Margo all those years ago. All he recalled were the constant arguments and recriminations and never feeling at one with her. With Clancy, it was different. Apart from the passion, she was the kindest, sweetest, most enthusiastic person he'd ever met and he could hardly wait until seven o'clock.

He was tidying his desk at six-fifteen when the phone rang. He grabbed the receiver with one hand while he lifted his jacket from the back of the chair with the other. "Yeah, Walker."

"Lieutenant, there's a Don Costello here. He's just made out a missing person's report for his wife, Barbara."

Zack's heart thudded. "Barbara Costello's missing?"

"Seems so, sir. Mr. Costello's been on a business trip and hasn't been able to contact his wife for the last two days."

"Send him in Rogers."

"Yes, sir."

Zack slung his jacket back on the chair and turned in time to see a small, stocky man follow Rogers into his office. The rookie handed the report to Zack and left.

Zack held out his hand. "Mr. Costello, please take a seat." The man nodded and sat on a chair facing the desk. Zack stayed by the window reading the report.

"So you only returned home today?"

"Yes."

"And you haven't spoken to your wife for three days?"

"That's correct. The first evening I called and she didn't answer, I wasn't too perturbed, because I thought maybe she was out with friends or walking the dog. However when she didn't answer my calls the next two evenings, I had a horrible feeling something was wrong."

Zack continued reading and his stomach churned when he came to the part that Costello had found the dog with no food or water and it had urinated and defecated in the kitchen. "Was there any sign of a break-in?"

Don shook his head. "No, nothing like that." He gave Zack a scared look. "It says *Homicide* on your door. Does that mean you think Barbara's—"

"No, not at all. Look, Mr. Costello, as you know there have been some local homicides and because I'm investigating those and the Alex Martell case, you were referred to me."

"Alex? What's happened to Alex?"

"Nothing, we hope. Let's get you some coffee and I'll bring you up to date with everything that's been happening and maybe you'll be able to throw some light on a few things."

Thirty minutes later, Zack wasn't any wiser. Don Costello had only known Alex and John Martell for two years since his marriage to Barbara and couldn't help with the location of their vacation home.

"All I know is that John had it when Alex married him. Maybe someone at his place of work knows more."

"Does John have any family?" Zack asked, stirring sugar into his third cup of coffee.

"Not that I've ever heard anyone speak of. I know both his parents are dead and he's an only child. Sorry I can't be more help, but I'm away such a lot with my job that I only see Alex and John socially."

"And Barbara gave no hint that she intended going away anywhere."

"No, she'd never leave Caesar alone, she adores him. When I'm away, I call her every evening at eight and we discuss our days. If she's going to be out she calls me on my cell phone to let me know."

Zack sipped his coffee, deep in thought. Things were not looking good. He tossed a furtive glance at Don Costello who sat with a bowed head wiping his eyes. "Will you be all right to drive home?"

"Yes, but this has been an awful shock."

"Well, you did the right thing filing a report. We'll begin an investigation immediately, and as soon as we discover anything, I'll be in touch."

Don struggled to his feet, mumbled his thanks, and left the room.

Zack exhaled loudly. This was all he needed—another missing person. He picked up his pack of cigarettes, flung his jacket over one shoulder and stomped out to keep his rendezvous with Clancy, leaving his cell phone on the desk.

A few minutes after seven o'clock, Zack peered through the glass door of Clancy's condo. He rang the doorbell again, but there was still no answer. He smacked his palm on the doorjamb and returned to his car. Disappointment flowed through him that his evening was not going as planned, so he pulled into the parking lot of the first bar he came to. Although he didn't drink, he yearned company, and wasn't looking forward to returning to a quiet, empty house.

A jukebox was playing a country song and a few people had butted some tables together to make room to dance, while a group of men played pool on the other side of the bar. Zack climbed onto a barstool, ordered a virgin pina colada and watched a football game on a silent TV mounted behind the bar. At time out, he dived into his jacket pocket for his cell phone. Damn, he'd left it at work. He ordered another drink and raked in his pant's pocket for some coins as he made his way to a payphone. Clancy's phone rang unanswered.

Soon the bar filled up with a noisy crowd of young people, so Zack tossed a bill onto the counter and moved over to a table in a quiet alcove. He sat observing the group of young people wondering if they were all of legal age to drink. At least two girls looked underage, but nowadays it was hard to tell. Now he was getting older, the next generation looked younger.

A young man with a tray picked up his empty glass. "Can I get you another," he asked.

"No thanks, I'm going now." Zack handed the youth a five dollar bill and went out to his car.

The roads were quiet and he hadn't realized it was so late until he glanced at the clock on the dash. No wonder he was hungry. He pulled into a fast food drive-in and ordered a pizza stopping to munch one, juicy slice in the parking lot before he started the engine and drove home.

Silence met his ears when he opened the front door. Although he'd had nothing left in common with Margo, he still missed her company and the way she'd made a cozy home for them. He kicked off his shoes and sidled over to the flashing answer machine. Before he could retrieve his messages, the phone rang.

"Yeah," he barked.

"It's me, sir." Clancy was breathless. "Where have you been? We've been trying to get hold of you all evening."

Zack's body tensed. "What's up? Where are you?"

"At Alex Martell's house. I still have the spare key she gave me when I was protecting her and I remembered you saying that Barbara also had a key, so when Don Costello filed the missing person's report, I thought I'd snoop around."

"And?"

"There's a woman's body here, and it's not Alex."

"Oh, shit! I'm on my way." Zack slammed the phone down and rushed back out to his car. He wound down the window, flipped a switch on the dashboard and clamped a red, flashing light to his car roof.

It took him thirty minutes to reach the house in Halcyon Lane and by the time he arrived, a long line of cars stretched outside. Light spilled through drawn curtains and radiated over the front yard, making it easy for him to spot the officer on duty. He gave his name, pulled on the protective coveralls and gloves and ducked under the yellow tape. In his haste, he almost fell in the front door in time to see a woman being zipped into a black body bag.

"Lieutenant Zack Walker, homicide," he flashed his badge to a room full of forensic personnel. "Do we know who she is?"

A tall, thin man strode forward and shook his hand. "Hi, Mike Temple, CCO. According to the victim's ID, her name's Barbara Costello."

Clancy's gloved hand held out a driver's license. "It's her, sir. The killer must have been here when she let herself in with her key."

"Any sign of a break-in?"

"Yes, he got in by smashing the kitchen lock."

Zack swung round to a small, balding man clutching a writing pad. "How long's she been dead?"

The pathologist was handing several swabs and samples to the CSM. "About two hours when we arrived. She's been strangled and there's also signs of sexual assault."

"DNA?"

The other man shrugged. "I'll let you know."

Zack dragged a hand down his face. Barbara was victim number six and unless the killer had been careless enough to leave clues at this scene, they were still no nearer to solving any of the crimes.

"Sir," Clancy interrupted his thoughts and pointed to a bagged, plastic lily. "It looks like the same guy again. I've spoken with the neighbors on the north side and they said there was a power outage about the time Barbara died."

Deep in thought, Zack slowly circled the room. He mulled the facts over in his mind. The killer must have broken in with the intention of murdering Alex and instead encountered Barbara Costello. If this happened during the power outage, did he know he'd killed the wrong woman? Then again, if he had a flashlight or the power came back on while he was still here, he would have realized his mistake. Either way, Barbara Costello had paid the ultimate price for trying to help her friend. Now he had the daunting task of telling her husband the terrible news.

Clancy held up two more plastic bags. "These cleaning materials were on the bottom step of the stairs, so it looks like our man cleaned up before he left by the front door."

"What makes you think he left by the front door? Maybe he went out via the kitchen and placed the cleaning materials on the stairs to mislead us."

Clancy rolled her eyes. "Not possible. My guess is that he started washing the floor at the kitchen door and finished in the foyer. That way he wouldn't have to walk on the clean floor and contaminate it. Anyway the front door wasn't locked when I arrived."

Clancy swaggered over to an officer and handed him the plastic bags.

Mike Temple signaled to his group of men and they paraded past Zack. Mike shook his hand. "We'll get our findings to you as soon as we can, but there's not much to go on unless Doc has something."

"Thanks, Mike, thanks guys."

One by one the pathologist, M.E. and forensic personnel departed, leaving Zack and Clancy alone.

"So, what happened to you?" Clancy blurted.

"I must have left my cell phone at work."

Clancy's dark eyes flashed. "And you didn't think to call mine?"

"I was annoyed, I thought you'd stood me up, so I went to a bar."

Clancy peeled off her protective clothing and flounced over to the front door. "Men!" she swore under her breath.

Zack removed his coveralls and took his pack of cigarettes from the breast pocket of his shirt, slipping one between his lips. "I'm sorry I should have called you, pax?"

Clancy's lips parted in a smile. "Sure I'll take a rain check."

"Come on, we can't do anymore here. Has the kitchen door been secured?"

"Yes, everything's under control." Clancy locked the front door with her key and they both avoided the yellow police tape.

Zack lit his cigarette and placed a hand on Clancy's arm. "Some evening this turned out to be."

Clancy tilted her lips in a smile. "Sorry, next time, I'll wait until morning before I act on a hunch."

Lilies of Death

"No, that was good detective work. It's just a pity that sonofabitch was here when Barbara arrived. Will you follow me to Don Costello's to break the bad news? God, I hate this part of the job."

Zack leaned his head on the back of the chair. Neither he nor Clancy had felt like socializing at that late hour after they'd broken the news of his wife's death to Don Costello. The man had taken it badly and Clancy had stayed with him until his brother-in-law arrived to give him support.

Before they split up to go their separate ways, Clancy told him of her next plan. On Saturday, she intended to go to The Manatee Gun Club on S.R. 64 where Alex had enrolled in classes.

"Wherever she's staying, she's sure to turn up. Every week of tuition will give her a better chance of defending herself. She's a smart lady and I reckon she's not going to miss a lesson."

"Let's hope you're right. If you are, this'll be a traumatic weekend for her, finding out her husband's dead and also her best friend." They both remained silent for a few moments before Zack leaned forward and kissed Clancy's cheek. "Nice work Sergeant, now go home and get some rest. We'll tackle the paperwork in the morning."

They both climbed into their cars and went to their separate homes.

Chapter 16

By the time Saturday rolled around, Alex's shooting had improved. Now she was able to hit the target seven out of twelve times and her arms didn't tire as easily when she held the loaded gun for lengthy periods. She'd started jogging through the woods early each morning and was becoming familiar with every twist and turn of the trails.

Her gun-handling lesson was at noon, so after her morning jog she took a shower and set off for the gun club. The roads were quiet until she joined S.R. 64, which was nose to tail traffic with cars making a beeline for the coast. At last, she reached her destination and pulled into the only vacant parking bay at the club next to a police car.

With box in hand she tugged open the glass swing door and stopped dead in her tracks. Sergeant Clancy was leaning against the reception desk in uniform, her bronze face set in a serious expression.

"Clancy, what are you doing here?"

"Hello, Miss Alex, I guessed you wouldn't miss your lesson today."

"Too right. Is something wrong?"

Clancy took her arm and pulled her aside. "Why don't you have your lesson first, and then we'll talk."

A feeling of trepidation gnawed at Alex's stomach. When there was no welcoming smile from Clancy, who she now regarded as a friend, she knew something was wrong. Unable to concentrate on her lesson, her aim suffered and she only hit the target once. She was all too conscious of Clancy in the background watching with a solemn face.

Lilies of Death

At one o'clock, Alex packed her gun and ear protectors back in their box and accompanied Clancy outside. Her pulse beat rapidly as Clancy stooped to unlock the cruiser.

Her heart was in her mouth as she faced the officer. "Is it bad news, Clancy? Please tell me, I need to know."

"Lieutenant Walker wants to see you first. It's not my place to go over his head. I'm sorry, but I have to follow orders."

Alex nodded and opened her car door. "Okay, I'll follow you to the precinct."

In a blur, she tailed Clancy's police car to their destination. Her heart thumping in panicky, double time, she mounted the precinct steps and refused a seat as Clancy entered Lieutenant Walker's office.

Silent seconds ticked by. Alex wanted to scream. At last, Clancy appeared in the office doorway and stepped to one side while she entered. Lieutenant Walker stood grimfaced by his desk and held out his hand. "Come in Mrs. Martell and take a seat."

Alex perched on the edge of the chair, her throat tight. "Sergeant Clancy said you wanted to see me. Is it bad news?"

Zack Walker gave a small nod and Alex held her breath. "We've discovered your husband's car," he paused, "with two bodies inside."

The room spun and Alex gripped the edge of the desk. "Two bodies? Is one of them John?"

"We think so. We'll know for certain once we have a positive ID."

Alex's stomach was nauseous. "You mean you want me to identify his body?"

"No, Mrs. Martell, neither is a pretty sight. Do you remember what your husband was wearing the last time you saw him?"

Alex nodded. "A white shirt and gray pants. He always wore that on weekdays. Is that what the man was wearing?"

"Yes, but it doesn't prove conclusively it's John. We'll need to get a positive ID from his dental records. Let me have the name of his dentist and I'll be in touch as soon as I know anything for certain. I'm very sorry,"

Alex managed to quash a strong feeling of nausea at the thought of her husband's decomposing body.

"And the other person?"

"A woman."

Alex clamped her lips together. "I see."

She attempted to choke back her flow of tears, but they slowly oozed from her eyes and trickled down her cheeks. Clancy placed a hand on her shoulder and Alex broke down unable to control the sobs wracking her body. For months, she'd steeled herself for this moment, but now it was finally here she didn't know how to cope.

Clancy handed her a wad of tissues and she wiped her eyes and blew her nose. "I'm sorry, Lieutenant, but I always hoped he was still alive."

"I understand. I'll try to keep my questions as brief as possible and spare your feelings, but murder's a dirty business and our priority is to catch this felon before he kills again."

"Again?" Alex echoed, confused.

"Yes, we think your husband and his friend were killed by the same person who murdered the other local women."

"And who's trying to kill you." Clancy finished Zack's sentence.

A wave of panic clutched Alex's throat and sweat trickled down her spine at the look that passed between Zack and Clancy. "There's something else, isn't there?"

Clancy drew in a deep breath and exhaled through puffed cheeks. "It's Barbara, she's dead."

Alex clasped a hand over her mouth. "No, no, what happened?"

"She went to check on your house and he was waiting for her." Clancy said in a low tone.

"He killed Barbara? But why?"

"Because he thought she was you. He thought he was killing you."

The words vibrated in Alex's brain, but she was having a hard time absorbing them. This was too much to take in.

Zack crossed to his desk and picked up a file. "In view of what's happened, the Commissioner has agreed to protection for you again. Your house is still a crime scene, so you can't return there. Where have you been staying?"

"At our mobile home out east."

Clancy gave Zack a nod. "That's why there's no records, sir. If the home's on rented land, it's classed as a motor vehicle and the owners don't pay property taxes, so it's not registered with the County." Then she turned to Alex. "I searched all the County records, but neither your name nor John's was on any other property except Halcyon Lane. We were alarmed when we needed to contact you and you didn't answer your cell phone."

"I'm sorry, I should have told you where I was going, but it didn't seem important at the time. I wanted to be somewhere quiet where I could practice my shooting." Her lips quivered uncontrollably as her thoughts turned to Barbara's husband. "Does Don, Mr. Costello, know about Barbara?"

"Yes, he has a family member staying with him. This is the last thing any of us expected."

"I should go and see him," Alex murmured.

Clancy patted her shoulder. "He's pretty cut up. Maybe you should leave it for a few days. I've been assigned as your protection again, so we can go together later."

Alex gestured her approval. Her mind was spinning so fast it was hard to hold onto a thought. There would be a funeral to arrange, John's work colleagues to notify, and she'd have to decide what to do with the rest of her life. The air conditioning cycled on in a quiet hum and Alex raised her eyes to Zack. "What do I do now?"

Clancy's heart went out to Alex. She looked so pale and fragile and seemed smaller than when she'd last seen her. "I can take you home," she said in a soft tone.

"Home? But the Lieutenant said it's still a crime scene."

"That's right, but we can go to the trailer park. We'll go in my car, you leave yours here, and you can collect it in a few days."

Clancy had expected Alex to object, but all the fight had gone out of her. She looked dazed and her eyes were huge in her ashen face.

Zack handed Clancy a wad of paperwork. "Make four-hourly reports, Sergeant, and we'll keep you up to date about things at this end."

"Yes, sir."

She helped Alex to her feet and she tottered beside her like a rag doll. At the top of the precinct steps, Clancy draped an arm around Alex's shoulder, the last thing she wanted was for her to pass out and topple down the steps. As they neared her cruiser, a man's voice shouted, "Alex!"

Juno plunged across the road dodging traffic. Alex stood as still as a statue, her expression blank. Juno divided a look between the two women. "What's happened?"

"There's a possibility we've found her husband," Clancy spoke in a hushed tone although Alex didn't appear to have heard. "Also her best friend's been murdered."

Breath streamed out of Juno's mouth as if he'd been slugged in the gut. "My God! Is she all right?"

"She will be when I get her home. She's in a state of shock."

"Stop speaking as if I'm not here," Alex said. "I'm fine. I just don't feel like talking."

This was more like the woman Clancy had come to know. No matter how defeated she was, she always bounced back like a jumping jack.

"Can I do anything?" Juno asked.

Alex gave a wan smile. "No, but thanks for asking."

Clancy lifted her shoulders in a resolute shrug as Alex opened the cruiser door and buckled her seat belt. While waiting for a gap in the oncoming traffic, Clancy peered in her rear view mirror. Juno hadn't moved and when she turned east onto the main road, he was still standing in the same position.

She wove through the lanes of traffic with ease and skill while Alex sat silent, staring straight ahead. The only time she spoke was to give Clancy directions. The car bounced over the uneven track and through the gates of the mobile home park. Alex jabbed a finger as they approached the woods. "It's that one there right at the bottom."

Clancy parked under the carport and climbed out. This was certainly an isolated spot. Her head swiveled round taking in the vast space between this home and the next. An attacker could come from all four sides, but the woods would be the most advantageous. In a way, it was a perfect place for Alex to hide, but it was also the most vulnerable home in the park.

Alex hobbled from the car with hunched shoulders and opened the front door while Clancy secured the car before following her inside. "Wow, this is pretty cute. How long have you had this place?"

"John bought it for his mother two years before we met, but she only visited it once before she died." She gulped back tears.

"Now he's dead, too. I suspected he was, but I still didn't expect to get such a shock when the lieutenant confirmed it."

Clancy remained silent, letting Alex blabber. Talking might help. Some people wanted solace and others needed to express themselves when they suffered trauma.

"I think he was having an affair. Probably with that woman who was in the car with him. I found his cell phone here, in the fruit bowl. That's where he always put it as soon as we got here. He must have forgotten it the last time they were here."

Alex paced the width of the room wringing her hands. Back and forth, back and forth, Clancy watched as her wooden-soled sandals clacked on the tiles. "He must have used this place for their rendezvous. Oh, damn, how could he do this to me? I loved him so much!"

A small sob escaped and she collapsed on the sofa, leaning her head on her arm.

Clancy felt helpless. Apart from Zack, she'd never had strong feelings for another human being. She'd never known her father, hadn't seen her mother in twenty-two years and didn't know if she was still alive. When her five-year affair with the doctor ended, she'd been devastated, but she'd soon realized that she hadn't loved him after the first passion had fizzled out and that she'd only stayed with him out of familiarity.

Alex raised a tear-stained face. "I think I'll go and lie down."

Clancy returned to the car and popped the trunk. She lifted out her sports bag, which she kept packed in case of emergencies, and took it inside. A quick snoop around confirmed there was only one bedroom, so she stashed the bag in the kitchen nook.

An hour later, Alex emerged from the bedroom, her face cleansed of make up and her hair combed. "When will I know for certain if it's John?" She plummeted onto the sofa next to Clancy.

"Two or three days, depending on how quickly John's dentist responds."

"I know it's him, Clancy. With the description the lieutenant gave me, it has to be. How will you find out who the woman is?"

"A law clerk called Sandra Barrett resigned and left your husband's office, the day he went missing. She's moved away from her apartment, so we'll be looking into the possibility that she's the dead woman."

Alex jumped up from the sofa. "It *is* her. A week ago someone sent me a letter meant for John written by a woman called Sandra."

Clancy's head snapped round. "What? Why didn't you tell us?"

"I didn't think it was important." She rummaged in her purse and handed the letter to Clancy.

Alex related how she'd arrived back at the office after conducting a short interview with a prominent local banker and the first thing she noticed was the stamped, cream envelope with spidery writing lying on her desk. She turned it over, looking for a return address, but none was there. When she'd taken her jacket off, sorted through the rest of the mail and sat at her desk, she opened the letter.

A smaller envelope inside was addressed to her husband, John, but had no stamp. Whoever had opened the letter had torn the top of the envelope, so she took a deep breath and pulled out a matching sheet of cream paper. Words written in neat cursive covered half the page.

'My dearest John,

How could I have lived these last few months without you? I know you think I should have left my boyfriend a long time ago, but it's not going to be an easy thing to do. I think he's suspicious about our plans, so I'd rather wait until things are a little better between us. Have you told Alex about us yet? I think she has a right to know what we're planning.

Whenever you want to leave is all right with me, so tell me a day and time and I'll make sure I'm ready. My life has been so much better since I opened my heart to you. Call me when you can.

Love,
Sandra.'

"No!" Alex had howled, crumpling the letter and hurling it across the room. John *had* been having an affair. Were the police right and he'd left her for this Sandra? Humiliation speared through her. She took the phone off the hook and locked her office door. All she wanted was to be alone.

Sometime later, the handle on her office door rattled, so before she rose to unlock it, she reached for a tissue, blew her nose and dabbed her eyes.

Charlie strolled in behind her. "You okay?"

She nodded, her throat too clogged to speak. "John was having an affair. Someone's sent me a letter." She indicated the crumpled paper in the corner of the room.

"May I?" Charlie didn't wait for her response, but picked up the paper and straightened it out on the desk. His face was stony when he looked up. "Inconclusive."

Alex sniffed. "I thought it was self explanatory."

Charlie leaned against the desk and folded his arms. "I prefer giving people the benefit of the doubt. What this Sandra's writing about isn't clear at all. She could be writing about anything."

"Like what?"

"Well," Charlie stalled. "John might have been helping her with something—er—a surprise party for her boyfriend, or some project she didn't want anyone to know about."

Alex grunted and sniffed.

"You don't write something as vague as that to someone you're having an affair with. The words would be all mushy and lovey-dovey. No," he analyzed the written words again, "this isn't a love letter. And anyway, how did someone end up with a letter that was meant for John?"

Alex shrugged. "I've no idea. There's no stamp on the original envelope, so it looks as if it wasn't mailed and John never received it."

Charlie turned the envelope over. "You see, it's probably all quite innocent. Somebody's playing with your mind."

All she wanted was to go home, take a long, hot bath and forget all about this nonsense. Charlie was right; there was no real evidence that John had been unfaithful.

"Go home and get a good night's sleep and things are sure to look better in the morning."

"Thanks, Charlie, I will."

All this talk of John brought back memories of their last morning together.

She awoke early, lying on her back and turned to look at him. He was facing her with his eyes closed, his face relaxed in sleep. She leaned forward and kissed the end of his nose. His brown eyes met hers.

"Did I wake you?" She asked, stroking his stubbly cheek.

"No, I was pretending to be asleep. Come here." His arm encircled her body and clutched her close. "Have I told you this morning that I love you, Alexandra Martell?" She shook her head. "Well, I do, I love you." His lips touched hers in a gentle kiss.

She wound an arm around his shoulder and flattened her body to his. He looped a leg over hers and slithered closer, his lower body hard against hers. She sighed. Gently he rolled her over and kissed her eyes, her mouth, her neck.

Engrossed in their lovemaking, the next thirty minutes passed swiftly until the buzzing of the alarm interrupted Alex's relaxed pose.

"Oh, my God, is that the time?" She flung back the covers and jumped out of bed. "I have a nine o'clock meeting and I'm gonna be late."

John laughed and grabbed hold of her right hand, dragging her back into bed while she struggled to be free. "So what, let Charlie stew for five minutes. You know he's in love with you and that he hates me?"

Alex didn't resist. "No he doesn't. He's jealous of you, that's different."

"What went on between you two before I came on the scene?"

"Nothing. I went out with Brett for nearly two years, but I've never even been on a date with Charlie. He's always been very protective of me, but I never realized he was in love with me until he didn't show up at our housewarming party."

Her lips sought John's. "I really must go, I'll see you tonight." She dashed toward the bathroom, but halted when he spoke.

"Sorry, love, but I've got a very early meeting on the east coast tomorrow, so I'm staying the night with one of the partners and won't be home for dinner."

"Oh, that's okay." She remarked with a shrug. "I have a good book to read."

They chatted over a brief breakfast and Alex was the first to rise from the table and grab her brief case. She dropped a small kiss on John's lips. "See you tomorrow, drive carefully."

Lilies of Death

"I will, I love you."

"Me too, bye." She closed the kitchen door and unlocked her car with the remote. While she adjusted her rear view mirror, she opened the garage door and shoved the stick into reverse. Once outside, she backed down the driveway, waved to John, who was standing by the window, and drove off.

That was the last time she'd seen him and her life had never been the same since.

Alex watched Clancy's brows twitch while she read the crumpled letter. "Do you think it's a love letter?"

The other woman made a face. "Dunno nobody's ever sent me one."

"Charlie says it's not lovey-dovey enough for a love letter and that the woman's writing about something else."

"Could be. It is a bit vague. Can I keep this for now? Lieutenant Walker'll let you have it back later."

All of a sudden, conflicting emotions inundated Alex and she couldn't stand the thought of being in the mobile home. "Yes, do what you want with it. I don't want to stay here if this is where John brought that woman. Let's go to a motel."

Clancy unfolded her legs from beneath her. "Are you sure? Why don't we stay here tonight and go somewhere tomorrow. It is kinda late."

Alex realized that what Clancy said made sense and acquiesced. "Okay, we'll talk about it in the morning."

The sun shining in dappled patterns on the bed woke Alex early. She dressed in her jogging clothes and peeped round the bedroom door. Clancy was still asleep on the sofa snoring softly, so she let herself out the front door, locking it behind her. When she'd said goodnight to Clancy the previous evening, she was sure she'd never sleep. This was a day she'd always remember, the day she knew that John was gone forever and that she'd lost her best friend, too. However, her sleep had not been fraught with apprehension and sorrow, but instant and refreshing.

Now, jogging through the woods on the familiar trails, she decided not to go to a motel, but stay where she was. She loved it here and there was no real proof that John had been having an affair. It was the knowledge that his cell phone was lying in the fruit bowl that niggled deep within her. He never went anywhere without it, why this time?

After two circuits of the trails, she loped out the woods, up the steps of the mobile home, and unlocked the front door.

Clancy was sitting in her robe on a stool in the kitchen drinking coffee and her full lips parted in a wide smile. "Good morning, you look all bright-eyed and bushy-tailed."

"Yes, I feel much better. Have you had breakfast?"

Clancy shook her dark head and looked sheepish. "I only woke up a few minutes ago."

"Is cereal and toast okay?"

"Sure, you do the cereal, I'll make the toast."

The two women sat in companionable silence, each with their own thoughts, eating cereal and munching toast.

Alex stretched before jumping up and depositing her bowl and plate in the kitchen sink. "Do you want to shower first? I still have my exercises to do."

"Thanks," Clancy picked up her bag from the floor in the nook and headed for the bathroom.

Chapter 17

The first thing Clancy did when she woke that morning was radio the precinct. Zack was already at his desk and listened to her report. Now, two hours later, energized with breakfast and a nice hot shower, she reported again.

"How's the widow?" Zack asked.

"Remarkably good, considering. Any news?"

"Not on the woman, but we've got a positive ID on John Martell. All being well, the coroner should release his body for burial later today."

A sinking feeling filled Clancy's stomach. Would Alex crumble when she knew that the male body was that of her husband? Only time would tell. The sound of running water ceased announcing that Alex was out of the shower and dressing. The bedroom door opened and Clancy quickly ended her bulletin.

At the sight of the radio, Alex's eyes widened in question and then clouded with pain.

Clancy tapped the seat of the sofa. "Come and sit down, Miss Alex."

"It's John, isn't it?" Clancy nodded and Alex gave a strangulated laugh. "You always call me *Miss Alex* when it's bad news, I can read you like a book."

"I'm very sorry."

"Don't be, I knew it was him, it had to be. He'd never let anyone else drive his car, he loved it too much. And the woman?"

Clancy shrugged. "Nothing positive yet."

"So, what happens now?"

"We wait until the coroner releases John's body and then you can organize a funeral. The lieutenant reckons that might happen later today."

Alex twitched her brows looking confused. "Why the long wait?"

"Formalities. Everything's done in a precise order. The coroner won't release any body until he's satisfied about the cause of death and that the collection of all evidence is complete."

Tears brimmed in Alex's eyes as she twisted a lock of hair with her index finger. "Thanks, Clancy, I really appreciate everything you've done."

Clancy fidgeted. She hated getting praise. In this instance, she wished she could do more. Alex had had a rough time and she had no one to turn to now Barbara was gone. Normally she didn't get emotionally involved in cases, but this one was an exception.

Alex felt adrift in an unfamiliar sea, before she'd always had someone to help her in times of crisis, but this time she was alone. With meticulous determination, she straightened her shoulders and stood. "Well, as soon as we hear something, I'll make a start. I want to get the funeral over as soon as possible. Will you come with me?"

"Of course, it's my job."

After lunch, they piled into Clancy's car and she drove to the precinct. While Alex picked up her Chevy, the Sergeant went inside and reported to Zack. When Alex pulled up outside the front steps, Clancy was waiting with a grim face, so she rolled down the window and held her breath.

"John's body's been released. Do you want to make the arrangements today?"

A cold feeling ran through Alex. The sudden finality of months of anxiety asphyxiated her and she felt as if she were choking. She knew she had to do this for John, so she raised her chin and looked Clancy square in the eyes. "Yes, let's do it now. Will you follow me in your car?"

They drove in convoy to the largest funeral home in Geyserville. The atmosphere was calming and peaceful and gave Alex confidence as she selected a classic, oak casket with brass handles. She felt serene and unruffled and realized that her subconscious must have been preparing her for this moment for the last five months. Her mind was tranquil and lucid as she arranged a time for the funeral the next afternoon and declined the offer of a limousine. What was the point? Clancy could drive her in her silver Chevy—John would have liked that.

Max cavorted through the front door the moment it opened. No birds sang as the wind whistled through the trees and Juno minced outside in his pajamas. A lock of dark hair dipped over his brow as he bent to retrieve the newspaper from the driveway. Where the sky had boasted a deep blue an hour ago, angry, dark clouds scudded across the sky, matching his somber mood.

"Max!" Juno waited, but the dog didn't respond. "Max!" He called again, frustration building inside. For the last two days, he'd been uneasy. Something niggled at him and he couldn't shake an atmosphere of uneasiness.

He tried to convince himself that an attorney's letter had sparked this sensation, but he knew better than that. His ex-wife, Veronica, had applied for more alimony, which she had no hope of getting, as her earnings by far superseded his. No, something else was unsettling him. His sleep had been fitful and he'd woken up in a foul mood. He kicked the trunk of the closest tree and swore when he hurt his foot. "Goddammit, Max, where are you?"

The dog strutted from between the trees and sat at his left heel while Juno massaged his right foot. With newspaper in hand, he limped into the house followed by the dog. The headlines glared at him the minute he opened the paper. '*Man missing for five months found murdered.*' His eyes ravaged the article and his heart pumped as he read the report. Alex, he must go to her.

Then he sobered. Whatever made him think she would want him when she was mourning her husband? Somehow he'd got his wires crossed and believed that she felt about him the way he felt about her. Which was what? Again, he tried to analyze the heavy feeling in his gut and before he went to take a shower, he concluded he was horny for sex.

His affair with Petra had tapered off recently, leaving him with no emotional outlet. He liked living in solitude, but he still hankered for the soft touch of a woman. Since moving to Florida, he'd had his choice of a parade of beautiful women, but for some reason they all bored him. All they wanted was to settle down and marry and that was the last thing he wanted. He'd tried that institution twice and didn't intend getting trapped again, not as long as young women threw themselves at him and kept his bed warm at night.

He poured another cup of coffee and perused the remainder of the news. The media had played down a small article at the bottom of the front page about Barbara Costello's murder. It didn't reveal many facts, only that her body was found in a friend's house. Out of curiosity, he turned to the next page and ran his eyes down the list of obituaries. He found the one for John Martell and noted the funeral was the following day.

Now he had to decide whether to attend. He guessed Zack Walker would be there along with Alex's protection, Sergeant

Clancy. Then he realized just how little he knew about Alex. She'd told him she was adopted and that her 'parents' were both dead. Now that her best friend, Barbara, was gone, did she have anyone to comfort her apart from work colleagues?

Then an alarming streak of jealousy took a stranglehold on him. He wanted to be the one she depended on and ran to in time of crisis, but he knew that was not going to happen. Most times they met, a long immeasurable span of silence filled the air and she lost patience with him. He raised his almost empty cup of coffee to his forehead and rolled it from side to side as if he was trying to iron out the furrows. However, he'd made his decision, he was going to attend John's funeral whether Alex liked it or not.

Outside the wind shrieked and howled and rain lashed the side of the mobile home, waking Alex at six-thirty. She cupped her hands behind her head and laid thinking about the rest of that day. There was a feeling of dread in the pit of her stomach. John's funeral would be momentous, indelibly printed on her mind along with the few short years they'd spent together as man and wife and now the rest of her life stretched ahead like a barren wasteland.

She turned on her side and welcomed the familiar draught of cool air wafting from the register as the air conditioning kicked in. Although the weather outside was foul, the heat in the bedroom was unbearable and damp hair stuck to the back of her neck. Unable to get back to sleep, she slipped on a thin, cotton robe and opened the bedroom door. Shock rippled through her at the sight of the empty sofa and no sign of Clancy.

Her heart developed a funny rhythm as she poked her head in the empty kitchen and nook. She tried to control her hectic breathing as she wavered to the front door and flung it open.

Clancy was sitting on the top step of the porch smoking a cigarette. She turned her head. "Hi, couldn't you sleep either?"

"No, I didn't know you smoked."

"I don't very often, but the storm kept me awake. How're you feeling?"

Alex leaned against the door with her arms crossed watching fat raindrops tumble from the carport. "I'm okay, nervous I guess, but okay."

Everywhere was in darkness and the only light was the faint glow from neighboring yard lamps blurred through the heavy deluge. Alex took a deep breath and her voice was little more than a whisper wafting through the sound of the incessant downpour. "I like being awake when everyone else is still in bed. I feel as if the whole world belongs to me and there's no one out there trying to harm me."

The two stared at each other in silence and Clancy blew a plume of smoke into the air. "You've had a tough time, but no one can foresee the accidents of life. I think you've been extraordinarily brave the way you'd handled everything. Once today's over, things can only get better."

Overhead the wind clacked the branches of the trees together as Alex stared at the puddles pimpled with rain. She scrunched her eyes shut and nodded. If only Clancy knew how scared she was, she'd think her a coward. The thought of the funeral filled her with sorrow, the idea that someone wanted her dead terrified her, and she was petrified at the thought of spending the rest of her life alone.

Clancy stubbed out her cigarette on the step and stood. "Come on, let's go inside, it's cooler there. I'll make you some coffee and toast."

Alex opened the door and a blast of cool air fanned her cheeks. She sat on a stool in the kitchen nook while Clancy scooped grounds into the coffee pot and stuffed bread into the toaster.

They dilly-dallied as long as they could over the meager meal, one of them getting up to monitor the weather every five or ten minutes. By the time they'd stacked their plates in the dishwasher, the wind had lessened, the rain had dried up, and the sky lightening from the east, was looking brighter.

"Are you going to run with me this morning?" Alex asked, watching Clancy's face register surprise.

"Are you still going to run today?"

"Of course, it's just another day. John died months ago and anyway, he's not in that casket, he's here in my heart." She pressed a hand to her breast. "I've had five months of sadness and mourning, there'll be plenty of time for a final goodbye this afternoon. Come on. Let's get changed."

The storm had washed away all trace of humidity and the air was fresh and cool as the two women set off jogging along the trails. They loped in Indian file, their running shoes pounding the track in unison, and arms swinging as one. In no time at all their hair and shirts were damp with sweat and rain droplets dripping from the trees.

They emerged from the woods with chests heaving and perspiration dotting their brows. Alex leaned her hands on her knees, drawing in deep breaths. She swung round and Clancy was jogging on the spot and shadow boxing.

"Wow, that was invigorating. I wish I had somewhere like this to run. My condo's in an apartment block downtown and there's nowhere suitable for miles. Using the gym at the precinct isn't the same."

"I've never jogged before I came to stay here. In fact, I'd never exercised either, but I love it."

They traipsed up the steps; Alex threw a small towel at Clancy and grabbed another, wiping her face and neck on it.

They took turns in the shower and by the time Alex dressed in her one and only black dress, her spirits had deteriorated. At last, the reality of burying John hit her and her lips trembled as she applied a coat of mascara to her lashes. She leaned both hands on the vanity and stared at her likeness in the mirror.

When a soft tap sounded, her eyes shifted to the door behind.

"Are you okay?" Clancy stood in the doorway wearing a long, black, acetate dress and jacket. She'd parted her hair and sleeked it down with gel.

"I-I think so. I know I have to do this, but I hope the media doesn't turn the funeral into a circus. I want it to be a quiet affair."

"Don't let anything upset you, just take it as it comes. I'll be close by to see that nobody pesters you."

Alex met Clancy's eyes in the mirror. "Thanks. Have you heard if Barbara's funeral's been arranged yet?"

"I'll ask Lieutenant Walker when I see him later. Ready?"

Alex took a deep breath, exhaled and nodded.

Clancy closed and locked the door and followed Alex to the Chevy parked under the carport. Both women clicked their seatbelts closed and Clancy turned the ignition and backed out onto the road. Traffic was light at that time of day and she pulled into the church parking lot twenty minutes later.

The first thing Alex saw was a van emblazoned with a local TV channel's logo. A weedy man with a beard stood on the path leading to the church with a large video camera mounted on his shoulder. At the sound of car doors closing, he swung the camera in Alex's direction, and followed her until Clancy, walking behind her, gave him a shove.

"Give Mrs. Martell some privacy please. This is a solemn occasion."

The man continued to film. "This is my job, lady and its news."

Clancy pulled her police badge from her pocket. "I'm not a lady, I'm a police officer." The man's face paled. "So keep your distance from the bereaved. I'd hate to arrest you for causing a public disturbance."

The man worked his face into a disgusted look, slunk back to the parking lot and stood beside the news van.

Clancy caught up with Alex and they waited in the church doorway until the hearse arrived. Four men in black suits lifted the flower-covered casket and carried it up the path. Alex vaguely remembered arranging for the funeral home to supply pallbearers and choosing white flowers, but everything else soon became a blur.

Several people entered the church and sat at the back before Alex and Clancy walked slowly down the aisle behind the casket and entered the front pew. A hand touched Alex's shoulder and she turned and looked into Juno's green-flecked eyes. "Hang in there," he mouthed.

That small gesture of encouragement caused tears to glisten in her eyes.

Clancy leaned forward nodding an acknowledgement to Lieutenant Walker in the front pew opposite and he reciprocated. The organ struck up a hymn, but Alex couldn't sing, her mouth wouldn't work. The minister's words about John went right over her head and didn't penetrated her brain.

After a short service, the pallbearers lifted the casket and carried it back up the aisle with Alex and Clancy close behind. At a newly dug grave in the churchyard, Clancy led Alex to a seat and handed her a spray of white roses. After a few more prayers, the two women deposited their flowers on the casket and Alex stumbled back to her seat.

Charlie and Brett stood opposite along with several others from the magazine. The partners from John's work filed in front of her, shaking her hand and offering words of condolence. Lieutenant Walker and two armed officers hovered on the perimeter, their eyes scrutinizing each guest. At the back of the crowd, Alex spotted Darren Winters. Was her attacker one of the people here? Was he plotting how and when he would strike next? Alex shuddered as a gray goose walked over her grave. The one person conspicuous by his absence was Barbara's husband, Don, but Alex hadn't expected him to come.

"Come on, let's go," Clancy took her arm and helped her to her feet. Together they crossed the grass to the Chevy and Alex climbed in. She felt empty inside.

Clancy stayed at the driver's door speaking in hushed tones with Lieutenant Walker. He gesticulated with his hands while Clancy listened and nodded. The other two officers roamed close by, hands on their weapons their eyes scanning the crowd. At last, Clancy opened the door and lowered her tall frame into the driver's seat.

"The lieutenant's going to tail us as far as the parking lot entrance and block it so that no one can follow us. As an extra precaution, I'm going to detour down a few streets, just in case our man has an accomplice."

"I feel as if I'm in the middle of a mystery movie," Alex remarked, turning in her seat to see the police car pull out behind the Chevy.

As Clancy reached the parking lot entrance, she turned left instead of right and when Alex looked back, the police car had swung round barricading the gateway.

Because of the circumstances of John's death, Lieutenant Walker had advised Alex not to invite any funeral guests for refreshments. As the car whizzed along, she was glad. For months she'd mourned John, but now she knew he was not coming back, she had to concentrate on staying alert, perfecting her firearm techniques, and trying to save her life.

Chapter 18

He stood at the back of the crowd. Because he'd attended funerals of other victims, he knew how the police operated, so he'd parked in a street adjacent to the church and entered by a side walkway usually taken by the bride and her father for a wedding. With long, even strides, he crossed to the path leading round the back of the church and the street where his car waited.

Before he turned the corner, he looked back. Alex and her bodyguard were leaving the graveside. He lengthened his stride and depressed the button on his remote to open the driver's door. Once seated, he cranked the ignition and crept to the end of the street. A few moments later, Alex's silver Chevy with the bodyguard driving, careered along the main road, passing the nose of his car.

A satisfied smirk spread across his face as the police car swung round blocking the parking lot entrance. Now the Chevy was a hundred yards ahead, so he executed a left turn and pulled out behind. At the first traffic light, the Chevy turned right. He knew the roads in that small community were a series of dead ends and that the Chevy would soon need to make a left and a right to rejoin to the main road, so he continued straight on at a slower pace.

The nose of the Chevy poked from a cul-de-sac and swung back in front of him. He tried hard to stifle a chuckle, but it progressed from his chest to his throat. Did these stupid women think they could outsmart him? He was a master of covert operations. After a term in the military, he'd been recruited by an underground organization and had spent several months as a mercenary tracking undesirable political figures and assassinating them. No one got the better of him. He was the best.

Now they were traveling east and leaving the town of Geyserville. Although he'd deliberately allowed two other cars to pull in front of him, the Chevy was still easy to spot if it made an unexpected turn. For ten minutes, the cars in front glided along never making a turn. As he approached a side road, a noisy, dirty truck pulled out and dove into the small gap between him and the SUV in front, causing him to stamp on the brake. He swore under his breath and at the first opportunity, he nosed in front of the truck until he was once again two cars behind the Chevy.

At the next crossroads, the turning signal of the SUV flashed and it veered off the road. He released his foot from the accelerator, allowing his car to drop back further from the red car in front. The noisy truck swerved round and tucked in between his car and the red one again. This time he was quite happy and hung back further, keeping his eyes glued to the silver car.

The cars gobbled up the miles until an orange blinking light signaled the intention of Alex's car to turn left. He sat bolt upright, hands gripping the wheel, his heart hammering in his chest. The Chevy completed the left turn and the red car and the noisy truck continued straight on. He braked and pulled over to the side of the road, craning his neck down the dirt track. His brows came together over the bridge of his nose. Why hadn't he thought of this place before? Of course, this is where his victim would bolt when she was cornered. It seemed quite appropriate that she would end her life in the same place as her husband. He swiveled his head. The main road was clear, so he turned down the dirt track just as the Chevy's red brake lights disappeared from view.

His car bucked and rocked as he gunned the engine trying to reduce the yardage between himself and the Chevy. With a reflex action, he ducked when a large branch scraped the car roof and Spanish moss dangled in front of the windshield obliterating his vision for a second.

Now he saw his destination, the mobile home park, the one he'd tailed his other victims to, months before. Although the dirt track continued round to the right, he drove straight through the park gates; his car now on the smooth blacktop road. He pursed his lips trying not to grin. How appropriate, mobile homes had carports, not garages. All he had to do was cruise to the back of the park until he spotted the parked silver Chevy.

He flexed and contracted his fingers around the steering wheel while his extremities tingled. Now the chase was nearing its end, his mind was spinning so fast it was hard to hold onto a thought, as excitement bubbled inside. He skirted the perimeter of the park and several people working in their yard looked up as he drove past. At the bottom, he followed the road round to where one home sat apart from the others backing onto a dense wood.

Now he knew where she was hiding, he berated himself. He should have realized she'd run here like a scared rabbit, just as his girlfriend had five months ago.

Back at the mobile home, Alex flopped on the sofa. The strain of the funeral had drained her of all energy. Clancy changed from her dress into jeans and a tee shirt and came through from the kitchen with a pot of coffee in her hand.

She inclined her head to the vessel. "Want some?"

"No, if I have anymore caffeine I'll never sleep tonight. You phoned the lieutenant on the way back here. What did he say?"

"Not much. Just that almost everyone he'd expected was present at the funeral. No one acted suspiciously, except Juno. He stayed in the background leaning against a tree. Other than that there was nothing out of the ordinary, no strangers lurking about."

At the mention of Juno's name, Alex glowed. She'd been so absorbed in trying not to cry, that she hadn't noted who was present. She vaguely remembered seeing Charlie, Brett and Darren Winters. No trees were close to the graveside, so Juno must have been standing to one side or behind her. She hadn't seen or heard from him since the day she'd met him at the police precinct.

"I don't think it's him," Clancy said, interrupting Alex's thoughts.

"Who?"

"Juno."

Alex shook her head. "No, I don't think so either. I still find it hard to believe it's someone I know. It could be some maniac who picks victims at random and I was unlucky enough to draw the short straw."

Clancy was silent for a moment before lifting her shoulders in a shrug. "He might be easier to catch if it was, but my gut tells me it's someone you know. Our criminal profilers maintain that people who've had a hard childhood and turn to a life of crime, are trying to gain recognition and parental praise or are killing the parent they hate over and over again. We're dealing with a dangerous psychopath, Alex, so you'd better believe it."

Juno watched Alex's car zoom onto the main road with Sergeant Clancy driving.

The previous evening, he'd ended his relationship with Petra. They'd sat in a quiet booth at the back of a restaurant and Juno waited until the server had left with their order before he spoke.

"I don't think we should see each other socially anymore," he said, looking down at his fingertips.

After a tense silence, he looked up, surprised at Petra's wild, dark eyes. "It's that skinny magazine writer, isn't it? I knew it the moment I first saw you together."

"No, this has got nothing to do with her. I just feel that our relationship has run its course and has nowhere else to go."

"Not as far as I'm concerned. I always thought we'd get married."

Juno gave a long, slow blink. "Excuse me? When have I ever mentioned marriage? I've tried that institution before and it doesn't work for me."

Petra's nostrils flared and she threaded her fingers through her hair. "Huh, and you think Miss Goody-Two-Shoes will be content to sleep with you without a ring on her finger? I don't think so. What's that simpering, little bitch got that I haven't? I suppose because she acts all lost and lonely, you want to protect her. Well, let me tell you this, Juno, my father's a powerful man and he can ruin you just like that." She snapped her fingers.

"Don't threaten me," Juno accused. "Your father told me you're a spoiled, conniving female when he first asked me to take you out, and I didn't believe him, so there's no need to prove him right." He stood and leaned forward supporting himself on his hands. "I'll pay the check on the way out." He turned on his heel and left.

Today, he felt as if someone had lifted a weight from his shoulders as he sat in his car in the church parking lot. Petra had been right about one thing, he couldn't get Alex Martell out of his mind. Today she'd looked as if she were a lost child, pale and lonely. He'd longed to sprint across the grass, take her in his arms and comfort her.

At last, the line of traffic started to move, but he remained in his car for a further fifteen minutes. The funeral had made him maudlin. His thoughts turned to his father who'd been a big inspiration to him. How he'd managed to put up with his mother's many foibles, he didn't know. She was a complex woman, whereas his father had been a straightforward man, honest and kind. Without another thought, he opened the car door reached his arms high and stretched. He maneuvered the few short steps to the path and trekked to the open church door.

A cool, peaceful aura purveyed as his footsteps echoed in the empty edifice. He tilted his head back and scrutinized the domed ceiling painted cobalt blue with gold stars. Carved wood decorated the pulpit and walls behind the transepts while in front of an arched, stained glass window, large displays of white flowers adorned the altar.

Halfway down the aisle, he sat on the end of one of the pews and closed his eyes. It was years since he'd been in a church, but today he felt the need to be alone in total seclusion to review the mistakes of his life. At forty-three, he had two broken marriages and scores of love affairs behind him, and was responsible for the death of one young woman. What did he have to offer Alex Martell? She was thirteen years younger than he, beautiful, a recent widow and hated his guts.

He laid his arm on the back of the pew in front and hung his head clearing his mind of all thoughts. When a hand touched his shoulder, his eyes flew open and he sat up. The minister who'd conducted the funeral service stood beside the pew.

"I'll be locking the church doors in fifteen minutes," he said. "Were you at the funeral?"

"Yes."

"Are you a friend of the deceased?"

Juno shook his head. "No, I'm a business colleague of Mrs. Martell."

The minister raised his eyes to the heavens before looking back down at Juno. "Ah, you know the beautiful Alex." His hand still grasped Juno's shoulder. "Are you the writer?"

"You know me?"

The minister chuckled. "Only from your books and what Alex's told me about you. I've known her since she was a child and I married her to John in this very church. These last few months have been hard on her, but she's very resilient and one day soon she'll be ready to pick up the pieces of her life again."

Juno was flabbergasted. "She's spoken about me?"

"Yes, in confidence of course, but I know she thinks very highly of your friendship." The minister gave a knowing nod. "I'll walk you to the door when I'm ready to lock up." He strolled down the remainder of the aisle disappearing through a door at the bottom.

Juno sat still staring straight ahead, trying to assess the meaning of the minister's words. Because Alex had mentioned his name didn't prove anything. She could have described his hostile attitude at the interview, or maybe her caustic words after they'd had dinner. However, that she'd told the minister about their meetings surely meant something. His heart gave a skip of anticipation.

The click of a door closing signaled the return of the minister and Juno stood as he approached.

"I can give you more time if you need it," he said, pausing by the pew.

"No thanks, I don't come to church often, but it seemed the right thing to do today."

Juno accompanied the minister in silence to the front door.

The minister pulled it closed, inserted a key in the lock and turned it. "It's a shame the church has to be locked, but we've had some vandalism over the years." He held out his hand and Juno shook it. "It was nice meeting you. Give Alex some time to get over this, goodbye."

Juno remained on the steps watching the minister walk to his car before he swiveled his head and noted a cluster of dark clouds rolling in from the north. He jogged to his car just as the first raindrops began to sprinkle. Jamming the key in the ignition he applied his foot to the accelerator, and when he reached the parking lot entrance, he turned onto the main road. The wipers swept aside the unrelenting rain and he was so absorbed in peering through the windshield beyond the deluge, that he didn't notice a dark car pulling out of a side road.

At the first clap of thunder, he approached the house and parked outside the front door. He bolted inside, his head and shoulders drenched, as raindrops dripped down his face onto the tiled floor. Max ran to meet him and he reached down to pat him.

"Good boy." He held the door open, but the dog took two steps backward. Juno gave him a gentle push. "Go on, you've been cooped up all day."

Max lollopped into the rain rounded the car and disappeared behind a tree. After many inquiries, no one had come forward to claim the dog and in a way he was glad, they were both misfits and melded well together.

Leaving the door ajar, Juno strode into the kitchen, reached for a towel and wiped his face and hair dry. He depressed the button on the answering machine, but there were no messages.

Back at the front door, he craned his neck through the torrent of water pouring from the gutters. "Max!" he called, cupping his hands round his mouth to amplify the volume of his voice. "Max!"

The wind gusting through the trees whipped the words from his mouth, so he hastened outside, still staying under the overhang of the roof. As he stood under the protection of the eaves, the rain sluiced down while the wind peppered raindrops over him. He called the dog's name again.

A frown furrowed his brow. Damn Max, he could go to the devil. One moment he didn't want to go outside and the next, he didn't want to come back in. Juno kicked the door closed and sauntered into the kitchen.

After he'd read his mail and made a pot of coffee, he opened the door and called the dog's name again. He studied his watch. Max never usually stayed out this long in the rain. Maybe he was sheltering somewhere. He tried to tamp down his rising anger and went to turn away, but something beyond the hood of his car caught his eye. He squinted through the downpour at a dark mass and covered the distance in a matter of seconds.

Under a live oak, Max lay on his side in a pool of blood, his tongue lolling from his open mouth, eyes staring. Juno fell to his knees and cradled the dog in his arms, rocking him as if he were a child. "Oh no, God no."

The sky looked as gray as he felt as he continued rocking, his eyes scrutinizing the area. Who and why would anybody want to do this? Max was no threat to anyone. There were no other houses for miles around, so it couldn't be because his barking aggravated neighbors. This was a deliberate execution, a warning.

Juno's jaw worked with pent-up rage as he surveyed his property. The incessant rain had saturated is clothes and water dripped from his hair and ran in rivulets down his face. He sidestepped a low branch and jogged down the concrete driveway. When he came to the end, he bent down. Imprinted in the mud were two sets of tire tracks, one that was his. He saw no reason to pursue the trespasser, he would be long gone, and so he jogged back.

Deep sadness overpowered him as he slid his arms under the still animal, carried him round to the lanai and laid him gently down, covering him with a throw he lugged from the back of a chair. Moving as if he were a zombie, he entered the house and locked all the doors and windows before stripping off his wet clothes. A short, hot shower helped bring him back to reality, but he bristled with fury as he toweled himself dry.

He seethed in silence for not confirming he wasn't being followed. As he circled the living room, he made a vow to find whoever had killed his dog and punish them. He tumbled into an armchair and covered his eyes with his hand, trying to blot out the unpleasant picture of the dead dog.

Two hours later, the rain had ceased, the sky was clear and the sun shining. This was typical of Florida's climate. While the weather was still foul, he'd rooted around in the basement and found a sturdy cardboard carton, large enough to accommodate Max. Now, he wrapped the dog in a large bath towel and placed him in the box. With a shovel in his hand, he marched out the kitchen door to the last tree at the back of his property where he stabbed the earth, soft from the recent storm, and began to dig.

With sweat dotting his brow, he returned to the house, loaded the box on a dolly and wheeled it to the newly dug hole. Angry pressure built inside as he thought of the waste and lowered the animal into the ground. Sorrow cut through him like a knife as he scooped dirt over the crate until the soft, warm soil blanketed it. With the back of the spade, he tamped down the earth until it was hard packed.

Sadness filled his inconsolable heart as he gazed down at the dog's last resting place. "Farewell, Max. I'm sorry I wasn't more careful and you had to die because of that." Full of emotion, he spun round and with stooped shoulders trudged back to the house.

Chapter 19

Because Clancy was playing watchdog to Alex Martell, Zack Walker had commandeered another woman officer to assist him in his investigations. Minnie LaTour was straight out of the Police Training Academy and as enthusiastic as a greyhound in its first race. She was small with spectacles and dark hair tied back in a ponytail. By all accounts, she was a whiz with computers and that was why Zack had chosen her. To further their investigation, he needed to discover the details of Alex Martell's adoption to see if there was a connection between her and Diane Bostock.

Minnie's cheeks glowed as she bustled into Zack's office. "I've spoken to the attorney about Alex Martell and he gave me the name of the institution where she was placed almost immediately after her birth. After extensive investigations I finally found out the name of the woman who put her up for adoption."

Zack returned the papers in his hand to the desk, his heart picking up its pace, as he observed the satisfied smirk on Minnie's face. "Go on, LaTour, I'm all ears."

A smug smile settled on her face as handed him a piece of paper.

Zack took the paper and when he read the name, he felt as if he'd been slapped. "Are you sure about this?" He didn't want to go off half-cocked by interviewing the wrong woman.

"Yes, sir, I'm positive. She already had one son when she gave birth to twin girls on September 5, thirty years ago in Boca Raton and put them up for adoption."

"How did you find all this out?"

"The Internet's a wonderful thing, sir, and there's more. There's no father's name on the birth certificates."

Zack was stunned into silence. If someone had poked him in the chest at that moment, he'd have toppled over. This was a breakthrough and a revelation. "Well done, LaTour. Do we have any idea of this woman's whereabouts?"

"Yes, sir. After her husband died, she moved from the northeast to Boca Raton and married an old friend of the family." She looked over the top of her gold-rimmed spectacles and wiggled her dark brows.

"The twins' father?"

LaTour shrugged. "It's a possibility."

Zack loved this aspect of police work, investigating facts and tracking down people. Not many things surprised him, but this had come as a shock. At least now, they had something to work on. His words came out as fast as rapid gunfire. "Find out this woman's new married name and her address. We're taking a trip to Boca Raton."

Max's premature death had thrown Juno for a loop. He needed someone to talk to and it was at times like this that he realized how few friends he had. The house felt empty and he wandered the rooms almost expecting the animal to emerge from behind one of the pieces of furniture. He wasn't in the mood to write and although John's funeral had helped fill his morning, he had no idea what to do with the rest of the day.

In the kitchen, he grabbed a bottle of beer from the refrigerator, released the cap and took a deep slug. His thoughts turned to Alex; she'd looked pale and tense at the graveside and without thinking, he dialed her cell phone number and was about to hang up when she answered.

"Hello." Her voice was soft and distant.

"Hi, it's Juno. How are you?"

She emitted a large sigh. "Oh, I'm okay, just glad the funeral's over."

"It was a nice service."

"Yes."

"I see you still have police protection. Is she there with you now?"

The silence that ensued teemed with tension. "Yes, the sergeant's with me twenty-four, seven. Why do you ask?"

"Because I'm interested." He closed his eyes. "I care what happens to you, Alex, that's why I gave you my cell phone number. Please call me if you need anything at any time."

"Thanks, I will."

The line went dead. He clicked the *off* button and hung his head. He'd wanted to say what was in his heart, but decided not to on the phone. The tightness between his shoulder blades had lessened since hearing Alex's voice. What he really needed was to see her. Since she'd been in hiding, the urge to find her had escalated to fever pitch, and she filled his every thought.

He finished the rest of his drink, plucked a jacket off the back of a chair and went out to the lanai. Once there, he tapped a cigarette from a package nestling in his shirt breast pocket, and lit it breathing smoke deep into his lungs. With one hand, he leaned against the screen supports gazing at the creek as dragonflies floated over the slow-moving current.

Two steps took him from the lanai to the gravel path where he shrugged on his jacket and set off for a walk at a brisk pace. He wandered down the track to his cabin, his thoughts divided between Alex and his dog. The house had acquired an uncanny stillness. Before the dog arrived, he'd never noticed the enveloping silence, but now he missed his constant company and the patter of his paws.

The cabin was now in sight, so he started to jog. As he neared, he slowed drawing his brows together, eyes trained on the front door. It was open and the lock looked as if someone had forced it. Eyes scouring the expanse around the cabin, he crept forward. He pushed the door with his left shoulder and peered inside. Everything looked intact. With his heart hammering against his ribs, he shoved the door wider and stepped inside.

His eyes scanned the room. The only thing out of place was his Underwood typewriter. Someone had lifted it from the desk and chucked it onto the rug in the middle of the floor. Still uncertain whether the burglar was present, he poked his head in the shower room and the bedrooms before he bent to retrieve the machine. He rifled through a stack of papers on the desk, but they hadn't been disturbed.

This was weird. Why would someone break in and steal nothing? Perhaps the perpetrator had expected to find things of value or money and had thrown the typewriter onto the floor as a sign of disapproval. If that were the case, Juno was lucky. Most of the time, thieves committed acts of vandalism if they didn't get what they expected. Unless this robber had accomplished what he came to do.

Zack Walker drove into Palm Beach County and whipped the steering wheel east toward the coast.

Minnie LaTour consulted the GPS clipped to the dashboard. "You turn left in half a mile, that'll take us down to the houses that back onto the water."

Zack executed the turn. "Where now?"

"Make another left and you should be on Osprey Point Circle."

Zack completed the exercise and reduced his speed, leaning forward to peruse the house numbers. Multi-million dollar homes on large lots lined the circle and Zack swung into a wide, paved driveway flanked by tall palm trees and parked outside impressive, double front doors. He made a face at LaTour. In reply, she rolled her eyes.

Zack contemplated the large exterior of over eight thousand square feet. Two stories high, the house was concrete block stucco painted pale peach with arched windows. Terra cotta barrel tiles covered the roof apart from in the center of the house where a large, domed, glass cupola rose like a gigantic bubble. To one side sat a three-car garage.

"Impressive," Zack said, as he climbed out and straightened his tie. "Let's hope the lady's at home."

Side by side, Zack and Minnie mounted the circular steps and he rang the doorbell. A young Cuban woman opened the doors and smiled.

Zack flashed his police ID. "Lieutenant Walker of Central County Precinct and this is Sergeant LaTour. We'd like to speak to Mrs. Anderson. Is she in?"

The young woman nodded. "Please come in."

Zack ushered Minnie in front and followed her into a spacious marble-tiled foyer with an ornate double staircase leading to a second floor gallery. The young Cuban disappeared into a door and Zack swiveled his head drinking in his opulent surroundings. The door to the left opened and the young woman gestured them to enter.

A huge room yawned before them. A series of sliding, patio doors overlooked a kidney-shaped swimming pool and bobbing on the ocean, a cabin cruiser at the end of a private dock. Alicia Anderson lounged on a Barcelona chair reading a fashion magazine.

She placed the periodical on a side table and stood, smoothing down a pair of black, sateen pants. She extended a manicured hand. "Won't you both be seated? Can Carmen get you something to drink?"

"No thank you, we'll only take a few moments of your time."

Alicia flapped a hand and the young Cuban, who'd been hovering in the doorway, left the room.

"Is this about my son?" She asked, returning to her chair.

"Why would you think that, Mrs. Anderson?"

"Because he's the only person we know in Central County."

Zack shook his head and decided to be blunt. "No, this is not about your son it's about your daughters."

Alicia paled beneath her golden suntan and raised beautiful, sculptured brows. "You are mistaken, Lieutenant, I don't have daughters, only one son."

Sergeant LaTour opened a manila folder and took out a piece of paper, handing it to the woman.

Alicia's took the paper and read it with a pinched face. "Where did you get this?"

"Everything in Florida's public record, Mrs. Anderson. I'm sorry if this has been a shock, but we need you to attest that you gave birth to twin girls and put them up for adoption thirty years ago."

Alicia lifted her chin high and looked down her nose at Zack. "Why do you need to know this?"

"Because someone has a grudge against them and they're in danger."

Alicia sat in stony silence reading the paper in her hand once again. She lifted her head and her eyes filled with distress. "My husband knows nothing of this. If he finds out, he'll be furious."

Minnie motioned with her chin to a large framed photo on the mantle shelf. "Is that him over there?"

"Yes, he's out playing golf at the moment."

Zack leaned forward clasping his hands together. "Look, Mrs. Anderson, we're not here to make trouble for you, but we need you to tell us if you know of anyone who might want to harm your daughters."

Alicia turned her head and looked out the window. "Don't be ridiculous, how would I know such a thing? I've never even met these women."

Outside a car door banged and Alicia's face blanched. "That's my husband." She rushed to her feet. "Please don't tell him why you're here."

Her eyes pleaded with Zack and he inclined his head.

"Darling," Alicia sidled across the room to a tall, silver-haired man and kissed him on the cheek. "You're home early. I thought you were going to have drinks with the Carleton's."

"I changed my mind and cut short the round of golf because of a headache." His eyes came to rest on Zack.

Zack took a step forward and proffered his hand. "Lieutenant Zack Walker of Central County Precinct, I'm a colleague of Mrs. Anderson's son. He asked me to look in on her while we're in the vicinity."

"Nice to meet you, Lieutenant. How is Balthazar?" Martin Anderson bent to shake Zack's hand.

"Very well, he's even helped me with a couple of cases."

"Excellent. That boy's got a good head on his shoulders, which is more than can be said for my son." He patted his wife on the shoulder. "Well, I'll leave you to catch up on the news with your new friends and I'll go and change."

Martin Anderson turned and exited the room.

Alicia returned to the Barcelona chair with a look of relief on her face. "Thank you Lieutenant, you don't know how much this means to me."

"You're welcome, ma'am. What did your husband mean about his son?"

Alicia raised her eyes to the heavens and sighed. "Martin's first wife, Emily, couldn't have children, so they adopted a two-month-old baby boy. He's two years older than Balthy, but the two are nothing alike. Carlos was always a cruel child, fighting with other children and torturing animals."

Alicia patted a few stray blonde hairs back into her French twist before continuing. "Martin organized all kinds of counseling for him, but that did no good. Much to everybody's surprise, he enlisted in the military and seemed to change. I say 'seemed' because no sooner had he been home for three months than he was a hanging out with the wrong type of people and had a police record. We haven't seen him in years and have no idea where he is or what he's doing now. Martin always says that if Emily had lived, Carlos would have broken her heart, she adored him."

While Alicia flapped her hands and fluttered her eyelids during her oration, Zack was making a mental note of everything she said. "And all this was while you were living in Pittsburgh?" Alicia nodded. "So when did you last hear from him?"

"Just before Martin and I married. He sent us a letter from New York saying that he'd found a nice girl, had started a new job and couldn't come to the wedding." Alicia lifted her shoulders in a shrug. "We've heard no more from him since."

Minnie had been silent all through this conversation taking notes in shorthand.

Zack rose and Minnie followed. "Thank you for your time Mrs. Anderson. We may need to talk to you again, but if we do, I'll make sure it's done in a discreet way."

Alicia presented a hand with red-painted nails to Zack. "Before you go, I'd like to ask you one question, Lieutenant. What are my daughters like?"

"They're beautiful, they have your eyes. And I'd like to ask *you* one further question. Is Martin their father?"

Alicia smiled and nodded. "I'll get Carmen to show you out." She lifted a small, brass bell from a side table and tinkled it.

The door opened and the young, Cuban woman dropped a curtsey. "Yes, ma'am?"

"Show the police officers to the door, please, Carmen." Alicia picked up her magazine and resumed her reading.

Outside in the car, Zack composed his face in a grin. "Can you imagine being called Balthazar? No wonder Juno doesn't use it."

Minnie giggled. "I dare you to call him by that name the next time you see him."

"No way, I wouldn't want anyone knowing my name was Balthazar either. Will you drive back?"

"Yes, sir." Minnie sprinted round the back of the car while Zack climbed over to the passenger seat.

With Minnie driving, he'd have more time to consider this newly-acquired information. Now they knew that Juno, Alex Martell and Diane Bostock were kin, he wondered if Juno was aware that he had twin sisters. Alex Martell obviously believed the story that her parents died in a car accident and therefore she had no notion. That left Diane Bostock. She must have discovered the truth about her family and relocated to find them, but someone had killed her before she could.

Then another thought crossed Zack's mind. Juno would most likely inherit the family money when his mother died, but what if he'd unearthed details of his twin sisters and decided to eliminate them? He must pursue this line of enquiry until he was satisfied that the writer was not a suspect.

Minnie swiftly maneuvered the traffic while these thoughts pulsed through Zack's mind.

"Are you going to tell Alex Martell, sir?" She asked.

"I'm not sure. Maybe we should go on letting her believe that her parents are dead."

"But her parents are alive, sir. Doesn't she have the right to know?"

Zack threw his hands in the air. "Oh, shit, what a mess. I'm not letting anyone know anything until we've narrowed down the list of suspects. All this tells us is that these people are related and not who killed Diane or who's trying to kill Alex. I need to interview Juno and make sure he's not involved. Call him and set up a time."

"Yes, sir." LaTour practically saluted as she set a course for the freeway.

Zack remained standing by the window when Juno walked in.

"Hey, how are you?" Juno leaned forward and shook Zack's hand. "I'm glad you asked to see me, I was going to call you."

Zack raised his eyebrows in a silent question.

"Someone killed my dog and broke into my cabin yesterday."

Juno elaborated on how someone had jimmied the cabin door and thrown his typewriter onto the floor.

"Was there much taken?" Zack asked, gesturing for Juno to sit.

"No, that was the strange thing, but what distressed me was that they slit my dog's throat."

Zack pulled out his chair and sat facing Juno "Why do you think they did that? Was he a nuisance?"

"No, I only let him out to do his business, the rest of the time I kept him in the house. I think someone was sending me a warning."

"About what?"

"I've no idea unless the person you're looking for wants me off the case. Anyway, I wanted to let you know about these recent happenings. Why did you want to see me?"

When Zack spoke, his tone was sterner than he intended. "I need to ask you some questions."

Juno stretched out his legs and crossed them at the ankles. "Fire away."

"How often do you see your mother?"

"My mother, why do you want to know that? Has something happened to her?"

"No, I just need you to tell me a bit about your family."

Squint lines extended from the corner of Juno's eyes as he narrowed them and nodded. "My father died twelve years ago and my mother moved to Boca Raton and remarried. I've seen her twice since her marriage."

"And her husband? Do you get on all right with him?"

"Martin? Oh yes, I've known him for as long as I can remember, he's an old friend of my father's."

Zack silently praised Officer LaTour; at least her findings were accurate. "Would you say your parents had a happy marriage?"

"As far as I know, yes. Look, Walker, what's this all about?"

Zack decided to lie. He didn't want Juno knowing the real reason for the questions in case he'd already discovered his mother's secret and was the perpetrator. "The County Commissioner's ordered me to dig into the background of anyone who's remotely connected to this case and that includes you. It's just routine." Zack planted himself right in front of Juno. "What do you remember about when you were thirteen?"

Juno's eyes telegraphed abject shock. "God, I don't know, that was thirty years ago. My father returned from a long business trip and bought me a new bike."

"And your mother?"

Juno tilted his head back and closed his eyes. "I think that was the year her sister, my aunt Teresa, was unwell. She spent some months in Boca Raton and my father took me on a trip to Europe."

"And when you got back, was your mother home?"

"Yes, she came back because she was sick. My father moved into the guest room and employed a housekeeper. I think my parents' marriage might have been going through a bad patch at that time, but whatever it was, they overcame it and were very close until he died."

Zack paused. "And you have no brothers or sisters."

"No. My mother used to say that she'd had a hard time having me and that one baby was enough. I hated being an only child."

Zack was content. Juno's answers had been swift and straight to the point. He was certain the writer had no knowledge of his half-sisters. He had only one more question to ask and leaned forward, his arms braced on the desk. "What happens when your mother dies, do you inherit the family money?"

Juno uncrossed his legs and laughed. "No, father left all his money to me when he died. Mom only got the house. Are you satisfied? Do I pass muster?"

Zack hated grilling Juno, but he had to be satisfied that he knew nothing of the twins and was not involved with the murders. "Yes, I'm sorry I had to put you through this, but I have my reasons. You're free to go."

Juno rose and faced Zack. "You know where to find me if you need me."

Zack nodded and waited until the door closed before he picked up the phone and called Minnie's extension. "Can you come in here?"

The woman officer knocked once before entering.

"I need you to find out all you can about the other suspects." Zack handed her a list of names and addresses. "Brett Etheridge, Darren Winters and Charlie Addison. It's unlikely it's one of these guys, but we'd better check them out before we move on to plan B."

"Which is, sir?"

Zack rubbed the side of his nose. "Give me five minutes and I'll think of something."

Chapter 20

Two evenings later, Alex and Clancy were playing a game of Trivial Pursuit. Alex sat in an armchair with her back to the window and Clancy on the sofa opposite with the game board positioned on the coffee table between them. Alex shook the dice, moved her piece the correct number of squares, and landed on a green one.

"A Science and Nature question," Clancy stated, reaching for the appropriate card from the box.

Alex scowled. "Oh no, I can never answer this category."

Clancy took a deep breath. "Which is the fastest land mammal?"

Alex squinted and crinkled her brow. "Can you give me a clue?"

Clancy shook her head. "Nah-ugh, that's *chea-ting*." She emphasized her last word breaking it into two separate syllables.

Alex grinned. "I know the cheetah."

Clancy displayed a mouthful of sparkling, white teeth and reached for the dice while Alex selected a green wedge.

A sudden, sharp crack sounded while Alex fitted the green wedge into her wheel. "It's your turn, Clancy, shake the dice."

When no reply came, Alex looked over at the police officer and suppressed a scream. A single bullet had channeled a neat path between Clancy's eyes and the back of her head had exploded in a bloody mass over the chintz-covered sofa. She'd died sitting upright with a look of surprise on her face and a silent scream on her lips.

Without thinking, Alex dropped to her knees in the gap between the coffee table and the armchair. No noise filled the yawning silence as she placed her elbows on the armchair seat and gradually raised her head until her eyes peeped over the chair back. A series of thin spidery cracks ringed a bullet hole in the center of the window.

Taking choppy, little breaths, she returned to her knees and hastily crawled toward the phone in the kitchen. Once inside, she struggled to her feet, tucking her hand back through the open door to switch off the living room light. In the dark kitchen, she felt for the phone and lifted the receiver. There was no dial tone. Her heart raced, she hared across the kitchen to retrieve her cell phone from her purse. A sob choked her and tears trickled down her cheeks as she fumbled in the near-empty bag, trying to remember where she'd left it. Her heart turned over. It was in the car. Clancy kept her radio there, too, so that she had privacy to report to the Lieutenant.

Although the windows and doors were locked, she knew that wouldn't deter the killer from getting in if he wanted to. He had her trapped without any form of communication. The moment she'd trained for had finally arrived. She must keep a clear head and her wits about her.

She stumbled through the dining nook to the bedroom and felt her way round the wall to the closet. Blood surged through her veins as she stripped off her jeans and sweater, changing into a jogging suit and cramming her feet into a pair of running shoes. Working methodically, she grabbed a handful of hair and pulled on a hair band before opening the nightstand drawer and withdrawing her gun. She inserted a full clip, stuffed a replacement one into her jacket pocket and zipped it shut.

Alex tiptoed over to the window, moving one of the curtains a smidgeon, and peeking outside. Everything looked and sounded normal. A soft glow spilled from the front yard light over the plants and shrubs close to the house. The street beyond was in darkness, but Alex could just distinguish it was empty. The carport was in shadow, but anyone could be hiding behind her Chevy. She considered it too risky to try to recover her cell phone or the radio from the car.

It was almost time for Clancy's next radio report. Her only chance was that the Lieutenant would investigate when he didn't hear from his sergeant. She slid to the floor, her back against the nightstand with a numb feeling in the pit of her stomach.

Her brow was damp with perspiration as she clutched the gun in both hands, her eyes trained on the door. The silence around her was unsettling and after she'd exhausted every option trying to think what to do, she decided to stay put and hope that help arrived soon. If this maniac broke into the home and forced his way into the bedroom, she could get off a shot before he realized what was happening. What she had to make sure was that his injury would prevent him from harming her.

After what seemed like hours, the gravel on the path outside the window crunched and Alex's neck stiffened, tension surging through her in waves. Footsteps passed the window and then halted before turning back. Then she heard it. Beginning as an almost hysterical cackle, it ended in a guttural sound, brimming with malice and a suffocating sensation tightened her throat.

Was this the same person who'd voiced the warning in her hospital room? Her blood pumped thick and hot as she struggled to her feet and sneaked over to the window. She positioned one eye at the crack, where the curtains didn't quite meet, and was in time to see a dark shape wielding something long, battering her car's side window. The sound of smashing glass rent the still, night air as the man continued to pummel the car and windows with the instrument.

Alex covered her ears with her hands, but persisted in watching. Then all was quiet and the figure's shoulders drooped. He flung aside his weapon, braced his hands on his knees, and turned his head toward the window. Alex jumped back. Could he see her, or did he sense she was watching? Unconsciously, she held her breath and returned her eye to the crack in the curtains in time to see the figure move away from the home and disappear into the woods.

Once he'd vanished, Alex launched into action. With her breath coming in short spurts, she dived across the bedroom snapping on the kitchen light, and wrenching her purse from the counter, at the same time rooting around for the car keys. As if a demon was hot on her tail, she snatched open the front door and clattered down the steps. In her anguish to escape, she left the door wide open, and ran pell-mell to the car.

Zack hated paperwork. He'd finally waded through a huge pile, so he reached for a cigarette from the package on his desk. The radio on the windowsill crackled, so he tilted his chair back and grabbed it. This would be Clancy; she was past due the time for her last transmission of the evening.

"Walker here. Do you copy Clancy? Over."

The radio was silent. Zack took a deep drag of his cigarette and blew a spiral of smoke upwards. "Come in Clancy, over."

When there was no reply, a sixth sense told him something was wrong. Clancy was never this late. He stubbed out his cigarette while shrugging on his jacket and tugging open his office door.

"Simmons, Carter, come with me." The two officers rose from their seats and dashed to join Zack. "Parker, have a car sent round to the front of the building. Now!"

Several faces lit up with excitement at Zack's sharp tone. "What's up, sir?" Parker asked.

"I think we may have an officer down. Have an ambulance sent to The Getaway Mobile Home Park on S.R 27 out by Lake Jackson. We'll be there long before them, so tell them to go to the south side of the park and look for our cars."

By the time Zack had finished his speech, he was striding along the corridor with the two officers following, and Parker repeating instructions into a radio. As Zack turned the corner to exit the front door, he almost bumped into Juno.

Juno took a swift step backward. "Hey, where's the fire?"

"It's Clancy and Alex. They've missed their regular transmission. We've had no communication from them for over four hours. You can follow if you want, but don't touch anything when we get there, and keep out of the way."

Juno's smile changed to an anxious expression as he swung round to retrace his steps.

Outside, Carter climbed into the driver's seat, Simmons in the back, and Zack in the passenger's side. The car's occupants clicked on their seat belts, Carter gunned the engine and pulled away from the curb with spinning wheels kicking up a shower of dust. As they approached the first set of traffic lights, Zack turned to ascertain that Juno's car was behind.

"Turn on the sirens and the lights." Zack ordered. "We need to get there as soon as we can. Every second might help save a life."

Carter flipped the knobs on the dashboard and when the cars in front slowed, he overtook them, his eyes constantly checking for motorists entering the highway from side roads. The car bowled along, eating up the miles, and every so often Zack verified that Juno was still on their tail.

The car swung left off the main road. Zack leaned forward switching off the sirens while he clutched the strap above the door. The car swayed and bucked over potholes down the dirt track, its headlights splitting the darkness and illuminating the park sign at the bottom.

"Follow the road round to the back." He barked as the car leveled out on the smooth, blacktop road.

Tires squealed as the car careened round the perimeter of the park and residents opened their doors craning their necks at the speeding police car.

"There!" Zack extended an index finger pointing to Alex's mobile home.

The car screeched to a halt. Zack tumbled out running past the empty carport. He stared at the light tumbling through the open door, and his right hand crept to his shoulder holster, withdrawing his automatic weapon. Carter and Simmons joined him. They all approached the open door with their guns in their hands. Zack motioned with his head for Carter and Simmons to wait by the door. Juno parked his car behind theirs and doused his lights.

Zack nudged the door wider with his shoulder, Simmons assumed a shooting stance, legs astride, knees locked and both arms outstretched.

"Police!" Zack shouted and darted past Simmons, adopting a similar pose. A muffled cry caught in his throat when he saw Clancy's body. He raised a hand to his brow and closed his eyes to shut out the gruesome sight of his lover.

Simmons strutted toward the bedroom, gun extended. He flipped on his flashlight and poked his head in, his gun sweeping the room. "No one in the bedroom, sir." He reported.

Zack was crying inside and it took him all his time to project a professional manner in front of his men. "Get a crime scene team out here, Carter. Seal off a wide area outside with tape Simmons, and send the ambulance away when it arrives."

Juno stood in the open doorway with an ashen face, his eyes never leaving Clancy.

Carter was finishing his radio report when another vehicle halted outside. "That's the ambulance, sir. Any sign of the other woman?"

"Not yet, we might need to comb the woods, she could be out there."

He took large strides to the window examining the bullet hole while brushing away the trace of tears with the back of his hand.

Zack hated sounding blasé, but he knew Clancy would have understood. The last thing she'd want was for everyone at the precinct to know about their affair. He acted as if he was re-examining the bullet hole while Simmons and Carter left.

With notebook in hand, he began documenting everything in the room, no noticeable smells, no signs of any other violence and no traces of an intruder. Taking extra care not to touch anything, he lowered his head and plodded onto the porch.

A hand touched his shoulder and he swung round to face Juno. "What about Alex?" He asked in a clipped tone.

"She's not here and her car's missing. I reckon she must have driven off after Clancy was killed."

"So, you don't think she's somewhere out there?" Juno hitched his chin in the direction of the woods.

"No, if she were, her car would still be here. Wherever she is, it's my guess that our man's long gone." Zack lit a cigarette and offered one to Juno. Both men smoked in silence for a few minutes.

"I'm sorry about your Sergeant," Juno said between drags. "She was a good officer."

"Yes, damn good, I'd like to get my hands on the motherfucker that did this." Zack's voice broke and he covered his mouth with his free hand to interrupt further expletives.

They continued smoking in silence, watching the other officers unwinding yellow tape and circling the mobile home and carport. Several park residents had congregated in a group and were discussing the situation.

Carter addressed the crowd. "There's nothing to see here folks, please go back to your homes."

A large man lumbered forward. "Has there been a break-in? Is someone hurt?"

"No, sir, we're investigating a report that the owner left the home in a hurry without locking the door. Everything's under control, please return to your homes."

Another murmured discussion took place and several minutes passed before the cluster of residents dispersed.

Zack had finished his second cigarette and was pacing the boards of the small porch when several cars pulled up and the crime scene officers arrived. Carter and Simmons took note of all their names and time of their arrival. Within minutes, a group of men in coveralls and surgical gloves stomped toward them carrying their equipment.

A man paused. "Were you first on the scene, Zack?"

"Yes, the front door was open, so nothing's been touched. Looks like one shot was fired from outside."

"Anyone we know?"

"Yes, Sergeant Clancy."

The man's breath hissed as he inhaled. "Anything else?"

"Just the dead sergeant and broken glass under the carport. The rest is up to you guys."

The man grinned showing stained, chipped teeth. "I always said you have the easy part. See you later."

The man followed the rest of the group inside and Zack turned to Juno who was lighting another cigarette. "Are you sure you want to stay? These guys'll be here for quite some time. I'll call you if we find anything."

Thick eyebrows sheltered Juno's eyes. "If you're going to search the woods tonight, I'd rather stay. I'd like to know if Alex is out there."

Zack faced Juno and gave him a candid look. "If you want my honest opinion, I don't think she is. If our man chased and killed her, he'd have left in his own vehicle, not hers. I think he let her escape and this is just another warning. He's thumbing his nose at us and saying he can do whatever he likes and get away with it. But I'm going to make sure he doesn't."

Chapter 21

Alex had no clue where she was going. She brushed broken glass off the driver's seat, not realizing she'd cut her fingers in several places, placed her gun on her lap and started the engine. Without looking, she backed out the carport, rammed the transmission into drive, and the car careened forward. She gritted her teeth as she hunched over the wheel, pressing her foot hard on the gas pedal.

Oblivious to everything in her attempt to get away, she didn't notice a car pull out behind her with no headlights. She was no sooner on the main road than the flickering low fuel warning light caught her eye. Her buoyant spirits sank like lead. She'd intended to fill up with gas the next morning, but at this time of night, the small gas station closest would have closed hours ago. The next one was too far away.

Her brain clicked and whirred. She slowed her speed and reached over to the glove box for her cell phone. Flipping it open, she dialed 911 and waited. The low battery signal flashed, so she rammed the phone into her pocket.

With eyes scouring the road, she jammed on the brakes when she saw the turning she'd taken to interview Juno a few weeks earlier. Heavy rain spattered the smashed windshield shining in diamond-like glints. The wiper blades jarred and juddered over the broken, uneven surface, blurring her line of vision, and restricting her view of the road.

Trying to control her hectic breathing, she glued her eyes to the beam projecting from her headlights and concentrated. A side road loomed, so she whipped the wheel round without slowing, praying she had enough gas to reach Juno's house. The car trundled on at a steady speed. All of a sudden, the engine began to misfire.

"No!" She wailed, her foot pumping the accelerator. "Please go a bit further."

The car edged forward before the engine spluttered and died. Drained of all energy, Alex leaned her head on the steering wheel. All she'd succeeded in doing was getting stranded in the middle of nowhere. She raised her head and blinked the scene beyond her headlights into focus. She was practically at Juno's property.

Garnered by a surge of hope, she flung open the car door, picked up her purse and gun and plodded up the road, her feet and ankles slopping around in a waterlogged pothole. She squelched past the car and lumbered up the road, the rain now coming down in hard-driving sheets. The sight of the two stone posts at the entrance to Juno's driveway, lifted her sprits. Now she was near to safety, her nerve endings were on fire, and she started to run, taking long, heaving breaths.

She welcomed the tall, dark silhouettes of the trees as she charged between them, her shoes sinking in mud to slow her. Tears of relief streamed down her face the nearer she got to her destination, and by the time she stumbled into the clearing around the house, her knees were ready to collapse.

She uttered a small sob as she pommeled the front door with her fist. "Juno, its Alex!" The silence was unsettling. Her last glimmer of hope died, her body went limp, her knees buckled, and she sagged onto the front steps.

A tear trickled down her cheek as all the fight went out of her. The last few hours had been harrowing, but she'd been sure that Juno would be here to help. Tired, wet and cold, her mind drifted back to the day of the interview, and her eyes snapped open. When she'd been sitting on the sofa questioning Juno, she remembered seeing a lanai at the back of the house.

Her back and legs ached as she battled to her feet. With the safety catch clicked on, she tucked the gun into the waistband of her jeans, slung her purse over her shoulder, and hand over hand, felt her way round the siding to the back of the house. A sliver of moonlight illuminating the lanai spurred her on until her fingers sought the screen door catch, and she almost fell in.

The house was in darkness as she pressed her nose against the sliding, glass door and squinted in. No one was home, not even the dog. It was not bright enough to see her watch, so she had no idea of the time. A white, plastic chaise lounge dripping with rain beckoned, and she slumped onto it feeling safe for the first time since Clancy died.

At the side of the road, hidden by a clump of trees, the engine of the truck idled in neutral and as soon as the Chevy lurched and bucked up the dirt track road, the man shoved the transmission into drive and followed without switching on his headlights. When he reached the main road, Alex's red taillights were visible for a moment before they disappeared round a bend. He depressed the accelerator and soon closed the gap between them.

All of a sudden, red brake lights lit up his windshield, and he slowed. The car in front swung left off the highway, so he emulated her action, but lagged further behind. She surprised him again by making a sharp right turn, and a smirk puckered his face. He knew where she was going. He'd tailed the writer here a few nights ago.

Then his mouth thinned into a slash of anger. Why was she running to Juno? When her car gradually slowed and trickled to a halt, he pulled to the side of the road. Raindrops peppered his windshield, as he watched Alex stagger from her car, and trudge along the road. By the light of her headlamps, he saw her turn left up the driveway to the house.

He shifted the transmission into reverse and backed along the road parking under the shelter of trees with low hanging branches. Once outside, he bolted up the road and vaulted over a chain link fence onto Juno's property. He landed with his legs astride and knees bent. Fat raindrops plopped from overhead branches, soaking his head and shoulders, as he forged between the dark shapes of trees toward the house.

The ground was soft and muddy and slowed his progress. When the building was in sight, he zigzagged from tree to tree, hiding behind the trunks, and poking out his head until he had a clear view of Alex in a heap on the front steps.

He had the chance to make his move now. How easy it would be to overpower her while she was in a weakened state and choke the life out of her. However, that wasn't how he wanted her to die. He needed her to recognize him, feel afraid of him, even plead with him before he claimed her body, and wrung her neck.

She was on her feet again and making her way round to the back of the house. He silently praised Juno for the thicket of trees, continuing to move in their shadows until he was level with her. She clawed at a lanai screen door before falling inside and collapsing on a piece of furniture.

He maintained his position behind a tree weighing up his options. If Juno didn't return and find her in a few hours, she might die of pneumonia or be too weak to go elsewhere for help. With the rain showing no sign of letting up, he decided to stay put and see what happened.

Juno stayed with Zack until forensics had finished and the coroner zipped Clancy into a body bag, and wheeled her on a gurney to his car.

Zack's eyes were wild in his pallid face. "This has become personal now. That sonofabitch has to be stopped. Deliberately killing an unarmed police officer is not only a cowardly action, but also one of a psychopath. This madman we're dealing with has no regard for human life."

Juno gripped Zack's shoulder. "I wish I could have helped more, but instead you've lost a good officer and close friend."

"And we've failed to protect Alex." Zack moseyed down the steps and kicked the remaining shards of glass under the carport. "Something else took place here, but until we find her, we won't know what happened. Come on, let's go. Maybe a good night's sleep will help put all this into perspective."

Juno angled his head from the driving rain and ran to his car backing away from the module followed by Zack in his police car. Ten minutes later Juno turned from the main road while Zack's car zoomed straight back to Geyserville.

The constant rhythm of the wipers lulled Juno into a soporific state. At this time of the evening, roads were quiet especially with the heavy rain. When he turned onto the road leading to his property, his headlights deflected on the taillights of a parked car.

He slowed to a crawl as the smashed back window of the car came into view. His heart began beating an irregular tattoo as he pulled alongside and observed broken side windows along with a smashed windshield. A faint glow emanated from the car's headlights, conveying they'd been on for some time and that someone had abandoned the silver Chevy.

A silver Chevy—the words thrashed through his brain. Alex drove a silver Chevy and they'd found splinters of broken glass under the carport. Spurred on by this thought, he revved the engine, swerved between the two posts, and roared up his driveway.

Breathless with fear, heart constricted, he leaped from his car and unlocked the front door. He began flinging doors open and running through each room, but then he halted. If Alex were here, she'd be somewhere outside.

He grabbed a flashlight from his desk, fled to the front door narrowing his eyes as the flashlight's beam shone on muddy footprints on the steps.

She'd been here. "Alex!" He shrieked, her name floating away on a gust of wind.

He cupped his hands round his mouth and called her name again, as he averted the low branches of the trees, swinging the beam of light around. Unaware that the rain had waterlogged his clothes, his voice became louder and more distraught, as he maintained a search of the grounds.

The only other sound, except for the rushing water in the nearby creek, was his rapid breathing and the steady plop of raindrops. The wind lambasted him as he rounded the side of the house, his wet hair tousled and flying in array around his head. Clouds covered the moon as he plodded toward the back of the house, brandishing his flashlight.

"Alex!" He called, his voice sounding hoarse.

He swiveled the beam of light over the lanai and his heart banged against his ribs when a small movement caught his eye. A bundle of wet clothes on the chaise lounge sat up.

Large, indigo eyes wide with fear dominated Alex's face.

"It's me, Juno," he shouted above the noise of the storm and released the screen door catch. He turned the flashlight on himself as she concealed a sob and weaved toward him.

When her knees buckled, he flung aside the flashlight and caught her, sweeping her into his arms. With long strides, he carried her round to the front of the house, and stomped in the front door, kicking it closed behind him. With water dripping all over the floor, he marched through to the living room and placed her on the leather sofa before rushing into the guest bedroom to grab a pillow, blankets and some towels.

Alex's face was deathly white. Juno felt for her pulse, it was faint but rapid. He lifted her into his arms again and gently laid her on the floor. Working rapidly, he toweled dry the sofa before removing her shoes, jeans, sweater and underwear and disposing of her gun with care. He laid a large, dry bath sheet on the sofa and placed Alex on top, massaging her body all over with another.

His nerve endings tingled as he noted firm, rounded breasts, a small waist and shapely legs. Once he'd removed his eyes from her nakedness, he noticed blood on her fingers and hands. Folding the blankets in two for extra warmth, he tucked them under her armpits and lifted her head onto the pillow. Next, he hared into the kitchen, filled a small bowl with warm water, and grabbed a roll of kitchen paper along with a box of Band-Aids.

Working on one hand at a time, he washed away the dried blood. Several small cuts were still bleeding, so he wrapped a bandage round each of those fingers, before tucking her arms under the blanket.

Now that Alex was comfortable, his next action was to lock the front door, strip off his wet clothes and dress in dry ones. He toweled his hair and poured a generous measure of brandy into a glass before taking a small sip. The liquor burned his throat and warmed him. Balancing the glass on the sofa's arm, he leaned over Alex, lifted her head and tipped a few drops of the golden liquid between her lips.

She moaned.

He tilted the glass again, this time she swallowed, coughed and her eyes opened. Juno sat on the edge of the sofa and brushed her damp hair back from her forehead. "Hi, how're you feeling?"

Alex sat bolt upright, the blankets slipping down to her waist. She squealed and hauled them back up to her chin. "Where are my clothes?"

"I took them off. I didn't want you catching pneumonia."

"*You* took them off? You took my clothes off while I was unconscious. What else did you do?" Her lips molded into a formidable line.

"What? What are you accusing me of? I carried you in here, removed your wet clothes, dried you and kept you warm. If that's all the thanks I get, you can put your wet clothes back on again." He held up her dripping wet jeans, sweater and shoes.

Two bright spots of color spread over her cheeks. "I-I'm sorry. I didn't mean to sound ungrateful." Tears pooled in her eyes. "I'm so pleased to see you. I was so scared."

Juno pulled her roughly forward into his arms. She still clutched the blankets under her chin, but she laid her head on his shoulder.

"You're quite safe now. You lie back, keep warm and tell me what happened at the mobile home. I was with Lieutenant Walker when he found Clancy."

With her voice full of tears, Alex related everything that had happened and by the time she'd finished, tears fell copiously onto the blanket.

"I hadn't filled the car with gas," she uttered trying hard to hold back her tears. "And when the low fuel light came on, I knew I couldn't drive very far, so I came here."

"Well, you almost made it. You lie still while I phone Lieutenant Walker and tell him you're here. You had us all very worried."

The space between them widened as Alex lay back and watched him pick up the phone. Her eyes never left him as he made the call. He replaced the receiver and returned to sit on the side of the sofa.

"Do you want to finish this brandy?" He held up the glass, but she shook her head. "Can I get you coffee or something to eat?" Again, she motioned the negative. "Do you want anything?"

"Would it be okay if I took a shower? I think that might warm me up."

She swung her legs round and Juno stood, helping her to her feet. "Do you think you can walk, or shall I carry you?"

She appeared smaller than he remembered as she stood in front of him clutching the blankets and looking up at him with enormous eyes. "I'm fine, thanks."

Her voice was little more than a whisper and he longed to take her in his arms and shower her with kisses.

His throat was tight as he persuaded his eyes to break from hers. "Follow me. I'll get you clean towels and some clothes. They may be a bit big, but at least they'll keep you warm."

He led the way through a hallway, across the master bedroom and into the master bath with Alex following, dragging the blankets behind. Once he'd opened a closet and withdrawn two large towels, he folded them and draped them over a towel rail.

"I've switched on the heated towel rail and the heat lamp, so both should be nice and warm by the time you've had your shower. I'll sort out some clothes and leave them outside the door. Call me if you need anything else."

Alex felt at a loss for words, so she nodded. Being in close proximity to Juno when she had no clothes on made her feel vulnerable. Also, knowing he'd seen her naked unsettled her. This was something she'd rather have happened while she'd been conscious because now she'd never know what his reaction had been. Did he stare and admire her, or was he too busy drying her to notice? She'd probably never know the answer to those questions.

She inspected the enormous bathroom. A large Jacuzzi tub filled one corner, double vanities lined a wall with a closet, and the shower she was about to step into, was almost as big as the bathroom in her house. Reflected in the mirrored wall opposite, gold plated faucets on the tub and sinks gleamed.

She looked frightful. Wet hair cloaked her shoulders like Raggedy Ann's and traces of mascara streaked her cheeks. A shiver rippled through her as she folded the blankets and laid them on top of a wicker, laundry basket. Steam billowed upward as she adjusted the shower control and lingered under the warm, cascading water.

Pulsing needles of water pounded her skin and revived her. She was surprised to see a wire rack crammed full of shower crèmes, shampoos and conditioners, and reached for one that was her favorite. By the time she'd soaped her body and shampooed her hair, she felt like a new person.

With one towel wrapped around her head like a turban, Alex's body glowed from the warmth of the second one, swathing her like a sarong. She poked her head out the door and saw a pile of neatly folded clothes. She retrieved them, closed the door and let the body towel fall to the floor.

She pulled on a gray tank top many sizes too big and stepped into a pair of boxer shorts that kept sliding down over her hips. Next, she donned a fleecy-lined sweatshirt that fell to her knees and folded up the cuffs several times. She held a pair of Juno's jeans against her and decided to pass on those. They would keep falling down and the legs were far too long.

With her hair almost dry and styled with her fingers, she opened the door and moseyed into the bedroom. A king-sized bed dominated the room along with a whole wall entertainment center housing a large screen, plasma TV and a sophisticated music system. Valances of heavy, gold brocade fabric wreathed the two floor-length windows and her feet sank into a cream, deep-piled carpet.

Her eyebrows furrowed with puzzlement. This room was much more luxurious than the living room, which had a few pieces of leather furniture and was stark by comparison. She muffled a small giggle. Was this where Juno experienced all his entertainment and the living room was where he worked? Whatever the reason for the décor, she liked it.

She jumped when Juno appeared in the doorway. "Ah, I see you're done. What happened to the jeans?" Alex held them in front of her, tilting her head at a jaunty angle. "Hmm, yes, they are a bit big. Would you like a belt for your *dress*?"

Before she could answer, he crossed to a closet and selected a diamante, elasticized belt from a hanger.

Her eyebrows arched inquisitively.

"It's not mine, one of my wives left it behind and I've never got round to throwing it out."

Alex clipped on the belt and handed back the pair of jeans. Her appearance in a full-length mirror across the other side of the room caused her to smile. The sweatshirt cuffs were as thick as padding, the shoulder seams hung almost to her elbows and the thick fleecy fabric ballooned out below the belt.

"I look like a dysfunctional circus act," She said, grinning from ear to ear.

Juno angled his head to one side. "Uh-huh, but I like it, you look different."

He stood rooted to the spot impaling her with his eyes. Her heart was pumping furiously and she felt as if she were a paralyzed rabbit caught in a car's headlights. He reached out and glossed the back of his knuckles over her cheek. She closed her eyes and swayed. Electricity surged through her veins as he took a step forward and circled her waist with his arm, pulling her close. His body heat filtered through the thick sweatshirt and her head fell back on her shoulders.

Delicious sensations, dormant for months, overwhelmed her as his lips hovered over hers for agonizing seconds before pressing against them. His hands caressed her back and hips and her arms crept around his neck as the kiss deepened. They clung to each other, their breathing hard and her bones felt as if they were melting.

"Alex," he murmured close to her ear, the word coming out in a breathy gust. "Damn you, Alex, this wasn't in the plan, this wasn't meant to happen."

She tunneled her fingers through his hair as he swung her off her feet and carried her to the bed. She knew this was madness, but it was what she needed right now, what she had dreamed of for so long.

His palms coasted up her thighs lifting the sweatshirt while her fingers traced the tufts of dark hair visible at the 'V' neck of his shirt. The oversized boxer shorts slid easily over her hips and she caught her breath as his fingertips charted the smooth, silkiness of her inner thighs.

He made a low, satisfied sound deep in his chest as she leaned forward and kissed his neck, his cheek, and his lips. Warmth soared through her body as his hands pushed the sweatshirt and tank top higher and he kissed her breasts, gently tugging her nipples with his teeth. Desire was a whimper in her throat as he unzipped his jeans and rolled them over his hips.

Alex's body was on fire as Juno lifted the cumbersome sweatshirt over her head and leaned over her, his arm muscles taut with the strain. Their eyes melted together and his blazed into her brain. He flicked his tongue softly over her lips and she moaned in pleasure, letting exquisite rivers of desire devour her.

She felt his warm, rigid flesh between her thighs. He gently prized apart her legs with his knee and she raised her hips to meet the first thrust of his sex. His entry was swift and deep and she rolled her hips, welcoming his rhythmic penetration. An avalanche of emotions overwhelmed her and she tried to draw him deeper, her hands clutching his buttocks. Blinding passion swamped her as their movements escalated and she thought she would dissolve with pleasure.

The erogenous parts of her body pulsed with luxuriant sensations and her ears pulsated with the drumming of her heartbeat. From between clenched teeth, Juno uttered a curse word before his body tensed and then relaxed with deep rippling vibrations.

He rolled onto his side and they lay facing each other while he rained small staccato kisses on her lips. His breath ghosted across her cheek as he pulled her into his arms, the full length of their bodies touching. Soaked in pleasure, she traced his features with her fingertips, and he grabbed and sucked her index finger when she touched his lips.

She smiled and a ripple of laughter gurgled in his throat. Then her face became serious. "Juno?" Her eyes searched his.

"Are you cold?"

"Na-ugh," she shook her head. "I shouldn't have let this happen—"

"Why not? We're both consenting adults. I for one enjoyed it. Didn't you?"

Alex felt as if he'd kicked her in the gut. She'd hoped he had some small feelings for her, but his casual attitude cut her to the quick, and it took her all her time not to cry.

"Yes, it was fine," she turned away and pulled the sweatshirt back over her head, fastening the belt around her waist. Inside, she was dying. She loved Juno and he was acting as if she were just another notch on his belt.

Alex was walking into to the bathroom when the doorbell rang. Juno gathered his jeans around his hips and hurried from the room. Closing the bathroom door, Alex leaned against it and gave a sob. Why had she thought Juno cared for her? He was a notorious womanizer, loving and leaving females at will. She felt a fool and wished she could turn back the clock, but you can't unring the bell.

Once she'd washed her hands and face and straightened her hair, she returned to the bedroom just as Juno entered.

"Oh, there you are. Come on through, Lieutenant Walker's here with a woman officer."

When Alex entered the room, the lieutenant was leaning on the mantle shelf smoking a cigarette and speaking in undertones to a slim, woman officer. The lieutenant flung the remnants of his smoke into the cinders before lunging forward and pumping her arm. "Alex, it's good to see you. Juno's just finished telling us about how he found you outside. What happened to your hands?"

Alex looked down at the Band-Aids. "I must have cut them when I brushed the glass off the car seat. Juno very kindly patched me up."

Her eyes met Juno's and he gave a mock bow. She sat on a leather chair and took the mug of coffee he offered.

"This is Sergeant LaTour," Walker said, slicing a hand toward the woman officer. "Now perhaps you can bring us up to date with what happened earlier this evening."

Breath filtered through Alex's teeth in a long sigh as she gripped the hot drink and related the details of Clancy's death. By the time she'd described the events, scalding tears clogged her throat and clouded her vision.

During her recital, Juno rested his chin on one hand, his eyes pinned to her face, while Sergeant LaTour took notes. They all lapsed into a weighty silence and Alex divided a scared look between the two men.

Then Lieutenant Walker spoke. "I hate to say this, Alex, but there's only one thing left to do." His eyes bounced between her and Juno. "To trap this bastard, you're going to have to act as bait."

Chapter 22

Lieutenant Walker and Minnie described what she needed to do. They were both still convinced that one of the three remaining suspects was the man they wanted, so they recommended Alex give the impression that she didn't have a care in the world and encourage each of them to deepen their relationship with her.

When she'd voiced her uneasiness, Lieutenant Walker had offered her the alternative of going away somewhere safe and not returning until the killer was caught.

"I couldn't do that. Two people have already died because this psycho wants me dead."

"This is probably the best way to flush him out," Minnie LaTour confirmed. "I know it isn't going to be easy, but we really need your help, and we'll work out a way to protect you."

Alex contemplated this for a short time. "Okay, but I just hope I live long enough to discover who this bastard is. I'd like the chance to come face to face with him and find out what he has against me."

Minnie smiled and nodded. "Good for you. We'd like to know the reasons behind this vendetta, too. I'll give you a call on your cell phone tomorrow and let you know what we've set up."

After the two police officers left, Alex felt uncomfortable. Juno acted as he always did, cool and friendly. When he spoke, his words held no trace of softness and no indication that a short time ago they'd been lovers. Her eyes toured his face but no pertinent emotions lingered there.

"Would you like some more coffee?" He asked, brandishing a glass pot.

"No thanks, I really should be going."

His eyebrows arched in incredulity. "Going? But where?"

His last question brought home the fact that she had nowhere to go. She couldn't go back to the mobile home where Clancy had been killed, and she didn't want to return to her house where Barbara had died.

"I'll get some of my things and probably go to a hotel. Do you have any gas I can borrow?" Although she spoke these words calmly, anger was building inside at Juno's blasé attitude.

"Sure, I always keep a spare can in the shed, but why go haring off to a hotel when you can stay here?"

She was gob smacked. Instead of allowing him to know her true reaction, she blurted. "Where's your dog?"

A closed expression passed over his face. "I no longer have him. It won't take me long to get the guest room ready. What do you say?"

"I'd say I'm a Jonah. Two people have already died because of me and I don't want anyone else getting hurt."

He quirked an eyebrow at her. "There you go fretting about me again."

Fresh anger ripped through her at his satisfied smirk. "Not really. I'm more interested in keeping my conscience clear."

His lips curved in a smile. "Don't bother about me. I can take care of myself. Will you at least stay tonight? Then in the morning, you can go to a hotel if you want, but I don't relish the idea of going out in this awful weather to put gas in your car and drive it up to the house."

Her brief entanglement with Juno had bruised her heart and filled her with hopeless longing and the last thing she wanted was to be in close proximity to him for the next twelve hours, but his proposal made sense.

She peeped out the window at the rain still battering down. "Thank you, I'd like to stay. Point me in the direction of the guest room and I'll get settled in."

She tailed Juno along a hallway to the guest bedroom. With pale blue wallpaper and coordinating quilt and shams, she marveled at his taste in décor. "This is nice. Did you do your own decorations?"

"Lord no, Petra had this and the master bedroom done for me."

"Oh," disappointment speared through her. So, Petra had designed the master bedroom to her taste, which implied that she stayed there frequently. Perhaps Juno intended to marry her. He hadn't introduced her as his fiancée, but many couples never got engaged, only married.

"The bathroom's through there," he gestured to a door. "It's not as big as the master, but I think you'll find it adequate. Do you need anything else?"

"No thanks, I have everything I need." '*Except you,*' she wanted to add, but didn't.

He paused in the doorway and looked back. "I'll see you in the morning, then. Do you want me to give you a call?"

"No, I'm not even sure I'll sleep, but thanks."

He closed the door and she sat on the bed feeling very alone, Juno filled her mind and her life. Being close to him in his house was purgatory, especially since they'd made love. Tomorrow she'd tell Sergeant LaTour where she was and find a hotel.

Alex pulled the over-sized sweatshirt over her head and climbed into bed wearing the tank top and boxers. The quilt was light and warm nestling around her body. Her last thought before she fell asleep was that her quest to help flush out the killer would give her some respite and help take her mind off Juno.

Alex breezed into the lobby of the *Everyday* magazine building and acknowledged the receptionist's welcome. During the ride in the elevator and the walk to her office, everyone greeted her warmly. Inside, she was trembling and her stomach churned. She still found it hard to believe that Brett, Charlie or Darren Winters was the perpetrator. After unlocking her office door and dumping her purse on the desk, thudding footsteps sounded in the hallway, and Charlie burst in.

"Alex, honey, why didn't you tell us you were coming back so soon? Brett said you'd be gone for weeks." He bent and kissed her cheek.

"I finished my business sooner than expected. How are you, Charlie? You look tired."

His lips formed a moue. "It's this libel case, I haven't been sleeping well. But, never mind me, how are you?"

Alex feigned a bright smile. "I'm great, never better. I hope you have a good story for me to get my teeth into, I'm raring to work."

"I'm afraid not, we didn't include you in this month's schedule, but I'm sure I can find you something good to get your teeth into."

Her heart gave a skip of anticipation. "Why don't I do a story on these recent murders? I could contact the lieutenant in charge and find out what leads he's following."

Charlie's eyebrows leapt up before they fused in a frown. "That's not such a good idea. We've tried doing stories on murder cases before, but they've always been vetoed. The police won't want the killer knowing how their investigation's progressing. No, I'm sure I can find you something better. Come to my office in a couple of hours." He squeezed her shoulder. "It's great having you back again." He leaned forward, pecked her on the cheek, and left.

Alex released a pent up sigh and wilted onto her chair. Acting as if everything was fine was exhausting. She was a jumble of nerves. The next thing was to visit Brett and sound out his reaction to her return. Then she planned to call Darren Winters to discuss his editorial and see how he responded to her relaxed, convivial attitude.

By mid-morning, Alex was bored stiff. She'd tried calling Darren Winters, but he was not available, so she left a message for him to return her call. Charlie was ensconced with legal bigwigs about the libel case and anticipated he'd be tied up most of the day, so it was a nice surprise when Brett burst into her office and gave her a hug.

"Alex, I couldn't believe it when Norma told me you were in work today. I guess you got the legal things tied up after the funeral quicker than you thought."

"Yes, everything turned out to be quite straight forward. John was a very organized person."

Brett hitched his left hip onto the corner of her desk and let his right leg swing loose. "You look depressed. Are you okay?"

Alex gave a false smile. "Sure, I did my mourning for John many months ago and I know he'd want me to get on with my life, so I've taken the first step and returned to work."

"And what you need now is to take step two and get out."

Alex's heart tripped over a few heartbeats. "Is that an invitation?"

Brett's eyes opened wide. "You mean you'd come out with me?"

"Sure, why not, we had some good times together." She grimaced. "It wouldn't be a proper date, just two work colleagues having dinner."

Brett's face flushed and he sprang off the desk. "Absolutely, how about tonight?"

"How about tomorrow, I have something arranged this evening."

"You're on. Gee Alex, you don't know how happy this makes me, wait until I tell mother. Think about where you'd like to go, and call me later." He hugged her and bounced out the door.

The rest of the day continued to drag and at four o'clock, Minnie LaTour phoned. The lieutenant had arranged for the sergeant to keep an eye on Alex and follow her wherever she went. This did nothing to allay Alex's fears. After all, the killer had wiped out Clancy with one single bullet and he could easily do the same with Minnie.

Alex woke once again in Juno's guest bed. This was the second night she'd spent there and knowing he was around made her feel safe. Her first day back at the office had been mundane and straightforward. Tonight she was going out with Brett. She'd called him the previous afternoon and proposed dinner at Luigi's, her favorite Italian restaurant.

She sashayed through to the kitchen in her terry robe and made a pot of coffee. After Juno had put enough gas in her car to get her back to the mobile home, she'd driven there to pack her things before taking her car in for repair, and picking up a rental. She still didn't know why she hadn't gone to a hotel—yes she did—she wanted to be close to Juno even although he had no feelings for her.

She sensed a movement behind and spun round to see the object of her thoughts leaning against the doorjamb watching her. "Good morning. How did you sleep?" He asked, his is dark hair tumbling over one eye.

"Fine, it's a very comfortable bed." She reached for two mugs, poured coffee into both and held one out to him.

He sauntered over and stood looking down at her, ignoring the mug in her hand. "My bed's even better." He leaned one arm on the counter bringing his face very close to hers.

"Oh and why would I need to know that?" She felt her face flush and her breath catch in her throat.

He stood in front of her, trapping her against the kitchen island and took both mugs from her, placing them on the counter. His warm breath drifted over her face, as he bracketed her jaw with one hand, and leaned forward to press his lips to hers. He lifted his head, his face still close to hers, and his eyes fenced with hers for a moment.

"No reason, I wanted you to know that I only buy quality furnishings." He picked up a mug and took a sip of coffee. "I won't be in this evening, I have a meeting, but I should be back by ten."

"I won't be here either. I'm having dinner with Brett."

"Lucky man. How far are you willing to go to trap this killer?"

To cover her frustration, she picked up the other mug and rolled it between her palms.

"What I do is no business of yours. Just because you've been kind enough to let me stay for a couple of nights, gives you no rights to question my morality. I'm getting my car back later today, so once I've collected my things, I'll move into a hotel."

He lifted his shoulders a fraction. "That's your choice, but you can stay here for as long as you like."

"Well, I don't think Petra will be very happy when she discovers I've been staying here."

"This is my house, I do as I please and anyway, Petra and I are through."

Her heart took on an extra beat at his words and her toes began to tingle. Now she was in a quandary. She liked it here with Juno, but felt it would be foolish to stay because if he made advances toward her again, she knew she wasn't strong enough to reject him. She loved him with all her heart, but it was a hopeless love.

He stood back and stretched. "Well, don't make any hasty decisions, the offer still stands to stay. See you later."

All day at work, Alex debated about whether to continue staying at Juno's or go to a hotel. Her heart wanted her to stay, but her head told her she shouldn't. Right now, she needed her wits about her if she was going to help the police catch this killer. By four o'clock she was exhausted and opted to stay where she was for the time being. She'd have to make sure that she acted aloof and didn't allow her feelings to escalate out of control.

After she picked up her car from the repair shop, she drove back to Juno's, took a shower and washed her hair. By the time she'd dressed and applied her make up, her stomach was turning cartwheels. She felt as if she were an undercover agent for the C.I.A. on an important mission. Although she knew Minnie LaTour was tailing her, and probably sitting outside waiting for her to leave, she hadn't spotted a car following her back from work. Satisfied with her appearance, she shrugged on a light jacket on the way to her car.

Brett was already in the foyer when she arrived at Luigi's. He smiled and bent to kiss her cheek. "You look lovely, Alex, but you always do. I hope you're hungry, they have some great specials tonight."

A seating hostess led the way to the back of the restaurant and showed them to a quiet booth with a bottle of Champagne cooling in an ice bucket.

Alex threw Brett a quelling look. "There was no need for Champagne, it's so expensive."

"Nothing's too good for you and besides, this is a celebration, we're back together again."

Oh dear, this was what she'd been afraid of. Sometimes Brett's world was a million miles from reality. She thought she'd made it clear that this wasn't a real date, just two friends having dinner.

He insisted on sitting next to her and placing his arm around her shoulder. His right hand kept straying to her thigh and she removed it several times, but he was persistent. Alex receded into the corner of the booth, Brett's closeness suffocating her.

"I think you should sit over there?" She proclaimed, pointing to the banquette opposite. "Then I can look at you when we talk and we'll both have more room to eat."

A hurt expression crossed his face. "You don't want me sitting next to you?"

"Not when we're about to eat spaghetti and meat balls," she laughed. "You have no idea what a messy eater I can be."

He moved away and relocated to the other side of the table. "Sorry, would you like some Champagne?" She nodded and he filled her flute almost full. He raised his glass. "To us, here's to getting back together again."

She took a sip of champagne and placed her flute on a coaster. "We're not back together again, Brett. I told you we're two friends having dinner."

"I know, but this is just the start of things to come. Now that you're free again, we might even end up getting married this time."

Alex stared at the bubbles floating upward in her glass, trying to find the right words to say. "Look Brett, you're not the only man I like. There's Charlie—"

"Charlie? You must be joking—he's way too old for you."

"Fifteen years isn't that much difference and besides, he loves me."

Brett's face clouded with anger and he drew his brows together in a demonic scowl. "Then why are you leading me on like this? I thought you wanted us to get back together again."

"You're the one that said that, not me. I told you I'd come out with you as a friend."

"What about Charlie? Is he more than a friend?"

Alex pondered the question. "He might be, he's been very good to me."

Brett bunched his jaw. He leaned over the table and spoke in a menacing voice. "I thought you were different from other women, but you're just the same as all the others, a little whore." He stood and turned to go. "I should have listened to my mother, she sussed you out from day one. Go and play your little games with someone else."

Alex blinked in amazement as he whipped round and hastened out. Tonight Brett had shown her a side she never suspected existed. She went over their conversation many times and wondered if she could have handled the situation differently. When the server arrived with their meals, she asked her to put them in a box. Once she'd paid the check, she carried the boxes to the car and drove off.

The next day, Darren Winters was waiting for her when she arrived at the office.

"Hi," he greeted her with a wide smile. "It's nice to see you again. Did you enjoy your vacation?"

"Who said I was on vacation? I had some time off to arrange my husband's funeral and to deal with legal matters."

Darren's face turned the color of putty. "Oh, my God, I'm so sorry, I must have misunderstood. I came by your office to see you about the editorial, and a young woman mentioned something about a vacation, so I thought she meant you."

"That's okay. The police said John must have died when he first went missing. I think I already knew he was dead, but it was still a shock when the police told me. Won't you sit down and I'll make us some coffee."

Darren remained standing while Alex filled the coffee machine with water and scooped grounds into the filter. She was conscious of his eyes following her every move and shivered as a twinge of uneasiness skittered through her.

"Are you cold?" He asked, walking round the desk toward her.

She took a step backward and rearranged the cups on the tray. "No, I'm fine. Sometimes I shiver when I feel a blast of cool air from the A/C. I'm a real hot house plant and keep mine much higher at home."

Today her nerves were raw and Darren's nearness troubled her. His face no longer looked boyish, his cheekbones seemed more angular and his whole face had a harder appearance. Alex filled two cups with coffee and set them down on the front of her desk with a bowl of sugar and some pots of cream. Now with the width of the desk between them, the tension left her shoulders and her confidence returned.

"Cream?" Darren brandished one of the small pots.

"No thanks, I take it black." Alex drew one of the cups toward her and stirred in some sugar. "I'm glad you liked the editorial, I hope it'll generate a lot more business for the company."

"When people phone, I've told Vera to ask clients where they heard about us and several have said they've read the editorial, so it looks as if it's already paying off. You did a great job."

"That's what I'm here for," she quipped.

"And what I'm here for is to see if you'll come to the theater with me. I have two tickets for Nana Mouskouri at the Van Wezel on Thursday. Will you come?"

A tiny thrill ran through her. She'd always admired the Greek singer and had several of her CDs. "What time does it start?"

"Eight o'clock."

She made a few, quick calculations. If she left the office at five, arrived at Juno's by six, she still had enough time to have a quick shower, change and drive to Sarasota in time for the concert. "Yes, I'd love to. I'll meet you outside the main doors at seven forty-five."

Darren's face softened and became boyish again when he beamed with pleasure. "It's a date." He reached for his coffee cup and emptied it in one gulp. "I'll see you Thursday."

Chapter 23

Alicia and Martin Anderson were eating breakfast seated on white, wrought iron chairs on their lanai that overlooked a kidney-shaped swimming pool. A young Cuban man wearing a large-brimmed, straw hat was pruning shrubs while another in similar garb retrieved leaves from the pool with a net.

Martin spooned a segment of juicy, pink grapefruit into his mouth as he watched his wife staring vacantly into thin air. "Not hungry, dear?" She jumped at the sound of his voice.

"No, I think I'll skip breakfast and have an early lunch. It's my bridge afternoon at the club."

Martin nodded. He pushed his empty dish away and reached for a pot of yogurt. He continued observing his wife while he ripped off the foil lid. For the last few days, she'd been preoccupied, not responding immediately to anything he said. The time had come for a confrontation.

He placed his yogurt pot down and took a sip of coffee. "You really should eat something. There's no point in crying over spilt milk."

Her eyes sliced directly to him. "What do you mean?"

He reached over and took her hand. "You've not been the same since those police officers paid you a visit."

Her face blanched. "Those police officers? What do you mean?"

"I'm not entirely stupid, Alicia, is Balthy in trouble?"

She looked down and motioned the negative.

"Is it Carlos?"

Again, she shook her head.

He allowed a few seconds to pass before he spoke. "Well, that only leaves the twins."

Alicia gave a strangled cry and buried her face in her hands. He waited until her shoulders had stopped shaking with silent sobs before he scraped his chair round to her side of the table and placed an arm around her.

She laid her head on his chest and soon his polo shirt was damp with warm tears. "You know?" She sat upright and wiped her eyes. "How long have you known?"

"Years, Teresa told me."

"My sister told you. Why?"

"Because she thought I had a right to know. It was not long after Emily died and Carlos had disappeared. I have to admit it came as a big shock." He looked her straight in the eyes. "For years, I've hoped you'd tell me."

Her eyes glossed with tears. "I'm sorry, I always wanted to, but I was so sure you'd hate me. I know how much you and Emily wanted children of your own."

"Did David know?"

"Yes. He'd been in Japan for nearly five months when I discovered I was pregnant, so he knew the baby couldn't be his." She smiled and kissed Martin's cheek. "It must have happened that summer you, me and Emily went to Cape Cod. Remember how she always liked to go fishing with the Taylor's and we spent each afternoon in bed?"

He smiled and nodded. "I often wonder if she knew about us. If she did, she never gave any indication."

"David had no idea until I became pregnant. We had a huge argument, he took off for Europe with Balthy, and I came down here to stay with Teresa. I had a difficult pregnancy, and after I put the twins up for adoption, I went home."

Martin cuddled her and remained silent as she continued.

"I hurt David very badly. For months, we slept in separate rooms and never spoke about you and me. Finally, we sat down and had a long talk. It was very civilized. He asked me to be totally honest with him, so I told him everything—how we'd been lovers for years—and how much I loved you."

Martin waggled his head in disbelief. Until the day David died, his attitude toward him had never changed and he wondered if he could have been that magnanimous if it had been Emily who'd been having a long-term affair. The strange thing was that he loved Emily as much as he loved Alicia, and he knew that Alicia loved David as much as him. They were two people trapped in a love triangle.

Alicia sighed. "The police came to verify I was the twins' mother, the lieutenant said they were in danger."

"Did he say what kind?"

"No, I was so taken aback by their visit, I couldn't think straight. Anyway, it's not my business now. I relinquished all rights to them when I gave them away."

He saw the glitter of tears on her lashes and his heart went out to her. "You're still their mother. Wouldn't you like to meet them?"

"I don't know. They may hate me for what I did."

"Well, *I'd* like to see them, so I'm going to contact the police and find out what I can. I think it's time we met our daughters and got to know them."

Alicia threw herself into his arms and began sobbing again.

Zack Walker managed to stifle his surprise when a rookie announced that Alicia and Martin Anderson were waiting to see him. He cleared a pile of papers off a chair and placed it next to a vacant one, so that Martin Anderson could sit next to his wife. Once the rookie had left the room and the Andersons sat, he spoke. "Now, how can I help you folks?"

"We want you to tell us where the twins are, we want to meet them." Martin said.

"What's brought this on?" Zack scowled at Alicia, "You said your husband didn't know about them."

"I didn't think he did, but my sister told him a long time ago, and we've decided we'd like to meet our daughters."

Zack sighed and worked his face into a grimace. This was the last thing he'd expected, now he had to bring these people up to date with what had been happening. He inhaled deeply and related everything.

Alicia's face crumbled and she started crying when she learned that someone had murdered Diane. Martin embraced his wife and asked with a scared look. "And the other twin?"

Zack smiled. "She's fine, a real feisty lady."

He offered the Andersons a cigarette before lighting one for himself and inhaling deeply. "Would you guys like some coffee?" he asked as he perched on the edge of his desk.

"No thanks," Martin relaxed, crossing one leg over the other.

Zack leaned back and steepled his fingers. Some things about this case were beginning to make sense, but others were still mystifying. This perpetrator was hell bent on harming Alex Martell and no one knew why. Was it because of her connections to the Andersons who were wealthy, or was it something to do with her late husband? Too many questions remained unanswered for his liking.

He puffed his cheeks out in exasperation. "Do you have any children, Mr. Anderson?"

"Yes, an adopted son, Carlos."

"Tell me about him."

Martin shrugged. "What would you like to know?"

"Where he's living."

Alicia's indigo eyes opened wide. "You think he's got something to do with all this?"

"To tell you the truth Mrs. Anderson, I don't know. Because we have no suspects, we suspect everyone. For instance, it's quite a coincidence that you suddenly decided you wanted to meet your daughter when she's in danger. Now that makes me wonder if it's connected to what's been happening—"

"But you were the one that told me about Alex. I only—"

Zack held up his hands to silence Alicia. "I'm sorry I didn't mean to infer that you or your husband was involved. Now tell me about Carlos."

Martin Anderson's lips thinned as he began talking about his adopted son. Zack listened and made notes while Martin told him he didn't know Carlos's whereabouts and related his son's misdemeanors. The last time Carlos had phoned his father was seven years earlier.

"You never told me." Alicia said.

"There was no need, my dear. All he said was that he'd moved and was no longer living in New York and that he'd send me his new address. Well, I never heard from him again, so I've no idea where he is now."

"What about his appearance?"

Martin drew his brows together in a deep frown. "Carlos has always been a smart dresser. He's almost six feet tall, 175 pounds and I would imagine he's still in good shape. He was in the military and a fitness fanatic."

"Hair?"

"Brown, always very short or in a crew cut."

"Eyes?"

"Brown, like mine."

"Would you say he has a temper?"

"Most definitely. That was one of the things my wife didn't like about adopting a child. She always said that you never knew what kind of genes were inbred in a child. As it turned out, Carlos had some bad blood in him, but I'm sure he'd never do anybody any real harm."

Zack finished writing his notes and stretched his back. "Have you made a will Mr. Anderson?"

"Of course."

"May I ask if Carlos is the only beneficiary?"

"You may ask, but I don't think it's any of your business."

"It is when someone's life's at stake. Who are the beneficiaries under your will Mr. Anderson?"

Alicia tucked her arm through Martin's and cooed. "Tell him darling. It's no secret."

Martin glowered at Zack. "On my death, half my estate goes to my wife and the other half is divided equally between Carlos, Diane and Alex."

Zack's insides churned—this could be the connection. "So now Diane's dead, one half will be divided between Carlos and Alex and if Alex dies, Carlos will get one half instead of one third of one half."

All the time he spoke Alicia's eyes grew wider and her look more incredulous. "You never told me the twins were in your will." She accused Martin.

He turned to his wife with a tender look. "Once your sister told me about them, I included them in my will. I didn't mention it because I kept hoping you'd tell me about them."

While the Andersons continued bantering, a thought struck Zack. If Carlos was the killer, Alicia's life might also be in danger. With her and Alex dead, Carlos would inherit everything once Martin died. His stomach was queasy with dread. Could Carlos be callous enough to murder the whole family? He became conscious of two pairs of eyes watching him, so he coughed and continued.

"Is the white Mercedes the only car you own, Mr. Anderson?"

"Yes, and my wife drives a Cabriolet. I don't see the need for us to have any more than two cars. Why?"

Zack ignored the question. "And I presume you keep both cars well maintained?"

"Naturally. Why is this important, Lieutenant?"

Zack took a deep breath and decided not to enlighten them about his hunch. "It's not. I was just making a general inquiry. With the price of gas now, two cars are quite enough to keep on the road."

Whereas what he'd really wanted to say was, 'Because both your lives may be in danger and the ideal way to get rid of you at the same time would be a car accident.'

Instead, he continued with his interrogation. "What else can you tell me about Carlos? Does he know the contents of your will?"

Martin snorted. "I shouldn't think so, but then—"

Zack watched a troubled look cross Martin's face. "You've thought of something else?"

"There was an incident several years ago while Carlos was living with us when the safe was broken into and some valuable antiques went missing from the house, but Carlos swore he'd nothing to do with it."

"Was your will in the safe?"

"Yes, it and other documents were stolen along with some money."

Zack stretched out his arms, palms to the ceiling and shrugged. "I rest my case."

By now, Alicia's face was as white as a sheet and Martin knitted his brows with annoyance. "I think you're barking up the wrong tree, Lieutenant. This is my son we're speaking about. He'd never steal anything or try to kill someone."

"Adopted son, Mr. Anderson, not a blood relation."

Lilies of Death

Neither Alicia nor Martin appeared to follow his line of thinking and Zack was glad. The last thing he wanted was to alarm them, but Carlos was looking more and more like the man they wanted.

"Can you provide us with a recent photo of your son?" Zack asked.

Martin shook his head. "Not recent. The only ones I have were all taken before he left twenty years ago."

Zack's hopes sank. Why did nothing go the way he wanted? He shrugged. "Well, when you get back home, send us what you have. It's just routine anyway."

After the Andersons left, Zack berated himself. What if he was wrong and Carlos was innocent? Somehow, this explanation was the most feasible. The problem was that no one had seen Carlos for years and chances were he'd changed his appearance, so even his immediate family might not recognize him. Alex certainly wouldn't know who he was. Now, he'd discarded the initial theory that the killer was one of the men Alex knew, he decided to concentrate on his latest hunch.

He set the wheels in motion by allocating several detectives the job of tracing Carlos Anderson. If they could discover where he was living, they'd be able to eliminate him from their inquiries. The more Zack thought about it, the more he was convinced there was a big chance that Carlos was their man. The detective to whom he assigned the neighboring counties gawped at him as if he'd just landed from outer space.

"Are you sure, sir? Why would a son living in close proximity to his father not contact him?"

Zack didn't want to go into his reasons. "Just do it, Wilson and let me know what you find out."

In his hotel room, the insistent ringing of the phone jarred Martin Anderson from a deep sleep. He fumbled for the bedside lamp and grabbed the receiver. Loud babbling filled his ear. "Hold on a minute. Is that you Alfonso?"

"Si Senor, something very bad has happened."

Heart pumping with apprehension, Martin sat bolt upright. "What?"

"The house, Senor, a fire."

By now, Alicia was wide-awake and clutching the covers under her chin.

"How bad? Are you hurt?"

"No, Senor. It is a hot night, so Maria and me were asleep on the lanai. A loud noise woke us, an explosion. We fled, but the house she is almost destroyed. We called 911 and the police and fire truck came quick, but the fire is so bad, the house is in ruins."

Martin ran a hand over his brow. "Thank you, Alfonso. You and Maria check into a hotel and get them to call me here for a credit card number. The main thing is that you're both all right."

"But, your beautiful house. Who would do such a thing?"

"I don't know, but a house can be fixed. You check into a hotel and call me in the morning."

"Thank you Senor."

Martin hung up and turned to a white-faced Alicia. "There's been an accident, a fire at the house. Alfonso and Maria are okay, but according to what he says, there's not much of the house left."

With a sharp intake of breath, Alicia covered her mouth with her hand.

Martin read fear in her eyes.

"Do you think it was deliberate?" she asked in a shaky voice.

Martin stared into Alicia's eyes. "Alfonso said there was an explosion, so it sounds very like arson to me."

"But who—?"

"I don't know, but at least Alfonso and Maria are all right. There's nothing we can do right now, so let's try to get back to sleep."

He doused the light, but knew he wouldn't be able to sleep. Every part of their conversation that afternoon with Lieutenant Walker bounced about in his brain. His mind worked overtime as he dwelled on the questions the lieutenant had asked. By the time it was dawn, he'd figured out what Walker had been getting at. All these questions about his will and if Carlos knew the contents, could mean only one thing, his son was a suspect.

Chapter 24

Thursday was a terrible day. Charlie was in a bad mood; Brett ignored Alex and her computer's hard drive crashed. She ended up writing an article on a typewriter, which took her twice as long as usual, because she constantly needed to alter some of the paragraphs, and she had to retype them again. For the first time she appreciated modern technology. By the time five o'clock came, she was more than ready to leave the office, and was looking forward to her evening at the theater.

Everywhere was quiet when she arrived at Juno's house. She covered her hair with a waterproof cap, took a quick shower and nibbled on a sandwich while she dressed in a lightweight cream suit.

The drive to Sarasota was uneventful and although she had to park in the northern parking lot farthest away from the Van Wezel auditorium, she still arrived on time. With her back to the main door, her eyes scanned eager faces approaching, but Darren was nowhere in sight. A hand touched her shoulder and she swung round to see him grinning and holding out a purple teddy bear. "I bought this for you."

"Thank you, he's lovely," she cuddled it close. "I'm going to call him Posh Paws."

They joined the line to enter the auditorium and found their seats. Right on time the performance began and Alex soon forgot her life was in danger as she sat in the darkness encompassed by melodic songs and music. She was entranced as Nana's beautiful soprano voice filled the theater and transported her away from her troubles.

All too soon, the concert ended and they filed from the theater, stepping into the cool, night air. In the parking lot, they paused by her car.

"Do you want to go on somewhere? There's a nice wine bar on Main Street where we could have something to eat."

Alex hesitated; it was almost ten o'clock. She knew she should fraternize with Darren, but she didn't want to be back too late. "I'd like that. Where's your car?" He gestured further up the same aisle they were standing in. "I'll wait 'til you back out and then I'll follow you."

While Darren walked to his car, Alex looked around hoping to catch a glimpse of Minnie LaTour. Everything appeared normal, so she climbed into the Chevy and waited until Darren's car passed before tailing him.

The wine bar had its own parking lot, so they pulled into adjacent bays and climbed out. Darren requested seats in the non-smoking section and a young man led them to a cozy table at the back of the room away from a musician playing a guitar. Alex took the offered menu and ordered a diet soda.

"Is that all you want?" Darren asked. "Why not have some wine?"

"No thanks, I'm driving and besides, if I drink alcohol at this time of night, I'm likely to fall asleep at the wheel."

Darren ordered a beer and moved closer. "It's nice here, isn't it? I used to come a lot at one time. What would you like to eat?"

Alex perused the menu and ordered a selection of onion rings, chicken nuggets, and breaded shrimp with a thick, spicy dip. Their server brought their drinks and Alex sipped her soda through a straw while Darren poured a half-full glass of frothy beer.

He raised his glass. "Well, here's to many more evenings like this."

Alex touched his glass with hers. "Thanks for the concert, I really enjoyed it."

He leaned closer, his eyes boring into hers. "This is the best evening I've had in a long time. I hope this is the start of things to come."

She lowered her eyes. "Yes I hope so, too."

The guitarist was playing a slow, love song and several couples were dancing in front of the stage. Darren reached for her hand, helped her to her feet and led her between the tables. Placing both hands round her waist, he pulled her close and Alex had nowhere to put her arms except around his neck. One of Darren's hands moved up and down her back urging her closer.

Alex relaxed and let her head fall onto his shoulder. He turned his head and dropped a kiss on her cheek. Suddenly, his body stiffened and Alex raised her head meeting the venom-filled eyes of Brett Etheridge. Darren moved to one side and Brett assumed Darren's former position.

"So, is he the reason you won't get back together with me?" Brett inquired through clenched teeth.

Alex had a sinking feeling in her stomach at the fury on Brett's face. "No, this is the first time I've been out with Darren, I hardly know him. He has nothing to do with us."

Brett's lip curled in a sneer as they slowly danced around the floor. "Well, you looked mighty cozy to me for a first date. I don't remember you being so *responsive* on our first date."

"I'm not being responsive. I was relaxing and dancing to the music." She pulled away and glared at him. "As far as I'm concerned, you and I are finished. What I do in my free time has nothing to do with you." She turned on her heel and marched back to join Darren at their table.

"Who was that?" He asked when she returned to her chair.

"Someone I work with. We dated for a couple of years before I was married and now he thinks we should pick up where we left off and start over. I'm sorry he interrupted our dance."

Darren lifted his shoulders in a shrug. "It doesn't matter. Did he upset you?"

"No, I'm fine." Alex dipped an onion ring into the thick sauce and took a sip of soda. "You can relax, now, I think he's gone."

Darren glanced over his shoulder and watched Brett flounce out the door with his face pinched in anger.

The tempo of the music had changed, couples moved in time to the lively tune and Alex tapped her toes. She was conscious of Darren watching her so she smiled. "Would you mind very much if I left soon? It's getting late and I have a busy day ahead of me tomorrow."

Darren looked at his watch. "Good heavens, I hadn't realized it was so late. Of course we can go."

He signaled to the server, and once he'd settled the bill, he took her hand and they strolled outside to their cars. In the well-lit parking lot, Darren let out a cry. "Oh, no!" Alex followed the trajectory of his eyes. "Someone's slashed my tires." He bent to explore the damage.

Alex examined the other cars including hers, but they were all unharmed. "Are you in an auto club?"

Darren nodded. "But all they can do is give me a tow, there's nowhere to get a new set of tires at this time of night. Who would do such a thing? You don't think that guy you work with had anything to do with this do you?"

"How could he. He doesn't know which car's yours. No I think it's probably a random act of vandalism."

Inside Alex shuddered. This was another sign that someone was watching and following her. With her heart thudding in her chest and her mouth so dry she could hardly swallow, her eyes circumnavigated the vicinity. Minnie LaTour should be close by, so had she seen the culprit?

"I can give you a ride home," Alex offered.

"No it's too far out of your way. I'm sorry the evening ended like this, but I'll call the auto club and then get a taxi to take me home." He leaned forward and kissed her cheek. "I guess this is fate's way of telling us the evening's over. Maybe next time we can end it on a better note."

"I'd like that. Do you want me to stay?"

"Good Lord no, it's late enough, I'll call you tomorrow."

Darren waited until she was safely in her car before he waved and returned to the bar.

Although it was late, Alex was now wide-awake. Tonight had more or less proved that Darren wasn't the person the police were looking for. Unless he'd arranged for someone to slash his tires in a bid to throw the police off the track.

A swift glimpse in the rear view mirror established that a distant car was tailing her. For the rest of the drive, she kept monitoring it, and once she turned into Juno's drive, the car halted at the end of the road. Alex smiled. Lieutenant Walker had guaranteed that Minnie LaTour was the most skilled officer for surveillance, and he was right.

Alex parked round the back and entered the house through the kitchen door. The soft glow from a lamp in the living room trickled into the kitchen allowing her to define the shape of the cabinets. She stepped out of her shoes, tiptoed across the hardwood flooring in the hallway, and entered the living room.

Juno was asleep on the sofa, his dark hair falling over his brow, a deep frown on his face. She stood in the doorway studying his prone form. His polo top had ridden up revealing a firm, tanned torso, one leg drooped on the floor and an arm rested at his side, while the other dangled on his leg.

She had to control the urge to rush over and kiss his full, pouting lips. In sleep, Juno looked vulnerable with his taut expression and deep lines spidering from the corner of his tightly closed eyes. Slowly, she took a few steps forward her eyes never leaving his face.

Green-flecked eyes flew open and bored into hers. "You're late!" He barked.

Stunned by his sudden awakening, Alex couldn't speak for a moment. "We went for a drink," she declared at last.

"And afterward?" His dark brows rose in question as he sat up. "Did you go back to his place?"

"No, and even if I had, it's no business of yours."

He reached out and grabbed her hand pulling her down next to him on the sofa. "As long as you live here it is."

Alex shied away from him. "I'm not living here. I'm staying for a short while. And now I think about it, it's not such a good idea if you're going to question my comings and goings."

She went to get up, but he pulled her down beside him again. "Living or staying here, it makes no difference. While you're here, you should respect my feelings."

Alex turned to face him, anger growing inside. "Feelings, what feelings? You're the coldest person I've ever met. Even after we made love, you acted as if we hardly knew each other."

All the time she spoke his eyes were cold and dark boring into hers. He grabbed her by the shoulders and planted a kiss on her lips. She wanted to struggle free, but found herself melting against him, longing for the kiss to last forever.

He lifted his head and raised one eyebrow. "Is that what you want? Passion? Because I'm not much good at wooing women, I just do what comes naturally."

Alex was dying inside. This man was cold, her heart was torn and tattered, and yet he mocked her. She gulped to prevent tears that filled her eyes from falling. "I think I'd better leave in the morning. I'll do as I originally planned and check into a hotel."

She was almost at the living room door when he swung her round and in one smooth movement, lifted her into his arms. In total darkness, he carried her down the hallway and kicked open the master bedroom door, stumbling toward the bed. His closeness made her helpless to object. Her head swam as they fell onto the bed and his mouth ravaged hers. With urgency, he pushed her skirt up to her waist and kissed her vee through her panties. Her breath hissed as warmth spread through the lower half of her body. She wanted this man more than she'd ever wanted any other.

With his thumbs in the waistband, he worked her panties over her hips. By the silver light of the moon shining in the window, she could just make out his tense expression, as he wriggled out of his pants. His breath was warm as he pushed her thighs apart and the tip of his tongue caressed her sensitive, fleshy mound while his fingers probed her dewy cleft.

Alex stiffened and let her senses take over, splintering her with pleasure. She tunneled her fingers through his hair as her whole body tremored with desire. Unbearable heat swamped her as his tongue continued to transport her to the brink of a crashing climax.

"Juno!" She cried out, as his body moved up over her and he buried his penis deep inside her.

He made a sound deep in his chest as he began to move and Alex could hardly breathe. Her body was perilously close to exploding as she clawed at his buttocks and their bodies throbbed together. Drowning in pleasure, a small sough escaped from her throat, as her pulsating release was shattering.

Juno continued to move enhancing her climax further until he gasped, his whole body rippling and convulsing. They clung to each other, their breathing hard. He levered himself up and rolled onto his side. With a small movement, he brought her round to face him and their eyes made contact in the gloom. His arm curled around her drawing her lower body up against his and soon their mouths melded in a long, deep kiss.

When they broke apart, her entire being flooded with joy and she closed her eyes leaning her head on his shoulder. He kissed the top of her head before laying his against her. Alex's senses sang as she drifted off to sleep in the arms of the man she loved.

When Alex awoke next morning, she was under the covers naked and alone. She raised herself on her elbows and looked around the master bedroom. Then she remembered. Sometime during the night, Juno had removed the remainder of her clothing and made love to her again. Draped over a chair was a pair of his jeans and the polo shirt he'd worn the previous evening, her cream suit and underwear was neatly folded on the dresser.

She lounged back on the pillow stretching her arms high over her head as she relived their actions of the early hours. Juno had no feelings for her so she couldn't allow them to become intimate again. To keep her dignity, she must move out and go to a hotel after work today. The other side of the bed was still warm, so she rolled over and luxuriated in the afterglow of spending the night with the man she loved.

The bathroom door clicked and Juno swaggered in, a towel wound round the lower half of his body and water dripping from his hair. "Oh good, you're awake. I was just going to wake you. It's turned seven-thirty." When he spoke, he looked at her with tender eyes and a wave of emotion engulfed her.

"Thanks. Are you finished in the bathroom?"

He nodded and stood by the bed watching her.

"Do you have a robe I could use?"

He grinned. "Nah, we country folks don't have luxuries like that." He extended his hand toward the bathroom door.

She knew he was testing her, so she flung back the covers and strutted buck-naked into the bathroom. She leaned against the closed door, her heart thudding in her chest. Although they'd been intimate and spent the night together, she still felt shy in his presence. After all, they were little more than strangers.

Showered and with a towel wrapped around her body, she collected her clothes from the dresser, hurried along to the guest room where she dried her hair and dressed for the office.

In the kitchen, she helped herself to a mug of coffee from a pot keeping warm on the burner and shoved a slice of bread into the toaster. At the sound of a car engine revving, she rushed through to the living room in time to see Juno's dark sedan disappearing down the driveway. Hurt speared through her. He hadn't even stayed to say goodbye. She'd never met anyone as complex and she didn't know how to cope with his attitude or her feelings for him.

Because she wasn't expected at the office until later, she began packing some of her belongings and stacked the full suitcases behind the guest bedroom door.

On the drive to the office, her mind kept going over what had happened with Juno. For a brief period, she'd managed to forget her life was in danger and that any day she could die. Now she wanted so badly to live. She could love Juno from afar even if he didn't love her. No one could take away the memory of the times they'd made love, those would have to last her a lifetime.

Five minutes after she arrived in her office, Charlie strode in with a frown on his face. "Where were you last evening? I tried calling you on your cell phone three times."

"Sorry, I went to the theater to see Nana Mouskouri and I left my phone at home. Was it important?"

Charlie gazed at her with a surly expression. "I called until well after midnight."

"Yes, after the show we went downtown to a bar for a drink and stayed pretty late."

"We?"

She wasn't used to Charlie giving her the third degree and a ripple of confusion ran through her. Why did everyone suddenly want to know where she was?

"Darren Winters took me to the theater and we went for a nightcap afterwards. Did you phone for something special?"

"Darren Winters? That guy you wrote the editorial for? Why would you want to go to the theater with him?"

Alex didn't reply for a moment. She knew Charlie was in love with her but he still had no right to question her.

"Because he's a friend of Don's and I met him at Barbara's. He only had *Everyday* do his editorial because he knew me."

"You never mentioned before that you knew him. Are you lovers?"

Alex couldn't believe her ears. She gawped at Charlie. "Whether we are or not is no business of yours, I have every right to go out with anyone I choose."

Charlie sliced the air with his hands. "I'm sorry, Alex, but I was disturbed when I couldn't get hold of you. Of course you have a right to go out with who you choose." He gave a wan smile. "Just remember to come out with me sometime, too."

Alex relaxed and smiled. "Of course, I'm sorry you were worried. Maybe we can get together over the weekend?"

"I'd like that. I'll call you tomorrow."

Before she could analyze her conversation with Charlie, the phone rang and another busy morning flew by. Lunch was a quick sandwich delivered from the local deli, and the afternoon flew by with a long staff meeting. By five o'clock, she was more than ready to leave. Between her late night with Darren Winters and only having a few hours sleep, she was exhausted.

Chapter 25

Driving back to Juno's, Alex noticed distant headlights shadowing her and she smiled, that would be Minnie LaTour. She turned off the country road between the stone pillars and was surprised to see Juno's dark sedan, a white Mercedes and a police car parked in front of the house.

Inside the hallway, she ventured through the archway into the living room where four pairs of eyes watched her entrance. She studied Lieutenant Walker standing by the window and Juno leaning on the mantle shelf, his face chiseled in stone. An older couple sat on the loveseat holding hands.

"Hi," Alex chirped. "Has something happened?" Her eyes swept over the four silent people staring at her.

The lieutenant was the first to speak. "Yes Alex, but this has nothing to do with the murders." He gestured to the older couple on the loveseat. "This is Juno's mother and her husband."

The older man stood and held out his hand.

"Nice to meet you," Alex shook his and the woman's hand.

Twenty seconds of silence ticked by as her eyes scanned everyone in the room. Juno's eyes were downcast, his jaw bunched in anger.

"Is someone going to tell me what's going on because it obviously affects me?" Alex folded her arms and waited by the sofa.

Juno raised his head and his eyes pierced hers. "These, my dear Alex, are your parents and as it turns out, we are brother and sister."

At first, Juno's words didn't sink in and they continued gazing at one another. Then the words slammed into her brain.

"What! Don't be ridiculous, my parents are dead. They died in an auto accident when I was a baby."

Juno shook his head. "That wasn't true. Your adopted parents were probably told that because the attorney couldn't reveal the real circumstances of your birth." He held out his hand in his mother's direction. "These are your real parents, believe me, it's true."

Alex looked at the woman on the loveseat. Her blonde hair was neatly styled, her nails beautifully manicured and her clothes were of the highest quality. The silver-haired man was tall and distinguished with a deep Florida tan and knife-like creases in his pants. They both looked at her, the woman with tears in her eyes.

Anger washed over Alex and she creased her face in disdain. "You knew you had a daughter yet it took you thirty years to find me. What kind of people are you?" She turned to leave, but Juno crossed the room in two swift strides and tugged her arm.

"Stay and listen to what they have to say, then you can go. Believe me, this was as big a shock for me, maybe even more so."

Then the severity of the situation hit her and she covered the lower half of her face with her hand. Juno was her brother and they'd made love. She stared at the woman, then the man and finally Juno, who nodded. The events of the previous night careened through her mind and a surge of hopelessness followed. All the fight went out of her, and she allowed Juno to lead her to a chair.

Martin Anderson started the conversation, but Alex was only half listening. All she could think of was her love for Juno. By the time she concentrated on what was being said, Alicia was speaking about their affair, and the reason for placing the twins for adoption.

Lilies of Death

"Twins?" Alex repeated. "I have a twin?"

A sad look crossed Martin's face and he shook his head. "Not anymore. She was one of the women murdered."

Alex cast Lieutenant Walker a questioning look.

"Yes, the second murder victim, Diane Bostock, was your twin." He affirmed.

Alex recalled her shock when she first saw Diane's photo in the paper and her heart felt heavy. The lieutenant described how Diane had discovered she had a twin and moved to Geyserville to find her. Whoever was trying to murder Alex must have made a mistake and killed Dianne instead. Now things were beginning to make sense.

"I'm so glad that you and Balthy are friends," Alicia gushed. "At least we know you have someone to look after you." She directed her next question to the lieutenant. "Have you any leads or any idea why Alex is in danger?"

"Not directly, ma'am, if we did, it might be easier to solve this case, but now you're here, let me have the name and phone number of your hotel."

Martin gave the lieutenant the information and the Andersons rose to leave. Alicia kissed Juno's cheek. "We must have dinner before we go back to Boca," She looked over at Alex. "You, too, Alex, if you want to."

"Yes, thank you, I'd like that."

When the three visitors had left, Alex and Juno sat in silence. Everything inside Alex stilled and her heart sprang to her throat. The air crackled with tension. She tried to speak, but no words came out.

"This alters things quite a bit," Juno said.

Alex couldn't speak, her tongue was paralyzed. Inside she was crying. She no longer cared if she was in danger; her dreams had been shattered along with her heart. Her shoulders drooped with dejection.

Juno poured a measure of golden liquid from a decanter into a glass and held it out to Alex.

She flapped a hand for him to take it away.

"You look like a ghost, drink it." He handed her the glass.

With shaking fingers, she took a small sip; the strong liquor burned her throat. She coughed. "This is crazy, I feel as if I'm in a movie."

"If the thought of me being your brother's bad, just thank your lucky stars that you're not related to Carlos."

"Who's Carlos?"

"Martin's adopted son, he's a real piece of work. When we were kids, he broke my arm twice and tried to bury me alive."

At this point, Alex realized how little she knew about Juno. The few details she'd gleaned were what she'd read in newspaper and magazine articles, not about the man, but about the life he led.

"Thank God we were sent to different boarding schools when I was eleven," he reminisced. "Otherwise he might have ended up killing me."

Alex was fascinated and listened while Juno elaborated about his childhood and how Carlos had enlisted in the military, gone on to join some rebel organization and then disappeared.

"He surfaced again a few years later, just after his mother died and Martin and he got on well for a time. Then strange things began happening. One year when Martin was on vacation, several valuable items disappeared from the house and the safe was broken into. Carlos swore it had nothing to do with him, but Martin's never been entirely sure.

"Once again he vanished and no one's heard from him for the last fifteen years, so we don't know where he is or if he's dead or alive. I say good riddance. I haven't seen him in thirty years, so I wouldn't recognize him if I passed him in the street."

Alex felt more normal now that the shock of the situation was wearing off. "What a sad story. I hope he's safe somewhere."

Juno guffawed. "You're too sentimental. The law's probably caught up with him and he's more than likely rotting away in jail somewhere."

Alex's stomach growled and she remembered she'd hardly eaten all day.

Juno's eyebrows arched. "Hungry?"

"Yes, I was busy at work and didn't have time for much lunch." She indicated her stomach. "Hence the growling."

"I didn't eat either. Shall I make us an omelet?"

She followed him through to the kitchen and sat on a barstool watching him crack eggs into a bowl and whisk them.

"Your mother's very beautiful." She opened a drawer and removed the silverware. "She seems very nice and obviously dotes on you."

"She's your mother, too," Juno griped. "And you'll soon discover she's a pain in the ass." They exchanged a long, intense look. "You have her eyes."

Alex nodded. "I still can't take all this in. This morning I was an orphan and this evening I have a mother, a father and a brother. Are you sure this isn't a plot from one of your books?"

"This is too bizarre to put in one of my books, no one would believe it." He passed a plate filled with a steaming, golden-crusted omelet to her. "I'm not much good at cooking, but I can make good eggs."

Alex broke off a corner with her fork and agreed as the cheesy-flavored egg melted in her mouth.

They ate in silence and when they were finished, Juno stacked the plates into the dishwasher. He stood with his back to the kitchen island and as he took a step toward her, a loud crack ripped through the silence.

Alex cried out as Juno slid to the floor bleeding from his left upper arm.

"Get down," he yelled, "you're in full view of the window."

Alex sank to her knees and crawled across to him. "Is it serious?" She opened the button on his shirt cuff and rolled up his sleeve.

"Nah, it's just a graze. Whoever's out there's a rotten shooter. Can you reach the phone from here?"

She nodded, grabbed the handset from the cradle and pressed the 'talk' button. "There's no dial tone," she informed him quietly. "Do you think it's *him* out there?"

Juno's face had turned a puce color and dots of sweat lined his brow. "Where the hell's Sergeant LaTour, she's supposed to be your shadow."

Blood oozed from the wound and ran in tiny rivulets down his elbow and forearm.

"You need a tourniquet for that arm, you're losing too much blood," Alex crept on her hands and knees across the kitchen. Another sharp crack sounded and a bullet smacked into the side of one of the base cabinets above her head.

Now she was scared. Whoever was out there was watching them. They were sitting ducks. She made a sudden decision. "I need to knock off the lights, so that he can't see in. I'm going to make a run for the door."

"No, it's too dangerous. That last bullet only missed you by inches, I'll go."

"No, please I need you."

They exchanged a long look.

He gave her a lopsided smile and Alex's heart did a flip.

"I'm already injured, so if he's lucky enough to hit me again, you'll still be safe and can protect yourself. If he shoots you, too, neither of us stands a chance.

She mulled over his words and realized they made sense. "Okay, but please be careful."

Their eyes met and held.

Juno swung his legs round until he was propped on his knees. From there, he raised himself into a squatting position with his head held low. "Well, here goes."

He scuffled across the floor, his injured arm hanging limply and leaving a wavy trail of blood on the tile. Before he reached the door, he rolled onto the floor behind a vegetable cart at the precise moment another shot slammed deep into the wall. Now he was only a few feet from his destination. He held up a thumb to signify he hadn't been hit again and darted for the door, dragging the light switch down in one swift movement. The kitchen plunged into darkness and Alex ran across the room and reached Juno, as he snaked to the floor.

Relief that he hadn't been hit again flooded through her and she threw her arms around him, resting her head on his shoulder. "Thank goodness you're all right. I'm going to run and get my gun and something to tie up your arm. Will you be okay?"

"Sure, just don't take too long. We don't know who we're dealing with and he may try to break into the house. When you come back, I'll fetch my gun, too. We need all the protection we can get."

Heart pounding and breath rasping in her throat, Alex bolted up the hallway and hauled open the nightstand drawer, her fingers groping in the dark. When she felt the cold metal, she extracted her gun and loaded a full clip. The spare one she rammed in her jeans pocket before fumbling around on a chair for a scarf. In the bathroom, she closed the door, switched on the light, grabbed a box of Band-aids, and ripped open a packet of sterile gauze and two surgical dressings. All this she achieved in a few minutes.

With her heart in her mouth, she scurried back down the hallway in the darkness, feeling her way along the wall until she came to the kitchen door. As she re-entered, her foot caught on something and she fell, her gun clattering and skidding across the tile. She emitted a moan. Slightly winded, she struggled to her feet, feeling around for her weapon.

Gun in hand, she edged over to the door and by the light of the moon streaming in the window, she saw Juno prone on the floor. She bent down and shook him. "Juno." There was no reply. Her fingers traced his face. His forehead felt clammy and his eyes closed. In the dim, shadowy light, she could just make out the rolled-up cuff of his sleeve, so she tied the scarf as tightly as she could above the bullet wound. Next, she applied the gauze to the wound, and wrapped the dressing tightly around his arm. She must get help; Juno was more hurt than he'd led her to believe.

Minnie LaTour braked and watched Alex turn between the pillars onto Juno's property. She pulled over to the left side of the road edging her unmarked cruiser onto a grassy verge under a large, leafy tree until lush, low branches almost obscured it.

She enjoyed surveillance work because she was a loner and happy in her own company. Although she had many male and female friends on the force, she preferred to work alone instead of with a team. Her stomach rumbled. Instead of reaching for the sandwiches in the glove box, she unscrewed the cap of a bottle of fruit juice and took a long slug.

Leafy branches brushed the roof and side windows of the car as a gentle breeze fluttered outside. Although parked in the shade, the car was already hot, so Minnie rolled up her sleeves and loosened the top button of her khaki shirt. She shuffled into a comfortable position and leaned her head back, her eyes never leaving the driveway entrance.

Lilies of Death

As the light began to fade, a popular tune invaded her mind and she began to hum, rocking her head from side to side in time with the music. From where she sat, she watched a police car pull out between the stone pillars followed by a white Mercedes. Minnie recognized the police car as Zack's and gave a grin. Things must be heating up with the investigation.

She flipped on the map light and inspected her watch. Alex wouldn't go out again at this time of night, so she settled down to listen to her personal CD player.

She selected a disc by Sting and donned her headphones. When that finished, she replaced it with another by Faith Hill, and after she'd changed the disc again, she yawned. It was time for some food.

A small movement outside caught her eye. She swung her head round. Leather-gloved hands plucked open the door, grabbed her shirt, and wrenched her from the car. Her headphones bounced off her head. She smacked down on her butt, winded. In the gloom, out the corner of her eye, she could just make out a boot approaching. She grabbed the heel with both hands and jerked with all her might. The dark form toppled backward. She rolled over and catapulted to her feet. The figure landed on his back.

Minnie charged to the car, leaned through the open door, and grabbed the radio's mike. A hand seized her ankle. She pressed the button. The radio crackled.

"Officer needs assistance—" Minnie's voice tailed off.

Bunched into a fist, a hand punched her in the face. Pain rocketed through her brain. Still on her stomach, she flipped onto her back and drew her knees upward. With perfect timing, she rammed her feet into the advancing figure's belly. A loud cry sounded. He backed off. Minnie sat up, but her next kick went wide and the hand clutched her ankle, dragging her out of the car.

Stunned for a second, she hardly saw the glove as another blow skimmed her cheekbone. She yelped. Not easily frightened, Minnie realized that she was no match for this strong, dark figure. Her mind recalled all the training she'd received at the police academy and she decided to follow rule number 141.

Moving slowly, she wriggled forward on her butt until her feet were between the figure's legs. She tilted her body upward supporting her weight on her elbows while her legs executed a scissor action, her boots making firm contact with the figure's genitals. He yowled and doubled up. Minnie rolled over, jumped up, was almost at the car when something in her brain snapped, and blackness consumed her.

Chapter 26

Alex began to sob. All her pent up feelings for Juno surfaced and she clutched him close to her chest, covering his face with tiny kisses. "Oh, don't die," she wailed. "Somebody please help us."

She allowed herself the luxury of releasing these emotions, but then she sobered. Sitting here feeling sorry for herself was not going to help matters. She must pull herself together and keep her wits about her. Although Juno was out cold, his wound's heavy bleeding looked as if it had lessened. To enable her to monitor it further, she applied a clean piece of gauze over the top of the dressing and secured it with two Band-aids. Now she'd be able to see how much blood seeped through.

That done, she took a deep breath and recalled everything Clancy had taught her. A rush of anger poured through her. Whoever this person was and whatever he wanted of her, she was not going down without defending herself. Right at that moment, she was determined to fight as she'd never fought before, and a raging fire surged through her veins. On her hands and knees, she skulked across the room to the window and poked her head up. All was quiet.

Fine strands of moonlight sifted through tree branches bending and dipping in the evening breeze and the creek gurgled as it flowed along. Alex flinched as her finger muscles went into spasm from gripping her gun too tightly. She changed the weapon to her other hand and flexed her cramped digits.

She peeped out the window again. This time something in the shadows moved. She gave a sharp intake of breath and bent low. Still uncertain what had caused the movement outside, she streaked across the kitchen and into the living room, flattening her back against the wall by the window and sneaking a swift look. Her spirits soared when she saw her car parked where she'd left it, behind Juno's.

Then they plummeted. A figure wearing a ski mask appeared from behind her car and stood with his arms folded over his chest, staring at the window. She didn't know whether or not he could see her, but he was a daunting opponent and Alex groaned. Unless she could disable this man with a bullet, Juno and she wouldn't have a chance of survival. His threatening stance testified to a well-toned, muscled body, someone who'd be able fell her with one single blow.

She took a deep breath and peeked out the window again. The figure had gone. Alex tensed. Where was he now? She flapped her head from side to side, her eyes straining in the darkness before rushing back to the kitchen to check on Juno. A dark patch on the gauze signified that more blood had seeped through the dressing.

A thump sounded. The kitchen door rattled. Alex stiffened. Her hands shook. She rested her right hand in her cupped left one to steady it and aimed the gun at the door. The door burst open. She pulled the trigger. A shot rang out. The doorway was empty. The door hung drunkenly by one hinge. All she could see was silhouettes of swaying branches. She smothered a sob. This man was playing with her. He must know how much stronger he was, and now he'd disabled Juno, he was terrorizing her.

She edged toward the open door. Standing to one side, she poked her gun out, and then her head—nothing. Her heart hammered against her ribs as she took a surreptitious step outside, sweeping the open expanse with her eyes and her gun. Now she felt vulnerable. She was sure the man could see her, so she scooted to the nearest tree, and dived behind its wide trunk.

A movement in front and to the left made her tense. With her gun at chest level, she hid behind the tree and waited. The grass rustled. Alex stared. She longed to blink but she was afraid she'd miss something. Scratching sounded. She gripped her gun. A possum poked his nose from behind a tree and Alex moaned with relief, her gun hand falling limply to her side. Damn him, damn Minnie LaTour, where was she?

A cloud passed over the moon plunging everywhere into sudden darkness, so Alex raced from behind the tree across to the house. With her back to the siding, she edged her way to the corner. Satisfied there was nowhere for a perpetrator to hide, she inched round to the front of the building toward her car.

A loud crack sounded. Pain seared through her right hand. Alex dropped her gun. A bullet had grazed her. She pressed her body against the siding and picked up the gun with her left hand. Now she knew her assailant was watching her every move, could take her out at any moment, and all her hopes faded. This man was like a chameleon blending into the blackness of the night in his demonic, dark clothing.

Alex sat on the damp ground, her breath labored with the intense pain ricocheting through her hand. Her thoughts turned to Juno. Would the man kill him, too?

She thought she heard someone call her name and she shook her head to clear it.

"Alex!" Her name drifted faintly on a gust of wind.

Her head shot up, swiveling from side to side, trying to determine which direction the sound was coming from. A small female silhouette zigzagged from tree to tree nearing Alex and the house—Minnie LaTour. Alex's heart beat wildly in anticipation and her hopes soared again. She struggled to her feet, gun in hand and scrambled along to the next corner.

Now Alex could see Minnie more clearly. Her usually neat hair was straggling around her shoulders and she was limping. The nearest tree to the house was fifteen feet away and as Minnie left the safety of it, a loud noise rang out and she fell to her knees with a surprised look on her face before toppling forward onto the gravel path.

Still gripping the gun, Alex froze like a statue. Minnie didn't move. Alex covered her mouth with her free hand as vomit filled her throat and threatened to spew from her mouth. Taking rasping breaths, she steadied herself and peered all around. There was no sign of the killer, but she was sure he was still watching her every move. Also, was Minnie dead or only wounded? A myriad of questions teemed through her mind.

Now she was angry. If her assailant had killed Minnie in cold blood, that proved he was a crazed maniac. She was not going to let him do that to her or Juno. The bullet graze to her right hand pained, the bleeding was not heavy, so she concentrated on overcoming the discomfort and in trying to disable the killer. If she'd been alone, she would have taken a chance and made a run for her car, but there was Juno to consider. Without him, she might as well be dead. Even if he was her half-brother, he meant the world to her and she loved him with all her heart.

All of a sudden, she was calm and alert as adrenaline pumped through her veins. Her mind was clear and her reactions heightened. Her shoulders tightened as a twig snapped at the other corner of the house. He was behind her. She crouched low and made a run for the nearest tree. A shot rang out. It missed by a long way. He was toying with her. Her pulses thumped and reverberated through every inch of her body.

Alex peeped round the tree's wide trunk and spied a figure in black standing in the shadows by the house, she couldn't go back there. The only alternative was to head for the creek and the cabin about which Juno had spoken. As she stood contemplating when to make another move, the heavens opened and torrents of water poured down. Even although the tree foliage was thick, fat raindrops plopped from the leaves and dripped down her neck.

With the sky dark and the moon and stars no longer visible, she reckoned that the curtain of heavy rain, rising from the ground in a fine mist, would obscure her flight to the next tree, so she scuttled out. In the matter of seconds, she was drenched to the skin. Rain trickled down her face and dripped off her nose. Undaunted, she barged into the darkness past the next tree and into the blackness beyond.

She copied Minnie LaTour and ran in a zigzag pattern from tree to tree, her breath rasping in her throat, hoping she was making a beeline for the cabin. Juno had said it was close to the creek, so she pressed on, her chest rising and falling with the effort of running. The cabin's silhouette loomed, and she emitted a small cry of relief, as she covered the last few feet with renewed verve.

She turned the knob and almost fell in the cabin's door. Her hand felt for a lock and twisted it into place. Next, she pawed the wall for a light switch and yanked it down—nothing—the power must be out. In a way she was glad, and realized that it had been a dumb move to try to turn on the lights. Near to collapse, she scampered through the small kitchen to another door and felt around for a lock, but it was already secured. That accomplished, she rested her hands on her knees and let her head hang between her shoulders. What now? She was exhausted from running and trapped in the middle of nowhere at the mercy of a ruthless killer.

Hysteria threatened to overpower her, but she straightened and dug her nails into her palms. That discomfort and the pain shooting through her right hand, gave her newfound energy. The fast falling rain sounded like a volley of gunfire as it drummed on the cabin's metal roof. The air inside was hot and stale and Alex's chest heaved with the effort to breath. Dark shadows danced across the walls as tree branches outside bent and flexed in the gusty wind.

All Alex's fears disappeared. The worst that could happen was that she would die. Her goal was to avert that and make sure it was quick and pain free if there was no eluding it. She decided to rest and rebuild her strength until the next confrontation with her killer.

Juno stirred. His head throbbed in unison with his arm. The kitchen was in darkness, but he could still make out the open door and the storm outside in the gloom. Where was Alex? Had she gone for help? He rolled onto his knees and pushed himself to his feet with the aid of the counter. His head swam. He took a few deep breaths and when he steadied, he plodded over to the open door and looked out. Rain sluiced down making it almost impossible to see beyond a few feet. He weaved across the kitchen, clutching the wall to keep his balance, before reeling into the living room.

Half way over to the window, he dived onto the arm of a chair and rested for a few moments. His knees were as limp as noodles, but he compelled himself to rise and cross to the window. Parked in front of Alex's car was his sedan.

The memory of the earlier attack caused every muscle in his body to tense and he spoke his thoughts aloud. "If you've harmed one hair of her head, I'll kill you." Then he added under his breath, "You bastard!"

Intense anger gave him new strength and he traipsed back to the kitchen. He flinched as a loud crack rang out. Alex—was someone shooting at her. He hurried through to his den, which overlooked the side of the house, but the stream of water gushing from the gutters restricted his view beyond the first set of trees. Out the corner of his eye, he spied a tall, dark figure racing from the house just as he reached in the desk drawer for his gun. He verified the clip was full, limped through the kitchen and out the door.

His shoes squelched in the mud as he set off as fast as his wobbly legs would allow, skipping from tree to tree in the wake of the dark figure. In a few seconds, the rain had saturated his clothes and hair. Blood was beating in his brain, and all he could think of was Alex's safety, as he hobbled into the darkness in pursuit.

Instinct led him on a familiar pathway until he could make out the shape of his cabin. When he was twenty feet away, he leaned against the trunk of a live oak. All was quiet except for the constant sound of falling rain. Gun in hand, he took a few steps onto the soggy grass, and dashed under the cabin's eaves for shelter.

He panted with the effort of running, and rested for a few moments, drawing in several long, deep breaths. With his back to the wall, eyes scanning the darkness, he edged along and slowly turned the door handle. It wouldn't budge. He fished in his jeans pocket and pulled out his bunch of keys, fumbling in the dark to find the one that opened the cabin. He selected a small silver key, inserted it into the lock, and the door opened.

Alex was crouching on the floor, her heartbeat hammering in her chest. She heard the door handle rattle and she stiffened. He was out there. She gripped her gun, stretched out her arms, took a firm stance feeling very calm, and aimed at the door. When it opened, she pulled the trigger, her right arm jerking with the recoil, and she knew immediately that her shot had gone high and wide, plowing into the architrave.

A shadow advanced.

"Alex, it's me, Juno."

She recognized his hoarse voice and her knees crumbled. "Juno!" She ran across the room and threw herself at the dark silhouette. His arms enfolded her and she lifted her face until her lips found his. All her feelings for him poured out.

"Wow, that was quite a welcome. Shall I go out and come in again?"

Alex laughed. "Sorry, I'm so relieved you're okay. I had no idea if he'd got you, too." Then she sobered. "He shot Sergeant LaTour. She's lying on the path, but I couldn't go to her, otherwise he'd have shot me, too. What are we going to do?"

Juno locked the door. His legs gave way. He clutched Alex and together they weaved across to the barstools in the kitchen. "I'm working on that," Juno said, wilting onto the seat. "At least we have an advantage being inside, now."

"Is there a phone here?"

"No, I usually have my cell phone when I come."

"Mine's in my car along with the sergeant's radio. If I thought I could sneak back and get it I would, but I know he's out there waiting for one of us to make a move." Alex reached over and touched Juno's hand. "How's the arm?"

"Hurting like hell, but I think the bleeding's almost stopped."

Darkness and a companionable silence shrouded them as the storm raged outside. A warm feeling blanketed Alex now that Juno was safe and by her side. Her distraught feelings melted away and her strength returned. It was as if he was a panacea. With him by her side, she felt as if she could cope with anything, even death.

"I'm sorry you've been drawn into this," Alex told him, breaking the long silence. "It's me this maniac's after. I didn't want anyone else to become involved or injured because of me."

"Nothing's that simple, and anyway, we're family now."

His words reminded her that he was her half-brother and a deep sadness flowed through her. Of all the men in Florida, she had to fall in love with her half-brother. What were the odds of that? She reckoned it must be thousands to one.

"If you want a hot drink, there's a small propane stove in that cupboard over there and a tea kettle on the counter." Juno extended his index finger.

Alex probed around in the dark for the handle and withdrew a two-ring stove connected to a propane canister and placed it on the counter. "Matches?"

Juno flipped open a book from his pants' pocket and tossed it to her.

With something to take her mind off the seriousness of the situation, she half-filled the kettle with water and placed it on a lighted burner. The glow from the flame revealed an ashen-faced Juno with wet clothes molded to his body. She shivered. Although it was hot and humid in the cabin, dampness seeped through her bones from her drenched clothes.

"We should get into something dry," Juno said. "Why don't I do that and then you can change, too."

"Great, in the meantime, I'll make us some tea?"

Juno nodded and trudged toward the hallway leading to the bedroom.

His face was set in a rictus of a smile as he watched Juno enter the cabin. So far so good, he had both victims trapped inside. Juno wasn't important, it was the woman who counted. If he also had the chance to dispose of Juno, he would. That way there would be no loose ends, nothing or no one to implicate him. Anyway, he'd be long gone before the police found these bodies and the remains of the others. Then he'd be free to move on and live life as he chose without anyone asking questions.

Amidst a gust of rain, he darted to the cabin and leaned against the soaking siding. His mounting adrenalin caused him to have a strong erection and he squirmed as his jeans became uncomfortably tight.

"Damn you," he muttered, visualizing Alex's lovely face. "You won't get away this time. Now I've got you cornered, even *he* can't save you." He covered his mouth with his hand and sniggered.

With his back against the building, he minced along to the first window and sneaked a look in the crack between the curtains. Two outlines sat on barstools, talking. He guessed that Juno had locked the door, but perhaps he hadn't had time to inspect the windows yet, so he scooted round to the next one. The curtains weren't drawn, so he lifted the sash. It opened. As swift and as stealthy as a commando, he bent double, writhed under a small gap, and dropped to the floor without a sound. He was in a bedroom.

In the gloom, he could make out a full-size bed and a small chest positioned by the door. From the space between the two windows, he reckoned there was a hallway outside this room that led to the living room and kitchen beyond. His tennis shoes made no sound on the soft carpet as he crept to the bedroom door and placed his ear against it. Slowly, he turned the handle and opened it an inch to enable him to position his right eye enough to see. As he suspected, a hallway stretched ahead.

He squeezed through the door opening and with his back against the wall, tiptoed to the end where the living room yawned ahead. One swift poke of his head established that Juno and Alex were still talking in the kitchen.

Now his victim was within easy reach, he had to make a plan. Rushing headlong into the living room and killing her in cold blood was not his goal. That fate was okay for Juno, he deserved nothing better, but Alex was different.

When Juno stood and began walking his way, his hand moved to his weapon lodged in his belt at the back of his jeans.

As quiet as falling snow, he tiptoed back into the bedroom and closed the door.

Chapter 27

Juno's head swam with weakness and nausea. When he lurched across the living room, pain sliced through his arm, cutting him like a knife. His lips quirked in a trace of a smile as the sound of Alex humming a jaunty tune wafted toward him. As soon as he reached the hallway, he propped one arm against the wall and leaned his head on it. The coolness on his forehead revived him enough to reach the bedroom door.

The hinges squeaked when the door opened. One of these days, he'd get round to oiling them, but in Florida's humidity, he knew they'd soon be creaking again, so it seemed a worthless exercise. Through the window, the moonlight twinkling on the rapid moving creek caught his eye. Leaning one hand on the bed to keep his balance, he reached out and snapped the window lock into place. The others needed locked, too. Normally he left them open, but tonight was an exception.

He shook his head to clear it. Still using the bed as a steadying device, he tottered round the room to the closet and opened the door. Clutching it for support, his right hand fished for some pants and sweaters, one for each of them. Taking two steps backward, he wilted onto the bed ripping off his dripping shirt and flinging it onto the floor.

Before he could undo the belt on his jeans, intuition made him turn in time to see a dark silhouette spring forward. As he rose to his feet, a blow caught him in the kidneys. He raised his left forearm and blocked a fist about to connect with his jaw. The figure stood with his legs apart. Juno's feet faltered. He staved off waves of nausea and fought to keep conscious.

The dark shadow bounced around on the balls of his feet, his fists jabbing Juno's stomach. He doubled up. Then a swift, sharp clip on the chin caused pyrotechnics to explode behind his eyes. Even if he'd been uninjured, Juno knew he was no match for his attacker. This man was a trained fighter and knew where to hit to do the maximum damage.

Forgetting the pain rivering through his injured arm, Juno threw a punch with his right hand, swiftly followed by his left. Bone and cartilage crunched as his fist made contact with the man's cheek. A shower of expletives bounced off every surface of the room followed by an enraged bellow.

"You little shithead!"

Confusion struck Juno motionless. Where had he heard that phrase before? He ransacked his mind, but it was numb.

The figure vaulted over the corner of the bed, butting his head into Juno's torso, winding him and paralyzing his lungs. His lungs gusted in an effort to draw in some air. The man then slammed his fists into Juno's belly like pistons. He felt no pain. His brain was numb. Next, a well-placed kick to the back of his knees toppled him to the floor. He was barely conscious as another kick to the head sent splintering pain through his skull and he spiraled into welcome oblivion.

Alex whirled round as a shout and a loud thump came from the bedroom. "Juno? Are you okay?"

When there was no answer, she waited a few moments before gingerly edging into the living room. "Juno?" Again, there was no reply. She had a lead weight in her chest as she took a few tentative steps toward the hallway. Had Juno passed out? Was that why he couldn't answer? A sixth sense told her that was not the case and a worm of apprehension niggled deep inside.

She swallowed around the knot of fear in her throat and paused at the entrance to the hallway. The bedroom door eased open. In the gloom, a figure materialized. Alex knew instantly this was not Juno. Shock paralyzed her. Her eyes widened and she blinked against the sudden glare of a flashlight shining in her eyes.

"Who are you? And what do you want?" She raised an arm to shade her eyes speaking calmly while fighting down rising panic.

"Surely you know, Alex?" He spoke in a high singsong voice as he forged toward her with a measured tread. "I want you dead."

She felt the blood drain from her face. "But why? I don't even know you."

He gave a sinister cackle. "You reckon?"

She reached for the wall and began backing into the living room. He advanced with silent steps. Her heart pumped with fear. In a few strides, he closed the distance between them. Then he turned the flashlight on himself. Alex held her breath. Her skin crawled. The eyes behind the ski mask telegraphed murderous fury. Adrenalin pumped through her brain giving her added bravado.

"Then why don't you take off your mask? Or are you a coward, too?"

A loud bellow erupted. Alex continued staring into his wild, dark eyes as he slowly peeled off the mask. Her mouth opened and closed and her heart seized up in her chest. The room rocked as if she were drunk.

"You! But why?" She tried to control her hectic breathing.

He barked a mirthless laugh. "Because you're a worthless tramp."

She winced at his words, shaking her head. "That's not true."

His mouth broke into a malicious smirk and his eyes glittered with resentment. "How can you say that when you've fucked everyone except me."

"And that's reason to kill me?"

"Not entirely, but it'll do for starters." He gave her a cold, remote stare.

Alex's eyes frantically explored the room.

"There's no way out, it's just you and me." His tone was low and menacing.

"What have you done to Juno?" Fear tightened around her heart.

"He won't be bothering us for a long time."

She felt the intensity of his eyes on her while her mind clicked at a fast, furious pace. Common sense told her she could never defend herself against this man. He was taller and much stronger and had been in the military. If only she'd brought her gun with her and not left it on the counter. Now, her only chance was to escape and hide outside in the darkness.

He moved toward her with slow, sinister steps. As she turned to run, she caught her foot and fell like a sack. He pounced. She held out an arm to stave him off. With one knee on either side of her body, he placed both hands on her shoulders, pinning her to the floor.

His hot lips sipped at hers and she thrashed her head from side to side. "No, get off me!"

Ignoring her cries, his large hands closed over the mounds of her breasts, his lips continuing to lave kisses on her neck and throat. One hand sifted through the strands of her hair while the other squished her nipples through her wet clothes. He threw his head back, his laughter spilling over her like a rolling wave.

Tears burned her eyes and she decided to plead with him. "Please don't, not like this. Let me get up and we can go into the other bedroom."

He rammed the heel of his hand against her windpipe. Colors swam before her eyes. "I'm not falling for that. I'm just going to have you right here on the floor."

He rose onto his knees and removed his hand from her throat to reach the zipper of his jeans. Alex jerked a knee into his genitals. He howled. Stimulated into action, she slid backward, jumped up and whipped herself forward; her feet hit the floor running.

In a listing gait, she was almost at the front door when he lunged at her. Just in time, she parried his attempt to grab her, turned and sped into the kitchen. Her hands explored the counter for her gun. He grabbed her. She shrank from him. He clutched her sopping wet clothes and flung her to the floor. A shock of pain traveled through her.

"Goddamn you—you bitch!"

The air crackled with intense dislike, he advanced and she inclined away from him. She struggled to her feet expecting pain as he raised one of his hands. Instead, he stroked her cheek with his knuckles.

"Oh, Alex, we could have had it all, you and I, but it turns out that you're one of them and every one of them has to die for me to get what I want."

"I don't know what you mean." She edged backwards toward the kitchen door. "One of whom?"

"The Andersons," he spat. "You're one of her daughters."

"But what difference does it make whose daughter I am, I thought you loved me. I thought you wanted us to be together."

He toured her with scornful eyes. "Don't come that with me. Surely, you know who I am. I'm Carlos."

Martin and Alicia Anderson exchanged a smile.

"Our daughter's wonderful," Martin said. "She looks just like you and even has your color of eyes."

Alicia had been on tenterhooks before meeting Alex, but one look at her daughter had dispelled her fears. "She has your smile," she told him, glowing inside with pride. "I wish you'd told me earlier you knew about the twins. That way we might have known Diane and prevented her death."

The Mercedes sped along Fruitville Road with Martin remaining silent, his eyes never leaving the road. Alicia leaned forward and fiddled with the radio until she found a station playing a Frank Sinatra song.

"I can't wait to get to know Alex. Isn't it strange that she and Balthy know each other?" When Martin didn't reply she turned to face him. "Martin? Is something wrong?"

He swung the wheel and turned into the driveway of their hotel, pulling up next to the valet parker. The young man opened the passenger door and Alicia stepped out with her brows drawn together. She followed her husband up the marble steps trying to keep up with his long strides until she eventually caught up with him in the corridor leading to the elevators. She was about to ask him what was wrong again, but the faraway look in his eyes silenced her.

As soon as they entered their suite, Martin made a beeline for the mini bar. He filled a glass with ice, topped it up with Scotch, and took a long drink. This action made Alicia's heartbeat quicken. Something was wrong. Martin never drank before dinner. He sauntered over to the sofa leaning his head on the high back.

"Are you all right, dear?" Alicia fussed with her hair in the mirror, trying to appear nonchalant.

"I'm just tired."

This again was unusual. Martin was always full of life and seldom flagged, even after strenuous exercise. She sneaked a sly look at him. He had his eyes closed and was pinching the bridge of his nose with his right thumb and forefinger.

Alicia sidled across the room and snuggled next to him on the sofa. "Where do you want to go for dinner tomorrow?

There's a few nice places on Longboat Key. We'd better make a reservation before we call Balthy and Alex."

Martin opened his eyes and looked at her as if he just realized she was in the room. "Huh?"

"I said we'd better make a reservation for dinner tomorrow, now there'll be four of us."

"You do it. I'm going to soak in the tub." He rose and left the room without looking back.

Alicia picked up the phone book and after a few minutes of perusing the restaurant section, she selected a popular eating-place on St. Armand's Circle and made a reservation for six-thirty the following evening. Next, she picked up the phone and dialed her son's number. She tapped her fingers and hummed as the tone rang at the other end of the line. When there was no answer, she dialed his cell phone and waited, but again there was no reply.

She lowered her eyebrows in a thoughtful frown. Strange, Balthy said he'd be around the house for the rest of the evening. An image of Alex filled her mind and she smiled. Life was good. She'd finally buried the ghosts of the past and acknowledged that she'd had twin daughters. No woman could ask for a better husband and father than Martin and a wave of love spilled over her when he appeared through the bathroom door with a towel wrapped around his lower body.

"I've made a reservation for tomorrow evening, but now I can't reach Balthy."

"Oh, he's probably gone out," Martin mused as he downed the last of his drink.

"But, he said he'd be in all evening."

"So, have you never changed your mind?" he barked.

Alicia opened her eyes wide and then narrowed them. "What's wrong, Martin. I know I can be a bit annoying at times, but usually you indulge me. Please tell me."

Martin stalled before he spoke. "I didn't want to scare you, dear, but we might be in danger, too."

"What? Why?"

"Because we're connected to Alex."

"Don't be so melodramatic."

A feeling of relief washed over her. Martin was taking Lieutenant Walker's words too seriously. However, she hated seeing him upset when he was only thinking of her well-being.

"Let's not dwell on something that's never going to happen. Tomorrow's our last day before we go back to Boca and tackle the insurance company about the house, I want to enjoy it with Balthy and our new-found daughter. She's quite something, isn't she?"

"Quite something, "Martin repeated. "No wonder Balthy's so taken with her."

Alicia puckered her brow in a frown. "What do you mean?"

"Surely you noticed the way they looked at one another."

Alicia raised a shoulder in indifference. "So, they're brother and sister, I'd expect them to be close."

"But they only found out about that today. Alex and Balthy were both shocked at our news. What if there's more than brotherly love between them."

Alicia placed a hand on each side of her face and stared. "Oh, Lordy! No wonder they looked surprised. Do you really think they might be lovers?"

"I think it's a distinct possibility. You know Balthy's reputation with women, no decent-looking female's safe."

With Balthy being thirteen years older than Alex, the idea that they were in love had never entered Alicia's head. She knew what it was like to love a man illicitly. She'd spent most of her married life as Martin's lover, knowing there was no chance of them ever being together. It was only when both partners died that they acknowledged their love, and finally married.

Now she was in a quandary, but before she panicked, she wanted to wait until tomorrow at dinner to observe her offsprings' actions, and if Martin was right, she had a big decision to make.

The first flash of lightning lit up the sky as Alicia tried to call Juno again. Thunder rumbled and drizzling rain quickly turned into a downpour. One look out their penthouse window convinced her to call room service for dinner. The streets were awash with water and the traffic created an incessant swish.

"I hope the weather's better by tomorrow," she pronounced, switching on a table lamp. "It won't be much fun eating outdoors."

"Don't worry, by tomorrow the sky'll be bright blue and there'll be no trace of the storm. This bad weather's coming from the east. You can't reach Balthy because the phone lines are probably down." Martin donned a pair of gold-rimmed spectacles and read the room service menu. "Come and choose what you want."

Alicia picked up a second menu, her eyes scanning the long list of food. They decided to order Clam Chowder, Salmon en Croûte and Strawberry Cheesecake, followed by Irish coffee. Until their meal arrived, Martin watched TV and tuned to a local news channel. It depicted the damage that was ravaging the Geyserville district.

"There," Martin motioned to the screen. "Look at that mess. I'm sure Balthy will call if he and Alex have a problem. Let's assume that *'no news is good news.'*"

Alicia nodded. As usual, Martin was right. She'd always been a fusspot where her son was concerned and now she had Alex to consider as well. At least if they were together, they'd be safe. Balthy had built a strong house, but the trees on his

Lilies of Death

property disturbed her, if one of those blew down, the damage to the house would be substantial.

After dinner, Alicia picked up one of her son's books that she hadn't finished reading. Martin watched TV, but each time she looked up, it was obvious he wasn't concentrating by the deep frown furrowing his brow. Agitation coursed through Alicia. What if Martin wasn't overreacting to the lieutenant's words, but who would want to harm them? At such a ridiculous idea, she smiled and returned to her book.

Martin couldn't settle. He kept getting up and looking out the window at the storm. Alicia had recovered from the shock of the house fire and was sitting calmly on the sofa reading. As he poured himself his third glass of Whiskey, she interrupted his thoughts. "For heaven's sake sit down. You told me not to fuss about Balthy and Alex and here you are prowling around like a bitch on heat."

"I'm not thinking about Balthy and Alex."

"Then what's wrong?"

Martin wondered if he was doing the right thing by telling his wife his fears. "I'm convinced the fire at the house the other night was no accident. Whoever set it thought we'd be home."

The color drained from Alicia's face. "You mean someone tried to kill us?" He chewed his bottom lip, nodding. "But who?"

"Carlos."

Alicia looked at him as if he'd just told her he was really the President of the United States. "Don't be ridiculous. Why would Carlos want to kill us?"

"The age old reason, money."

"But Carlos will get all your assets and money eventually, why kill you now?"

As she spoke the words, the reason dawned on Alicia and her eyes flew wide open.

Martin nodded. "He obviously knows that you inherit when I die and then him and the twins. He's already disposed of Diane and now he's trying to kill Alex, so that he can have everything. My God, I've raised a monster."

Chapter 28

Alex watched Carlos's mouth curl in a sneer. He opened his hands, both palms facing her at shoulder level. "Surprise! Don't look so shocked, I'm sure you've heard all about me."

She nodded, her throat paralyzed.

His hand grabbed her shirt, snatching her closer. "Speak to me, you little bitch. Tell me you're sorry for the way you've treated me."

In a flash, Clancy's words returned. *'Get angry, more angry that you've ever been, that'll start the adrenaline flowing and help you defend yourself.'* Her whole body boiled with anger.

"No I'm not sorry. You're just a sick individual who can't keep a woman. Why should I say I'm sorry?"

He voiced an expletive and she cringed as he sprang forward grabbing her round the throat. She couldn't breath. Her eyes watered and her ears hummed. Anger surfaced again and she fashioned her hands into fists, forgetting her grazed, bleeding hand, and punched his neck and shoulders. He released one hand to secure hers. She flinched as pain ricocheted up her arm. With her free fist, she punched his face, skin split and blood spurted, it might have been hers. He cursed. Her lungs felt as if they'd been crushed and her breathing was choppy and quick. She took huge breaths trying to fill her lungs with air and to ward off losing consciousness. Blindly, she ran for the door.

Outside, the driving rain stung her face and the wind lambasted her. She tipped her head down and ran for the trees. Oblivious as to whether he was following she teetered on; tree branches scratching her face and neck. The wind whipped her wet hair around her head and whispered her name as she ran from the safety of the trees. The creek was straight ahead threshing with a swift current. With shoulders slumped she paused, her breath tearing at her burning lungs.

From somewhere behind, he pounced. Alex landed hard in the mud. He squatted down, flipped her onto her back, grabbed her shoulders and shook her roughly. Her head swam as it bounced off the muddy grass. She howled as rockets of pain exploded in her skull. His breath was hot on her cheek as he spoke in her ear. "Get ready to die, Alex. At least you'll go while I—"

Another figure appeared in the darkness and drove a fist into the man's nose. His head jarred back. Alex dug her heels into the mud and skidded backward into Juno's bent form.

"Run!" he shouted, the word hardly audible above the noise of the roiling creek.

"No!" she hollered back. "I can help you."

The man jackknifed into a sitting position and jumped to his feet. The rain had lessened and a slice of moon slithered from behind the clouds, bathing them in its pale light. Juno's face was lined and drawn.

The man's face distorted with malice. "I've always hated you," he jabbed a finger at Juno's chest. "You always got everything I ever wanted, but not this time, you're not having her. You don't imagine I did all this for nothing."

Alex quaked at his words. Carlos reached for her, but Juno planted himself between them enough to neutralize his lunge at her and took a blow to the side of the head. He went down like a ninepin. Alex now knew there was no hope. She was no match for this man's strength.

She braced her feet firmly apart and gave a militant tilt to her chin. "Come on then, kill me and get it over with. I'm not afraid to die."

This elected a smile from him. "Not so fast. First I want to make love to you."

"Never, you'll have to kill me first."

"On the contrary, sweet Alex, I'll kill you after." His tone was now as soft as velvet.

The next few seconds happened in slow motion. He leaned forward. Alex cringed. His hand grabbed her clothes. She tried to wriggle free. He jerked her closer. She closed her eyes. A shot rang out swiftly followed by a second one. Her eyes flew open as surprise flashed across Carlos's face and he doubled up, a guttural sound escaping. He plummeted to the ground in front of her. She couldn't breathe. A small figure tottered forward.

Minnie LaTour's feet faltered. "Are you okay?"

Galvanized into action, Alex clambered over Carlos and knelt beside an unconscious Juno, feeling for his pulse. "He's been shot," Alex's knees threatened to collapse, so she knelt on the ground, cradling Juno's head in her lap.

"Lieutenant Walker and an ambulance are on their way," Minnie said, swaying on her feet. "I told them to drive past the house and follow the track to the creek."

The will to move had deserted Alex and every inch of her body ached. "Thank you," she whispered. "Thank you very much."

Even although her face was the color of putty, Minnie still managed a grin. "You're welcome. I was only doing my job."

Alex gesticulated toward Carlos. "Is he dead?"

"No, only unconscious, I hit him in the back of thigh and then in the shoulder. Are you hurt?"

Alex held up her injured hand. "It's only a graze, how do you feel?"

"Weak, I must have passed out after I was shot, but luckily enough it's not a serious wound. How's Juno?"

"Out cold. He took a bullet in the arm and this sicko kicked him in the head."

The two women sat in amiable silence as squealing, distant sirens moved closer and dark silhouettes approached. Lieutenant Walker and three other officers raced across the grass with four paramedics carrying two gurneys in their wake. In no time at all, they had administered IVs to Minnie, Juno and Carlos and dressed Alex's hand.

"Can I go with Juno?" Alex asked, wrapping a blanket around her shoulders. "He is my brother."

"Sure, you'll need to have that hand looked at anyway." Zack Walker turned Carlos over. "Do you know him?"

Alex's throat muscles closed around her vocal chords, so she nodded.

"Who is he?"

"My editor, Charlie Addison."

"Alias Carlos Anderson. Okay boys, you take these guys to the hospital. There's another ambulance on its way, so I'll wait until it arrives and removes Carlos."

A young police officer held Alex's elbow as they trudged behind the paramedics to the ambulances parked further down the track. Alex jumped in and sat beside Juno, stroking back a tousled lock of hair from his forehead.

The engines whirred and the vehicles rocked their way over the uneven ground until they reached the road where the drivers turned the sirens on. They sped toward the hospital in Geyserville with Alex clutching Juno's hand and murmuring words of comfort.

She was bone tired and staggered into the emergency room as the paramedics wheeled Minnie and Juno straight through to waiting doctors. A second police officer had traveled with Minnie and he spent some time at the check-in desk until the third arrived in a patrol car. Alex felt close to tears as a nurse called her name and she trekked behind her into a room.

The nurse washed the scratches on her face and neck with antiseptic and then took her to x-ray before dressing her hand again.

"No permanent damage done, Mrs. Martell," the doctor reported, writing up a chart. "Just a chipped bone in your wrist that'll heal itself in time."

"Do you know the condition of Mr. Juno?"

"Not offhand, but I'll find out if you want to return to the waiting area. Are you related?"

It pained Alex to say it, but she had to, "Yes, he's my brother."

Time passed in a blur until the doctor returned and she went limp with relief when he said, "Mr. Juno has recovered consciousness and he'll undergo surgery in the morning to remove the bullet from his arm. Why don't you go home and get some sleep. You'll be able to visit him later tomorrow."

She nodded, tension flowing from her body. Her hand had begun to throb, so she scrunched her eyes shut and jumped when someone spoke. "I can take you home now, Mrs. Martell."

She urged her eyes open and saw the young police officer who'd escorted her in the ambulance and followed him rubber-kneed to his patrol car.

It felt strange going back to the house where a few hours earlier she'd been terrorized. She longed for the comfort of Juno's arms, even as a brother, so she decided to sleep in his bed. Too tired to take a shower, she flung off her clothes and tumbled between the sheets. His body aroma lingered and cuddling into one of the pillows, she was soon asleep.

The phone ringing off the hook coerced her back to consciousness. She gritted her teeth as she reached for the receiver with her injured hand. "Hello?"

"Alex? It's Mother." Her insides tumbled at the unexpected greeting. "Lieutenant Walker's just left and I couldn't wait until morning to find out how you are."

"I'm fine. How's Juno?" She asked with sleepy huskiness.

"Oh, my poor boy, the lieutenant says he's got to have surgery. I phoned the hospital, but they won't let me see him until tomorrow."

"That's right they're going to remove the bullet in the morning. I'm sure he'll be okay, he's in a very good hospital. What time is it?"

A few seconds silence passed. "Just after midnight. Look, I'll let you get back to sleep. Will we see you at the hospital tomorrow?"

"Yes, I'll be there, goodnight."

Alex flopped back on the pillow. Now wide-awake, she analyzed the recent conversation. How strange it had sounded when Mrs. Anderson announced herself as 'Mother', but then that's what she was. It was going to take some time to get used to having parents. She knew she'd never be able to get it into her head that Juno was her brother, that thought still hurt.

A bright moon leaked through a gap in the curtains projecting dark shadows on the ceiling that no longer seemed ominous and Alex was soon lulled back to sleep.

As dawn broke, the dark horizon lightened in shades of pink and gray, shrouding the house in violet hues. Hardly a breeze stirred the air, fresh and cool after the previous evening's storm. By seven-thirty, bright sunlight diffused by the sheers streamed over Alex, waking her. At first, she had no clue where she was, but then she remembered the events of the previous evening and quivered. Her whole body ached, so she decided to take a bath.

Relaxing in warm water with her injured hand dangling outside the tub, she had time to analyze her feelings for her parents. Her father had said very little, it was her mother who'd made excuses and tried to explain. Brows drawing together, she wondered what she'd have done in the same circumstances. There were many things to take into account. Thirty years ago, people regarded having a child out of wedlock a social no-no. Then there would have been her mother's husband and Juno to consider. Having her mother's illegitimate children living with them would have put a tremendous strain on the marriage.

By the time she climbed from the tub and struggled into a terry robe, she realized that she'd probably have done the same thing as her mother. She'd been lucky to be adopted by fantastic parents and had had a wonderful childhood, which the lieutenant said, had not been the case for Diane. Her heart filled with sadness for the sister and twin she would never know.

Feeling better now, her stomach rumbled and she realized she'd had very little to eat the day before, except for the omelet she'd eaten before Juno was shot. Once she'd made a pot of coffee and sat down to a plate of steaming scrambled eggs, reflections of the past cascaded through her mind. The great times she'd had with her adopted father, the first time she'd met her husband, John, the huge influence he'd had on her life and the times she'd made love with Juno.

Tears dewed her eyelashes and her head drooped into her hands. Once she started sobbing, she couldn't stop. She cried for her deceased parents, her short marriage and for her dead twin. Now Juno was another matter. She'd wanted a life with him, which she could still have, but not the way she longed for, only as a brother.

After her little pity party, she felt calmer. At least she wasn't badly hurt like Minnie and Juno, or dead like Clancy, she'd been very fortunate and had everything to live for including her new family.

After she'd picked at a salad for lunch, she phoned the hospital. A nurse told her that Juno's surgery had gone well, he was awake and that she could visit him after three o'clock. Her heart soared with gladness. Contrary to her earlier mood, she hummed as she selected what to wear to visit him.

Dressed in a velour jogging suit, she rifled though her suitcase and found her personal CD player. As she left the house to drive into Geyserville, birds floated in a liquid, blue sky and it was hard to believe there had been such a violent storm the night before. Her first deed was to stop and buy a 'get well' card, before dropping by a music store for a classical CD.

Butterflies filled her stomach as she entered the hospital's automatic doors and headed for reception. Riding the elevator to the fourth floor, she looked around for room 422.

A loud babble met her ears when she pushed open the door. Her mother sat to the left of Juno chattering, while her father stood by the window engrossed in conversation with a tall, mustached man.

Juno's face wreathed in smiles. "Here she is, come in Alex."

Before she could get halfway across the room, her mother rose and embraced her. "My dear, Alex, we've been so worried about you." She touched the dressing on her daughter's hand. "Are you in much pain?"

"No, it's nothing compared to Juno's injury." Her eyes skittered over to his and held. "How are you?" She stepped closer to the bed

His eyes bored into hers in a steady gaze. "All the better for seeing you." He pulled a spare chair closer to the bed. "Come and sit down."

She thrust forward the card, the CD and the player. "I brought you this. I thought it might help while away the hours."

He turned the CD case over and read the back. "Clever girl, it's one of my favorites, thank you."

Lilies of Death

Their eyes made sizzling contact again and hot color surged to her cheeks. She suddenly realized that the others in the room had ceased talking and were watching them. Her gaze swung to her mother's distraught face.

Her father coughed, breaking the awkward silence and placed an arm around her mother's shoulder. "Well we don't want to tire Balthy too much, so we'll go and let you two have some time together."

Alex smiled into his warm, brown eyes. "Please stay, you don't need to go on my account."

"No, we've been here long enough and besides, Alicia and I have some serious talking to do." Martin held her mother's elbow, helped her to her feet and said to Juno, "We'll come back and see you again tomorrow."

Her mother bent and kissed Juno's cheek. "Take care."

Juno settled back on the pillows. "Okay Mom, bye Martin."

Juno wafted a hand introducing the tall, dark man. "This is my agent, Sam Grant, my sister, Alex."

Alex shook hands with the man who promptly stated that he had a meeting to attend and left.

Now alone with Juno, shyness engulfed her. Try as she might, her feelings for him hadn't changed. Her body yearned for his and she longed for his kiss.

He used his good arm to scoot further up the bed and open the top drawer of his nightstand withdrawing his cigarettes and lighter.

She queried him with raised eyebrows. "Are you allowed to smoke in here?"

"Who knows, but I'm dying for a cigarette."

The room seemed to close around them in taut intimacy. Sighing with contentment, he leaned back filling his lungs with the cigarette's smoke. "Oh, that feels good. I still have the taste of that vile anesthetic in my mouth. They won't let me have anything to drink, so I'll to make do with a cigarette."

Heartbeats thundered through her veins and she was unable to stop tears filling her eyes, so she turned away, lowering her lashes to hide her eyes.

Juno stubbed out his cigarette in a nearby plant and with the slightest pressure brought her round to face him. "Don't cry. It's all over now and you're safe."

She nodded, words lodged in her throat not able to reach her mouth.

He smoothed his hand up and down her back whispering words of comfort. All this was too much for her and oblivious to the pain she might cause him, she collapsed in his arms.

With a sharp intake of breath, he groaned.

As she lifted her face from his chest, he swept away her tears with his fingers and she blinked him into focus. "I'm sorry. I guess it's just a delayed reaction to all that's happened. I don't usually break down like this."

Gently he pushed her away. "Don't apologize. You've been under a terrible strain lately. Lieutenant Walker dropped by last evening and brought me up to date with everything. Imagine Carlos being your editor, I didn't recognize him that day I had lunch with you both, he looked so different. I can hardly believe it."

"Me neither, I've worked for him for years and he was the last person I'd have expected to be a killer."

"I think Martin's pretty cut up. Although he and Emily adopted Carlos, he still thought the world of him. The lieutenant doubts there'll be a trial. He feels sure that a psychiatric evaluation will prove that Carlos is insane and that he'll be committed to an institution."

"Sometimes money makes people do crazy things. They don't realize there's more to life than riches."

Lilies of Death

His brows rose in a taunt. "Like what—love?"

Her throat was tight as she nodded. "Yes, love is one of the most important parts of life. Without your parents' love, you wouldn't be the person you are."

"Your adopted parents must have loved you very much. You turned out okay."

The room door swung open and a nurse strode in. "It's time for Mr. Juno's injection. Can you wait outside please?"

Alex rose. "I'd better go, you need your rest."

Juno placed a hand on her arm to restrain her and with fire dancing in his green eyes, said. "It's okay, nurse, my sister's seen my butt before."

Alex lowered her hot face and muttered in an undertone. "Just behave yourself, I'm going." She leaned forward and kissed his cheek. "I'll see you tomorrow."

"I might be getting home tomorrow." He cocked one brow and winked.

Her insides quivered at that small gesture and she hurried out, not trusting herself to look back.

Chapter 29

The bright light of the evening star, Venus, glittered in the blue sky and the road shimmered with heat that had built up during the day as Alex turned into the driveway of Juno's house. Before she left the hospital, she verified with one of the nurses that he'd be discharged the next day, so she decided to place a call to their mother when she arrived home. Home—it would never be that for her—yet that's the way she thought of it as she peered up at the building and tall trees bathed in purple shadows.

Even although she'd taken painkillers, her hand pulsated in time with a headache. She was exhausted and resolved to have an early night. Locking the front door, she stared in the foyer mirror at her tired, scratched face and frowned. Before she made something to eat and went to bed, she wanted to make the call to her mother, so she picked up the phone in the living room and plopped down on the sofa.

When the hotel receptionist answered, she asked for the penthouse and waited. Her father spoke. "Hello?"

"Hi, it's Alex. Is…is my mother there?"

"No, she's lying down, she has a headache."

"Oh, well I thought I'd let you know that Juno's being discharged before lunch tomorrow and I wondered if you wanted to meet me at the hospital."

Her father didn't reply straight away and Alex thought they'd been cut off until he suddenly broke the silence. "Er, no, you pick him up and take him home. We'll swing by later in the afternoon. Your mother wants to have a word with you both."

Alex scowled, wondering what her mother had to say. "Okay, I can do that. I'll see you later tomorrow then."

Too tired to rack her brain for explanations, she changed into her pajamas, slammed an instant dinner in the microwave and scoffed it. With her teeth cleaned and hair combed, she returned to Juno's bed and slept.

"Are you ready to go?" Alex poked her head round Juno's room door and pushed in a wheelchair.

Juno's face was set in stone. "The sooner I get out of this hospital the better. Why people say you're in the best place when you're sick or injured is beyond me. Ever since I've been admitted, nurses have poked me, doctors have examined me and the infernal bleeping from that monitor has kept me awake all night." He then looked at his mode of transport with disdain. "I'm not sitting in that thing."

Alex's eyes rounded with surprise. "But it's a hospital rule. What happens if you feel dizzy and fall when you get to your feet?"

He opened his mouth as if to say something, but instead took two steps and wilted down on the canvas seat.

The room door swung open and a nurse scurried in, holding out a bag to Alex.

"This is Mr. Juno's medication. One pill three times a day and if he gets a fever or there's any sign of inflammation around his wound, he must see a doctor."

Juno snatched the bag from the nurse's hand. "Thank you, I'm quite capable of carrying my own pills."

She held the door open and Alex wheeled him out.

Alex waited while Juno absorbed the fresh air for a few moments before he climbed into the passenger seat of her car and she drove off. Sensing his bad mood, her hands gripped the wheel and her eyes never veered from the road. Watching the town and countryside fly past, she wished she could think of something to say to fill the awkward silence, but she thought it best to stay silent. It was obvious that Juno didn't feel like talking.

The car barreled along and she stole a glance at Juno, but his expression hadn't changed. She pulled up outside the front door of his house and he got out of the car without a word, entered the house, headed for his bedroom and closed the door.

When Alex had spoken to the nurse the previous evening, she'd explained that sometimes patients experienced depression after the trauma of a bullet wound. With this in mind, she tossed a salad and made a pot of coffee. If Juno were hungry, he'd soon venture from his solitude to seek food. Otherwise, she'd wait until her parents arrived and hope he was in a better frame of mind.

Just before three, Juno appeared in the kitchen and poured a mug of coffee.

Alex smiled. "Are you feeling better?"

"Yes, I was exhausted. That short nap has put me to rights."

"Are you hungry? I've made salad, but I can cook if you want something else."

"No, coffee's fine just now. And yes, I have had my pill." He sallied through to the living room and stood looking out the window.

"I don't remember asking."

"No, but I thought you might." He groaned. "Oh no, my parents' car's coming up the driveway."

Alex craned her neck. "Yes, they said they'd be dropping by this afternoon."

She wandered through the archway and opened the front door at the same time the Mercedes braked to a halt. As her mother kissed her cheek, Alex could see that she'd been crying. Her father waited until she'd closed the door before he joined them in the living room.

Vibes of doom and gloom bounced off the walls when Alex entered the living room. Juno's face was petrous, her mother sat on the sofa wringing a hankie and her father stood with his back to the fireplace, a dour expression on his face.

"Can I get either of you a drink?" Alex asked brightly.

"I'll have whiskey," her father requested.

Alex looked over at her mother and raised her brows in question.

"Nothing for me, dear."

An ominous silence pervaded the room as Alex poured golden liquid onto ice and handed it to her father. She focused first on her mother and then her father.

He spoke in the stillness of the room, peering at his wife and nodding. "Your mother has something to tell you both."

Alex composed herself in an armchair and waited.

A multitude of expressions crossed her mother's face. Twice she opened her mouth as if to speak, but no words came.

"This is very difficult," she eventually admitted, still wringing the hankie. The next words she directed to Alex. "Your father and I have noticed that you and Balthy are very close." She cleared her throat and looked at her husband again. "We suspect that your feelings for him run deeper than brotherly love."

Unbearable heat rushed to Alex's face and she was unable to meet her mother's eyes.

"We don't blame you. Balthy exudes a mystique that women can't resist." She laughed. "Believe me he's no saint. What I'm trying to say is—" Her eyes pleaded with her husband, but he flapped a hand. This time she looked at Juno. "I hope you think your father and I gave you a good home life. I know I was a nuisance when I wouldn't allow you to go to camp with your friends, but I only did it because I love you."

The scowl on Juno's face deepened. "What's this all about mother? You obviously have something to say, so spit it out."

"Your father was a very proud man and had difficulty acknowledging his short comings. We were married for many years before you came along and only then it was because he knew it would please me to adopt a child."

Juno looked as if his mother had thrown a bucket of water over him.

"You were three months old when we adopted you. We always knew your father couldn't have children and when we married it didn't matter, I loved him so much. However, as the years went by, and I saw how happy Emily and Martin were with Carlos, I wanted a family, too." She looked over at Alex. "That's another reason I couldn't keep you and Diane. That would have been like rubbing David's nose in it, him knowing that I could have children with another man." She hung her head. "I'm sorry."

"Sorry!" Juno exploded. "You come here and tell me I'm adopted and then say you're sorry. My God!" Puce with fury, he flounced around the room. "Why are you telling me this now? Why not when I was a child?"

"Because I never wanted you to know. The only reason I'm telling you now is because you need to know that you and Alex are not related."

She swiveled round and her eyes poured over her daughter.

Alex stared at her mother in disbelief. The words hit her like the impact from a sledgehammer. This was straight out of her dreams. Juno was not her brother. By now, her mother had dissolved into tears and Alex placed an arm around her shoulder.

Juno continued to pace, his eyes fiery and her father placed a hand on his arm bringing him to a standstill. "I know this has been a shock, but nothing's changed except that you're not related to Alex. You'll always be your mother's son."

All this time, Alex had found it hard to come to terms with the knowledge that Juno was her brother, now there was no need. Her eyes sought his and he quirked his lips in a small smile. Her heart did a somersault. She glowed with happiness.

Her father finished his drink and helped his wife to her feet. "We'll go now. You two must have a lot to talk about."

Her mother flung her arms around Juno. "Please say you don't hate me."

"I don't hate you. I just wish you'd told me before."

"We have to get back to Boca this evening. We've still the insurance claim on the house to deal with. Will you and Alex come and visit us sometime?"

Alex exchanged a smile with Juno. "We'd love to. We've got a lot of catching up to do."

Her mother's eyes misted with tears as she clasped her daughter to her breast. "I'll call you both."

Alex closed the door behind her parents and her feet danced back through to the living room where Juno was leaning on his uninjured arm against the mantle with his feet crossed, the same pose he'd struck on the day of the interview.

"Hmm, what do we do now?" He bobbed his eyebrows and grinned. "At least we didn't commit incest." He wiggled his eyebrows again.

Alex's gaze swung up to his. "Why do we need to do anything?"

"Because I love you. I've loved you from that first day you came here with your silly voice recorder."

Her whole body tingled with joy. She was afraid that if she spoke she'd burst into tears, so she mouthed, 'I love you, too.'

Quick as a flash, he crossed the room, clasped her close with his uninjured arm and looked at her with tender eyes. A frisson of pleasure teemed through her as she wound her arms round his neck and he pressed his soft lips to hers.

"I wish I could make love to you," he whispered, "but this arm hurts too damned much."

"There'll be plenty of time for that. I'm still trying to digest everything that's happened. Have you heard what condition Carlos is in?"

"The police told Martin he's going to be fine. At least that part of him'll mend, which is more than can be said for his mind."

Alex shuddered and laid her head on Juno's chest. "I still can't believe I'm no longer in any danger. It seems strange not to look over my shoulder anymore."

She quivered with exquisite pleasure as he stamped his mouth over hers again.

Juno's injury healed fast and three weeks later, Alex drove them to Boca Raton. She pulled up outside the impressive façade of a luxury hotel. "Wow, this is nice."

Juno gave a low, throaty chuckle. "When you get to know our mother a little better, you'll realize that this is her style, the more ostentatious the better. You should have seen the huge mausoleum I grew up in. Her house here is only about a quarter the size."

"Really? My small house would probably fit into the foyer."

They climbed from the car and mounted marble steps. Lit by glittering, crystal chandeliers and decorated with enormous bouquets of fresh, tropical flowers, the hotel's cool interior was a welcome change from the burning heat outside. Juno led the way to the elevators and pressed the button for the penthouse. Ornately carved double doors faced them and Juno rang the doorbell.

A young Cuban woman opened the door.

Juno ushered Alex in. "Hello, Carmen, Mom's expecting us."

The young woman bobbed a curtsey and Juno strode past her into a massive room with panoramic windows overlooking the coastline.

"Balthy! Alex! Their mother jumped up from a chaise lounge and embraced them. "You're early. I didn't expect you until lunch time."

Juno extricated himself from his mother's arms and sat on a velvet-covered chair. "Alex was anxious to get here, so we left at the crack of dawn. Where's Martin?"

"Need you ask," her mother answered in an exasperated tone. "Nothing short of world war three'll make him abandon his precious golf." They all laughed.

"Have they started with the house repairs, yet?" Juno reached for a grape from a large bowl of fruit.

"Not yet. The builders think it could take up to a year to finish." Her mother's eyes surveyed the luxury around her. "I don't think I could stand living here for that long, I need my own things around me. However, I did manage to get you a room on the seventh floor. It's nothing spectacular, so I hope you'll be comfortable."

Alex's eyes scanned the luxurious penthouse taking in every detail and wouldn't have minded spending one night there. "I'm sure the room will be very nice."

"If we'd been able to rent a larger suite, you could have stayed here with us, but Carmen has the second bedroom and I couldn't manage without her."

"It's okay, Mom," Juno rolled his eyes at Alex. "A room'll suit us fine."

Their mother picked up a small bell and tinkled it. Carmen hurried in. "You can bring in the tray of drinks now."

The young woman nodded. "Yes, ma'am."

Juno crossed to the window. "What a great view from here, you can see for miles."

Carmen placed a tray on a table and silently left the room.

Their mother poured iced lemonade into tall glasses and handed one to Alex. "Yes, it's all right. We really wanted to stay at the hotel on the beach, but they couldn't provide us with a penthouse, so we had to make do with here. Of course if we'd given them more notice, we could have got what we wanted, but when it's a case of needs must, one has to improvise."

Now Alex understood what Juno meant when he said their mother was a 'pain in the ass.' Raised in such a privileged family had spoiled her for everyday things. No wonder Juno liked to live simply and could only take her in small doses.

"So Alex, Balthy says you have something to ask us."

"Yes," her eyes met Juno's. "We want to invite you to our wedding."

A stunned expression crossed her mother's face before she began to cry. She dabbed her eyes with a lace handkerchief. "Oh, this is just wonderful. We couldn't have hoped for better news. Of course we'll come. When's the magical day?"

"In four weeks. There's no reason to wait, we want to be together always."

"And I'm sure you both will. As this is a celebration, I'll call your father on his cell phone and ask Carmen to put a bottle of Champagne on ice."

She excused herself and left the room.

Juno lowered his tall frame next to Alex on a love seat. "See, I told you she'd be pleased." He curled his hand round the back of her neck, pressed his lips to hers and swept her along on a wave of ecstasy.

They jumped apart when the door opened and their mother returned.

"Your father's on the eighteenth green, so he'll be home shortly. In the meantime, bring me up to date with what you've both been doing."

They took turns in relating the happenings of the last few weeks. First Alex spoke about how she'd placed her house and the mobile home in the hands of a realtor and had moved in with Juno.

Then he outlined his plans to build another wing onto the house and remodel it. "I want Alex to feel that the house is hers and to decorate every room any way she wants."

"Wouldn't you be better buying a new place, somewhere closer to town instead of in the boonies?"

"No, this is what we both want. Alex has given up her job at the magazine and she's going to help me with my writing."

Their mother arched her neatly plucked brows. "Really? Well if it's what you both want. I hope you'll be very happy."

Alex linked her arm through Juno's and nestled close. "We will."

Chapter 30

The metal gate clanged as it trundled aside and Zack Walker waited until it was fully open before he strutted through. His brain was churning a mile a minute. A few grains of doubt still gnawed at his insides as to whether Carlos Anderson was telling the truth, but somewhere deep inside, he knew he was. Yet it was still hard to believe. After a week of intensive interviews, the most amazing story had surfaced.

Once he was outside the secure building, he jogged to his car, climbed in and headed for the precinct. First, he wanted one of the clerks to make a transcript of the interviews. Next, he planned to speak to the Police Commissioner and suss out his reaction to this new evidence. No, that was the wrong word—there was no evidence—that was the problem. Psychiatrists had diagnosed Carlos insane and he wondered if anyone else would believe this voluntary confession.

Zack was a stickler for justice. If someone broke the law, he believed the punishment should be commensurate with the severity of the crime. He'd worked many cases where there was no real proof or hard evidence and that person had got away with the crime even although it was widely known they were guilty. He was not going to let that happen this time. Angry with himself for not following his usual instincts and believing everything was straightforward; he barged into his office and summoned a clerk.

After the female rookie left with the information to type, Zack called the Police Commissioner's secretary and requested an emergency meeting as soon as possible. His hopes took a dive when she told him her boss had left town earlier that day to attend a family reunion. Pouring his ninth cup of coffee of the day, he thanked her and resigned himself to the fact that the meeting couldn't take place for a few days, so he decided to go home and get a good night's sleep.

That was easy to say. He was still awake at two thirty, so he jammed his feet into a pair of old slippers and padded through to the living room in his pajamas. He smoothed a hand over his eyes and wondered how this felon could have duped him so easily. Normally he was skeptical about each detail of every case, but this time he'd allowed his judgment to be clouded by a hardened trickster. God, he felt so stupid. As soon as he could arrange a meeting, he'd grovel to the Commissioner and beg for extra assistance in bringing this criminal to justice.

The honking of a car horn woke Zack from a deep sleep. He looked around and was surprised to see the hands of the clock at nine-thirty. His meeting with the Commissioner was at ten that morning. He scrambled to the window and pulled aside the sheers. Sergeant LaTour sat at the wheel of a patrol car. He acknowledged her blaring of the horn with a wave and ran through to get dressed.

There was no time for a shower. He rammed his legs into pants, pulled a shirt over his head and buckled on his weapon. On the way to the kitchen, he grabbed a comb and ran it through his hair before buttoning up his jacket, hauling on socks and shoes and rushing out the door.

"Good morning, sir." LaTour twittered as Zack tumbled into the car.

"No it's not, put your foot down, I've got a ten o'clock meeting with 'God.'"

The sergeant sniggered. "I love the way you call him that, the name's so appropriate."

Zack fastened his seat belt as LaTour overtook a slow-moving truck with a fanfare of sirens and flashing lights.

Sergeant LaTour had recovered swiftly from her injuries and although she was back at work part-time, her duties consisted mostly of driving and paperwork. During Zack's continued investigation of the local murders, she hadn't been assigned to him and therefore she knew nothing of the latest developments. While Zack ran his battery-operated shaver over his chin, he briefly spouted his reason for the meeting with 'God.'

"You're kidding! Do you believe all this stuff Carlos's been saying?"

"Sure, now I think back, many things I couldn't figure out then, make more sense now. Maybe he's not as crazy as we thought."

Minnie skillfully negotiated the traffic, pulling up at the back door of the precinct in record time. "Good luck with your meeting, sir. I'm finishing my shift at one-thirty and then I'm going to Alex and Juno's wedding."

Zack stuck his head back inside the car before he closed the door. "If my meeting goes according to plan, I'll see you later."

Minnie waved and turned into the parking lot.

Alex assessed her image in the mirror and smiled. Her parents had driven from Boca Raton the previous day and were staying at the same hotel, only in the penthouse. Her modest room had a balcony overlooking the shining waters of Sarasota Bay and Lido Key beyond. It had taken one look at the three-piece outfit she was wearing, to know that this was what she wanted for her wedding to Juno. A delicate shade of cream, the skirt had a handkerchief hemline while the top was sleeveless, embellished with tiny crystals at the neckline, and the belted jacket boasted matching decorations around the collar and cuffs.

Someone knocked on the door. She opened it to a bellboy holding out a long, flat box.

He gave a small bow "Flowers for Mrs. Martell."

Alex ripped off the ribbon bearing the florist's name and lifted the lid. Lying in tissue was a bunch of white Calla Lilies. She scratched around the box looking for a card and extricated one from under the tissue. She was stricken dumb as she read one word, 'Carlos.'

For what seemed endless minutes the universe rocked. The breath labored in her chest. Surely, this was a joke. Why would he send her these on her wedding day? She remembered Barbara saying that lilies were for funerals and how she'd received a bowl of them the day of the hit and run accident. Then she calmed down. Carlos was in custody and couldn't hurt her anymore, this must his idea of a sick joke.

The phone rang—her cue that the limo had arrived, so she gathered up a small bouquet of pink orchids that matched the ones decorating her hair and left the room.

Her father was waiting when the elevator ground to a halt on the first floor. He lifted her hand and kissed it. "You look very beautiful, my dear. How do you feel?"

"A little nervous, I don't know why, because I know I'm doing the right thing. Where's Mother?"

"Balthy picked her up and they've gone on ahead."

By the time they'd crossed the wide, high, concrete bridge leading to Lido Key, Alex felt as if she'd left her stomach behind. It jiggled and churned and she couldn't remember feeling this nervous when she married John.

The limo pulled up under the awning of a beachside restaurant and an attendant dressed in a tuxedo opened the car door at her father's side. He thanked the man and rounded the car to extend a hand to Alex.

The restaurant's automatic doors opened and the manager welcomed them, bowing. "Good afternoon, Mr. Anderson.

Everyone in the wedding party's seated on the beach. Would the bride like to freshen up before the ceremony?"

Alex's face felt tight when she smiled. "No thanks, I'm fine."

Light classical music wafted through doors that led to the beach and the sight of the seated crowd turned Alex's knees to jelly. Her father led her to a flower-decked archway to wait until the music changed—the signal for them to begin their walk down the red-carpeted aisle.

Juno was talking to the minister next to a gazebo, every inch covered in pink, red and white roses, and at the sight of him, all her doubts flew away. He wore a lightweight ivory suit, a stark contrast to his collar-length dark hair, and a green shirt that was almost the color of his eyes. Alex spotted her mother's large-brimmed, pink hat and smiled.

The music changed, her father squeezed her hand. "You don't know how proud it makes me to walk you down the aisle. In my wildest dreams, I could never have hoped for a more beautiful daughter. Are you ready?"

"Very," her heart overflowed with love as Juno turned and their eyes met. The guests stood as strains of *The Trumpet Voluntary* heralded her arrival and she began a slow walk toward the gazebo and her future.

Her parents had insisted on making all the wedding arrangements and all she and Juno had done was give them a list of people they wanted to attend. Until this moment, she had no idea who had accepted and who had declined. Every time she'd called her mother, she was either too busy to go into details or out shopping, so it was a pleasant surprise to spot Darren Winters, Brett Etheridge and Minnie LaTour among the invited guests.

Her father placed her hand in Juno's and went to stand next to her mother who was dabbing her eyes with a handkerchief.

Lilies of Death

As she turned to Juno, the minister led them up the steps of the gazebo and positioned them in the center facing each other. A large, orange sun sank slowly into the waters of the Gulf of Mexico, casting long, purple shadows over the beach. Alex hardly heard the words the minister said, as he began quoting the start of the marriage service. The congregation faded to a blur and she was only conscious of Juno looking at her with love in his eyes.

This was a momentous day, one she'd remember for the rest of her life. They both had painful pasts, but today was a new beginning, erasing all the bad luck and unhappiness they'd managed to overcome.

Alex's throat was tight as she listened to Juno repeating the minister's words. She was psyching herself up for her own recitation when a shout sounded at the back of the crowd.

The minister raised his head, a deep frown lining his brow. Lieutenant Zack Walker assisted by two deputies, sprinted down the aisle and stormed up the gazebo steps.

"What's the meaning of this interruption?" the minister demanded in a surly tone.

The two deputies bounded toward Juno. One held his arms while the other clicked on a pair of handcuffs.

"I can't allow this wedding to go on," the lieutenant replied. "This man is under arrest for conspiracy to murder."

The deputies turned Juno to face the lieutenant and he read him his 'Miranda rights'.

Alex's heartbeat pounded in her ears. "There must be some mistake. Juno's done nothing wrong. Has he—?" She let the question hang there.

At her words, Juno underwent a sudden metamorphosis. His face became as hard as granite and his false smile turned brittle at the corners. Then he dropped his bombshell. "You were so easy to deceive, my dear Alex."

She shrank from him, her eyes widening in horror.

"I relied on your romantic notions not allowing you to see reality and I was proved right."

She shook her head in denial, her mind dwelling on what he'd just said.

He went to take a step toward her, but the deputies stopped him and bundled him down the steps. He looked back. "If it's any consolation I do love you and after I'd got rid of those two." He hitched his chin in the direction of her parents. "I was going to kill you gently."

His words pierced Alex to the core and she winced.

"I would have made our short time together memorable, but I love money more than you, so you had to die for me to get what I wanted." He spoke to the lieutenant. "I guess I was wrong when I thought you wouldn't believe Carlos."

Alex's head reeled and her father hastened up the steps and caught her before she fell. A deep pain ripped through her heart. She was having a hard time piecing together what had transpired in the last few minutes, but the outcome was the same, Juno had been going to kill her. She wasn't thinking on all cylinders, so at the moment the reason wasn't clear.

Her father helped her to a seat in the front row next to her mother. Then tears were streaming down her face as she choked back sobs. She had loved Juno with all her heart and now she wanted to die.

Some of the wedding congregation was standing and talking in whispers while others had already started to leave. Her mother and father helped her to her feet and led her to the waiting limo.

The ride back to the hotel was hazy along with the ascent to the penthouse and her mother undressing her and putting her to bed. Profound agony, as deep and as dark as a chasm, ripped through her along with great gulping sobs until exhausted, she fell asleep.

Two weeks later, seconded in her parents' penthouse at Boca Raton, Alex gazed out over the sparkling waters of the Atlantic Ocean. The last year had been a nightmare. First John had disappeared and months of anguish followed until she met and fell in love with Juno.

A few days after her doomed wedding, Lieutenant Zack Walker drove to Boca Raton and elaborated on the plot that Carlos and Juno had hatched between them years before.

"This all started when Juno and Carlos were teenagers. They discovered they were cousins and always kept in touch, even if you," he nodded at Martin and Alicia Anderson, "didn't know where Carlos was. Juno went through all the money his father left him in a very short time, so he and Carlos devised a plot whereby they could share the remainder of the family money."

"But, where do I come into all of this?" The question tumbled out as Alex's mind whirred with bewilderment.

"When Carlos broke into your father's safe and took a copy of his will, he found out about you and Diane and that you'd both inherit along with him when your parents died. It must have been a great shock and it probably took him years to track you both down, but he did."

"But where did Balthy fit into all this?" Her mother asked.

Zack grinned. "Being a charmer, his part of the plan was to woo Alex and Diane and if necessary, kill them."

Alex took a moment to orient herself. "But we met by accident when I interviewed him for *Everyday* magazine."

Zack nodded. "And who arranged that? Your editor Charlie, alias Carlos. Now perhaps you can see how intricate this plot was. When they discovered that you and Diane lived in Florida, Carlos applied for a transfer and Juno relocated here, too. There was nothing they wouldn't do to get their hands on Martin's family money."

Zack turned and addressed Martin. "You must be worth a fortune."

Martin sighed and nodded. "My family made their money in steel several generations ago."

Zack continued. "In order to avoid suspicion, they had to disguise your murders, so Carlos killed Myrtle Bixby and another woman earlier, so that we'd think a serial killer was at work."

"Did he kill John, too?" Alex asked in a small voice.

"Yes, he had to otherwise John would have inherited your portion of the money when you died."

"So that poor woman with John was an innocent victim?"

"Not exactly. Carlos went out of his way to get to know Sandra Barrett because he knew she worked with John. He set about charming her and when she eventually moved in with him, he began abusing her, so that she'd turn to John for help. By now, Carlos had developed a liking for killing, his days as a mercenary had fueled a dormant psychosis, and so these murders gave him immense pleasure."

With a wolfish smile, the lieutenant continued. "Then things went horribly wrong. You didn't die in the hit and run accident and we gave you protection making it hard for Carlos and Juno to get close to you. However they had plenty of time, they needed to dispose of your parents first."

Alex shuddered. This was worse than any movie she'd ever seen. She still found it hard to believe that Juno could be so cold and callous. He may have been distant at times, but overall he'd acted gentle and kind.

"The original idea was that after Diane died, they'd kill you and then your parents, leaving Carlos the sole inheritor and he'd split the money with Juno. However, Juno didn't trust Carlos,

Lilies of Death

so he improvised on the plot. To make sure he got his half of the money, he made plans to marry Alex before her parents died and after a reasonable length of time he'd kill her, too, thus ensuring he'd get his half of the fortune."

Alex felt sick to her stomach. She flinched at the memory of the times she'd made love with Juno and realized that she'd had a lucky escape. She wanted to ask so many questions but the words damned up in her throat.

"But, Balthy was so shocked when we told him Alex was his sister," her mother piped up. "You mean to say he knew all along?"

"Uh huh," Zack agreed, "this guy's a very good actor as well as a pathological liar. He also knew he was adopted, but he needed you to tell him, so that he'd be free to marry Alex."

"But, who set the fire at the house in Boca Raton?" Martin asked.

"That was Carlos. He knew how to make Molotov cocktails from his mercenary days. He jumped the gun and botched that assassination attempt, not realizing you were both out of town."

"And my wedding day lilies?" Alex wanted to know the whole story.

"Again, that was Carlos. Once he realized what Juno's intentions were, he wanted to stop him marrying you. It was his way of sending you a warning, because despite all his attempts to kill you, in his deranged mind, he believed he loved you."

Alicia Anderson rang a small, brass bell. "I think we should all have some tea. My mind needs some stimulation to take all this in. Do you like Lapsong Souchong, Lieutenant?"

Zack looked askance at Alex who shrugged. "No thanks, I'd better get back to the precinct."

Alicia gave instructions to Carmen and sat down, smoothing the skirt of her lime green suit. "You've done a remarkable job,

Lieutenant, my husband and I want to thank you for saving Alex's life, she's very precious to us."

"You're welcome, ma'am. Although I have to admit, without Carlos's help, none of this might have become known until it was too late." He patted Alex's hand. "You've been through a lot, but with the help of your folks here, I'm sure you'll pull through."

"What will happen to them?" Alex asked.

"The psychiatric evaluation on Carlos revealed all kinds of mental defects and I suspect the outcome of Juno's will be similar. The courts will decide whether they're fit to answer charges or whether they'll be detained indefinitely in a mental institution. Either way, it's very unlikely that either will ever have their freedom again."

Alex sighed, "Thank you Lieutenant. I'll walk you out."

Zack shook hands with her parents and followed her through the penthouse's double doors. When the elevator stopped, the sliding doors swished apart and Darren Winters stepped out.

His face cracked in a wide smile. "Hi, I thought I'd drop by and see how you're doing."

Alex glanced at Zack. He raised his eyebrows and grinned before the elevator doors closed.

She returned Darren's smile. His blond hair was shorter than when she saw him last and his face sported a golden tan. Ivory slacks hung on slim hips and his blue polo shirt matched the color of his eyes.

"Would you like to come and meet my parents?" She queried, leading the way to the double doors.

"Yes, thanks, I'd like that." Darren held out a bouquet of carnations. "I hope you like flowers?"

Alex hesitated. "Er, yes, I love them, but promise you'll never buy me lilies."

Educated in England and Scotland, Jordan Hall has had a variety of careers including hair stylist, accounts clerk, photographer and children's nanny. While holding down these jobs, she always found time to write poetry and short stories.

Well traveled, she has visited the Far East, the Caribbean and many U.S. states. Her novels feature places she has visited, sights she has seen and events she has experienced.

She now lives in Florida with her husband and enjoys traveling when she takes time off from writing.

Printed in the United States
131383LV00004B/32/P